THE NIGHT WATCH

THE
NIGHT
WATCH

SERGEI LUKYANENKO

Translated from the Russian by Andrew Bromfield

ANCHOR CANADA

Anchor Canada and colophon are trademarks.

Library and Archives Canada Cataloguing in Publication has been applied for.

ISBN-13: 978-0-385-66365-6
ISBN-10: 0-385-66365-X

First published in Russian under the title Ночной Дозор by AST, 2004

Printed and bound in Canada

Published in Canada by
Anchor Canada, a division of
Random House of Canada Limited

Visit Random House of Canada Limited's website: www.randomhouse.ca

TRANS 10 9 8 7 6 5 4 3 2

This text has been approved for distribution as conducive to the cause of the Light.
The Night Watch

This text has been approved for distribution as conducive to the cause of the Dark.
The Day Watch

Story One

DESTINY

PROLOGUE

THE ESCALATOR strained slowly upward. In an old station like this, what else would you expect? But the wind swirled like a wild thing inside the concrete pipe – ruffling his hair, tugging the hood off his head, sneaking in under his scarf, pressing him downward.

The wind didn't want Egor to go up.

The wind was pushing him back.

Strange, but no one else seemed to notice the wind. There was hardly anyone around – it was midnight and the station was already emptying. Only a few people riding down towards Egor and hardly anyone on the up escalator either. One ahead of him, two or three behind. That was it.

Except, of course, for the wind.

Egor stuck his hands in his pockets and turned to look back. For a couple of minutes already, from the moment he stepped off the train, he'd had the feeling he was being watched. It wasn't a frightening kind of feeling at all, it felt interesting, a sudden, pricking sensation.

Down at the bottom of the escalator there was a tall man in uniform. Not police, a soldier. Then there was a woman with a sleepy little child, clutching her hand. And another man, young, wearing a bright orange jacket, with a walkman. He looked just about dead on his feet too.

Nothing suspicious. Not even for a boy going home so late. Egor looked up again, at the policeman lounging against the gleaming handrails, dejectedly trying to spot some easy prey in this sparse stream of passengers.

Nothing to be afraid of.

The wind gave Egor one last nudge and suddenly dropped away, apparently resigned that the struggle was pointless. The boy glanced back once more and started running up the moving steps as they flattened out under his feet. He had to hurry. He didn't know why, but he had to. Again he felt a pricking sensation of senseless anxiety and a cold shudder ran through his body.

It was the wind again.

Egor slipped out through the half-opened doors and the piercing cold assailed him with renewed fury. His hair, still wet from the pool – the dryer was broken again – was instantly stiff with ice. Egor pulled the hood back over his head, darted past the vendor kiosks without stopping and hurried into the underpass. Up on the surface there were far more people, but he still had the feeling of alarm. He glanced back now, without slowing down, but there was no one following him. The woman with the small child was walking towards a trolleybus stop, the man with the walkman had paused in front of a kiosk, inspecting the bottles, the soldier still hadn't come out of the subway.

The boy speeded up through the underpass. There was music coming from somewhere, so quiet he could hardly hear it, but it was incredibly soothing. The delicate trill of a flute, the strum of guitar strings, the chime of a xylophone. The music was calling to him, telling him to hurry. Egor dodged past a group of people hurrying towards him, overtook a happy little drunk who was barely staggering forward. All thought seemed to have been blown out of his head, he was almost running now.

The music was calling.

And now there were words weaving themselves into it . . . not clearly, still too quiet to make out, but just as alluring. Egor bounded out of the underpass and stopped for a moment, gulping in the cold air. A trolleybus was just rolling up to the stop. He could ride just one stop, almost all the way to his house . . .

The boy set off towards the trolleybus, walking slowly, as if his legs had suddenly become numb. It halted for a few seconds with its doors open, then the hinged flaps swung together and it moved away. Egor watched it go with dull, glazed eyes, the music getting louder all the time, filling the whole world, from the semicircular lobby of the high-rise hotel to the 'box on stilts' – his own building – that he could see not far away. The music was prompting him to walk. Along the wide, brightly lit avenue, where there were still plenty of people around at this hour. His home was only five minutes away.

But the music was even closer . . .

When Egor had walked about a hundred metres, the hotel was suddenly no longer sheltering him from the wind. The icy blast stung his face, almost drowning out the music that was calling to him. The boy began to stagger, nearly coming to a stop. The enchantment was shattered, but the feeling of being watched was back, this time with a strong undercurrent of fear. He glanced back. Another trolleybus was approaching the stop. And he caught a glimpse of an orange jacket in the light of the streetlamps. The man who had ridden up the escalator with him was walking behind him. Still with his eyes half closed in the same way, but with surprising speed and purpose, as if he could see Egor.

The boy started to run.

The music began again louder than ever, breaking through the curtain of the wind. He could now make out words . . . he could, but he didn't want to.

The right thing to do now was to walk along the avenue, past the shops, which were closed but still brightly lit, alongside the late-nighters on the pavement, in full view of the cars rushing by.

But Egor turned into an alleyway. To where the music was calling him.

It was almost completely dark, the only things moving were two shadows by the wall. Egor seemed to see them through a dense haze, as if they were lit up by some ghastly bluish glow. A young man and a girl, very lightly dressed, as if the night air wasn't twenty degrees below zero.

The music rose to a final, crashing, triumphant crescendo. And stopped. The boy felt his body go limp. He was covered in sweat, his legs giving way, he wanted to sit down on the slippery, ice-covered pavement.

'A pretty one . . .' said the girl in a quiet voice. She had a thin face, with sunken cheeks and a pale complexion. Only her eyes seemed to be alive: black, huge, magnetic.

'You can leave . . . just a little bit . . .' the young man said with a smile. They were as alike as brother and sister, not in their features, but in some indefinable quality that they shared, as if their faces were covered by a dusty, semi-transparent gauze.

'For you?' For a moment the girl turned her gaze away from Egor. The numbness eased slightly and terror flooded his mind. The boy opened his mouth, but his eyes met the young man's and he couldn't shout. As if he was suddenly wrapped in some cold, elastic membrane.

'Yes. You hold him!'

The girl gave a mocking snort. Turning her gaze back to Egor, she stretched out her lips as if she were blowing a kiss. In a quiet voice she pronounced those familiar words, the ones that had been woven into the alluring music.

'Come, come . . . come to me . . .'

Egor stood without moving. He had no strength to run, despite the horror, despite the scream that had burst from his lungs and stuck in his throat. But at least he could simply stand.

A woman walked past the end of the alley with two huge German shepherds on leads. Walking in slow motion, as if she were moving underwater, as if she were part of his terrible dream. Out of the corner of his eye, Egor saw the dogs turn sharply towards the alley, tugging at their leads, and for a moment an insane hope flared up in his soul. The German shepherds started growling uncertainly, with loathing and fear. The woman stopped for a moment and glanced suspiciously into the alley. Egor caught her glance – indifferent, as if she was looking into empty space.

'Come on!' She tugged at the leads and the dogs gladly moved back to her side.

The young man laughed quietly.

The woman quickened her step and disappeared from view.

'He's not coming to me!' the girl exclaimed petulantly. 'Look, will you, look, he's not coming!'

'Try harder,' the young man said curtly. He frowned. 'Learn.'

'Come! Come to me!' the girl said, emphasising each word. Egor was less than two metres away, but it seemed to be important to her that he came over to her.

Egor realised that he had no more strength to resist. The girl's gaze held him, as if binding him with an invisible elastic tether, the words summoned him and he could not help himself. He knew that he should not move, but still he took a step forward. The girl smiled, and he saw her white, even teeth. She said:

'Take off your scarf.'

He couldn't hold out any longer. His hands trembled as he threw back his hood and pulled off his scarf without unwinding it. He stepped towards those alluring black eyes.

Something was happening to the girl's face. Her lower jaw was stretching down, her teeth were moving, curving. He saw the flash of long fangs that were not human.

Egor took another step.

CHAPTER 1

THE NIGHT got off to a bad start.

It was barely even dark when I woke. I just lay there, thinking things over, watching the final gleams of daylight fading away in the cracks of the blinds. This was the fifth night of the hunt – and there was still nothing to show for it. And I wasn't likely to get lucky today either.

It was cold in the apartment, the radiators hardly gave any heat at all. The only thing I like about winter is that it gets dark quickly, so there aren't many people out on the streets. If not for that, I'd have dropped the whole business ages ago and left Moscow for some place like Yalta or Sochi. It would have to be the Black Sea, not some far away islands in a warm foreign ocean: I like to hear the sound of my mother tongue around me . . .

Stupid dreams, of course.

It's still too soon for me to be thinking of retiring to somewhere a bit warmer.

I haven't earned it yet.

The telephone must have been waiting for me to wake up – it started ringing in that loathsome, nagging way it has. I fumbled for the receiver and held it to my ear – quietly, without saying a word.

'Anton, answer.'

I didn't say anything. Larissa's voice was brisk and focused, but already tired. She obviously hadn't slept all day.

'Anton, shall I put you through to the boss?'

'No, don't do that,' I growled.

'That's more like it. Are you awake?'

'Yes.'

'It's the same again for you today.'

'Anything new?'

'No, not a thing. Have you got anything for breakfast?'

'I'll find something.'

'Okay. Good luck.'

It sounded feeble and unconvincing. Larissa didn't have any faith in me. No doubt the boss didn't either.

'Thanks,' I said to the dial tone. I got up and made the usual trip to the toilet and the bathroom. I was just about to spread toothpaste on the brush when I realised I was getting ahead of myself and put it back down on the edge of the basin.

It was completely dark in the kitchen, but of course I didn't bother turning on the light. I opened the door of the fridge – the small light bulb I'd screwed out of its socket lay there freezing with the food. I looked at the saucepan with the colander sitting on top of it. Lying in the colander was a lump of half-defrosted meat. I lifted out the colander, raised the saucepan to my lips and took a gulp.

If anyone thinks pig's blood tastes good, then they're wrong.

I put the saucepan with the rest of the thawed-out blood back in the fridge and walked back to the bathroom. The dull blue lamp hardly lightened the darkness at all. I took a long time cleaning my teeth, brushing furiously, then I gave in, went back to the kitchen and took a gulp of icy vodka from the fridge. Now my stomach didn't just feel warm, it felt hot. A wonderful set of sensations: frost on my teeth and fire in my stomach.

I hope you— I started thinking, about the boss, but I caught myself just in time. He was quite capable of sensing even a half-formed curse. I went through into my room and started gathering together the clothes scattered all over the place. I discovered my trousers under the bed, my socks on the windowsill, and for some reason my shirt was hanging on the mask of Chkhoen.

The ancient king of Korea eyed me disapprovingly.

'Why can't you just watch over me?' I muttered, and then the phone started screeching again. I paced around the room until I found the receiver.

'Anton, was there something you wanted to say to me?' the disembodied voice asked.

'Not a thing,' I said sullenly.

'I see. Now add "glad to serve, your honour" to that.'

'I'm not glad. And there's nothing to be done about it . . . your honour.'

The boss paused for a moment.

'Anton, I really would like you to take this situation we have on our hands a bit more seriously. All right? I expect you to report back in the morning, in any case. And . . . good luck.'

I didn't exactly feel ashamed. But I wasn't feeling quite so irritated any more. I put my mobile phone in my jacket pocket, opened the cupboard in the hallway and wondered for a while what I ought to take to round out my kit. I had a few novel items of equipment that friends had given me the previous week. But I settled on the usual lot anyway – it's fairly compact and gives pretty good all-round coverage.

Plus the minidisc walkman. I don't need my sense of hearing for anything, and boredom is an implacable enemy.

Before I went out I took a long look at the staircase through the spy-hole. Nobody there.

And that was the beginning of one more night.

*   *   *

I rode the metro for about six hours, switching aimlessly from line to line without any system, sometimes dozing, letting my conscious mind take a break and my senses roam. There was nothing going down. Well, I did see a few interesting things, but they were all utterly ordinary, tame beginner's stuff. It wasn't until about eleven, as the metro got less crowded, that things changed.

I was sitting there with my eyes closed, listening to Manfredini's Fifth Symphony for the third time that evening. The minidisc in the player was totally wild; a personal selection, medieval Italian composers and Bach alternating with the rock group Alisa, Richie Blackmore and Picnic. It's always interesting to see which music comes up for which event. Today it was Manfredini.

I felt this sudden cramp – all the way up from my toes to the back of my head. I even hissed as I opened my eyes and glanced round the carriage.

I picked the girl out straight away.

Very pretty, young. In a stylish fur coat, with a little handbag and a book in her hands. And with a black vortex spinning above her head like I hadn't seen for at least three years.

I suppose the look I gave her must have made me look insane. The girl sensed it, glanced back at me and immediately turned away.

Try looking up instead!

No, of course she's not going to see the twister anyway. The most she could possibly feel is a slight sensation of alarm. And she can't get any more than the vaguest glimpse of that flickering above her head, out of the corner of her eye . . . like a swarm of midges swirling round and round, like the air trembling above the tarmac on a hot day . . .

She can't see a thing. Not a thing. And she'll go on living for another day or two, until she misses her step on the black ice, falls and bangs her head so hard it kills her. Or ends up under a car. Or runs into a thug's knife in the hallway, a thug who has no real idea why he's killing this girl. And everyone will say: 'She was so young, with her whole life ahead of her, everybody loved her . . .'

Yes. Of course. I believe it, she's a very good person, kind. There's weariness there, but no bitterness or spite. When you're with a girl like that you feel like a different person. You try to be better, and that's a strain. Men prefer to be friends with her kind, flirt a bit, share confidences. Men don't often fall in love with girls like that, but everybody loves them.

Apart from one person, who's hired a Dark Magician.

A black vortex is actually fairly ordinary. If I looked closely, I could make out another five or six hanging above other passengers' heads. But they were all blurred and pale, barely even spinning. The results of perfectly standard, non-professional curses. Someone had simply yelled after someone else: 'I hope you die, you bastard.' Someone had put it even more simply and forcefully: 'Go to hell, will you?' And a little black whirlwind had moved over from the Dark Side, draining good fortune and sucking up energy.

But an ordinary, amateurish, formless curse lasts no more than an hour or two, twenty-four hours at most. And its consequences may be unpleasant, but they're not fatal. That black twister hanging over the girl was the genuine article, stabilised and set in motion by an experienced magician. The girl didn't know it yet, but she was already dead.

I automatically reached for my pocket, then remembered where I was and frowned. Why don't mobile phones work in the metro? Don't the people who have them ride underground?

Now I was torn between my principal assignment, which I had to carry through, even with no hope of success, and the doomed girl. I didn't know if she could still be helped, but I had to track down whoever had created that vortex . . .

Just at that point I got a second jolt. But this time it was different. There was no cramp or pain, my throat just went dry and my gums went numb, the blood started pounding in my temples and my fingertips started itching.

This was it!

But the timing couldn't have been worse.

I got up – the train was already breaking as it pulled into a station. I walked past the girl and felt her eyes on me, following me. She was afraid. There was no way she could see the black vortex, but it was obviously making her feel anxious, making her pay close attention to the people around her.

Maybe that was why she was still alive.

Trying not to look in her direction, I put my hand into my pocket and fingered the amulet – a smooth cylinder carved out of cool onyx. I hesitated for a moment, trying to come up with some other plan.

No, there was no other way.

I squeezed the amulet tight in my hand, feeling a prickly sensation in my fingers as the stone began to warm up, giving out its accumulated energy. The sensation was no illusion, but you can't measure this heat with any thermometer. It felt as if I was squeezing a coal hot from a fire . . . it was covered with cold ash, but still red hot at the centre.

When I'd drained the amulet completely, I glanced at the girl. The black twister was shuddering, leaning over slightly in my direction. This vortex was so powerful that it even possessed a rudimentary intelligence.

I struck.

If there'd been any Others in the carriage, or even anywhere in the train, they'd have seen a blinding flash that could pierce through metal or concrete with equal ease.

I'd never tried striking at a black vortex with such a complex structure before. And I'd never used an amulet with such a powerful charge.

The effect was totally unexpected. The feeble curses hanging over other people's heads were completely swept away. An elderly woman who'd been rubbing her forehead looked at her hand in amazement: her vicious migraine had suddenly disappeared. A young guy who'd been gazing dully out the window shuddered. His face relaxed and the look of hopeless misery disappeared from his eyes.

The black vortex above the girl was tossed back five metres, it even slipped halfway out of the carriage. But it maintained its structure and came zigzagging back through the air to its victim.

This was real power!

With real perseverance!

They say, though I've never actually seen it myself, that if a vortex is pushed even two or three metres away from its victim, it gets disoriented and attaches itself to the nearest person it can find. That's a pretty lousy thing to happen to anyone, but at least a curse meant for someone else has a much weaker effect, and the new victim has a good chance of escape.

But this vortex just came straight back, like a faithful dog running to its master in trouble.

The train was stopping. I threw one last glance at the vortex – it was back in place, hanging there above the girl's head, it had even started to spin faster . . . And there was nothing, absolutely nothing I could do about it. The target I'd been hunting all over Moscow for a week was somewhere close, right here in the station. My boss would have eaten me alive . . . and maybe not just in the figurative sense . . .

When the doors parted with a hiss, I gave the girl a final glance, hastily memorising her aura. There wasn't much chance of ever finding her again in this vast city. But even so, I would have to try.

Only not right now.

I jumped out of the carriage and looked around. It was true, I was a bit short of field work experience, the boss was quite right about that. But I didn't like the method he'd chosen for training me at all.

How in hell's name was I supposed to find the target?

Not one of the people I could see with my normal vision looked even slightly suspicious. There were plenty of them still jostling against each other here – it was the circle line, after all, Kursk station, there were passengers who'd just arrived on the main line, street traders making their way home, people in a hurry to change trains and head for the suburbs . . . But if I closed my eyes I could see a more intriguing picture. Pale auras, the way they usually are by evening, and in among them the bright scarlet blobs of fury, the strident orange glow of a couple obviously in a rush to get to bed, the washed-out brownish-grey stripes of the disintegrating auras of the drunks.

But there was no sign of the target. Apart from the dryness in my throat, the itching in my gums, the insane pounding of my heart. The faint taste of blood on my lips. A mounting sense of excitement.

The signs were all circumstantial, but at the same time they were too obvious to ignore.

Who was it? Who?

The train started moving behind me. The feeling that the target was near didn't get any weaker, so we still had to be close to each other. Then a train going in the opposite direction appeared. I felt the target tremble and start moving towards it.

Forward!

I crossed the platform, weaving between the new arrivals staring up at the indicator boards, then set off towards the back of the train – and my sense of the target began to get weaker. I ran towards the front of the train – there it was again . . . closer . . .

It was like that children's game, first I was 'cold', then I was 'warm'.

People were boarding the carriages. I ran along the train, feeling sticky saliva filling up my mouth, my teeth starting to ache, my fingers starting to cramp up. The music was roaring in my earphones.

> In the shadow of the moon
> She danced in the starlight,
> Whispering a haunting tune
> To the night . . .

How appropriate. The song was bang on.

But it was a bad omen.

I jumped in through the closing doors and froze, concentrating on what I could feel. Had I guessed right or wrong? I still couldn't get a visual fix on the target . . .

I'd guessed right.

The train hurtled on round the circle line. My instincts were raging, calling to me: 'Right here! Beside you!'

Maybe I'd even got the right carriage.

I gave my fellow passengers a surreptitious looking-over and dropped the idea. There was no one here worth taking any interest in.

I'd just have to wait, then . . .

> Feel no sorrow, feel no pain,
> Feel no hurt, there's nothing gained . . .
> Only love will then remain,
> She would say.

At Marx Prospect I sensed the target moving away from me. I jumped from the carriage and set off toward the other line. Right here, somewhere right beside me . . .

At the radial line station the feeling of the target became almost unbearably strong. I'd already picked out a few likely prospects: two girls, a young guy, a boy. They were all potential targets, but which one of them was it?

My four candidates got into the same carriage. That was a stroke of luck at last. I followed them in and waited.

One girl got out at Rizhskaya station.

The feeling of the target didn't get any weaker.

The young guy got out at Alekseevskaya.

Great. Was it the girl or the boy?

I risked a stealthy glance at both. The girl was plump and pink-cheeked, she was absorbed in reading her *MK* newspaper, showing no signs of any kind of agitation. The boy, in contrast, was skinny and frail, standing by the door and tracing his finger across the glass.

In my opinion the girl was a lot more . . . tempting. Two to one it was her.

But then, in judgements like that the question of sex decides pretty much everything.

I'd already begun hearing the Call. Still not verbalised yet, just a slow, gentle melody. I immediately stopped hearing the sound from my earphones. The Call easily drowned out any other music.

Neither the girl nor the boy showed any signs of alarm. The target either had a very high threshold of resistance or had simply succumbed straight away.

The train stopped at Exhibition. The boy took his hand away from the glass, stepped out on to the platform and marched off rapidly towards the old exit. The girl stayed on the train.

Damn!

They were both still too close to me, I couldn't tell which one I was sensing.

And then the music of the Call soared triumphantly and words began to insinuate themselves into it.

A female voice!

I jumped out between the closing doors, and hurried after the boy.

The hunt was nearing its end at last.

But how was I going to handle things with no charge on my amulet? I didn't have a clue.

Only a few people had left the train and there were five of us on the up escalator. The boy at the front, a woman with a small child behind him, then me, followed by an ageing, seedy-looking army colonel. The colonel's aura was beautiful, a glittering mass of steel grey and light blue tones. I thought with weary humour that I could call on him to help. Even these days people like that still believe in the idea of 'officer's honour'.

Except that any help I could get from the colonel would be about as much use as a fly-swat on an elephant hunt.

I dropped the stupid idea and took another look at the boy. With my eyes closed, observing his aura.

The result was disheartening.

He was surrounded by a shimmering, semi-transparent glow. Sometimes it was tinged with red, sometimes it was flooded with a dense green and sometimes it flared up in dark blue tones.

This was a rare case. A destiny still undefined. Undifferentiated potential. This boy could grow up to be a great villain, he could become a good and just person, or he could turn out to be a nobody, an empty space, which is actually what most people are anyway. It was all still ahead of him, as they say. Auras like that are normal for children up to the age of two or three, but they disappear almost completely as people get older.

Now I could see why he was the one the Call was addressed to. There was no denying it – he was a real delicacy.

I felt my mouth starting to fill up again with saliva.

This had all been going on for too long, far too long . . . I looked at the boy, at the thin neck beneath his scarf, and I cursed my boss and the traditions, the rituals – everything that went to make up my job. My gums itched, my throat was parched.

Blood has a bitter, salty taste, but this thirst can't be quenched by anything else.

The boy hopped off the escalator, ran across the lobby and out through the glass doors. Just for a moment I felt relieved. I slowed down as I followed him out, and just caught a sense of movement out of the corner of my eye as he ducked down into an underpass. He was already running, physically drawn by the lure of the Call.

Faster!

I ran over to a kiosk and said, trying not to show my teeth:

'The stuff that's six roubles, with the ring pull.'

The young guy with a pimply face handed me the quarter-litre bottle with a slow, sluggish movement – as though he'd been taking a drop himself to keep warm on the job. He warned me candidly:

'It's not great vodka. Not gut-rot, of course, it's Dorokhov, but, you know . . .'

'Got to look after my health, anyway,' I joked. The vodka was obviously fake, but right now that was okay by me. With one hand I tore off the cap with the ring pull and with the other I took out my phone and switched it to repeat dial. The young salesman stared – he must have been shocked that someone who could afford a mobile phone would buy such bad vodka. I took a swallow as I walked along – the vodka stank like kerosene and tasted even worse, it was definitely moonshine, bottled in the back of someone's garage – and ran to the underpass.

'Hello.'

Larissa wasn't there any more. Pavel's usually on night duty.

'This is Anton. It's somewhere near the Cosmos hotel, in the back alleys. I'm in pursuit.'

'You want the team?' The voice was beginning to sound interested.

'Yes. I've already discharged the amulet.'

'What happened?'

A street bum bedded down halfway along the underpass reached out a hand as if he was hoping I'd give him the bottle I'd just started. I ran on past him.

'Something else came up . . . Make it quick, Pavel.'

'The guys are already on their way.'

I suddenly felt as if a red-hot wire had been stuck through my jaws. Hell and damnation . . .

'Pasha, I can't answer for myself,' I said quickly and rang off. I pulled up short, facing a police patrol.

Isn't that always the way? Why do the human guardians of law and order always turn up at the most inappropriate moments?

'Sergeant Kampinsky,' a young policeman announced briskly. 'Your papers . . .'

I wondered what they were planning to pin on me. Being drunk in a public place? That was probably it.

I put my hand into my pocket and touched the amulet. Just barely warm. But this wouldn't take a lot.

'I'm not here,' I said.

The four eyes that had been probing me in anticipation of easy pickings went blank as the last spark of reason in them died.

'You're not here,' they echoed in chorus.

There was no time to program them. I blurted out the first thing that came into my head:

'Buy some vodka and take a break. Now. Quick march!'

The order clearly fell on fertile ground. The policemen linked arms like kids out looking for fun and dashed off along the under-pass towards the kiosks. I felt vaguely uncomfortable, picturing the consequences of my instructions, but there was no time to put things right.

I hurtled out of the underpass, certain I was already too late. But oddly enough, the boy still hadn't got very far. He was just standing there, swaying slightly, less than a hundred metres away. That was serious resistance. The Call was so loud now, it seemed strange to me that the occasional passers-by walking down the street didn't start dancing, that the trolleybuses didn't swing off the main avenue, forcing their way down along the alley towards their sweet fate . . .

The boy glanced round. I thought he looked at me. Then he set off again, walking quickly.

That was it, he'd broken.

I followed him, frantically trying to decide what I was going to do. I ought to wait for the team – it would only take them ten minutes to get here, at most.

But that might not turn out so good – for the boy.

Pity's a dangerous thing. I gave way to it twice that day. The first time in the metro, when I spent the charge of the amulet in a useless attempt to displace the black vortex. And now the second time, when I set out after the boy.

Many years ago someone told me something that I flatly refused to accept. And I still don't accept it now, despite all the times I've seen it proved right.

'The common good and the individual good rarely coincide . . .'

Sure, I know. It's true.

But some truths are probably worse than lies.

I started running towards the Call. What I heard was probably not what the boy did. For him the Call was an enchanting melody, sapping his will and his strength. For me it was just the opposite, an alarm call stirring my blood.

Stirring my blood . . .

The body I'd been treating so badly all week was rebelling. I was thirsty, but not for water – I could quite safely slake my thirst with the dirty city snow without doing myself any harm. And not for strong drink either – I had that bottle of lousy vodka with me and even that wouldn't do me any damage. What I wanted was blood.

Not pig's blood, or cow's blood, but real human blood. Curse this hunt . . .

'You have to go through this,' the boss had said. 'Five years in the analytical department's a bit too long, don't you think?' I don't know, maybe it is a bit too long, but I like it. And after all, the boss himself hasn't worked out in the field for more than a hundred years now. I ran past the bright shop windows with their displays of fake Gzhel ceramics and stage-set heaps of food. There were cars rushing past me along the avenue, a few pedestrians. That was all fake too, an illusion, just one facet of the world, the only one accessible to humans. I was glad I wasn't one of them.

Without breaking my rapid stride, I summoned the Twilight.

The world sighed as it opened up. It was as if airport searchlights had suddenly come on behind me, casting a long, thin, sharp shadow. The shadow swirled up, gaining volume, the shadow was drawing me into itself – into a dimension where there are no shadows. The shadow detached itself from the dirty tarmac, swirling and swaying like a column of heavy smoke. The shadow was running ahead of me . . .

Quickening my stride, I broke through the grey silhouette into the Twilight. The colours of the world dimmed and the cars on the avenue slowed, as if they were suddenly heavy.

I was getting close to my goal.

As I dodged into the alleyway, I thought I would just catch the final scene. The boy's motionless, ravaged body, drained dry, the vampires disappearing.

But I wasn't too late after all.

The boy was standing in front of a girl vampire who had already extended her fangs, slowly taking off his scarf. He was probably not afraid now – the Call completely numbs the conscious mind. More likely he was longing to feel the touch of those sharp, gleaming fangs.

There was a young male vampire standing beside them. I sensed immediately that he was the leader of the pair: he was the one who was initiating her, he was introducing her to the scent of blood. And the most sickening thing about it was that he had a Moscow registration tag. Bastard!

But then, that only improved my chances . . .

The vampires turned towards me in confusion, not under-standing what was going on. The boy was in their Twilight, I shouldn't have been able to see him . . . or them either.

Then the male vampire's face began to relax, he even smiled – a calm, friendly smile.

'Hi there . . .'

He'd taken me for one of his own. And he could hardly be blamed for his mistake: I really was one of them now. Almost. The week of preparation had not been wasted: I had begun to sense them . . . but I'd almost gone over to the Dark Side myself.

'Night Watch,' I said. I held my hand out, holding the amulet. It was discharged, but that's not so easy to sense at a distance. 'Leave the Twilight!'

The male vampire would probably have obeyed me, hoping that I didn't know about the trail of blood he'd left behind him, that the whole business could just be written off as 'an attempt at unauthorised interaction with a human'. But the girl lacked his self-control, she didn't have the wit to get it.

'A-a-a-agh!' She threw herself at me with a long, drawn-out howl. It was a good thing she still hadn't sunk her teeth into the boy; she was out of her mind now, like a desperate junkie who's just stuck a needle in his vein only to have it jerked back out again, like a nymphomaniac after her man's pulled out just a moment before coming.

That dash would have been too fast for any human, no one could have parried it.

But I was in the same dimension of reality as the girl vampire. I threw up my arm and splashed vodka from the open bottle into her hideously transformed face.

Why do vampires tolerate alcohol so poorly?

The menacing scream became a shrill squeal. The girl began whirling around on the spot, beating her hands against her face as it shed layers of skin and greyish flesh. The male vampire swung round, all set to run.

This was going too easily altogether. A registered vampire isn't some casual visitor I have to fight on equal terms. I threw the bottle at the girl, reached out my hand and grabbed hold of the cord of the man's registration tag, which had unravelled on command. The vampire gave a hoarse croak and clutched at his throat.

'Leave the Twilight!' I yelled.

I think he realised things were looking really bad now. He flung himself towards me, trying to reduce the pressure from the cord, extending his fangs and transforming as he came.

If the amulet had been fully charged, I could have simply stunned him.

As it was, I had to kill him.

The tag – a seal on the vampire's chest that gave off a faint blue glow – made a crunching sound as I gave the silent order. The energy implanted in it by someone with far greater skill than me flooded into the dead body. The vampire was still running. He was well fed and strong, other people's lives were still nourishing his dead flesh. But he couldn't possibly resist such a powerful blow: his skin shrivelled until it was stretched as taut as parchment over his bones, slime gushed from his eye sockets. Then his spine shattered and the twitching remains collapsed at my feet.

I swung round – the girl vampire could have regenerated already. But there was no danger. She was running across the yard between the buildings, taking huge strides. She still hadn't left the Twilight, so I was the only one who could see this extraordinary sight. Apart from the dogs, of course. Somewhere off to one side a small dog broke into hysterical barking, transfixed simultaneously by hatred and fear, and all the other feelings that dogs have felt for the living dead for time immemorial.

I didn't have enough strength left to chase her. I straightened up and captured a 3D image of her aura – grey, desiccated, rotten. We'd find her. There was nowhere she could hide now.

But where was the boy?

After he emerged from the Twilight created by the vampires, he could have fainted or fallen into a trance. But he wasn't in the alley. He couldn't have run past me . . . I ran from the alley into the yard and saw him. He was bolting, moving almost as fast as the vampire. Well, good for him! That was wonderful. No help required. It was unfortunate that he would remember everything that had happened, but then who would believe a young boy? And before morning all his memories would fade and assume the less menacing features of a fantastic nightmare.

Or should I really go after him?

'Anton!'

Igor and Garik, our inseparable duo, came running down the alley from the avenue.

'The girl got away!' I shouted.

Garik kicked out at the vampire's shrivelled corpse as he ran, sending a cloud of rotten dust flying up into the frosty air. He shouted:

'The image!'

I sent him the image of the girl vampire running away. Garik frowned and ran faster. Both operatives headed off in pursuit. Igor shouted as he ran:

'Clear up the trash!'

I nodded, as if they needed an answer, and emerged from my own Twilight. The world blossomed. The operatives' silhouettes melted away and their invisible feet even stopped leaving tracks in the snow lying in the human dimension of reality.

I sighed and walked over to the grey Volvo parked at the kerb. There were a few primitive implements lying on the back seat: a heavy-duty plastic sack, a shovel and a small brush. It took me about five minutes to scrape up the vampire's feather-light remains and put the sack in the trunk. I took some dirty snow from a melting pile left by a careless yard-keeper, scattered it in the alley and trampled it a bit, working the final dusty, rotten remains into the slush. No human burial for you . . .

That was that.

I went back to the car, got into the driving seat and unbuttoned my jacket. I felt good. Very good, in fact. The senior vampire was dead, the guys would pick up his girlfriend and the boy was alive.

I could just imagine how delighted the boss would be.

CHAPTER 2

'Sloppy work!'

I tried to say something, but the next remark stung like a slap on the cheek and shut me up.

'You screwed up!'

'But . . .'

'Do you at least understand your own mistakes?'

The boss had cooled off a bit and I took the risk of raising my eyes from the floor and saying cautiously:

'It seems to me . . .'

I like being in that office. It stirs the child's heart in me to see all those amusing little trinkets on the shelves in the bullet-proof glass cupboards, hanging on the walls. Everything there – from the old Japanese fan to the jagged piece of metal with a deer welded on to it – the symbol of some car plant – each had its own history. If you were lucky and the boss was in the right mood, you could hear some very interesting stories.

Only I don't seem to find him in that kind of mood too often.

'Okay.' The boss stopped striding round the office, sat down in a leather armchair and lit up. 'Let's hear it.'

His voice had turned businesslike, matching his appearance. To the human eye he looked about forty years old, and he belonged to that narrow circle of businessmen that the government likes to rely on so much.

'What do you want to hear?' I asked, at the risk of provoking another tirade.

'The mistakes. Your mistakes.'

Right then . . . Okay.

'My first mistake, Boris Ignatievich,' I said with a perfectly innocent air, 'was that I failed to understand the nature of the mission correctly.'

'Oh, really?'

'Well, I assumed my goal was to track down a vampire who had begun actively hunting in Moscow. To track him down and . . . er . . . neutralise him.'

'Go on, go on . . .' the boss encouraged me.

'In actual fact, the essential purpose of the mission was to ascertain my suitability for operational activity, for field work. Starting from my incorrect understanding of the mission, that is, following the principle of "separate and protect" . . .'

The boss sighed and nodded. Anyone who didn't know him too well might even have thought he was ashamed.

'And did you contravene this principle in any way?'

'No, and that's why I botched the mission.'

'How did you botch it?'

'Right at the beginning . . .' I squinted sideways at a stuffed snowy owl standing on shelf behind the glass. Had it really moved its head? 'Right at the beginning I drained the amulet in a futile attempt to neutralise a black vortex . . .'

Boris Ignatievich frowned. He brushed his hair back with his hand.

'Okay, let's start with that. I've studied the image, and if you haven't touched it up . . .'

I shook my head indignantly.

'I believe you. Well, a vortex like that can't be removed with an amulet. Do you remember the classification?'

Damn! Why hadn't I looked at my old notes?

'I'm sure you don't. But it doesn't matter. There is no class for this vortex. There's no way you could possibly have dealt with it . . .' The boss leaned across the desk and continued in a mysterious whisper: '. . . and you know what . . .'

I was all ears.

'There's no way I could have either, Anton.'

This confession was unexpected, and I couldn't think of anything to say. Maybe no one had ever actually said out loud that the boss could do anything, but that was what everyone at the office believed.

'Anton, a vortex as strong as that can only be removed by the person who created it.'

'We have to find him . . .' I said uncertainly. 'I feel sorry for the girl . . .'

'This isn't about her. Not just about her.'

'Why?' I blurted out and then hastily corrected myself. 'We have to stop the Dark Magician, don't we?'

The boss sighed.

'He might have a licence. He might be entitled to cast the curse . . . This isn't even about the magician. A black vortex as powerful as that . . . You remember the plane that crashed last winter?'

I shuddered. It wasn't that we'd done anything wrong, it had more to do with a loophole in the law: a pilot who was under a curse had lost control and his airliner had crashed into a residential area of the city. Hundreds of innocent lives . . .

'Vortices like that can't act selectively. The girl's doomed, but it won't just be a brick that accidentally falls off some roof on to her head. More likely a building will explode, there'll be an epidemic, or someone will drop an atom bomb on Moscow by mistake. That's the real problem, Anton.'

The boss suddenly swung round and cast a withering glance at the owl. It folded its wings away quickly and the gleam in its glass eyes faded.

'Boris Ignatievich,' I said, horrified. 'I'm at fault . . .'

'Of course you are. There's only one redeeming aspect, Anton.' The boss cleared his throat. 'When you gave way to pity, you acted quite correctly. The amulet couldn't completely detach the vortex, but it has postponed the Inferno for a while. And now we have a day to work with, maybe even two. I've always believed that ill-considered but well-intentioned actions do more good than actions that are well considered but cruel. If you hadn't used the amulet, half of Moscow would already be in ruins.'

'What are we going to do?'

'Look for the girl. Protect her . . . as well as we can. We'll be able to destabilise the vortex again once or twice. And in the meantime we'll have to find the magician who cast the curse and make him remove the vortex.'

I nodded.

'Everybody will be involved in the search,' the boss said casually. 'I've recalled everyone from holiday, Ilya will be back from Sri Lanka by morning and the others will be here by lunchtime. The weather's bad in Europe. I've asked our colleagues in the European office to help, but by the time they can disperse the clouds . . .'

'By morning?' I asked, glancing at my watch. 'Another whole day.'

'No, this morning,' the boss replied, as if unaware of the midday sunshine outside the window. 'You'll be searching too. Maybe you'll get lucky again . . . Shall we continue with our analysis of your mistakes?'

'Can we afford to waste the time?' I asked timidly.

'Don't worry, it won't be wasted.' The boss got up, walked over to the glass cupboard, took out the owl and set it down on the desk. From close up you could see it really was a stuffed bird, with no more life in it than a fur collar. 'Let's move on to the vampires and their victim.'

'I lost the girl vampire. And the guys didn't catch her,' I confirmed penitently.

'No complaints there. You fought worthily enough. The point is – the victim . . .'

'Sure, the boy still had his memories. But he took off so fast . . .'

'Anton! Wake up! They hooked the boy with the Call from several kilometres away. When he walked into that alley he ought to have been a helpless puppet. And when the Twilight disappeared, he ought to have fainted. Anton, if he was still able to move after everything that had happened, he possesses extraordinary magical potential!'

The boss paused.

'I'm an idiot.'

'No, but you have been sitting on your backside in the lab far too long. Anton, this boy is potentially more powerful than I am!'

'Oh, come on . . .'

'Drop the flattery.'

The telephone on the desk rang. It was obviously something important, as not many people know the boss's direct number. I don't.

'Quiet!' the boss snapped at the phone. It stopped. 'Anton, you have to find that young boy. The girl vampire who got away isn't dangerous in herself. Either our guys will find her or an ordinary patrol will pick her up. But if she drinks the boy's blood or, even worse, initiates him . . . You've no idea what a fully fledged vampire's like. And these modern ones are mere mosquitoes compared with some Nosferatu. And he, with all his airs, he still wasn't one of the worst . . . So the boy must be found, examined and, if possible, taken into the Watch. We have no right to let him go over to the Dark Side, the balance of power in Moscow would completely collapse.'

'Is that an order?'

'Given under licence,' the boss said darkly. 'I have the right to issue that kind of order, you know that.'

'Yes, I know,' I said quietly. 'But where do I start? That is, who do I start with?'

'Whoever you like. I'd say with the girl. But try to find the boy too.'

'Shall I go now?

'Catch up on your sleep first.'

'I've slept long enough, Boris Ignatievich.'

'I doubt it. I'd recommend an hour at least.'

I didn't understand. I'd got up at eleven and gone straight to the office, I felt perfectly fresh and full of energy.

'Here's someone to help you.' The boss flicked the stuffed owl with his finger. The bird stretched out its wings and started screeching indignantly.

I swallowed hard and risked a question:

'Who is it? Or what is it?'

'Why do you need to know?' asked the boss, looking into the owl's eyes.

'To decide whether I want to work with it!'

The owl glanced at me and hissed like an enraged cat.

'That's the wrong way of putting it,' said the boss, shaking his head. 'Will *she* agree to work with you, that's the real question.'

The owl started screeching again.

'Yes,' said the boss, talking to the bird now, not to me. 'There's a lot of truth in what you say. But who was it that requested a new appeal?'

The bird froze.

'I promise I'll intercede for you. And this time there is a chance.'

'Boris Ignatievich, in my opinion—' I began.

'I'm sorry, Anton, that doesn't bother me . . .' The boss stretched out his arm, the owl took a clumsy stride with its fluffy legs and stood on his open hand. 'You don't know just how lucky you are.'

I had no answer to that. The boss went across to the window, opened it wide and stuck his hand out. The owl flapped its wings and went hurtling downward.

'Where has . . . it . . . gone?'

'To your place. You'll be working as partners.' The boss rubbed the bridge of his nose. 'Oh yes! Don't forget, her name's Olga.'

'The owl?'

'The owl. Feed her and take care of her and everything will be fine. And now . . . get a bit of sleep. No need to come into the office when you get up, just wait for Olga to arrive and get on with the job. Check out the circle line on the metro, for one . . .'

'How can I get back to sleep . . .' I began. But the world around me was already turning dim, fading away, dissolving. The corner of a pillow jutted painfully into my cheek.

I was lying in my own bed.

My head felt heavy, my eyes full of sand. My throat was parched and painful.

'Aagh . . .' I gasped hoarsely, turning over on to my back. Through the heavy curtains I couldn't see whether it was still night or whether the day was well advanced. I squinted at the clock: the glowing figures showed eight.

It was the first time I'd been granted an audience with the boss in my sleep.

It's not a very pleasant business, especially for the boss – he must have broken through into my mind.

Time must really be short if he'd decided it was necessary to hold his briefing in the world of dreams. And it had all seemed much more real than I would have expected. The mission analysis, that stupid owl . . .

The sound of tapping on the window made me start. A rapid, gentle tapping that sounded like claws. I heard a muffled screeching.

But what else was I really expecting?

I jumped up, awkwardly adjusted my shorts and hurried over to the window. All the garbage that I'd swallowed as part of the preparation for the hunt was still affecting me, and I could distinguish the outlines of objects quite clearly.

I tore the curtains aside and raised the blind.

The owl was sitting on the windowsill. From down in the street, of course, it would have been hard to tell what kind of bird had landed on the tenth-floor window. But if the neighbours had happened to glance out, they'd have got a real surprise. A snowy owl in the heart of Moscow . . .

'What the hell . . .' I muttered.

I felt like being more specific. But that was a habit they'd cured me of when I first started working for the Watch. Or rather, I'd cured myself. Once you've seen a couple of Dark twisters above the heads of people you've cursed at, you soon learn to hold your tongue.

The owl was looking at me. Waiting.

All the other birds around were going wild. A swarm of sparrows sitting in a tree not far away started chirping crazily. The crows were a bit bolder. They settled on the next-door balcony and on the nearest trees and started cawing, every now and then launching off from the branches and circling near the window. Their instincts told them this surprising new neighbour meant trouble.

But the owl didn't react at all. She couldn't give a damn about the sparrows, or the crows.

'Just who are you?' I said as I threw open the window, ripping away the paper strips glued over the cracks. The boss really had lumbered me with this new partner . . .

The owl flapped its wings once and flew into the room. It landed on the wardrobe and closed its eyes. As if it had always lived here. Maybe it had got cold on the way over. But then it was a snowy owl . . .

I started to close the window, trying to think what to do next. How would I communicate with her, what would I feed her and how could this feathered creature possibly help me?

'Is your name Olga?' I asked, when I'd finished with the window. There was a draught from the cracks now, but I could fix that later. 'Hey, bird!'

The owl half opened one eye, taking no more notice of me than of the fussy, chattering sparrows.

I was feeling more awkward with every moment. In the first place I had a partner I couldn't even talk to. And in the second place my partner was a woman.

Even if she was an owl.

Maybe I ought to put my trousers on. I wasn't really awake yet, standing there in just my crumpled shorts, I hadn't shaved . . .

Feeling like a total idiot, I grabbed my clothes and hurried from the room. The phrase I muttered to the owl as I left added a finishing touch: 'Excuse me, I'll just be a moment.'

If this bird really was what I thought it was, I couldn't have made the best impression.

What I really wanted was to take a shower, but I couldn't afford to waste that much time. I made do with a shave and sticking my buzzing head under the cold tap. On the shelf, between the shampoo and the deodorant, I found some eau de cologne, which I don't normally use.

'Olga?' I called as I stuck my head out into the corridor.

I found the owl in the kitchen, on the fridge. Just sitting there looking dead, like a stuffed dummy stuck up there as a joke. Almost the way it had looked on the boss's shelves.

'Are you alive? I asked.

One amber-yellow eye peered at me.

'All right,' I said, spreading my hands. 'Why don't we start from the beginning? I realise I haven't come across very well. And I'll be honest about it, I do that all the time.'

The owl was listening.

'I don't know who you are,' I said, straddling a stool and facing the fridge. 'And you can't tell me either. But I can introduce myself. My name's Anton. Five years ago I discovered that I was one of the Others.'

The owl made a sound that was more like a muffled laugh than anything else.

'Yes,' I agreed. 'Only five years ago. That was just the way things went. I had a very high level of resistance. I didn't want to see the Twilight world. So I didn't. Until the boss found me.'

The owl seemed to be getting interested.

'He was doing a practical exercise, briefing agents on how to identify secret Others. When he came across me . . .' I laughed as I remembered. 'He broke through my resistance, of course. After that it was very simple . . . I did the adaptation course and started working in the analytical section . . . Nothing in my life really changed that much. I became one of the Others, but it was like I hadn't really noticed. The boss wasn't too pleased, but he didn't say anything. I was good at my job, and he had no right to interfere in anything else. But a week ago this vampire maniac turned up in town, and they gave me the job of neutralising him. Supposedly because all the agents were busy. But really to get me out there in the firing line. Maybe they were right. But during the week another three people were killed. A professional would have caught that couple in a day . . .'

I really wanted to know what Olga thought about all this. But the owl didn't make a sound.

'What's more important for maintaining the balance?' I asked anyway. 'Giving me some operational experience or saving the lives of three innocent people?'

The owl said nothing.

'I couldn't sense the vampires with the usual methods,' I went on. 'I had to attune myself to them. I didn't drink human blood, though, I made do with pig's blood. And all those drugs . . . but then, you know all about those, I expect . . .'

When I mentioned the drugs I got up, opened the little cupboard above the cooker and took out a glass jar with a tight-fitting ground-glass stopper. There was only a little bit of the lumpy brown powder left, it made no sense to hand it back in to the department. I tipped the powder into the sink and rinsed it away – the kitchen was filled with a pungent, dizzying odour. I rinsed out the jar and dropped it into the rubbish bin.

'I almost went over the edge,' I said. 'I was well on the way. Yesterday morning, on my way back from the hunt, I ran into the little girl from next door in the entrance. I didn't even dare say hello, my fangs had already sprouted. And last night, when I felt the Call summoning the boy . . . I almost joined the vampires.'

The owl was looking into my eyes.

'Why do you think the boss gave me the job?'

A stuffed dummy. Clumps of dusty feathers stuffed with cotton wool.

'So I could see things through their eyes?'

The doorbell rang in the hallway. I sighed and shrugged: it was her own fault, after all, anyone would be better to talk to than this boring bird. I switched the light on as I walked to the door and opened it.

Standing there in the doorway was a vampire.

'Come in, Kostya,' I said, 'come in.'

He hesitated at the door, but then came in. He ran his hand through his hair – I noticed that his palms were sweaty and his eyes restless.

Kostya's only seventeen. He was born a vampire, a perfectly ordinary city vampire. It's really tough: with vampire parents a child has almost no chance of growing up human.

'I've brought back the CDs,' Kostya muttered. 'Here.'

I took the pile from the boy, not even surprised there were so many. I usually had to nag him for ages to bring them back: he was terribly absentminded.

'Did you listen to them all?' I asked. 'Did you copy any?'

'No . . . I'll be going . . .'

'Wait.' I grabbed him by the shoulder and pushed him into the room. 'What's going on?'

He didn't answer.

'You already know?' I asked, beginning to catch on.

'There aren't many of us, Anton,' said Kostya, looking me in the eye. 'When one of us passes away, we sense it immediately.'

'Okay. Take your shoes off, let's go into the kitchen and have a serious talk.'

Kostya didn't argue. But I was desperately trying to figure out what to do. Five years earlier, when I became an Other and the Twilight side of the world was revealed to me, I'd made plenty of surprising discoveries. And one of the most shocking was the fact that a family of vampires was living right above my head.

I remember it like it was yesterday. I was on my way home from classes that seemed so ordinary, they reminded me of my old college. Three double lectures, a lecturer, heat that had the white coats glued to our bodies – we rented the lecture hall from a medical college. I was fooling around as I walked home, dropping into the Twilight in short bursts – I couldn't manage any longer back then. Then I began feeling out the people walking down the street, and at the entrance I ran into my neighbours.

They're really nice people. I wanted to borrow a drill from them once, and Kostya's father, Gennady, he's a builder, just came round and had some fun helping out with the concrete walls, demonstrating conclusively that the intelligentsia can't survive without the proletariat . . .

And now suddenly I could see they weren't humans at all.

It was terrifying. The brownish-grey auras, the hideous pressure. I stopped dead, staring at them in horror. Polina, Kostya's mother, looked surprised, the boy froze and turned his face away. But the head of the family walked towards me, moving deeper into the Twilight as he came, walking with the elegant stride that only vampires, alive and dead at the same time, have. The Twilight is their natural habitat.

'Hello, Anton,' he said.

The world around me was grey and dead. I'd dived into the Twilight after him without even noticing it.

'I knew you'd cross the barrier some day,' he said. 'Everything's okay.'

I took a step back – and Gennady's face quivered.

'Everything's okay,' he said. He opened his shirt and I saw the registration tag, a blue imprint on the grey skin. 'We're all registered. Polina! Kostya!'

His wife also crossed into the Twilight and unfastened her blouse. The boy didn't move and it took a stern glance from his father to get him to show his blue seal.

'I have to check,' I whispered. My passes were clumsy, I lost track twice and had to start again. Finally the seal responded. 'Permanent registration, no known violations . . .'

'Is everything okay?' asked Gennady. 'Can we go now?'

'I . . .'

'Don't worry about it. We knew you'd become an Other some day.'

'Go on,' I said. It was against the rules, but that was the last thing I was bothered about.

'Yes . . .' Gennady paused for a moment before he left the Twilight. 'I've been in your home . . . Anton, I return to you your invitation to enter . . .'

Everything was just as it should be.

They walked away and I sat down on a bench, beside an old granny warming herself in the sunshine. I lit a cigarette, trying to sort out my thoughts. The granny looked at me and said:

'Nice people, aren't they, Arkasha?'

She was always getting my name wrong. She only had two or three months left to live, I could see that quite clearly now.

'Not exactly . . .' I said. I smoked three cigarettes, then trudged off into the building. I stood in the doorway for a moment, watching the grey 'vampire's trail' fade away. I'd just learned how to see it that very day . . .

I moped into the evening. I leafed through my notes, which meant I had to withdraw into the Twilight. In the ordinary world, the pages of those standard exercise books were a pure, unsullied white. I wanted to call our group's supervisor or the boss himself – I was his personal responsibility. But I felt I had to make the decision myself.

When it was dark I couldn't stand it any longer. I went up to the next floor and rang the bell. When Kostya opened the door, he shuddered. But he actually looked perfectly ordinary, like all of his family . . .

'Call your parents, will you?' I asked.

'What for?' he muttered.

'I want to invite you all for tea.'

Gennady appeared behind his son's back, out of nowhere, he was far more skilful than me, the newly fledged adept of the Light.

'Are you sure, Anton?' he asked doubtfully. 'There's no need. Everything's okay.'

'I'm sure.'

He paused and then shrugged.

'We'll come round tomorrow. If you invite us. Don't rush things.'

By midnight I was feeling absolutely delighted they'd refused. At three I tried to get to sleep, reassured in the knowledge that they couldn't enter my home and never would be able to.

In the morning, still not having slept a wink, I stood at the window, looking out at the city. There weren't many vampires. Very few, in fact. There wasn't another within a radius of two or three kilometres.

How did it feel to be an outcast? To be punished, not for committing a crime, but for the potential ability to commit it? And how did it feel for them to live . . . well, not live, some other word was required here . . . alongside their own guard?

On the way back from classes I bought a cake for tea.

And now here was Kostya, a fine, intelligent young man, a physics student at Moscow University, who had the misfortune to have been born a living corpse, sitting beside me and raking the spoon around in the sugar bowl like he was too shy to take any. What could have made him so bashful?

At first he used to call round almost every day. I was his direct opposite, I was on the side of the Light. But I let him into my home, and he didn't have to pretend with me. He could simply sit and talk, or he could plunge into the Twilight and boast about the new abilities he'd developed. 'Anton, I actually transformed!' – 'And now my fangs have started to grow, r-r-r-r!'

And the strange thing was, it all felt entirely normal. I laughed as I watched the young vampire's attempts to transform himself into a bat – that's a trick for a top-flight vampire, but he's not one of them and, may the Light grant, he never will be. Just sometimes I would scold him: 'Kostya . . . you mustn't ever do that. Do you understand?' And that felt entirely normal too.

'Kostya, I was only doing my job.'

'You shouldn't have.'

'They were breaking the law. Do you understand? Not just our law, mind you. It's not just the Light Ones who have accepted it, all the Others have. That vampire—'

'I knew him,' Kostya suddenly said. 'He was a laugh. Did he suffer?'

'No.' I shook my head. 'The seal kills instantaneously.'

Kostya shuddered and squinted down at his own chest for a second. If you enter the Twilight, you can see the seal even through a vampire's clothes, and if you don't, you'll never find it. I don't think he actually moved across. But how should I know what the seal feels like to a vampire?

'What was I supposed to do?' I asked. 'He'd already killed. Killed innocent people, who had absolutely no defence against him. He initiated a girl . . . by crude force – she should never have become a vampire. Yesterday he almost killed a boy. Just for the sake of it. Not because he was hungry.'

'Do you know what our hunger's like?' Kostya asked after a pause.

He was growing up. Right in front of my eyes.

'Yes. Yesterday I . . . almost became a vampire.'

Just a moment's silence.

'I know. I could feel it . . . I was hoping.'

Damn. While I was conducting my hunt, they'd been hunting me too. Or rather, lying in ambush for me, hoping the hunter would turn into the hunted beast.

'No,' I said. 'Sorry, no way.'

'Okay, so he was guilty,' Kostya went on stubbornly. 'But why did you have to kill him? He should have been tried. A tribunal, a lawyer, a proper charge, the way the law says things should be done . . .'

'The law says that humans mustn't be involved in our business!' I roared. And for the first time that tone of voice failed to make any impression on Kostya.

'You were human for too long,' he said.

'And I don't regret it for a moment.'

'Why did you kill him?'

'If I hadn't, he would have killed me!'

'Initiated you.'

'That's even worse.'

Kostya didn't answer. He put down his tea and stood up. A perfectly ordinary, slightly insolent and morally pained young man.

Except that he was a vampire.

'Wait.' I stepped across to the fridge. 'Take this, they issued it to me, but I didn't need it.'

I pulled out the two-hundred-gram bottles of donor's blood from between the bottles of Borzhomi mineral water.

'No thanks.'

'Kostya, I know this is always a problem for you. It's no use to me. Take it.'

'Are you trying to bribe me?'

I started getting angry.

'Why would I need to bribe you? It's just stupid to throw it out, that's all. It's blood. People gave it to help someone.'

Kostya suddenly laughed. He reached out, took one of the bottles and opened it, tearing off the tinfoil cap with practised ease. He raised the bottle to his lips, laughed again and took a swallow.

I'd never seen them feed. And never really wanted to.

'Stop that,' I said. 'Don't play the fool.'

Kostya's lips were covered in blood and there was a fine trickle of it running down his neck. Not just running down, but soaking into the skin.

'Do you find the way we feed ourselves unpleasant?'

'Yes.'

'So you find me unpleasant as well? All of us?'

I shook my head. We'd never talked about this before. It had been easier that way.

'Kostya, in order to live, you need blood. And, sometimes at least, human blood.'

'We don't live.'

'I meant in the more general sense. In order to move, think, speak, dream.'

'What do you care about a vampire's dreams?'

'Listen, son. There are plenty of people living in the world who need regular blood transfusions. There are at least as many of them as you. And then there are hospital emergencies. That's why people give blood, that's why it's thought to be such an honourable and respected thing to do . . . I know about your kind's contributions to the development of medicine and the way you promoted the giving of blood. Kostya, if someone needs blood in order to live, to exist − that's no big deal. And whether it goes in through the veins or the stomach is irrelevant too. The important thing is how you get hold of it.'

'Empty words,' Kostya snorted. I got the feeling he'd crossed over into the Twilight for an instant and then come straight back out. The boy was growing up, all right. And he was getting really strong.

'You showed the way you really feel about us yesterday.'

'You're wrong.'

'Ah, drop it . . .' He put the bottle down, then changed his mind and turned it upside down over the sink. 'We don't need your—'

I heard a hoot behind me and swung round. I'd completely forgotten about the owl, but now it had turned its head towards Kostya and spread its wings.

'Agh . . .' he said. 'What . . .'

The owl folded its wings and closed its eyes.

'Olga, we're talking,' I growled. 'Just give us a moment . . .'

The bird didn't respond. Kostya glanced from me to the owl and back again. Then he sat down and folded his hands on his knees.

'What's wrong with you?' I asked.

'Can I go now?'

He wasn't just surprised or frightened, he was in shock.

'Okay. But take this, will you?'

Kostya began grabbing the bottles and putting them in his pockets.

'Take a plastic bag, you dunce! What if there's someone in the hallway?'

The vampire obediently packed all the bottles into a plastic bag bearing the noble inscription: 'For the resurrection of Russian culture!' He gave the owl a sideways glance, went out into the hall and hastily began putting on his shoes.

'Call again,' I said. 'I'm not your enemy. Not until you cross that line, I'm not.'

He nodded and shot out of my apartment like a bullet. I shrugged and closed the door, then went back into the kitchen and looked at the owl.

'Well? What happened there?'

It was impossible to read anything in those amber-yellow eyes. I threw my hands up.

'How can we work together? Eh? How are we going to collaborate? Do you have any way of communicating? I'm trying to be frank with you, do you hear me? To have a frank conversation!'

I didn't go all the way into the Twilight, just reached in there with my thoughts. It's not good to trust anyone you don't know like that, but the boss wouldn't have given me a partner I couldn't trust, would he?

No answer. Even if Olga could communicate telepathically, she wasn't going to.

'What shall we do? We need to look for that girl. Will you accept her image?'

No reply. I sighed and tossed the scrap of my memory at the bird anyway.

The owl stretched its wings and soared across on to my shoulder.

'Ah, so we do hear when we're spoken to? But we don't condescend to reply. All right, have it your own way. What should I do?'

The owl still wouldn't speak.

In fact, I knew what to do. There was no hope of success, but that was a different matter.

'And how am I going to wander round the streets with you sitting on my shoulder?'

A mocking glance, definitely mocking. And the bird on my shoulder shifted into the Twilight.

So that was it. An invisible observer. And no ordinary observer – Kostya's reaction to the owl had been very instructive. Apparently I'd been given a partner that the powers of the Dark knew better than the rank-and-file servants of the Light did.

'Right,' I said cheerfully. 'I'll just grab a bite to eat, okay?'

I took out some yoghurt and poured a glass of orange juice. The very thought of what I'd been feeding myself with for the last week – half-raw steaks and meat juices that were not much different from blood – made me feel sick.

'Maybe you'd like a bit of meat?'

The owl turned away.

'Have it your own way,' I said. 'No doubt when you get hungry you'll find some way to communicate.'

CHAPTER 3

I LIKE WALKING round town inside the Twilight. You don't actually become invisible, or you'd have people bumping into you all the time. They just somehow look straight through you and don't notice you. But this time I'd have to work out in the open.

The day's not our time. Odd as it may seem, the followers of the Light work at night, when the Dark Ones become active. And just at the moment there wasn't so much the Dark Ones could do. During the day vampires, werewolves and Dark Magicians are obliged to live like ordinary people.

Most of them, that is.

I was walking round Tulskaya metro station. Following the boss's advice, I'd worked through all the stations on the circle line where the girl with the black vortex could possibly have left the metro. She should have left a trail behind, a weak one maybe, but still detectable. Now I'd decided to work my way out along the radial lines.

It's a stupid station in a stupid district. Two exits quite some distance apart. A market, that pompous-looking skyscraper occupied by the tax police, a massive apartment block. With all those dark emanations all around, any chance of picking up the trail of the black vortex was looking pretty doubtful.

Especially if it had never even been there.

I walked round everything, trying to sense the girl's aura, sometimes glancing into the Twilight at the invisible bird nesting on my shoulder. The own was dozing. It couldn't sense anything either, and for some reason I felt sure its reconnaissance skills were better than mine.

Once a militiaman checked my papers. Twice I was pestered by crazy blokes who wanted to give me, absolutely free – that is for only fifty roubles – a Chinese fan, a child's toy and a dirt-cheap Korean mobile phone.

And again I couldn't control myself. I brushed aside the next street salesman who pestered me and performed a remoralisation. Only a little one, right at the very edge of what's allowed. Maybe he would start looking for a different kind of work. Or maybe he wouldn't . . .

But just at that moment someone grabbed hold of my elbows. A second earlier there was no one there – then suddenly there was a young couple. An attractive-looking girl with red hair and a solid-looking man with a surly expression on his face.

'Stop there,' said the girl. She was the leader, I could tell that straight off. 'Day Watch.'

Light and Dark!

I shrugged and looked at them.

'Your name,' the girl demanded.

There was no point in lying, they'd captured the image of my aura already, and after that identifying the individual is only a matter of time.

'Anton Gorodetsky.'

They waited.

'Other,' I confessed. 'Night Watch agent.'

They lifted their hands off my elbows, and even took a step back. But they didn't seem disappointed.

'Okay, let's enter the Twilight,' said the man.

They didn't look like vampires. That was one good thing. At least I could hope for a certain degree of objectivity. I sighed and shifted from one reality into the other.

The first surprise was that they turned out to be genuinely young. A witch of about twenty-five and a warlock of about thirty, the same age as me. I thought that if I needed to, I could probably even recall their names, there weren't that many witches and warlocks born in the late 1960s.

The second surprise was that the owl wasn't there on my shoulder. Or rather, it was: I could feel its claws and I could see it, but only with some effort. It was as if the bird had shifted realities at the same time as I had and moved into a deeper level of the Twilight.

This was getting really interesting!

'Day Watch,' the girl repeated. 'Alisa Donnikova, Other.'

'Pyotr Nesterov, Other,' the man muttered.

'You have some kind of problem?'

The girl drilled me with one of those speciality 'witch's glances'. She started to look more attractive and appealing with every moment. Of course, I'm protected against direct influence, it's not possible to bewitch me, but it certainly looked impressive.

'We're not the ones with the problem. Anton Gorodetsky, you have entered into unsanctioned contact with a human.'

'Yes? And what was that?'

'Only a seventh-degree intervention,' the witch admitted reluctantly. 'But an offence is an offence. And you also urged him towards the Light.'

'Are we going to draw up a charge report?' I suddenly found the situation amusing. Seventh degree was next to nothing – a level of influence on the borderline between magic and ordinary conversation.

'We are.'

'And what are we going to write? A Night Watch agent slightly increased one human's aversion to deception?'

'Thereby disrupting the established balance,' the warlock barked out.

'Really? And what harm does it do to the Dark? If the guy stops working as a petty crook, his life is bound to get worse. He'll be more moral, but unhappier too. Under the terms of the commentaries on the Treaty on the balance of power, that's not regarded as a violation of the balance.'

'Sophistry,' the young woman said curtly. 'You're a Night Watch agent. What might be pardonable for an ordinary Other is not acceptable from you.'

She was right. It was still a violation, even if it was petty.

'He was obstructing me. I have a right to use magical intervention in the course of conducting an investigation.'

'Are you on duty, Anton?'

'Yes.'

'Why during the day?'

'I have a special assignment. You can direct your enquiry to my superiors. Or rather, you have the right to address your enquiry to your superiors.'

The witch and the warlock exchanged glances. No matter how opposed our goals and moralities might be, the two hierarchies had to collaborate.

Only, to be quite frank, nobody really liked involving the bosses.

'Very well,' the witch agreed reluctantly. 'Anton, we will limit ourselves to a verbal warning.'

I looked around. All round me there were people, moving slowly through the grey gloom. Ordinary people, incapable of moving out of their own little world. We were Others, and though I stood on the Light Side and the other two were on the Dark Side, we had far more in common with each other than with any of those ordinary humans.

'On what terms?'

You should never try to second-guess the Dark. You should never make any concessions. And it's even more dangerous to accept any gifts from it. But rules are only made to be broken.

'No terms.'

Well, that was a surprise!

I looked at Alisa, trying to figure out the catch. Pyotr was obviously indignant at his partner, he was angry, he wanted to expose an adept of the Light as a criminal. That meant I didn't have to worry about him.

But where was the trap?

'That's unacceptable to me,' I said, with a sigh of relief – I'd spotted the catch. 'Alisa, thank you for your offer of a peaceful resolution. I can accept it, but in a similar situation I am bound to forgive you a minor magical intervention, up to and including the seventh degree.'

'Very well, Other,' Alisa agreed readily. She held out her hand and I automatically shook it. 'We have a personal agreement.'

The owl on my shoulder flapped its wings. There was a furious screech right in my ear. And a moment later the bird materialised in the Twilight world.

Alisa took a step back and the pupils of her eyes rapidly extended into vertical slits. The young warlock took up a defensive stance.

'We have an agreement,' the witch repeated sullenly.

What was going on?

I realised too late that I shouldn't have entered into an agreement while Olga was there. But then – what was so terrible about what had happened? As if I hadn't been there when other guys from the

Watch had concluded alliances like this, made concessions, agreed terms for co-operating with the Dark Ones, even the boss himself had done it! Sure, it's undesirable, but sometimes you have to.

Our goal is not to exterminate the Dark Ones. Our goal is to maintain the balance. The Dark Ones will only disappear when people conquer the Evil in themselves. Or we'll disappear, if people decide they like the Dark better than the Light.

'The agreement's been made,' I told the owl. 'Cool it. It's no big deal. Just standard collaboration.'

Alisa smiled and gave me a wave. She took the warlock by the elbow, and they started moving off. A few moments later they were out of the Twilight and setting off along the pavement. An ordinary young couple.

'What's wrong with you?' I asked. 'Well? Field work has always been built on compromises.'

'You made a mistake.'

Olga's voice was strange, it didn't match her appearance. Soft, velvety, musical. The way werecats talk, not birds.

'Oh! So you can talk now?'

'Yes.'

'Then why didn't you say anything before?'

'Everything was okay before.'

I laughed, remembering the old joke about the child that didn't speak for years.

'I'll leave the Twilight, okay? And meanwhile you can explain what mistake I've made. Minor compromises with the Dark Ones are inevitable in this line of work.'

'You're not well enough qualified to make compromises.'

The world around me became coloured. It was like switching modes on a video camera, when you change from 'sepia' or 'old movie' to the standard view. The comparison is really quite apt in some ways: the Twilight *is* an 'old movie'. A really old one that

humankind has managed to forget. They find it easier to live that
way.

I set off towards the steps down into the metro, snarling to my
invisible companion on the way:

'And just what have qualifications got to do with it?'

'A high-ranking Watch member is able to foresee the
consequences of a compromise. Whether it's no more than just a
minor trade-off and the effects are self-neutralising, or a trap, a
trick.'

'I doubt if a seventh-grade intervention's likely to lead to
disaster.'

A man walking along beside me glanced at me in surprise. I was
just about to say something like: 'I'm harmless, the non-violent
kind of psycho.' It's a great way of curing excessive curiosity. But
the man had already lengthened his stride, probably having come
to a similar conclusion himself.

'Anton, you can't predict the consequences. You overreacted to
a minor annoyance. Your little piece of magic led to intervention
by the Dark Ones. You agreed a compromise with them. But the
saddest thing of all is that there was no need for magical
intervention in the first place.'

'Okay, okay, I admit it. So now what?'

The bird's voice was sounding more lifelike now, developing
more expression.

I suppose it must have been a long time since she'd last spoken.

'Now – nothing. We'll have to hope for the best.'

'Are you going to tell the boss what happened?'

'No. At least, not yet. We're partners, after all.'

I felt a warm glow. This sudden improvement in relations with
my partner made any mistakes worthwhile.

'Thanks. So what do you advise?'

'You're doing everything right. Look for the trail.'

I'd have preferred rather less standard advice . . .

'Let's go.'

By two o'clock, along with the circle line, I'd combed the entire grey line too. Maybe I am a lousy operational agent, but there was no way I could have failed to spot the trail from yesterday, when I'd captured the image myself. The girl with the black vortex spinning over her head hadn't got out here. I'd have to go back and start again from the point where we'd met.

At Kurskaya I went up the escalator and out of the metro and bought a plastic tub of salad and a coffee from a van on the street. The very sight of the hamburgers and sausages made me feel sick, even though the amount of meat in them was strictly symbolic.

'Will you have something?' I asked my invisible companion.

'No, thank you.'

Standing there with the fine snow falling on me, I picked at my salad with a tiny plastic fork and sipped the hot coffee. A bum who'd been counting on me buying a beer, so that he could have the empty bottle, hung about for a bit and then took off into the metro to get warm. Nobody else paid any attention to me. The girl behind the counter served the hungry passers-by, faceless streams of people flooded from the station and back towards it. The salesman at a bookstall was trying wearily and unenthusiastically to foist some book or other on a customer, who didn't like the price.

'I must be in a bad mood or something . . .' I muttered.

'Why?'

'Everything looks dark and miserable. All the people are low-lifes and idiots, the salad's frozen, my boots feel damp.'

The bird on my shoulder screeched.

'No, Anton, it's not just your mood. You can sense the approach of the Inferno.'

'I'm not noted for being particularly sensitive.'

'That's just the point.'

I glanced at the station and tried to get a close look at people's faces. Some of them were sensing it too. The ones who stood right on the line between human and Other were tense and depressed. They couldn't understand why, so they were compensating by acting cheerful.

'Dark and Light . . . What will it be when it happens, Olga?'

'Anything at all. You delayed the time of the eruption, but now when the vortex strikes the consequences will be absolutely catastrophic. That's the effect of delay.'

'The boss didn't tell me that.'

'Why should he? You did the right thing. Now at least there's a chance.'

'Olga, how old are you?' I asked. Between humans the question might have been taken as an insult. But for us age doesn't have any particular limits.

'Very old, Anton. For instance, I can remember the uprising.'

'The revolution?'

'The uprising on Senate Square, in 1825.' The owl chortled. I didn't say anything. She could be even older than the boss.

'What's your rank?' I asked.

'I don't have one. I was stripped of all rights.'

'I'm sorry.'

'No problem. I came to terms with it a long time ago.'

Her voice was still cheerful, even mocking. But something told me Olga had never come to terms with it.

'If you don't mind me asking . . . Why did they shut you in that body?'

'There was no other option. Living in a wolf's body is much harder.'

'Wait . . .' I dropped the remains of the salad in a bin. I looked at my shoulder, but, of course, I didn't see the owl – to do that I would have had to withdraw into the Twilight. 'What are you? If you're a shape-shifter, then why are you with us? If you're a magician, then why such an unusual punishment?'

'That's got nothing to do with the job, Anton.' For just a moment there was a hint of steel in her voice. 'But it all started with me compromising with the Dark Ones. Only a small compromise. I thought I'd calculated the consequences, but I was wrong.'

So that was it . . .

'Was that why you started talking? You wanted to warn me off, but you were too late?'

No answer.

As if Olga was already regretting being so frank.

'Let's get on with the job,' I said. And just then the phone buzzed in my pocket.

It was Larissa. What was she doing working two straight shifts?

'Anton, listen carefully . . . They've picked up that girl's trail. Perovo station.'

'Shit,' was all I said. Working the commuter suburbs was hell.

'Right,' Larissa agreed. She was no field operative . . . that was probably why she was sitting by the phone. But she was a bright girl. 'Anton, get over to Perovo. All our team are concentrating over there, they're following the trail. And another thing . . . they've spotted the Day Watch there.'

'I get the picture.' I folded away my phone.

I didn't get it. Did the Dark Ones already know everything? Were they just yearning for the Inferno to erupt? Then maybe it was no accident that they'd stopped me?

Rubbish. A major disaster in Moscow was hardly in the interests of the Dark. But of course, they wouldn't try to stop the twister either: that would be to go against their nature.

So I didn't go by metro after all. I stopped a car. It ought to save me a bit of time, even if not much. I sat beside the driver, a swarthy intellectual about forty years old. The car was new, and the driver gave the impression of doing very well for himself. It seemed a bit odd for him to be earning a bit on the side by offering a taxi service.

. . . Perovo. A large city district. Crowds of people. Light and Dark, all twisted up together into a knot. And a few institutions, casting beams of Dark and Light in all directions. Working there would be like trying to find a grain of sand on the floor of a crowded disco with the strobe lights on.

I wouldn't be much use to anyone, or rather, I wouldn't be any use at all. But I'd been ordered to go, so I had to. Maybe they'd ask me to identify the girl.

'For some reason I was sure we'd get lucky,' I whispered, gazing at the road ahead. We drove past Elk Island Park, a pretty grim place where the Dark Ones gather for their sabbaths. And when they do, the rights of ordinary people aren't always respected. Five nights a year we have to put up with anything. Well, almost anything.

'I thought so too,' whispered Olga.

'I can't compete with the field agents,' I said, shaking my head.

The driver glanced sideways at me. I'd accepted the price without haggling, and he'd seemed happy enough to go in my direction. But a man talking to himself always arouses suspicion.

'I just blew this job,' I told the driver with a sigh. 'That is, I made a mess of it. I thought I could make up for it today, but they managed without me.'

'So what's your hurry?' the driver asked. He didn't look like the talkative type, but he was interested.

'I was ordered to go,' I said.

I wondered who he thought I was.

'So what do you do?'

'I'm a programmer,' I answered. And I was telling the truth too.

'Fantastic,' the driver commented, and laughed. What was so fantastic about it? 'Do you make a living?'

He didn't really have to ask. After all, I wasn't riding the metro. But I answered anyway:

'Enough.'

'I wasn't just asking out of curiosity,' my driver unexpectedly confided. 'My system administrator's leaving me . . .'

My system administrator . . . Well, well!

'I personally see the finger of fate in this. I give a man a lift and he turns out to be a programmer. I think you're already doomed.'

He laughed, like he was trying to make light of his over-confidence.

'Have you worked with local networks?'

'Yes.'

'A network of fifty terminals. It has to be maintained. We pay well.'

I felt myself starting to smile. It was a good offer. A local network. Decent money. And no one sending you out at night to catch vampires, making you drink blood and sniff out trails on the frozen streets . . .

'Shall I give you my card?' The man slipped one hand into his jacket pocket. 'Think about it . . .'

'No thanks. I'm afraid no one just leaves my kind of work.'

'KGB, is it?' the driver asked with a frown.

'More serious than that,' I answered. 'Much more serious. But something like that.'

'Oh, well . . .' the driver said, and paused. 'A pity. And I thought it was a sign from on high. Do you believe in fate?'

He'd slipped into a familiar tone quite naturally. I like that.

'No.'

'Why not?' asked the driver, genuinely surprised, as if he'd only ever met fatalists his whole life.

'There's no such thing as fate. It's been proved.'

'Who by?'

'In the place I work.'

He laughed.

'That's great. So it's not meant to be! Where shall I stop?'

We were already driving down Zelyony Avenue.

I peered hard through the layer of ordinary daily reality, into the Twilight. I couldn't make anything out clearly, my powers weren't strong enough. I sensed it rather than saw it – a cluster of dim lights in the grey gloom. Almost the entire central office was there.

'Over there . . .'

While I was still in ordinary reality I couldn't see my colleagues. I walked over the murky city snow towards the little square buried under snowdrifts between the apartment blocks and the avenue. A few frozen trees, a few lines of footsteps – either kids had been having fun, or a drunk had just staggered across.

'Wave to them, they've spotted you,' Olga suggested.

I thought for a moment and followed her advice. Let them think I could see clearly from one reality into the other.

'A meeting,' Olga said mockingly. 'An emergency briefing.'

I glanced round, just for form's sake, then summoned the Twilight and stepped into it.

The entire central office really was there. The whole of the Moscow department.

Standing in the middle was Boris Ignatievich. Lightly dressed in a suit and a thin fur cap, but wearing a scarf for some reason. I could just imagine him scrambling out of his BMW, surrounded by his bodyguards.

The field operatives were standing beside him. Igor and Garik – they were the ones really suited to the role of front-line fighters. Thick-set, stony faces, square shoulders, dull eyes – impervious. You can tell at a glance what kind of education they've had: eight years of secondary school, technical college and the special forces.

And as far as Igor's concerned that's exactly right. But Garik has two full college degrees. The appearance is similar, the behaviour almost identical, but the content's completely different. By comparison, Ilya looks like some refined intellectual, but it would be a mistake to be misled by those round spectacles with the thin frames, that high forehead and naïve expression. Semyon's was another exaggerated character: short, stocky, with a cunning gleam in his eyes, wearing a cheap nylon baseball jacket. A provincial, come up to the big city, from somewhere straight out of the 1960s, from the prize-winning collective farm Lenin's Stride. Absolute opposites. But what Ilya and Semyon had in common was a beautiful tan and dejected expressions. They'd been pulled out of Sir Lanka mid-holiday, and they weren't enjoying the Moscow winter too much. Ignat, Danila and Farid weren't there, although I could sense their fresh trails. But standing right behind the boss, not exactly like they were trying to hide, but not really noticeable unless you looked hard, were Bear and Tiger Cub. I was taken aback to see those two. They're not ordinary front-line fighters, they're really good, and they don't let minor details stand in their way.

There were lots of people from the office there too.

The analytical section, all five of them. The research team – everyone except Yulia, but that wasn't surprising, she's only thirteen. The only ones missing were from the archives section.

'Hi,' I said.

Some nodded, some smiled. But I could see they all had more important things than me on their minds. Boris Ignatievich gestured for me to come closer and then carried on from where he'd got to before I turned up and interrupted him:

'Not in their interest, and we welcome that. We won't get any help from them . . . well, fine, that's just great . . .'

Clear enough. He meant the Day Watch.

'We can search for the girl without interference, and Danila and

Farid are already getting close. I'd say, another five or six minutes
. . . But we've still been given an ultimatum.'

I caught Tiger Cub's eye. Oh, that was her ominous smile.
That's right, *her* smile. Tiger Cub's a woman, but there was no way
'Tigress' would have stuck.

Our agents don't much like the word 'ultimatum'.

'We don't get to hold on to the Dark Magician,' the boss said,
looking round at everyone with a dissatisfied expression. 'Got that?
We'll have to find him in order to disarm the vortex. But after that
we hand the magician over to the Dark Ones.'

'We hand him over?' Ilya queried.

The boss thought for a second.

'Yes, that's a fair point. We don't eliminate him and we don't
prevent him from contacting the Dark Ones. As far as I've been
able to tell, they don't know who he is either.'

The operatives' faces were turning sourer by the moment. Any
new magician on the territory they monitored was a big headache.
Even if he was registered and observed the terms of the Treaty. But
a magician this powerful . . .

'I'd prefer a slightly different scenario,' Tiger Cub said quietly.
'Boris Ignatievich, in the course of our work, situations can crop
up over which we have no control . . .'

'I'm sorry, but we can't allow such situations to arise,' the boss
snapped. Tiger Cub backed off immediately.

I'd have done the same.

'Well, that's about it . . .' The boss glanced at me. 'I'm glad you
got here, Anton. There's something I especially wanted you to
hear.'

I automatically tensed up.

'You did a good job yesterday. Yes, it's true, the only reason I
sent you out to look for the vampires was to test you. And not just
to see how good an operative you are, either . . . you've been in a

difficult situation for a long time, Anton. Killing a vampire is a lot harder for you than for anyone else here.'

'That's just where you're wrong, boss,' I said.

'I'd be glad if I'm mistaken. I want to thank you on behalf of the entire Night Watch. You destroyed one vampire and captured the image of the female vampire's trail. Captured it very accurately. You still don't have enough experience for investigative work. But you know how to record information clearly. The same thing goes for this girl. It was a completely non-standard situation, but you made a humane decision . . . and that's won us some time. The image of her aura was excellent. I knew immediately where to look for her.'

That really stung. No one was smiling or laughing, no one was smirking at me, but I still felt humiliated. The owl, whom nobody had seen yet, twitched on my shoulder. I took a deep breath of the Twilight air, that cold, tasteless air that isn't air at all. I asked:

'Boris Ignatievich, then what was the reason for sending me round the circle line? If you already knew the right district.'

'I could have been wrong,' the boss replied, a note of surprise in his voice. 'That's another thing . . . you have to understand that when you're working out in the field, you can't afford to rely on any opinion, no matter from how high up. One man in the field is a warrior – if he knows he's alone.'

'But I wasn't alone,' I said. 'And this assignment is absolutely crucial for my partner, you know that better than I do. By sending us to check districts you knew were empty, you deprived her of a chance to redeem herself.'

The boss's face is made of stone, you can't read anything in it if he doesn't want you to.

But even so, I felt like I'd hit the target.

'Your assignment isn't over yet, Anton and Olga,' he replied. 'There's still the female vampire, who has to be neutralised. No one has any right to interfere with us there: she violated the terms of the Treaty. And there's still the boy who showed such exceptional resistance to magic. He has to be found and turned to the Light. Plenty to be getting on with.'

'And this girl?'

'Already detected. The specialists will now try to neutralise the vortex. If that doesn't work, which it won't, we'll have to figure out who cast the curse. Ignat, over to you.'

I turned round. There indeed was Ignat standing not far away. Tall, well built and handsome, with blond hair, the figure of Apollo and the face of a movie star. He moved soundlessly, but even so in ordinary reality he couldn't avoid attention from women.

Real attention.

'That's not my way of working,' Ignat said glumly. 'Not an MO I'm particularly fond of.'

'You can choose who you sleep with on your own time,' the boss barked. 'But when you're working, I make all your decisions for you. Even when you go to the lavatory.'

Ignat shrugged. He glanced at me as if looking for sympathy and growled to himself:

'That's discrimination . . .'

'We're not in the States,' the boss said, his voice becoming dangerously polite. 'Yes, it's discrimination. Making use of the most appropriate available member of staff without taking his personal inclinations into account.'

'Couldn't I take that assignment?' Garik asked quietly.

That released the tension immediately. Garik's incredibly bad luck with women was no secret. Someone laughed.

'Igor and Garik, you carry on looking for the female vampire.' The boss almost seemed to have taken the suggestion seriously. 'She needs blood. She was stopped at the last minute, so she's going insane with hunger and frustration. Expect new victims at any moment. Anton, you and Olga look for the boy.'

That was clear enough.

Again, the most pointless and least significant assignment.

Somewhere in the city there was an Inferno waiting to erupt, somewhere in the city there was a wild, hungry female vampire, and I had to go looking for a kid who might, potentially, possess great magical powers.

'Permission to proceed?' I asked.

'Yes, of course,' said the boss, ignoring my quiet hint of revolt. 'Proceed.'

I swung round and left the Twilight as a sign of protest. The world flickered as it filled with colours and sounds. I was left standing there on my own in the middle of the square. To any outsider watching it would have looked really crazy. And then there were no footprints . . . I was standing in a snowdrift, sur-rounded by a shroud of virgin snow.

That's how myths are born. Out of our carelessness, out of our tattered nerves, out of jokes that go wrong and flashy gestures.

'It's okay,' I said and set off straight for the avenue.

'Thank you . . .' a gentle voice whispered affectionately in my ear.

'For what, Olga?'

'For not forgetting about me.'

'It really is that important to you to succeed in this, isn't it?'

'Yes, it is,' the bird answered after a pause.

'Then we'll try really hard.'

I skipped over the snowdrifts and some stones lying around – a glacier must have passed that way, or maybe someone had been playing at Zen gardens – and came out on to the avenue.

'Have you any cognac?' asked Olga.

'Cognac . . . yes. Why?'

'Good cognac?'

'It's never bad. If it's genuine cognac, that is.'

Olga sniffed scornfully.

'Then why don't you offer a lady coffee with cognac?'

I pictured to myself an owl drinking cognac out of a saucer and almost laughed out loud.

'Certainly. Shall we take a taxi?'

'Don't push it, kid!'

Hmm. Just when had she been locked into that bird's body? Or maybe it didn't stop her reading books?

'There's such a thing as television,' the bird whispered.

Dark and Light! I'd been certain my thoughts were safely concealed.

'Experience of life is an excellent substitute for vulgar telepathy . . . a long experience of life,' Olga went on slyly. 'Your thoughts are closed to me, Anton. And anyway, you're my partner.'

'I wasn't really . . .' I gave up. It was stupid to deny the obvious. 'And what about the boy? Are we just dropping the assignment? It's not all that serious . . .'

'It's very serious,' Olga exclaimed indignantly. 'Anton, the boss has admitted that he made a mistake. He's given us a headstart, and we've got to make the most of it. The girl vampire is focused on the boy, don't you see? For her he's like a sandwich she never got to eat, it was just taken right out of her mouth. And he's still on her leash. Now she can lure him into her lair from any side of the city. But that gives us an advantage. Why go looking for a tiger in the jungle, when you can tether a goat out in a clearing?'

'Moscow's just full of goats like that . . .'

'This boy is on her leash. She's an inexperienced vampire. Establishing contact with a new victim is harder than attracting an old one. Trust me.'

I shuddered, trying to shake off a foolish suspicion. I raised my hand to stop a car and said sombrely:

'I trust you. Absolutely and completely.'

CHAPTER 4

THE OWL emerged from the Twilight the moment I stepped inside the door. She launched into the air – for just an instant I felt the light prick of her claws – and headed for the fridge.

'Maybe I ought to make you a perch?' I asked, locking the door.

For the first time I saw how Olga spoke. Her beak twitched and she forced the words out with obvious effort. To be honest, I still don't understand how a bird can talk. Especially in such a human voice.

'Better not, or I'll start laying eggs.'

That was obviously an attempt at a joke.

'Sorry, I didn't mean to offend you,' I replied. 'I was just trying to lighten things up.'

'I understand. It's all right.'

I rummaged in the fridge and discovered a few odd bits and pieces. Cheese, salami, pickles . . . I wondered how forty-year-old cognac would go with a lightly salted cucumber. They'd probably find each other's company a bit awkward. The way Olga and I did.

I took out the cheese and the salami.

'I don't have any lemons, sorry.' I realised just how absurd all these preparations were, but still . . . 'At least it's a decent cognac.'

The owl didn't say anything.

I took the bottle of Kutuzov out of the drawer in the table that I used as a bar.

'Ever tried this?'

'Our reply to Napoleon?' the owl asked with a laugh. 'No, I haven't.'

The situation just kept getting more and more ridiculous. I rinsed out two cognac glasses and put them on the table, glancing doubtfully at the bundle of white feathers. At the short, crooked beak.

'You can't drink from a glass. Maybe I should get you a saucer.'

'Look the other way.'

I did as she said. There was a rustling of feathers behind my back. Then a faint, unpleasant hissing sound that reminded me of a snake that's just been woken up, or gas escaping from a cylinder.

'Olga, I'm sorry, but . . .' I said as I turned round.

The owl wasn't there any more.

Sure, I'd been expecting something like this. I'd been hoping she was allowed to assume human form sometimes at least. And in my mind I'd drawn this portrait of Olga, a woman imprisoned in the body of a bird, a woman who remembers the Decembrist uprising. I'd had this picture of Princess Lopukhina running away from the ball. Only a bit older and more serious, with a wise look in her eyes, a bit thinner . . .

But the woman sitting on the stool was young, in fact she was really young. About twenty-five. Hair cut short like a man's, dirt on her cheeks, as if she'd just escaped from a fire. Beautiful, with finely moulded, aristocratic features. But that dirty soot . . . that crude, ugly haircut . . .

The final shock was the way she was dressed.

Stained army trousers 1940s style, a padded jacket, unbuttoned, over a dirty-grey soldier's shirt. Bare feet.

'Am I beautiful?' the woman asked.

'Yes, as a matter of fact, you are,' I replied. 'Light and Dark . . . why do you look that way?'

'The last time I assumed human form was fifty-five years ago.'

I nodded.

'I get it. They used you in the war.'

'They use me in every war,' Olga said with a sweet smile. 'In every serious war. At any other time I'm forbidden to assume human form.'

'There's no war on now.'

'Then there's going to be one.'

She didn't smile that time. I restrained my oath and just made the sign to ward off misfortune.

'Do you want to have a shower?'

'I'd love to.'

'I don't have any woman's clothes . . . will jeans and a shirt do?'

She nodded. She got up – moving awkwardly, waving her arms bizarrely and looking down in surprise at her own bare feet. But she managed to walk to the bathroom as if it wasn't the first time she'd taken a shower at my place.

I made a dash for the bedroom. She probably didn't have much time.

A pair of old jeans one size smaller than I wear now. They'll still be too big for her . . . A shirt? No, better a thin sweater. Underwear . . .

'Anton!'

I raked the clothes into a heap, grabbed a clean towel and dashed back out. The bathroom door was open.

'What kind of tap is this?'

'It's foreign, a ball mechanism . . . just a moment.'

I went in. Olga was standing naked in the bath with her back to me, turning the lever of the tap left and right.

'Up,' I said. 'You lift it up for pressure. Left for cold, right for hot.'

'Okay. Thanks.'

She wasn't even slightly embarrassed. Not surprising, considering her age and rank . . . even if she no longer held one.

But *I* felt embarrassed. So I tried to act casual.

'Here are the clothes. Maybe you can pick something out. That is, if you need anything.'

'Thank you, Anton . . .' Olga looked at me. 'Take no notice. I've spent eighty years in a bird's body. Hibernating most of the time, but I've still had more than enough.'

Her eyes were deep, fascinating. Dangerous eyes.

'I don't think of myself as a human, or an Other, or a woman any longer. Or as an owl, either, come to that. Just . . . a bitter, sexless old fool who can sometimes talk.'

The water spurted from the shower. Olga slowly raised her arms and turned round, revelling in the sensation of the firm jets.

'Washing off this soot is more important to me than . . . the embarrassment of an attractive young man.'

I swallowed the 'young man' without argument and left the bathroom. I shook my head, picked up the cognac and opened the bottle.

One thing at least was clear: she was no werewolf. A werewolf wouldn't have kept the clothes on its body. Olga was a magician. A female magician about two hundred years old who'd been punished eighty years ago by being deprived of her body, but still hoped for a chance to redeem herself. She was a specialist in conflicts involving physical force and the last time she'd been used for a job had been about fifty years earlier . . .

That was enough information to search the computer database. I didn't have access to the complete files, I wasn't senior enough. But fortunately senior management had no idea how much information an indirect search could yield.

Provided, of course, that I really wanted to find out who Olga was.

I poured the cognac and waited. Olga came out of the bathroom about five minutes later, drying her hair with a towel. She was wearing my jeans and sweater.

I couldn't say she was transformed . . . but she was definitely looking a lot more attractive.

'Thanks, Anton. You've no idea how much I enjoyed—'

'I can guess.'

'Guessing's not enough. That smell, Anton . . . that smell of burning. I'd almost got used to it after half a century.' She sat down awkwardly on a stool and sighed. 'It's not good, of course, but I'm glad of this crisis. Even if they don't pardon me, it's a chance to get clean . . .'

'You can stay in this form, Olga. I'll go out and buy some decent clothes.'

'Don't bother. I only have half an hour a day.'

Olga screwed up the towel and tossed it on to the windowsill. She sighed:

'I might not get another chance to take a shower. Or drink cognac . . . Your health, Anton.'

'Your health.'

The cognac was good. I took a sip and savoured it, despite the total muddle in my head. Olga downed hers in one and pulled a face, but she observed politely:

'Not bad.'

'Why won't the boss let you assume your normal form?'

'That's not in his power.'

Clear enough. So it wasn't the regional office that had punished her, but the higher authorities.

'Here's to your success, Olga. Whatever it was that you did . . . I'm sure your guilt must have been expiated by now.'

She shrugged.

'I'd like to think so. I know people find me easy to sympathise with, but the punishment was just. Anyway, let's get down to business.'

'Okay.'

Olga leaned across the table towards me and spoke in a mysterious whisper:

'I'll be honest with you: I've had enough. I've got strong nerves, but this is no way to live. My only chance is to carry through an assignment so important that our superiors will have no option but to pardon me.'

'Where can you find a mission like that?'

'We already have it. And it has three stages. The boy – we protect him and then bring him over to the side of the Light. The girl vampire – we destroy her.'

Olga's voice sounded so confident that suddenly I believed her. Protect one, destroy the other. No problem.

'But that's only the small change, Anton. An operation like that will get you promoted, but it won't save me. The really important part is the girl with the vortex.'

'They're already dealing with her, Olga. They've taken me . . . us off the assignment.'

'Never mind that. They won't be able to handle it.'

'Oh no?' I asked ironically.

'They won't. Boris Ignatievich is a very powerful magician. But this isn't his field.' Olga half closed her eyes in a mocking smile. 'I've been dealing with Inferno eruptions all my life.'

'So that's why it's war!' I exclaimed, catching on at last.

'Of course. You don't get sudden eruptions of hatred like that in times of peace. That bastard Adolf . . . he had plenty of admirers, but he would have been incinerated in the very first year of war. And the whole of Germany with him. The situation with Stalin was different, adoration on a monstrous scale like that is a powerful shield. Anton, I'm a simple Russian woman . . .' – the smile that flitted across Olga's face showed what she really felt about the word 'simple' – 'and I spent all the last war shielding the enemies of my own country against curses. For that alone I deserve to be pardoned. Do you believe me?'

'I believe you.' I got the impression she was already getting slightly drunk.

'It's lousy work . . . we all have to go against our human nature, but that was too much . . . Anyway, Anton, they won't be able to handle it. I can at least try, though even I can't be sure I'll succeed.'

'Olga, if this is all so serious, you should put in a report.'

She shook her head and pushed back her wet hair.

'I can't. I'm forbidden to associate with anyone except my partner on the assignment and Boris Ignatievich. I've told him everything. All I can do now is wait. And hope that I'll be able to deal with this – at the very last moment.'

'But doesn't the boss understand all that?'

'I think he understands it all very well.'

'So that's the way . . .' I whispered.

'We were lovers. For a very long time. And we were friends too, something you don't find so often . . . Okay, Anton. Today we solve the problem of the boy and the crazed vampire. Tomorrow we wait. We wait for the Inferno to erupt. Agreed?'

'I have to think about it, Olga.'

'Fine. Think. But my time's up already. Turn away.'

I didn't have time. It was probably Olga's own fault. She'd miscalculated how much time she had left.

It was a truly repulsive sight. Olga shook and arched over backwards. A shudd er ran through her body and the bones bent as if made of rubber. Her skin split open, revealing bleeding muscles. A moment later, and the woman had been transformed into a formless, crumpled bundle of flesh. And the ball kept shrinking, getting smaller and smaller and sprouting soft, white feathers . . .

The owl launched itself off the stool with a cry that sounded half human, half bird, and fluttered across to her chosen place on the fridge.

'Hell and damnation!' I exclaimed, forgetting all the rules. 'Olga!'

'Isn't it lovely?' The woman's voice was gasping, still distorted by pain.

'Why? Why like that?'

'It's part of the punishment, Anton.'

I reached out my hand and touched one outstretched, trembling wing.

'Okay, Olga, I'm with you.'

'Then let's get to work, Anton.'

I nodded and went out into the hallway. I opened the cupboard where I keep my equipment and moved into the Twilight – otherwise you simply can't see anything in there except clothes and a load of old junk.

A light body settled on my shoulder.

'What have you got?'

'I discharged the onyx amulet. Can you recharge it?'

'No, I've been deprived of almost all my powers. All they left me is what's required to neutralise the Inferno. And my memory, Anton . . . they left me my memory. How are you going to kill the girl vampire?'

'She's not registered,' I said. 'I've only got the old folk methods.'

The owl gave a screeching laugh.

'Are poplar stakes still popular?'

'I don't have any.'

'Right. Because of your friends?'

'Yes. I don't want them to shudder every time they step inside the door.'

'What, then?'

I took a pistol out of a hollow gouged in the bricks and glanced sideways at the owl – Olga was studying the gun.

'Silver? Very painful for a vampire, but not fatal.'

'It has explosive bullets.' I slid the clip out of the Desert Eagle. 'Explosive silver bullets. Four four calibre. Three hits and a vampire's totally helpless.'

'And then?'

'Traditional methods.'

'I don't believe in technology,' Olga said doubtfully. 'I've seen a werewolf regenerate after being torn to pieces by a shell.'

'How long did it take to regenerate?'

'Three days.'

'Well, there you are then.'

'All right, Anton. If you have no faith in your own powers . . .'

She was disappointed, I realised that. But then I was no field operative. I was a staff worker assigned to work in the field.

'Everything will be fine,' I reassured her. 'Trust me. Let's just focus on finding the bait.'

'Okay, let's go.'

'This is where it all happened,' I told Olga. We were standing in the alley. In the Twilight, of course.

The occasional passers-by looked odd skirting round me, yet unable to see me.

'This is where you killed the vampire.' Olga's tone couldn't have been more brisk. 'Right . . . I understand. You did a poor job cleaning up the mess, but that's not important.'

As far as I could see, there wasn't a trace left of the dead vampire. But I didn't argue.

'The girl vampire was here . . . you hit her with something here . . . no, you splashed vodka on her . . .' Olga laughed quietly. 'She got away . . . Our operatives have completely lost their touch. The trail's still clear even now!'

'She changed,' I said morosely.

'Into a bat?'

'Yes. Garik said she did it at the very last moment.'

'That's bad. This vampire's more powerful than I was hoping.'

'She's completely wild. She's drunk living blood and killed. She has no experience, but plenty of power.'

'We will destroy her,' Olga said sternly.

I didn't say anything.

'And here's the boy's trail.' There was a note of approval in Olga's voice. 'Yes indeed . . . real potential. Let's go and see where he lives.'

We walked out of the alley and set off along the pavement. The houses surrounded a large inner yard on all sides. I could sense the boy's aura too, but it was very weak and confused: he clearly walked round here all the time.

'Straight ahead,' Olga commanded. 'Turn left. Further. Turn right. Stop.'

I stopped facing a street with a trolleybus crawling slowly along it. I didn't emerge from the Twilight yet.

'In that building,' Olga told me. 'Straight ahead. That's where he is.'

The building was a monster, an immensely high, flat slab set on tall legs or stilts. At first glance it looked like some gigantic monument to the matchbox. Look again and you could see it as an expression of a morbid gigantomania.

'That's a good house for killing in,' I said. 'You could go insane in there.'

'Let's try both,' Olga agreed. 'I've got plenty of experience.'

⋆   ⋆   ⋆

Egor didn't want to go out. When his parents left to go to work and the door slammed behind them, he felt the fear immediately. And he knew that outside the empty apartment the fear would turn into terror.

There was nothing that could save him. Nothing anywhere. But at least his home gave him the illusion of safety.

Last night the world had crumbled, completely collapsed. Egor had always admitted quite openly – at least to himself, if not to others – that he wasn't really brave. But he wasn't exactly a coward either. There were some things it was only right to be afraid of: young thugs, maniacs, terrorists, disasters, fires, wars, deadly diseases. He thought of them all lumped together – and all equally distant. All these things really did exist, but at the same time they remained beyond his everyday experience. Follow simple rules, don't wander the streets at night, don't go into unfamiliar districts, wash your hands before eating, don't jump on the railway lines. It was possible to be afraid of unpleasant things and at the same time know there wasn't much chance they would mess up your life.

Now everything had changed.

There were some things you couldn't hide from. Things that shouldn't exist, that couldn't exist.

But vampires did exist.

He remembered it all distinctly, the horror hadn't wiped his memory clean, the way he'd vaguely hoped it would yesterday, when he was running home, breaking the rules by running across the street without looking. And his timid hope that in the morning everything that had happened would turn out to be a dream had proved wrong too.

It was all true. It couldn't possibly be true, but it was . . .

It had happened yesterday. It had happened to him.

He'd been late coming home, sure, but he'd come home later

than that before. Even his parents who, Egor was quite certain, hadn't realised yet that he was almost thirteen, thought nothing of it.

When he left the swimming pool with the other guys . . . yes, it was ten o'clock already. They'd all piled into McDonald's and sat there for about twenty minutes. That was the usual thing too, after training everyone who could afford it went to McDonald's. Then . . . then they all walked to the metro together. It wasn't far. Along a brightly lit street. Eight of them together.

Everything was still fine then.

It was in the metro that he'd started feeling uneasy. He looked at his watch, stared round at the other passengers. But there was nothing suspicious.

Except that Egor could hear music.

And then things that couldn't happen had started happening.

Without knowing why, he'd turned into a dark, stinking alleyway. He'd walked up to a girl and a young guy who were waiting for him. They'd lured him there. And he offered his own neck to the girl, to her long, sharp fangs that weren't even human.

Even now, at home on his own, Egor could feel that chill – that sweet, enticing tingle running across his skin. He'd wanted it to happen! He'd been afraid, but he'd wanted the touch of the gleaming fangs, the sharp, short pain, and then . . . and then . . . there'd be something else . . . there had to be . . .

And no one in the whole world could help him. Egor remembered the way the woman who was walking her dogs had looked straight through him. An alert glance, not at all indifferent – she hadn't been frightened, she simply couldn't see what was happening. Egor had only been saved by the third vampire turning up. That pale guy with the walkman who'd started trailing him back in the metro. They'd fought over him the way hungry, full-grown wolves quarrel over a deer they've cornered but not killed yet.

Then everything had got confused, it all happened too fast. Someone had shouted something about some watch or other, about the twilight. There was a flash of blue light, and one vampire just crumbled into dust right there in front of his eyes, just like in the movies. The girl was howling because she'd had something splashed into her face.

Then he'd fled in panic . . .

And now he realised something terrible, even more terrible than what had happened: he couldn't tell anyone anything. They wouldn't believe him. They wouldn't understand.

Vampires don't exist.

It's not possible to look straight through people and not see them.

Nobody just burns up in a swirl of blue flame, and turns into a dried mummy, a skeleton, a handful of ash.

'They do!' Egor told himself. 'They do exist. It is possible. It does happen!'

But even he could hardly believe it . . .

Egor didn't go to school, but he did clean up the apartment. He wanted to do something. Several times he went across to the window and looked carefully round the yard.

Nothing suspicious.

But would he be able to see them?

They would come. Egor didn't doubt it for a second. They knew he remembered them. Now they would kill him, because he was a witness.

But they wouldn't just kill him. They'd drink his blood and turn him into a vampire!

The boy walked over to the bookshelf, where half the shelves were filled with videos. Maybe he could look for advice here. *Dracula. Dead and Loving It* – no, that was comedy. *Once Bitten* – total garbage. *Night of Terror* . . . Egor shuddered. He remembered that film. And now he'd never dare watch it again. What was the line? 'A crucifix helps, if you believe in it.'

But how could a crucifix help him? He wasn't even baptised. And he didn't believe in God. At least, he hadn't believed before.

Maybe he ought to start now.

If vampires existed, then so did the devil, and if the devil existed, then did God too?

If vampires existed, then so did God?

If Evil existed, then so did Good?

'It's all rubbish,' said Egor. He stuck his hands into the pockets of his jeans, went out into the hallway and looked in the mirror. He saw his reflection. A bit miserable-looking, perhaps, but just a normal kid. That meant everything was still okay, so far. They hadn't managed to bite him.

Just to make sure, he twisted this way and that, trying to see the back of his neck. No, there were no marks, nothing. Just a skinny neck, maybe not too clean . . .

The idea suddenly hit him. Egor ran into the kitchen, frightening the cat off its comfortable spot on top of the washing machine. He started rummaging through bags of potatoes, onions and carrots.

There it was, the garlic.

Egor hastily peeled an entire head and started chewing it. The garlic was fierce, it burned his mouth. Egor poured a glass of tea and started taking a mouthful after every clove. It didn't help much, his tongue was on fire and his gums itched. But it was sure to help, wasn't it?

The cat looked back into the kitchen, its eyes wide with apparent amazement, gave a disappointed miaow and stalked away, as if it couldn't understand how anyone could eat anything so disgusting.

Egor chewed up the last two cloves, spat them out into his palm and started rubbing them on his neck. He could have laughed at himself for doing it, but he wasn't going to stop now.

His neck started to sting too – it was good garlic. A single breath would be the end of any vampire.

The cat began howling restlessly in the hallway. Egor pricked up his ears and peered out of the kitchen. No, nothing there. The door was secured with three locks and a chain.

'Stop that noise, Grey!' he told the cat sternly. 'Or I'll make you eat garlic too.'

The cat took the threat seriously and raced into the parents' bedroom. What else could he do? Silver was supposed to help. Egor frightened the cat again by going into the bedroom, opening the wardrobe and taking his mother's jewellery box out from under the sheets and towels. He took out a silver chain and put it on. It would smell of garlic, and he'd have to take it off before evening. Maybe he should empty his moneybox and buy himself a chain. With a crucifix. And wear it all the time. Say he'd started believing in God. Didn't it happen sometimes that people didn't believe for a long, long time, and then suddenly started believing after all?

He walked across the sitting room, sat down with his feet up on the sofa and looked round the room thoughtfully. Did they have anything made of poplar wood? He didn't think so. And what did poplar wood look like, anyway? Maybe he should go to the botanical gardens and cut himself a dagger from a branch.

That was all great, in theory, but what good would it do? If the music started playing again . . . that soft, alluring music . . . What if he took the chain off himself, broke the poplar-wood dagger and washed the garlic off his own neck?

Soft, gentle music . . . invisible enemies. Maybe they were already there with him. He simply couldn't see them. He didn't know how to look. And a vampire might be sitting right there, laughing at him, looking at this naïve kid preparing his defences.

And he wasn't afraid of any poplar stake, he wasn't scared by the garlic. How could you fight against something invisible?

'Grey!' Egor called. The cat didn't respond to the usual 'kss-kss', he was an awkward character. 'Come here, Grey!'

The cat was standing in the doorway of the bedroom. His fur was standing on end and his eyes were blazing. He was looking past Egor, into the corner, at the armchair beside the coffee table. At an empty chair . . .

The boy felt the familiar chilly shiver run over his body. He jerked forward so violently that he went flying off the sofa and landed on the floor. The armchair was empty. The apartment was empty and locked. Everything turned dark, as if the sunlight outside the window had suddenly dimmed . . .

There was someone there with him.

'No!' Egor shouted, crawling away. 'I know! I know you're here!'

The cat gave a hoarse screech and darted under the bed.

'I can see you,' shouted Egor. 'Don't touch me!'

The entrance of the building looked gloomy and miserable enough. But viewed from inside the Twilight, it was a genuine catacomb. Concrete walls that were simply dirty in ordinary reality were overgrown with a dark blue moss in the Twilight. Disgusting. There clearly wasn't a single Other living here to clean up . . . I passed my hand over a really thick growth – the moss stirred, trying to creep away from the warmth.

'Burn!' I ordered it.

I don't like parasites. Not even if they don't do any particular harm and only feed on other creatures' emotions. No one's ever proved the hypothesis that large colonies of blue moss are capable of unbalancing the human psyche and causing depression or mania. But I've always preferred to play safe.

'Burn!' I repeated, transmitting a small amount of power through my hand.

A hot, transparent flame spread across the layer of tangled blue felt. A moment later the entire entrance was ablaze. I stepped away towards the lift, pressed the button and got in. The cabin was a lot cleaner.

'Ninth floor,' Olga prompted. 'Why waste your powers like that?'

'That's just small change . . .'

'You might need everything you've got. Let it grow.'

I didn't answer. The lift crawled slowly upwards – the Twilight lift, the double of the ordinary one that was still standing on the first floor.

'Suit yourself,' said Olga. 'The uncompromising passion of youth . . .'

The doors opened. The fire had already reached the ninth floor and the blue moss was blazing wildly. It was warm, a lot warmer than it usually is in the Twilight. There was a slight smell of burning.

'That door there,' said Olga.

'I can see.'

I could sense the boy's aura behind the door. He hadn't even taken the risk of coming out today. Excellent. The goat was tethered with a strong rope, all we had to do was wait for the tiger.

'I suppose I'll go in,' I said. I pushed the door.

The door didn't open.

That couldn't happen!

In the real world all the locks on the door could be closed, but the Twilight has its own laws. Only vampires need an invitation to enter someone's home, that's the price they pay for their strength and their gastronomic approach to humans.

In order to lock a door in the Twilight, you had at least to know how to enter it.

'Fear,' said Olga. 'Yesterday the boy was in a state of terror. And he'd just been in the Twilight world. He locked the door behind him, and without knowing it, he locked it in both worlds at the same time. Come deeper. Follow me.'

I looked at my shoulder – there was no one there. Summoning the Twilight while you're in the Twilight is no simple trick. I had to raise my shadow from the floor several times before it acquired volume and hung there, quivering in front of me.

'Come on, come on, you're doing fine,' whispered Olga.

I entered the shadow, and the Twilight grew thicker. Space was filled with a dense fog. Colours disappeared completely. The only sound left was the beating of my heart, slow and heavy, rumbling like a drum being beaten at the bottom of a ravine. And there was a whistling wind – that was the air seeping into my lungs, slowly stretching out the bronchi. The owl appeared on my shoulder.

'I won't be able to stand this for long,' I whispered, opening the door. At this level, of course, it wasn't locked.

A dark grey cat flitted past my feet. For cats there is no ordinary world or Twilight – they live in all the worlds at once. It's a good thing they don't have any real intelligence.

'Kss-kss-kss,' I whispered. 'Don't be afraid, puss . . .'

Mostly to test my own powers, I locked the door behind me. There, kid, now you're a little bit better protected. But will it do any good when you hear the Call?

'Move up,' said Olga. 'You're losing strength very fast. This level of the Twilight is a strain even for an experienced magician. I think I'll move up a level too.'

It was a relief to step out of it. No, I'm not an operational agent who can stroll around all three levels of the Twilight just as he likes. But I don't normally need to do that kind of thing.

The world turned a little brighter. I glanced around. It was a cosy apartment, not too polluted by the products of the Twilight world. A few streaks of blue moss beside the door . . . nothing to worry about, they'd die, now that the main colony had been exterminated. I heard sounds too, from the direction of the kitchen. I glanced in.

The boy was standing by the table, eating garlic and washing it down with hot tea.

'Light and Dark,' I whispered.

He looked even younger and more helpless than the day before. Thin and awkward, but you couldn't call him weak, he obviously played sport. He was wearing faded jeans and a blue sweatshirt.

'The poor soul,' I said.

'Very touching,' Olga agreed. 'It was a clever move of the vampires to spread that rumour about the magical properties of garlic. They say it was Bram Stoker himself who thought it up . . .'

The boy spat into his hand and started rubbing garlic on to his neck.

'Garlic's good for you,' I said.

'Oh yes. It protects you. Against flu viruses,' Olga added. 'How easily the truth is lost, and how persistent lies are . . . But the boy really is strong. The Night Watch could do with another agent.'

'But is he ours?'

'He's not anyone's yet. His destiny's still not been determined, you can see for yourself.'

'But which way does he lean?'

'There's no way to tell, not yet. He's too frightened. Right now he'd do absolutely anything to escape from the vampires. He's equally ready to turn to the Dark or the Light.'

'I can't blame him for that.'

'No, of course. Come on.'

The owl fluttered into the air and flew along the corridor. I walked after her. We were moving three times faster than humans now: one of the fundamental features of the Twilight is the way it affects the passage of time.

'We'll wait here,' Olga announced, when we were in the lounge. 'It's warm, light and comfortable.'

I sat in a soft armchair beside a low table and glanced at the newspaper lying there.

There's nothing more amusing than reading the press through the Twilight.

'Profits on loans down', said the headline.

In the real world the phrase was different: 'Tension mounts in the Caucasus'.

I could pick up the newspaper now and read the truth. The real truth. What the journalist was thinking when he wrote on the topic he'd been assigned. Those crumbs of information that he'd received from unofficial sources. The truth about life and the truth about death.

Only what for?

I'd stopped giving a damn about the human world a long time ago. It's our basis. Our cradle. But we are Others. We walk through closed doors and we maintain the balance of Good and Evil. There are pitifully few of us, and we can't reproduce – it doesn't follow that a magician's daughter automatically becomes an enchantress, and a werewolf's son won't necessarily be able to change his form on moonlit nights.

We're not obliged to like the ordinary, everyday world.

We only guard it because we're its parasites.

I hate parasites!

'What are you thinking about now?' asked Olga. The boy appeared in the lounge. He raced across into the bedroom – very quickly, bearing in mind that he was in the everyday world. He started rummaging in the wardrobe.

'Nothing much. Just feeling sad.'

'It happens. During the first few years it happens to everyone.' Olga's voice sounded completely human now. 'Then you get used to it.'

'That's what I'm feeling sad about.'

'You should be glad we're still alive. At the beginning of the twentieth century the population of Others fell to a critical threshold. Did you know there were debates about uniting the Dark Ones and the Light Ones? That programmes of eugenics were developed?'

'Yes, I know.'

'Science came close to killing us off. They didn't believe in us, they wouldn't believe. That is, while they still believed science could change the world for the better.'

The boy came back into the lounge. He sat down on the sofa and started adjusting the silver chain round his neck.

'What is better?' I asked. 'We were people once, but we've learned to enter the Twilight, we've learned to change the nature of things and other people. And what's changed, Olga?'

'At least vampires don't hunt without a licence.'

'Tell that to the person whose blood they drink.'

The cat appeared in the doorway and fixed his gaze on us. He howled, glaring angrily at the owl.

'It's you he doesn't like, Olga,' I said. 'Move deeper into the Twilight.'

'Too late,' Olga replied. 'Sorry, I let my guard down.'

The boy sprang up off the sofa. Far faster than is possible in the human world. Clumsily, without even knowing what was happening to him, he entered his shadow and immediately fell on the floor, looking up at me. Through the Twilight.

'I'm leaving . . .' the owl whispered as she disappeared. Her claws dug painfully into my shoulder.

'No!' shouted the boy. 'I know! I know you're here!'

I started to get up, spreading my hands.

'I can see you! Don't touch me!'

He was in the Twilight. He'd done it, just like that. Without any help from anyone, without any courses or stimulants, without any magician to tutor him, the boy had crossed the boundary between the ordinary and the Twilight worlds.

The way you first enter the Twilight, what you see and what you feel there goes a long way to determine who you'll become.

A Dark One or a Light One.

'*We have no right to let him go over to the Dark Side, the balance of power in Moscow would completely collapse.*' The boss's words came back to me.

Okay, kid, you're right on the edge.

That was more terrifying than any inexperienced vampire.

Boris Ignatievich was entitled to have the boy taken out.

'Don't be afraid,' I said, not moving from the spot. 'I'm your friend and I won't do you any harm.'

The boy crawled as far as the corner and froze there, never once taking his eyes off me. He clearly didn't understand that he'd shifted into the Twilight. It looked to him as if the room had suddenly turned dark, a silence had fallen and I'd appeared out of nowhere . . .

'Don't be afraid,' I repeated. 'My name's Anton. What's your name?'

He didn't say anything. He kept gulping, over and over again. Then he pressed his hand against his neck, felt for the chain and seemed to calm down a bit.

'I'm not a vampire,' I said.

'Who are you?' the boy yelled. It was a good thing that piercing shriek couldn't be heard in the everyday world.

'Anton. A Night Watch agent.'

His eyes opened wide, as if he were in pain.

'It's my job to protect people against vampires and all sorts of vermin.'

'You're lying . . .'

'Why?'

He shrugged. Good. He was trying to assess his actions so far and explain his reasons. That meant the fear hadn't completely paralysed his mind.

'What's your name?' I asked again. I could have influenced the boy and removed his fear. But that would have been an intervention, and a forbidden one.

'Egor.'

'A good name. My name's Anton. Do you understand? I'm Anton Sergeevich Gorodetsky. A Night Watch agent. Yesterday I killed a vampire who was attacking you.'

'Just one?'

Excellent. Now we had the makings of a conversation.

'Yes. The girl got away. We're searching for her now. Don't be afraid, I'm here to guard you . . . to destroy the vampire.'

'Why is everything so grey?' Egor suddenly asked.

Good boy. That's really good going.

'I'll explain. Only first let's agree that I'm not your enemy. All right?'

'We'll see.'

He held on to his absurd little chain, as if it could save him from anything. Oh, kid, if only everything in this world was that easy. Silver won't save you, or poplar wood, or crucifixes. It's life against death, love against hate . . . and power against power, because power has no moral categories. That's how simple it is. In the last couple of years I've come to realise that.

'Egor,' I said, walking slowly across to him. 'Listen, I want to tell you something.'

'Stop!'

He shouted the command as sharply as if he were holding a weapon in his hands. I sighed and stopped.

'All right. Now listen. Apart from the ordinary world that the human eye can see, there is also a shadow world, the Twilight world.'

He thought. Despite his fear – and he was terribly afraid, I could feel the waves of his suffocating horror washing over me – the boy was trying to understand. There are some people who are paralysed by fear. And there are some whom it only makes stronger.

I was really hoping he would be one of the second kind.

'A parallel world?'

There, now he was bringing in science fiction. But never mind, it didn't matter. Names are nothing more than sounds.

'Yes, and only people with supernatural powers can enter that world.'

'Vampires?'

'Not only. There are werewolves, witches, black magicians . . . white magicians, healers, seers.'

'And they all really exist?'

He was soaking wet. His hair was clumped together, his sweatshirt was clinging to his body, beads of sweat were rolling down his cheeks. But still the boy never took his eyes off me and was getting ready to repulse me. As if he really had the power to do it.

'Yes, Egor. Some people can enter the Twilight world. They take the side of either Good or Evil. Light or Dark. They are the Others. That's what we call each other, the Others.'

'Are you an Other?'

'Yes, and so are you.'

'Why?'

'You're in the Twilight world right now. Take a look around, listen. All the colours have turned grey. The sounds have faded away. The second hand on the clock is barely moving. You entered the Twilight world . . . you wanted to see the danger and you crossed the boundary between worlds. Time moves more slowly here, everything is different here. This is the world of the Others.'

'I don't believe it.' Egor glanced round quickly, then looked back at me. 'Then why's Grey here?'

'The cat?' I smiled. 'Animals follow their own laws, Egor. Cats live in all the dimensions at once, for them there is no difference.'

'I don't believe you.' His voice was trembling. 'It's all a dream, I know! When the light fades like that . . . I'm asleep. It's happened to me before.'

'So you've had dreams about turning on the light and the bulb not lighting up?' I already knew the answer, and anyway I could read it in the boy's eyes. 'Or it lights up, but only very, very faintly, like a candle? And you're walking along with the Dark all around you, and you hold out your hand and you can't even make out your own fingers?'

He didn't answer.

'That happens to all of us, Egor. Every Other has dreams like that. It's the Twilight world creeping into us, calling us, reminding us of itself. You are an Other. Still a young one, but you are. And you're the only one . . .'

I didn't realise straightaway that his eyes had closed and his head was slumped to one side.

'You idiot!' Olga hissed from my shoulder. 'This is the first time he's entered the Twilight independently. He hasn't got the strength for this. Pull him out quickly, or he'll stay here for ever!'

Twilight coma is a novice's problem. I'd almost forgotten about it, because I'd never worked with young Others.

'Egor!' I leapt across and shook him, grabbing him round the shoulders. He was light, very light – it's not only time that changes in the Twilight world. 'Wake up!'

The boy didn't respond. He'd already done what it takes others months of training to do – entered the Twilight on his own. And the Twilight world sucks the strength out of you.

'Pull him out!' said Olga, taking command of the situation. 'He won't wake up himself.'

That was the hardest thing of all. I'd done the emergency rescue courses, but I'd never had to drag anyone out of the Twilight for real.

'Egor, snap out of it!' I slapped him on the cheeks. Gently at first, then I started putting real force into it. 'Come on, kid. You're slipping away into the Twilight world! Wake up!'

He was getting lighter and lighter, melting away in my arms. The Twilight was drinking his life, the final ounces of his strength. The Twilight was changing his body, claiming it as permanent resident. What had I done?

'Seal yourself off!' Olga's sharp voice focused my mind. 'Seal yourself off, and him too.'

It always used to take me more than a minute to form a sphere. This time I did it in five seconds flat. I felt a stab of pain – as if a small shell had exploded inside my head. I threw my head back when the sphere of exclusion emerged from my body, shrouding me like a shimmering soap bubble. The bubble expanded, reluctantly enveloping me and the boy.

'That's it, now hold it there. I can't do anything to help you, Anton. Hold that sphere!'

Olga was wrong. She'd already helped me, with her advice. I'd probably have realised that I ought to form a sphere, but I could have lost precious seconds along the way.

It started getting lighter. The Twilight was still draining our strength – mine with an effort, the boy's with ease – but now it only had a few cubic metres of space to operate with. The ordinary laws of physics don't apply here, but there are parallels.

A balance was being established between our living bodies and the Twilight.

Either the Twilight would dissolve and release its prey, or the boy would remain an inhabitant of the Twilight world. For ever. It's what happens to magicians who have pushed themselves beyond the limit, either through carelessness or because they have no choice. It's what happens with novices who don't know how to protect themselves against the Twilight properly and allow it to take more than they should.

I looked at Egor: his face was turning grey. He was slipping away into the infinite expanses of the shadow world.

I threw the boy across my right arm, took a penknife out of my left pocket and opened the blade with my teeth.

'That's dangerous,' Olga warned me.

I didn't answer. I just slashed my wrist.

When the blood spurted out, the Twilight hissed like a red-hot frying pan. Everything blurred. It wasn't just the loss of the blood, my very life was seeping away with it. I'd ruptured my own defences against the Twilight.

But the dose of energy was too large for it to absorb.

The world turned brighter, my shadow leaped on to the floor and I stepped through it. The rainbow film of the sphere of exclusion burst, releasing us into the everyday world.

CHAPTER 5

A THIN STREAM of blood splashed on to the carpet. The boy was slumped in my arms, still unconscious, but his face was beginning to turn pink. The cat was yowling in the next room as if his throat was being cut.

I lowered Egor on to the sofa, sat down beside him and told Olga to find a bandage.

The owl launched off my shoulder and dashed away like a white streak into the kitchen. She must have slipped into the Twilight on the way, because she was back in a few seconds with a bandage in her beak.

Egor opened his eyes just at the moment when I took the bandage from the owl and started binding up my wrist. He asked:

'Who's that?'

'An owl. Surely you can see that!'

'What happened to me?' he asked. His voice was hardly trembling at all.

'You lost consciousness.'

'Why?' His eyes wandered anxiously over the traces of blood on the floor and my clothes. I'd managed not to get any on Egor.

'It's my blood,' I explained. 'I cut myself by accident. You have to be careful when you enter the Twilight, Egor. It's an alien environment, even for us, the Others. While we're in the Twilight world, we have to expend our strength constantly, feeding its vital energy. But a little at a time. If you don't keep control of the process, the Twilight will suck all the life out of you. It's just a price we have to pay.'

'And I paid more than I should have done?'

'More than you had. And you almost stayed in the Twilight world for ever. It's not death – but maybe it's worse than death.'

'Let me help . . .' The boy winced as he sat up – he must have felt dizzy. I held out my hand and he started bandaging my wrist, clumsily but trying hard. The boy's aura hadn't changed, it was still iridescent, neutral. He'd already entered the Twilight, but it still hadn't left its mark.

'Do you believe I'm your friend?' I asked.

'I don't know. Not my enemy, I suppose. Or you can't do anything to me!'

I reached out and touched the boy's neck and he instantly tensed up. I unfastened the chain and took it off his neck.

'You see?'

'So you're not a vampire?' His voice was slightly husky.

'No. But that's not why I could touch the garlic and the silver, Egor. They won't stop a vampire.'

'But in all the films . . .'

'And in all the films the good guys always beat the bad guys. Listen, kid, superstitions are dangerous, they give people false hope.'

'Isn't there any real hope?'

'No. Not really.' I got up and felt the bandage. Not bad, it was quite tight and holding firm. In half an hour I'd be able to heal the wound with a spell, but I didn't have enough strength yet. The boy looked up at me from the sofa. Yes, he was a bit calmer now. But he still didn't trust me. It amused me that he paid no attention to the owl dozing on the television with an innocent air. It looked as if Olga had influenced his mind after all. That was all to the good: explaining who the talking owl was would have been rather tricky.

'Have you got any food?' I asked.

'What kind?'

'Any kind. Tea with sugar. A piece of bread. I used up a lot of strength too.'

'I'll find something. How did you get cut?'

I didn't go into the details, but I didn't lie about it either.

'It was deliberate. I had to do it to get you out of the Twilight.'

'Thanks. If it's true.'

He was a bit cheeky, but I liked that.

'You're welcome. If you disappeared into the Twilight, my boss would have my head.'

The boy snorted and got up. But he was still keeping his distance from me.

'What boss is that?'

'A very strict one. Well, are you going to pour me some tea?'

'Anything for you.' Yes, he was still afraid. And he was hiding his fear by being cocky and familiar.

'Get this straight – I'm not a human being. I'm an Other. And you're an Other.'

'But what's the difference?' said Egor, looking me up and down challengingly. 'You don't look any different.'

'Until you give me some tea, I won't say a word. Didn't anyone teach you how to treat guests?'

'Uninvited ones? How did you get in?'

'Through the door. I'll show you. Later.'

'Come on then.' It looked like I was going to get my tea after all. As I set out after the boy, I couldn't help recoiling at the smell. I just had to say something.

'You know what, Egor, why don't you wash your neck first?'

The boy shook his head without looking round, busying himself with making the tea.

'It any case, it's stupid only to protect your neck. There are five points on the human body where a vampire can bite.'

'Oh yeah?'

'Yeah. That is, I mean on a male body, of course.'

Even the back of his neck turned red.

When Egor passed me my tea, I tipped five heaped spoons of sugar into the mug and winked at him.

'Pour me a glass of tea with two spoons of sugar . . . I want to try it before I die.'

He obviously didn't know that old joke.

'And how many should I take?' he asked.

'How much do you weigh?'

'I don't remember.'

I estimated his weight by eye.

'Put four in. To prevent hypoglycaemia.'

Gulping down his tea, he said:

'Explain!'

This wasn't anything like the way I'd planned. Follow the boy when the Call reaches him. Kill or capture the vampire. And take the grateful boy to the boss – he'd be able to explain everything properly.

'Once upon a time . . .' I said. 'Like the beginning of a fairy tale, that, isn't it? Only this isn't a fairy tale.'

'I'm listening.'

'Okay. I'll start with something else. There is a human world.' I nodded towards the window, the little courtyard outside and the cars crawling along the road. 'There it is. All around us. And most people can't move beyond it. That's the way it's always been. But sometimes we turn up. The Others.'

'And vampires?'

'Vampires are Others too. They're a different kind of Other, though, their powers are determined in advance.'

'I don't understand,' said Egor, shaking his head.

Okay, so I'm no tutor. I'm no good at expounding the basic truths, I don't enjoy it . . .

'Imagine two shamans who have gorged themselves on narcotic mushrooms, beating on their tambourines,' I said. 'A long, long time ago, back in prehistoric times. One of the shamans is putting one over on the hunters and the chief. The other one suddenly sees his shadow, which was trembling on the floor of the cave, gain volume and rise up until it stands erect. He takes a step forward and enters the shadow. He enters the Twilight. And that's when the most interesting part begins. You understand?'

Egor didn't say anything.

'The Twilight changes the person who has entered it. It's a different world, and it makes people into Others. But who you become depends entirely on you. The Twilight is a raging river flowing in all directions at once. Decide who you want to be in the Twilight world. But make up your mind quickly, you don't have much time.'

Now the boy understood. His pupils contracted and his skin turned slightly paler. An excellent stress response, he really would make a good operational agent . . .

'Who can I become?'

'You? Anybody you like. Your choice still hasn't been made. And you know what the basic choice is? Good or Evil. Light or Dark.'

'And are you Good?'

'First and foremost I'm an Other. The difference between Good and Evil lies in your attitude towards ordinary people. If you choose the Light, you won't use your powers for personal gain. If you choose the Dark, that will be what you do most of the time. But even a black magician is capable of healing people and finding people who have been lost. And a white magician can refuse to help people.'

'Then I don't see what the difference is.'

'You will. You'll understand when you choose one side or the other.'

'I'll never choose!'

'It's too late, Egor. You've already been in the Twilight, and you're already changing. In a couple of days the choice will have been made.'

'If you choose the Light . . .' Egor got up and poured himself some more tea. I noticed it was the first time he hadn't been afraid to turn his back on me. 'Then who are you? A magician?'

'A magician's apprentice. I work in the office of the Night Watch. Someone has to.'

'And what can you do? Show me, I want to see.'

There it was, straight out of the textbook. He'd been in the Twilight, but that hadn't convinced him. Petty fairground tricks are far more impressive.

'Watch.'

I held my arm out towards him. Egor froze, trying to understand what was going on. Then he looked at his cup.

The steam had stopped rising from his tea. The tea was crackling as it turned into a cylinder of muddy brown ice with tea leaves frozen into it.

'Oh,' said the boy.

Thermodynamics is the simple part of manipulating matter. I allowed the Brownian motion to start up again, and the ice boiled. Egor shrieked and dropped his cup.

'Sorry!' I jumped up and grabbed the cloth from the sink, then squatted down to wipe up the puddle on the lino.

'Magic's nothing but trouble,' said the boy. 'That was a good cup.'

'Just a moment.'

My shadow raced towards me, I entered the Twilight and looked at the broken pieces. They still remembered the whole, and it hadn't been the cup's destiny to get broken so soon. I raked the shards together with my hand. A few of the smallest pieces that had fallen under the cooker eagerly moved a bit closer.

I emerged from the Twilight and put the white cup on the table.

'Now you only need to pour more tea into it.'

'Fantastic.' Apparently this little trick had made a big impression on Egor. 'And can you do that with any kind of thing?'

'Almost any kind.'

'Anton . . . what if something was broken a week ago?'

I couldn't help smiling.

'No, sorry, then it's too late. The Twilight gives you a chance, but you have to take it quickly, very quickly.'

Egor's face darkened. I wondered what it was he'd broken a week ago.

'Now do you believe me?'

'Is that magic?'

'Yes. The most primitive kind. It takes almost no effort to learn.'

I probably shouldn't have said that. The boy's eyes lit up. He was already figuring out his prospects. His profit.

Light and Dark . . .

'But an experienced magician, he can do other stuff too?'

'Even I can.'

'And control people?'

'Yes,' I said. 'Yes, we can do that.'

'And do you? How come terrorists take hostages? You could creep up in the Twilight without being seen and shoot them. Or make them shoot themselves! How come people die of diseases? Magicians can cure them, you said so yourself.'

'That would be Good,' I said.

'Of course! But you're the magicians of the Light!'

'If we do any deed that is unconditionally good, it gives the Dark Magicians the right to do an evil deed.'

Egor looked at me in amazement. Too much had happened over the last twenty-four hours for him to take it all in. But he was handling it pretty well.

'Unfortunately, Egor, Evil is stronger by its very nature. Evil is destructive. It's much easier for Evil to destroy than it is for Good to create.'

'Then what do you do? This Night Watch of yours . . . Do you fight against the Dark Magicians?'

I mustn't answer. I knew that with a devastating clarity, just as I knew I should never have confided in the boy. I should have put him to sleep and withdrawn deeper into the Twilight. But not tried to explain anything to him, not a single thing.

I wouldn't be able to prove anything to him.

'Do you fight against them?'

'Not exactly,' I said. The truth was worse than a lie, but I had no right to tell a lie. 'We keep an eye on each other.'

'Getting ready to fight?'

I looked at Egor, thinking what a bright kid he was. But still a kid. And if I told him now that the great battle between Good and Evil was approaching, that he could be one of the new Jedi of the Twilight world, then he'd be ours.

Only not for long.

'No, Egor. There aren't very many of us.'

'The Light Others? You mean there are more Dark Ones?'

Now he was all set to leave home, abandon Mum and Dad, put on his shining armour and set out to die for the cause of Good . . .

'There aren't many Others in general. Egor, the battle between Good and Evil has been going on for thousands of years, with the balance shifting all the time. Sometimes Good has won, but if you only knew how many people, who had no idea the Twilight world even existed, were killed in the process. There aren't many Others, but every one of them can get thousands of ordinary people to follow him. Egor, if the battle between Good and Evil breaks out, half the people in the world will be killed. That's why almost fifty years ago a treaty was signed. The Great Treaty between Good and Evil, Dark and Light.'

His eyes now opened really wide.

I sighed and went on:

'It's a short treaty. I'll read it out to you – in the official Russian translation. You already have a right to know.'

I closed my eyes and peered into the darkness. The Twilight swirled into life behind my eyelids. A grey banner unfurled, covered with blazing red letters. The Treaty must not be recited from memory, it may only be read:

We are the Others,

We serve different forces,

But in the Twilight there is no difference between
the absence of Dark and the absence of Light.

Our struggle is capable of destroying the world.

We have concluded a Great Treaty, a truce.

Each side shall live according to its own laws,
Each side shall have its own rights.

We delimit our own rights and our own laws.

We are the Others.

We establish the Night Watch,
So that the forces of Light may monitor the forces of Dark.

We are the Others.

We establish the Day Watch,
So that the forces of Dark may monitor the forces of Light.
Time will decide for us.

The boy's eyes grew even bigger and rounder.

'Light and Dark live in peace?'

'Yes.'

'Those . . . the vampires . . .' He kept coming back over and over again to the same subject. 'They're Dark Ones?'

'Yes. They're people who have been totally transformed by the Twilight world. They acquire immense powers, but they lose the gift of life itself. And they can only carry on existing by using the energy of other beings. Blood's the most convenient form for transferring it.'

'And they kill people!'

'They can exist on donor's blood. It's like processed foods, it doesn't taste so good, but it's still nutritious. If the vampires just went out hunting—'

'But they attacked me!'

He was only thinking about himself right now. That wasn't good.

'Some vampires break the law. That's why we need the Night Watch, to police the observance of the Treaty.'

'Then . . . vampires don't just go around hunting people, right?'

I felt a breath of wind against my cheek from invisible wings. The claws dug into my shoulder.

'Now what are you going to tell him, Night Watch agent?' Olga whispered from out of the depths of the Twilight. 'Will you risk telling him the truth?'

'Yes, they go hunting,' I said. Then I added the thing that had struck me as most terrible of all five years earlier. 'If they have a licence. Sometimes . . . sometimes they need living blood.'

He didn't ask straight off. I could read everything the boy was thinking in his eyes, everything he wanted to ask. And I knew I'd have to answer all the questions.

'Then what do you do?'

'We make sure there's no poaching.'

'Then they could have attacked me . . . under that Treaty of yours? With a licence?'

'Yes,' I said.

'They could have drunk my blood? And you would have just walked by and looked the other way?'

Light and Dark . . .

I closed my eyes. The Treaty blazed brightly in the grey mist. Stark words, the product of thousands of years of war, costing millions of lives.

'Yes.'

'Go away!'

The boy was as tense as a coiled spring. On the brink of hysteria, on the brink of insanity.

'I came to protect you.'

'Don't bother!'

'The girl vampire's on the loose. She tried to attack—'

'Go away!'

Olga sighed.

'Now you've done it!'

I stood up. Egor shuddered and moved his stool further away from me.

'You'll understand some day,' I said. 'We have no other option . . .'

I didn't believe the words I was saying. And it was pointless to argue now. It was getting dark outside, pretty soon it would be hunting time . . .

The boy followed me, as if he wanted to make sure I left the apartment and didn't hide in the cupboard. I didn't say another word, just opened the door and went out into the stairwell. The door slammed shut behind me.

I walked up one flight of stairs and squatted down by the window on the landing. Olga didn't say anything and neither did I.

You can't just go revealing the truth like that out of the blue. It's not easy for a normal person even to admit that we exist. But to come to terms with the Treaty . . .

'There was nothing we could have done,' said Olga. 'We underestimated the boy, both his powers and his fear. We were discovered. We were obliged to answer his questions and to tell the truth.'

'Are we drawing up a report?' I asked.

'If you only knew how many reports like that I've drawn up . . .'

There was a smell of decay from the garbage chute. Outside, the noisy avenue was slowly descending into the evening dusk. The streetlamps were already beginning to flicker. I sat there, toying with my mobile phone and wondering if I ought to call the boss now or wait for him to call. Boris Ignatievich was probably observing me.

He was bound to be.

'Don't expect the boss to be able to give you too much help,' said Olga. 'He's up to his ears already with that black vortex.'

The phone in my hand started ringing, and I answered it.

'Yes?'

'Where are you, Anton?'

The boss sounded tired, worn out. I'd never heard him sound like that before.

'On a landing in a big, ugly apartment block. Beside the garbage chute. It's quite warm here, pretty comfortable really.'

'Did you find the boy?' the boss asked, sounding entirely uninterested.

'Yes.'

'Good. I'll send you Tiger Cub and Bear. There's nothing for them to do here anyway. And you come to Perovo. Now.'

I was just reaching for my pocket when the boss added:

'If you haven't got any money . . . even if you have, stop a militia car and get them to bring you here as fast as they can.'

'Do you really mean that?' I asked.

'Absolutely. You can leave straight away.'

I looked out of the window into the darkness.

'Boris Ignatievich, it's not a good idea to leave the kid alone. He really is potentially very powerful . . .'

'I know that . . . Okay. The guys are on their way. There's no danger to the boy once they're there. Wait for them to arrive, then come straight here.'

He hung up. I put away my phone and looked sideways at my shoulder.

'What do you make of that, Olga?'

'Odd.'

'Why? You said yourself they wouldn't be able to handle it.'

'It's odd that he wanted you to go, not me . . .' Olga said thoughtfully. 'Maybe . . . no, it can't be that. I don't know.'

I took a look through the Twilight and spotted two little specks right on the horizon. The field operatives were coming so fast they would reach me in about fifteen minutes.

'He didn't even ask the address,' I commented glumly.

'He didn't want to waste any time. Didn't you feel him take the co-ordinates?'

'No.'

'You need more training, Anton.'

'I don't work in the field.'

'You do now. Let's go downstairs. We'll hear the Call.'

I got up – that spot on the staircase had begun to feel really comfortable, just like home – and set off down the stairs. I was miserable, I had a really bad feeling about this. A door slammed behind my back. I turned round.

'I'm afraid,' Egor said, coming straight to the point.

'Everything's fine.' I started walking back up. 'We're guarding you.'

He chewed on his lips, shifting his gaze from me to the gloom of the staircase and back again. He didn't want to let me back into the flat, but he couldn't bear to be alone any longer.

'I think someone's watching me,' he said eventually. 'Are you doing that?'

'No. Most likely it's the vampire.'

The boy didn't even shiver. I hadn't told him anything new.

'How does she attack?'

'She can't come in through the door unless she's invited. That's one thing about vampires that the fairy tales have right. You'll feel like you want to go out yourself. In fact, you already want to go out.'

'I won't go out!'

'When she uses the Call, you'll go. You'll understand what's happening, but you'll still go anyway.'

'Can you . . . can you tell me what to do? Anything?'

Egor had given in. He wanted help, any help he could get.

'I can. Trust us.'

He only hesitated for a second.

'Come in.' Egor stepped back from the door. 'Only . . . Mum will be back from work any moment.'

'So?'

'Are you going to hide? What should I tell her?'

'That's no problem,' I said dismissively. 'But I—'

The door of the next-door apartment opened cautiously, just a crack, on the chain. A wrinkled, old woman's face peeped out.

I touched her mind, lightly, just for an instant, as carefully as possible so as not to do any more damage to a reason that was already shaky.

'Ah, it's you . . .' the old woman said with a beaming smile. 'You, you . . .'

'Anton,' I prompted her politely.

'And there was I wondering who the stranger was, wandering up and down,' said the old granny, taking off the chain and coming out on to the landing. 'The times we live in, the outrageous things people get up to, they just do whatever they like . . .'

'It's all right. Everything's going to be all right. Why don't you turn on the TV, there's a new series just starting.'

The old woman nodded, shot me a friendly glance and disappeared into her apartment.

'What series?' asked Egor.

I shrugged.

'I don't know. There must be something. Isn't there always some soap opera or other?'

'And how do you know our neighbour?'

'I don't.'

The boy said nothing.

'Just one of those little things,' I explained. 'And I won't come in, thanks, I have to go now.'

'What?'

'There'll be different guards here to look after you, Egor. And don't worry – they're far more professional than I am.'

I took a glance through the Twilight; two bright orange lights were just approaching the entrance of the building.

'I . . . I don't want them,' said the boy, panicking immediately. 'I want you to stay!'

'I can't. I have another assignment.'

Down below, the entrance door slammed and there was a

clatter of footsteps on the stairs. The action heroes disdained to use the lift.

'I don't want them!' Egor grabbed hold of the door as if he'd decided to shut himself in. 'I don't trust them!'

'You either trust all of the Night Watch or you don't trust anybody,' I told him firmly. 'We're not supermen in red and blue cloaks who work alone. We're just employees. The police of the Twilight world. What I say goes for the Night Watch.'

'But who are they?' The kid was beginning to accept it. 'Magicians?'

'Yes, but highly specialised ones.'

Tiger Cub appeared below me on the bend of the staircase.

'Hi there, guys!' she exclaimed cheerfully, bounding up an entire flight in a single leap.

It was a superhuman leap. Egor flinched and took a step back, staring watchfully at Tiger Cub. I shook my head: she was clearly poised on the very edge of transformation. She was enjoying it, and just at that moment she had good reason to be feeling frisky.

'How are things over there?' I asked.

Tiger Cub sighed loudly and then smiled.

'Oh . . . a laugh a minute. Everybody's in a panic. You get going, Antoshka, they're waiting for you . . . So it's you I'm looking after, right?'

The boy looked her over without saying anything. To be honest, the boss had made a great choice when he decided to get Tiger Cub to protect Egor. Everyone, from young children to old people, liked her and trusted her. They do say even some of the Dark Ones have sometimes been charmed by her. But then, that was their mistake . . .

'No one's looking after me,' the boy answered at last. 'My name's Egor.'

'And I'm Tiger Cub,' said the girl, already inside the apartment.

She gave the boy a friendly hug round the shoulders. 'Show me round the battlefield! Let's start preparing our defences!'

I started down the stairs, shaking my head as I went. In five minutes Tiger Cub would be showing Egor how she got her name.

'Hello,' Bear rumbled as he walked up towards me.

'Hi.' We shook hands quickly. Of all the Watch agents, Bear was the one I had the most mixed feelings about.

Bear was a little bit taller than average, strongly built with a face that gave nothing away. He didn't like to talk a lot. Nobody knew where he spent his time when he wasn't working, or where he lived, except maybe Tiger Cub. There were rumours that he wasn't even a magician, but a shape-shifter. They said that first he used to work for the Day Watch and then, during some mission, he suddenly switched over to our side. But that was all a load of nonsense. Light Ones don't become Dark Ones, and Dark Ones don't turn into Light Ones. But there was something about Bear that made you stop and wonder.

'Your car's waiting,' the field agent told me without bothering to stop. 'The driver's a real pro. You'll be there before you know it.'

Bear had a slight stammer, so he kept his sentences short. He was in no hurry, Tiger Cub was already on guard. But I had no time to hang around.

'Are things tough over there?' I asked, walking faster. The answer came from above me now:

'Worse than that.'

I bounded down several steps at a time and belted out of the entrance. The car was there all right – I slowed down for a moment to admire it. A classy maroon BMW, the latest model, with a flashing light carelessly stuck on the roof. Both doors on the side facing the building were open. The driver was leaning out of the car, hastily smoking a cigarette, and I could just make out the bulge of a holster beneath his jacket. Standing by the back door was an absolutely monumental middle-aged man. Under his open coat he was wearing a very expensive suit, with a Duma deputy's badge glinting on his lapel. The man was speaking on his mobile:

'Who is he anyway? I'll get there when I can! What? What damned girls? Have you gone crazy? Can't you do a single thing on your own?'

Seeing me, the deputy narrowed his eyes, cut short his conversation without saying goodbye and got into the car. The driver took a deep drag, tossed his cigarette away and took hold of the wheel. The engine howled softly and I barely had time to get into the front seat before the car moved away. Icy branches scraped across the outside of the door.

'You gone blind, or something?' the deputy barked at his driver, though I was the one to blame for what had happened. But as soon as the owner of the car turned to face me his tone changed: 'You need to get to Perovo?'

It was the first time I'd ever taken a ride with a representative of authority. And this guy was either a top man in the militia or a gangland boss. I realised in theory that there was no difference as far as a Night Watch agent's powers were concerned, but I'd never tried to experiment before.

'Yes, back to where the guys came from. And make it quick . . .'

'Hear that, Volodya?' the deputy said to the driver. 'Step on it!'

Volodya stepped on it so hard I started feeling a bit queasy and I even glanced into the Twilight to see if we were going to get there in one piece.

It seemed like we were. Only not just because of our driver's skill or because, like any Night Watch agent, I have an artificially elevated success coefficient. It looked like someone had gone through the probability field, weeding out all the accidents, tailbacks and overzealous traffic cops.

The only person in our department who could have done that was the boss himself. But what for?

'I'm feeling a bit frightened too,' whispered the invisible bird on my shoulder. 'When I was with Count—'

She stopped short, as if she'd realised she was speaking a bit too freely.

The car drove through a red light at an intersection, following an incredible twisting route, dodging between the saloons and station wagons. Someone at a bus stop waved a hand in our direction.

'Like a sip?' the Duma deputy enquired amiably, holding out a small bottle of Remy Martin and a plastic cup. It seemed so bizarre, I poured myself thirty grams without even thinking about it. Even at that speed the car was a smooth ride, and the cognac didn't spill.

I handed back the bottle, nodded, took the walkman earphones out of my pocket, put them on and clicked play. Out came this ancient song, 'Sundays' – my favourite.

> It was a small town, no bigger than a child's toy,
> There'd been no plagues or invasions there since long ago.
> The cannon rusted in silence on its fortress tower,
> And the travellers' roads passed it by.
> And so year after year, no holidays or work days –
> The whole town slept,
> Dreaming dreams of lands with empty cities
> And dead cliffs . . .

We emerged on to the main highway. The car just kept on picking up speed, I'd never travelled that fast in Moscow before. Or anywhere else, come to that . . . If the probability field hadn't been cleared, I'd have made them slow down, but it was pretty terrifying anyway.

> The music sounded among the cold cliffs,
> While the town slept . . .
> Calling to where?
> Calling to whom?
> That no one knew . . .

I couldn't help remembering that Romanov was an Other. Only he wasn't initiated, he'd been spotted too late . . . They'd offered him the chance, but he'd refused.

That's one option.

I wondered how often he heard this music in the night.

> All who left their windows open in the hot night
> Are gone now
> Gone away to seek a land where life is full of life,
> Following the song . . .

'Like some more?' The deputy was Mr Conviviality in person. I wondered what suggestions Bear and Tiger Cub had implanted in his mind. That I was his best friend? That he was eternally in my debt? That I was the president's illegitimate but favourite son?

But that's all rubbish. There are hundreds of different ways of making people trust you and like you and want to help you. The Light has its own methods, but unfortunately the Dark has plenty as well. It's all rubbish.

The question was: what did the boss need me for so badly?

CHAPTER 6

ILYA WAS waiting for me beside the road, standing there with his hands stuck in his pockets, staring up in disgust at the sky through a flurry of fine snowflakes.

'You took your time,' was all he said after I'd shaken the deputy's hand and got out of the car. 'The boss is getting impatient.'

'What's going on here?'

Ilya grinned, but it wasn't his usual cheerful smile.

'You'll see . . . let's go.'

We set off along a trampled path, overtaking women with shopping bags rambling home from the supermarket. How strange it is that we have supermarkets now, just like the real things. But people still walk the same old tired way, as if they'd spent an hour standing in line for little blue corpses described as chickens.

'Is it far?' I asked.

'If it was, we'd have taken a car.'

'How did our sexual giant make out? Couldn't he handle it?'

'Ignat tried his best,' was all Ilya said. I felt a brief pang of vengeful satisfaction, as if it were in my interests for handsome

Ignat to screw up. If a mission required it, he was usually in someone else's bed within two hours of being given his assignment.

'The boss has declared a state of readiness for evacuation,' Ilya suddenly said.

'What?'

'At a moment's notice. If the vortex isn't stabilised, the Others quit Moscow.'

He was walking ahead of me, I couldn't look into his eyes. But what reason would Ilya have to lie?'

'And is the vortex still . . .' I began. Then I stopped. I could see it.

Above the dismal nine-storey block facing us, a black tornado was revolving slowly against the background of the dark, snowy sky.

You couldn't call it a twister or a vortex any longer. It was a tornado. It rose up out of the next building along, hidden by the one we could see. And judging from the side-angle of the dark cone, it went almost down to the ground.

'Damn . . .' I whispered.

'Watch what you say,' Ilya snapped. 'It could easily come true.'

'It's thirty metres high . . .'

'Thirty-two. And still growing.'

I cast a hasty glance at my shoulder and saw Olga sitting there. She'd emerged from the Twilight.

Have you ever seen a bird frightened? Frightened like a human?

The owl looked ruffled. Can feathers really stand on end? There was an orange-yellow flame blazing in her amber eyes.

The shoulder of my poor jacket was torn into tiny shreds, and the claws carried on scraping, as if they wanted to scrape right through to my body.

'Olga!'

Ilya turned back and nodded.

'Now you see . . . The boss says the vortex at Hiroshima wasn't that high.'

The owl flapped its wings and soared smoothly into the air, without a sound. A woman shrieked behind me – I swung round and saw a stupefied face, glazed eyes following the bird's flight in amazement.

'It's a crow,' Ilya said quietly, half turning his head to glance at the woman. His reactions were far quicker than mine. A moment later the accidental witness was overtaking us, muttering about the narrow path and people who liked to block the way.

'Is it growing fast?' I asked, with a nod at the tornado.

'In bursts. But it's stabilising now. The boss called Ignat off just in time. Come on . . .'

The owl made a wide circle round the tornado, then flew lower and over our heads. Olga still looked very self-possessed, but her careless emergence from the Twilight showed how agitated she really was.

'Why, what did he do wrong?'

'Nothing really . . . except for being overconfident. He got to know the girl. Then he started pushing things along and that made the twister start to grow . . . and how!'

'I don't understand,' I said, confused. 'It can only grow that way if it's being fed with energy by the magician who summoned up the Inferno . . .'

'That's the whole point. Someone must have tracked Ignat and started shovelling coal in the firebox. This way . . .'

We entered the building that stood between us and the vortex. The owl flew in after us at the last moment. I gave Ilya a puzzled look, but I didn't ask any questions. Anyway, it was clear soon enough why we were there.

An operations centre had been set up in an apartment on the first floor. The heavy steel door, firmly closed in the human world, was standing wide open in the Twilight. Without stopping, Ilya dived into the Twilight and walked through. I fumbled for a few seconds, raising my shadow, and followed him.

It was a large apartment, with four rooms, all very comfortable. But it was also noisy, smoky and hot.

There were more than twenty Others there, including the field operatives and us back-room boys. No one took any notice when I arrived, they just glanced at Olga. I realised that the old Watch members knew her, but no one made any attempt to say hello or smile at the owl.

What could she have done?

'Go through into the bedroom, the boss is in there,' Ilya said briskly, turning off into the kitchen, where I could hear glasses clinking. Maybe they were drinking tea, or maybe it was some-thing a bit stronger. I glanced in quickly as I passed and saw I was right. They were reanimating Ignat with cognac. Our sexual terrorist looked completely knackered, crushed. It was a long time since he'd suffered this kind of failure.

I walked on by, pushed open the first door I came to and looked inside.

It was the children's room. A child of about five was sleeping on a little bed, and his parents and teenage sister were on the carpet beside it. Clear enough. The owners of the apartment had been put into a sound, healthy sleep so they wouldn't get under our feet. We could have set up the entire operations office in the Twilight, but why waste all that energy?

Someone slapped me on the shoulder and I looked round – it was Semyon.

'The boss is this way,' he told me. 'Come on . . .'

It seemed like everyone knew I was expected.

When I entered the next room, I was taken aback for just a moment.

There couldn't be any more absurd sight than a Night Watch operations centre set up in a private apartment.

There was a medium-size magic sphere hanging in the air above a dressing table stacked with cosmetics and costume jewellery. The sphere was transmitting a view of the vortex from above. Lena, our best operator, was sitting on a chair beside it, silent and intense. Her eyes were closed, but when I came in she raised one hand slightly in greeting.

Okay, so that was usual enough. Sphere operators see space in its totality, there's no way to hide anything from them.

The boss was reclining on the bed, propped up with pillows. He was wearing a bright-coloured robe, soft oriental slippers and an embroidered skullcap. The room was filled with the sweet fumes of a portable hookah. The owl was sitting in front of him. It looked as if they were communicating silently.

That was all usual enough too. In moments of exceptional stress, the boss always reverted to the habits he'd picked up in Central Asia. He'd worked there at the end of the nineteenth century and the beginning of the twentieth, first disguised as a mufti, then as a Muslim guerrilla leader, and then as a red commissar, and finally he spent ten years as the secretary of a district party committee.

Danila and Farid were standing by the window. Even with my powers I could make out the purple glimmer of the wands hidden in their sleeves.

A perfectly standard arrangement. At moments like this the headquarters was never left unprotected. Danila and Farid weren't the strongest fighters we had, but they were experienced, and that was often more important than crude strength.

But what was I supposed to make of the last Other in the room?

He was squatting modestly and unobtrusively in the corner. As thin as a rake with sunken cheeks, black hair cut short, military style, and big, sad eyes. It was impossible to tell how old he was, maybe thirty, maybe three hundred. He was dressed in a dark, loose-fitting suit. A human would probably have taken the stranger for a member of some obscure sect. And he would have been half right.

He was a Dark Magician. And a powerful one too. When he glanced briefly at me, I felt my protective shell – which wasn't installed by me – crack and start to buckle.

I took an involuntary step backwards. But the magician had already lowered his eyes to the floor as if to show me that the momentary probing had been accidental . . .

'Boris Ignatievich.' I could hear my voice wheezing slightly.

The boss nodded curtly, then he turned to the Dark Magician, who immediately fixed his eyes on him.

'Give him an amulet,' the boss ordered brusquely.

The Dark Magician's voice was sad and quiet, the voice of someone burdened with all the woes of the world.

'I'm not doing anything forbidden by the Treaty . . .'

'Neither am I. My colleagues must be immune against observers.'

So that was it! We had an observer from the Dark Side in our headquarters. That meant Day Watch had a headquarters somewhere close by, and one of us was there.

The Dark Magician put his hand in his jacket pocket. He took out a carved ivory medallion on a copper chain and held it out to me.

'Throw it,' I said.

The magician smiled gently with the same air of melancholy sympathy and flicked his hand. I caught the medallion. The boss nodded approvingly.

'Your name?' I asked.

'Zabulon.'

I hadn't heard the name before. Either he wasn't that well

known, or he was somewhere right up at the top of the Day Watch.

'Zabulon . . .' I repeated, glancing at the amulet. 'You no longer have any power over me.'

The medallion grew warm in my hand. I put it on over my shirt, nodded to the Dark Magician and walked over to the boss.

'You can see how things are, Anton,' the boss said, mumbling slightly, because he hadn't taken the mouthpiece of the hookah out of his mouth. 'There you are, look.'

I looked out the window and nodded.

The black vortex sprouted out of a nine-storey block just like the one we were in. Its slim, flexible stalk ended somewhere around the first-floor level. By reaching out through the Twilight, I could locate the precise apartment.

'How could this have happened, Boris Ignatievich?' I asked. 'This is a lot more serious than a brick falling on someone's head, or even a gas explosion in a hallway.'

'We're doing everything we can.' The boss seemed to think he had to justify himself to me. 'All the missile silos are under our control, the same measures have been taken in the US and France, and they're just being put in place in China. Things are a bit trickier with the tactical nuclear weapons. We're having big problems locating all the operational laser satellites. The city's full of all sorts of bacterial garbage . . . an hour ago there was almost a leak from the Virological Research Institute.'

'You can't cheat destiny,' I said guardedly.

'Exactly. We're plugging the holes in the bottom of the ship, and the ship's already breaking in half.'

I suddenly noticed that everyone – the Dark Magician, and Olga, and Lena, and the warriors – was looking at me. I began to feel uncomfortable.

'Boris Ignatievich?'

'You're linked to her.'

'What?'

The boss sighed and took the hookah tube from his mouth. The cold opium smoke streamed out on to the floor.

'You, Anton Gorodetsky, a programmer, unmarried, of average abilities, are linked to the girl with that vile black filth hanging over her head.'

The Dark Magician in the corner sighed softly. I couldn't think of anything better to say than 'Why?'

'I don't know. We sent Ignat to her, and he did a good job. You know he can seduce anyone.'

'But it didn't work with her?'

'It did. Only the vortex started to grow. They spent half an hour together and the vortex grew from a metre and a half to twenty-five metres. We had to call him off . . . quickly.'

I glanced sideways at the Dark Magician. Zabulon appeared to be looking at the floor, but he immediately raised his head. This time my defensive shield didn't react: the amulet gave me secure protection.

'We don't need this,' he said in a low voice. 'Only a savage would kill an elephant to get a small steak for his breakfast.'

The comparison shocked me. But he seemed to be telling the truth.

'We don't require destruction on this scale very often,' the Dark Magician continued. 'At the moment we don't have any ongoing projects that require such a large-scale discharge of energy.'

'I really hope you don't . . .' said the boss, in a strange, grating voice. 'Zabulon, what you have to understand is that if this disaster does happen, we'll squeeze everything we can out of it too.'

The shadow of a smile appeared on the Dark Magician's face.

'The number of people who will be horrified by what has happened, who will spill tears of sympathy with others' grief, will be very great. But there will be more, infinitely more, who will sit with their eyes glued greedily to their TV screens, who will take pleasure in other people's suffering, feel glad that it passed their city by and make jokes about the retribution meted out to the Third Rome . . . retribution from on high. You know that, my enemy.'

He wasn't gloating, the highest-ranking Dark Ones don't react in such primitive ways. He was stating a fact.

'Nonetheless, we're ready,' said Boris Ignatievich. 'You know that.'

'I know, but we are in a more advantageous position. Unless you have a pair of aces up your sleeve, Boris.'

'You know I always have all four.'

The boss turned towards me as if he'd completely lost interest in the Dark Magician.

'Anton, the vortex isn't being nourished by the Day Watch. Whoever created it is working on his own. An unknown Dark Magician of terrible power. He sensed Ignat's presence and accelerated the pace of events. Now you're our only hope.'

'Why?'

'I told you Anton, you're linked. There are three divergences in the probability field.'

The boss waved his hand and a white screen unfurled in the air. Zabulon frowned, he must have been caught by the edge of the energy discharge.

'The first path along which events can develop,' said the boss. A black stripe ran across the white sheet that hung in the middle of the room without any visible means of support. Then it blurred, spreading out in an ugly blot that extended beyond the edge of the screen.

'This is the most probable path. The vortex attains its maximum power and the Inferno erupts. Millions killed. A global cataclysm –

nuclear, biological, asteroid impact, a twenty-point earthquake. You name it.'

'And a direct infernal discharge?' I asked cautiously, glancing sideways at the Dark Magician. His face remained impassive.

'No. I don't think so. The threshold's still a long way off.' The boss shook his head. 'Otherwise, I think the Day Watch and the Night Watch would have wiped each other out already. The second path . . .'

A thin line, leading away from the black stripe. Broken off abruptly.

'Elimination of the target. If the target dies, the vortex will disperse . . . of its own accord.'

Zabulon stirred and said politely:

'I'm prepared to help with this little initiative. The Night Watch cannot carry it out on its own, I believe? We are at your service.'

Silence. Then the boss laughed.

'As you wish,' said Zabulon with a shrug. 'I repeat, for the time being we offer you our assistance. We don't want a global catastrophe that will wipe out millions of people in an instant. Not yet.'

'The third path,' said the boss, looking at me. 'Watch carefully.'

Another line, branching off from the main root, gradually growing thinner and fading away to nothing.

'That's what happens if you get involved, Anton.'

'What do I have to do?' I asked.

'I don't know. Probability forecasting has never been an exact science. I only know one thing: you can remove the vortex.'

I suddenly had the stupid idea that maybe I was still being tested. A field work test . . . I'd killed the vampire, and now . . . But it couldn't be. Not with such high stakes.

'I've never removed any black vortices.' My voice sounded different, not exactly frightened, more surprised. The Dark Magician Zabulon giggled repellently, in a woman's voice.

The boss nodded.

'I know that, Anton.'

He stood up, pulled his gown around him and walked up to me. He looked absurd, or at least his oriental garb seemed like an awkward parody in the setting of an ordinary Moscow apartment.

'Nobody has ever removed any vortices like this one. You'll be the first to try.'

I said nothing.

'And don't forget, Anton, if you mess this up, even just a tiny bit, anything at all, you'll be the first to burn. You won't even have enough time to withdraw into the Twilight. You know what happens to Light Ones when they're caught in an Inferno eruption?'

My throat went dry. I nodded.

'Pardon me, my dear enemy,' Zabulon said mockingly, 'but don't you allow your colleagues the right to choose? In such situations, even in wartime, it has always been usual to call for volunteers.'

'We've already made our call for volunteers,' the boss snapped without turning round. 'We've all been volunteers for a long time already. And we don't have any choice.'

'But we do. Always.' The Dark Magician laughed again.

'When we acknowledge that humans have the right to choose, we deprive ourselves of it, Zabulon,' said Boris Ignatievich, with a glance at the Dark Magician. 'You're playing to the wrong audience here. Don't interfere.'

'I say no more.' Zabulon lowered his head and shrank down again.

'Give it your best shot,' said the boss. 'Anton, I can't give you any advice. Try. I beg you, please, try. And . . . forget everything you've been taught. Don't believe anything I've said, don't believe what you wrote in your course notes, don't believe your own eyes, don't believe what anyone else says.'

'Then what do I believe, Boris Ignatievich?'

'If I knew that, Anton, I'd walk straight out of this headquarters and over to that building myself.'

We both looked out the window simultaneously. The black vortex was still swirling, swaying from side to side. Someone walking along the pavement suddenly turned to face into the snow and started making a wide circle round the stalk of the vortex. I noticed a path had already been trodden along the edge of the road: the people couldn't see the Evil straining to strike their world, but they could sense its approach.

'I'll watch Anton,' Olga said. 'Back him up and maintain communications.'

'From outside,' the boss agreed. 'Only from outside. Anton, go. We'll do the best we can to screen you from any kind of observation.'

The owl flew up off the bed and landed on my shoulder.

I glanced at my friends, then at the Dark Magician – he looked like he'd gone into hibernation – and walked out of the room. The noise in the rest of the apartment faded immediately.

They showed me out in total silence, without any unnecessary words, without any shoulder-slapping or helpful advice. After all, what I was doing wasn't such a big deal. I was only on my way to die.

It was quiet.

Too quiet somehow, even for a Moscow commuter suburb at that late hour. As if everyone had shut themselves in at home, turned out the lights and huddled down with their heads under the blankets, keeping quiet, saying nothing. Quiet, but not sleeping. The only movement was the trembling of the blue and red spots in the windows – the TVs were switched on everywhere. It's become a habit already, when you're afraid, when you're suffering – switch on the TV and watch absolutely everything, from the teleshopping to the news. People can't see the Twilight world. But they are capable of sensing how close it is.

'Olga, what can you tell me about this vortex?'

'Nothing definite.'

So that was it?

I stood at the entrance, watching the stalk of the vortex flexing like an elephant's trunk. I didn't feel like going in just yet.

'When . . . what size of vortex can you extinguish?'

'Five metres high, and I have a shot at it. Three metres and it's a sure thing.'

'And would the girl survive if you did that?'

'She might.'

There was something bothering me. In this unnatural silence, with even the cars in the street trying to avoid this doomed district of the city, there were still some sounds left . . .

Then it hit me. The dogs were howling. In all the apartments in all the buildings on all sides, the miserable dogs were complaining to their owners – in quiet, pitiful, helpless voices. They could see the Inferno moving closer.

'Olga, information about the girl. All of it.'

'Svetlana Nazarova. Twenty-five years old. Physician, employed in polyclinic number seventeen. Has never previously come to the attention of the Night Watch. Has never previously come to the attention of the Day Watch. No magical powers detected. Her parents and younger brother live in Brateevo, she maintains occasional contact with them, mostly by phone. Four close girl-friends, currently being checked, so far nothing exceptional. Relations with other people equable, no serious hostility observed.'

'A doctor,' I said thoughtfully. 'That's a lead, Olga. Some old man or old woman dissatisfied with their treatment. There's often an upsurge of latent magical powers in old age.'

'That's being checked out,' Olga replied. 'So far nothing's turned up.'

There was no point, it was stupid making wild guesses, people cleverer than I am had already been working on the girl for half a day.

'What else?'

'Blood group O. No serious illnesses, occasional mild cardiac arrhythmia. First sexual contact at the age of seventeen, with one of her peers, out of curiosity. She was married four months, has been divorced for two years, relations with her ex-husband have remained equable. No children.'

'The husband's powers?'

'He hasn't any. Neither does his new wife. That's the first thing that was checked.'

'Enemies?'

'Two female ill-wishers at work. Two rejected admirers at work. A school friend who tried to get a fake sick-note six months ago.'

'And?'

'She refused.'

'Well, well. And how much magic have they got?'

'Next to none. Their malevolence quotient is ordinary. They all have only weak magical powers. They couldn't create a vortex like this one.'

'Any patients died? Recently?'

'None.'

'Then where did the curse come from?' Yes, now I could see why the Watch had got nowhere with this. Svetlana had turned out to be a thoroughgoing goody-two-shoes. Five enemies in twenty-five years – that was something to be proud of.

Olga didn't answer my rhetorical question.

'I've got to go,' I said. I turned towards the windows where I could see the two guards' silhouettes. One of them waved to me. 'Olga, how did Ignat try to work this?'

'The standard approach. A meeting in the street, the "diffident intellectual" line. Coffee in a bar. Conversation. A rapid rise in the mark's attraction level. He bought champagne and liqueurs, they came here.'

'And after that?'

'The vortex started to grow.'

'And the reason?'

'There was none. She liked Ignat, in fact she was starting to feel strongly attracted. But at precisely that moment the vortex started to grow catastrophically fast. Ignat ran through three styles of behaviour and managed to get an unambiguous invitation to stay the night. That was when the vortex shifted gear into explosive growth. He was recalled. The vortex stabilised.'

'How was he recalled?'

I was frozen through already, and my boots felt horribly damp on my feet. And I still wasn't ready.

'The "sick mother" line. A call to his mobile phone, he apologised, promised to call her tomorrow. There were no hitches, the mark didn't get suspicious.'

'And the vortex stabilised?'

Olga didn't answer, she was obviously communicating with the analysts. Then:

'It even shrank a little bit. Three centimetres. But that might just be natural recoil when the energy input's cut off.'

There was something in all this, but I couldn't formulate my vague suspicions clearly.

'Where's her practice, Olga?'

'Right here, we're in it. It includes this house. Patients often come to her apartment.'

'Excellent. Then I'll go as a patient.'

'Do you need any help implanting false memories?'

'I'll manage.'

'The boss says okay,' Olga replied after a pause. 'Go ahead. Your persona is: Anton Gorodetsky, programmer, unmarried, under observation for three years, diagnosis – stomach ulcer, resident in this building, apartment number sixty-four. It's empty right now, if necessary we can provide backup on that.'

'Three years is too much for me,' I confessed. 'A year. One year, max.'

'Okay.'

I looked at Olga and she looked at me with those unblinking bird's eyes, and somewhere in there I could still see part of that dirty, aristocratic woman who'd drunk cognac with me in my kitchen.

'Good luck,' she said. 'Try to reduce the size of the vortex. Ten metres at least . . . then I'll risk it.'

The bird flew up into the air and instantly withdrew into the Twilight, down into the very deepest layers.

I sighed and set off towards the building's entrance. The trunk of the vortex swayed as it tried to touch me. I stretched my hands out, folding them into the Xamadi, the sign of negation.

The vortex shuddered and recoiled. Not really afraid, just playing by the rules. At that size the advancing Inferno should already have developed powers of reason, stopped being a mindless, target-seeking missile and become a ferocious, experienced kamikaze. I know that sounds odd – an experienced kamikaze – but when it comes to the Dark, the term's justified. Once it breaks through into the human world, an Inferno vortex is doomed, but it's only a single wasp out of a huge swarm that dies.

'Your hour hasn't come yet,' I said. The Inferno wasn't about to answer me, but I felt like saying it anyway.

I walked past the stalk. The vortex looked like it was made of blue-black glass that had acquired the flexibility of rubber. Its outer surface was almost motionless, but deep inside, where the dark blue became impenetrable darkness, I could vaguely see a furious spinning motion.

Maybe I was wrong. Maybe its hour had come . . .

The entrance didn't even have a coded entry system. Or rather, it had one, but it had been smashed and gutted. That was normal. A little greeting from the Dark. I'd already stopped paying any attention to its tracks, even stopped noticing the words and the dirty paw marks on walls, the broken lamps and the fouled lifts. But now I was wound up tight.

I needn't have asked for the number. I could sense the girl – I kept on thinking about her as a girl, even though she'd been married – I knew which way to go, I could even see her apartment, or rather, not see it, but perceive it as a whole.

The only thing I didn't understand was how I was going to get rid of that damned twister.

I stopped in front of the door. It was an ordinary one, not metal, very unusual on a first floor, especially in a building where the entrance lock is broken. I gave a deep sigh and rang the bell. Eleven o'clock. A bit late, of course.

I heard steps. There was no sound insulation . . .

CHAPTER 7

SHE OPENED the door straight away.

She didn't ask who it was, she didn't look through the spy-hole, she didn't put on the chain. In Moscow! And at night! Alone in her apartment! The vortex was devouring the final remnants of the girl's caution, the caution that had kept her alive for several days. That was usually the way people died when they had been cursed . . .

But to look at, Svetlana still seemed normal. Except maybe for the shadows under her eyes, but who knew what kind of a night she'd had? And the way she was dressed – a skirt, a smart blouse, shoes – as if she was expecting someone or was all set to go out.

'Good evening, Svetlana,' I said, already noticing a faint gleam of recognition in her eyes. Of course, she had a vague memory of me from the previous day. And I had to exploit that moment when she'd already realised we knew each other but still hadn't remembered from where.

I reached out through the Twilight. Cautiously, because the vortex was hanging right there above the girl's head as if it was attached to her, and it could react at any second. Cautiously, because I didn't really want to deceive her.

Not even if it were for her own good.

It's only the first time that's interesting and funny. If you still find it amusing after that, the Night Watch is the wrong place for you. It's one thing to shift someone's moral imperatives, especially when it's always towards the Good. It's quite another to interfere with their memory. It's inevitable, it has to be done, it's part of the Treaty, and through the very process of entering and leaving the Twilight we induce a momentary amnesia in the people around us.

But if you ever start to enjoy toying with someone else's memory – it's time you quit the Watch.

'Good evening, Anton.' Her voice blurred slightly when I forced her to remember things that had never happened. 'What's happened?'

I smiled sourly and slapped myself on the stomach. By now there was a hurricane raging in Svetlana's memory. My control wasn't so great that I could implant a fully structured false memory in her mind. Fortunately, in this case, I could just give her a couple of hints, and from then on she deceived herself. She put my image together out of one old acquaintance I happened to resemble and another person she'd known and liked even earlier than that, but not for long, as well as a couple of dozen patients my age and some of her neighbours in the building. I only gave the process a gentle nudge, helping Svetlana towards an integrated image. A good man . . . a neurasthenic . . . quite often unwell . . . flirts a bit, but no more than a bit – very unsure of himself . . . lives on the next stairwell.

'Are you in pain?' She gathered her thoughts. She really was a good doctor. With a genuine vocation.

'A bit. I had a drink yesterday,' I said, trying to look repentant.

'Anton, I warned you . . . come in . . .'

I went in and closed the door – the girl hadn't even bothered to do it. While I was taking off my coat, I had a quick look round, in the ordinary world and in the Twilight.

Cheap wallpaper, a tattered rug on the floor, an old pair of boots, a light bulb in a simple glass shade on the ceiling, a radio telephone on the wall – cheap Chinese junk. Modest. Clean. Ordinary. And the important thing here wasn't that the profession of district doctor doesn't pay very well. It was more that she didn't feel any need for comfort. That was bad . . . very bad.

In the Twilight world the apartment made a slightly better impression. No repulsive plant life, no trace of the Dark. Apart from the black vortex, of course, just hanging there . . . I could see the entire thing, from the stalk, swirling round above the girl's head, up to the broad mouth, thirty metres higher.

I followed Svetlana through into the only room. At least things were a bit more cosy in here. The sofa had a warm orange glow – not all of it, though, just the part by the old-fashioned standard lamp. Two walls were covered with single-box bookshelves stacked on top of each other, seven shelves high.

I was beginning to understand her, not just as a professional target and a potential victim of a Dark Magician, not just as the unwitting cause of a catastrophe, but as a person. An introverted, bookish child, with a mass of complexes and her head full of crazy ideals and a childish faith in the beautiful prince who was searching for her and would surely find her. Work as a doctor, a few girlfriends, a few male friends and lots and lots of loneliness. Conscientious work almost in the spirit of a builder of communism, infrequent visits to the café and occasional loves. And each evening like every other one, on the sofa, with a book, with the phone lying beside her, with the television muttering something soapy and comforting.

How many of you there still are, girls and boys of various ages, raised by naïve parents in the seventies. How many of you there are, so unhappy, not knowing how to be happy. How I long to take pity on you, how I long to help you. To touch you through the Twilight – gently, with no force at all. To give you just a little confidence in yourself, just a bit of optimism, a gram of willpower, a crumb of irony. To help you, so that you can help others.

But I can't.

Every action taken by Good grants permission for an active response by Evil. The Treaty! The Watches! The balance of peace in the world?

I have to live with it or go crazy, break the law, walk through the crowd handing out unsolicited gifts, changing destinies, wondering which corner I'll turn and find my old friends and eternal enemies, waiting to dispatch me into the Twilight. For ever . . .

'Anton, how's your mother?'

Ah, yes. As Anton Gorodetsky, the patient, I had an old mother. She had osteochondrosis and a full set of old folks' ailments. She was Svetlana's patient too.

'Not too bad, she's okay. I'm the one who's—'

'Lie down.'

I pulled off my shirt and sweater and lay down on the sofa. Svetlana squatted down beside me. She ran her warm fingers over my stomach and even palpated my liver.

'Does that hurt?'

'No . . . not now.'

'How much did you drink?'

As I replied to the doctor's questions, I looked for the answers in her mind. No need to make it look like I was dying. Yes . . . I had dull pains, not too sharp . . . After food . . . I'd just had a little twinge . . .

'So far it's just gastritis, Anton,' said Svetlana, taking her hands away. 'But that's bad enough, you know that. I'll write you a prescription.'

She got up, walked to the door and took her handbag off the peg.

All this time I was observing the vortex. There was nothing

happening, my arrival hadn't triggered any intensification in the Inferno, but it hadn't done anything to weaken it either.

'*Anton . . .*' I recognised the voice coming through the Twilight as Olga's. '*Anton, the vortex has lost three centimetres of height. You must have made a right move somewhere. Think, Anton.*'

A right move? When? I hadn't done anything except invent a reason to visit.

'Anton, do you have any of your ulcer medicine left?' Svetlana asked, looking across at me from the table. I nodded as I tucked in my shirt.

'Yes, a few capsules.'

'When you get home, take one. And buy some more tomorrow. Then take them for two weeks, before you go to bed.'

Svetlana was obviously one of those doctors who believe in pills. That didn't bother me, I believed in them too. All of us – the Others, that is – have an irrational awe of science; even in cases when elementary magical influence would do the job, we reach for the painkillers and antibiotics.

'Svetlana, I hope you don't mind me asking,' I said, looking away guiltily. 'Have you got problems of some kind?'

'Where did you get that idea, Anton?' she asked, carrying on writing and not even glancing in my direction. But she tensed.

'Just a feeling. Has someone offended you somehow?'

She put down her pen and looked at me with curiosity and gentle sympathy in her eyes.

'No, Anton. There's nothing. I expect it's just the winter. The winter's too long.'

She gave a forced smile and the Inferno vortex swayed above her head, shifting its stalk greedily.

'The sky's grey, the world's grey. And I don't feel like doing anything . . . everything seems meaningless. I'm tired, Anton. It'll pass when spring comes.'

'You're depressed, Svetlana,' I blurted out before I realised that I'd drawn the diagnosis out of her own memory. But she didn't pay any attention.

'Probably. Never mind, when the sun comes out . . . Thanks for your concern, Anton.'

This time her smile was more genuine, but it was still pained.

I heard Olga's voice whispering through the Twilight:

'Anton, it's down ten centimetres. The vortex is losing height. The analysts are working on it, Anton. Keep talking to her.'

What was I doing right?'

That question was more terrifying than 'What am I doing wrong?' Make a mistake, and all you have to do is make a sharp change of approach. But if you've hit the target without knowing how you did it, then you're in a real bind. It's tough being a bad shot who's hit the bull's eye by chance, struggling to remember how you moved your hands and screwed up your eyes, how much pressure your finger applied to the trigger . . . and not wanting to believe that the bullet was directed to the target by a random gust of wind.

I caught myself sitting and looking at Svetlana. And she was looking at me. Seriously, without speaking.

'I'm sorry,' I said. 'I'm sorry, Svetlana, forgive me. I came barging in late in the evening, and now I'm interfering in your private life . . .'

'That's all right, Anton. Actually, I like it. Now, would you like some tea?'

'Down twenty centimetres, Anton! Say yes!'

Even those few centimetres skimmed off the height of the vortex were a gift from the gods. They were human lives. Tens or even hundreds of lives snatched away from the inevitable catastrophe. I didn't know how I was doing it, but I was increasing Svetlana's resistance to the Inferno. And the vortex was beginning to melt away.

'Thanks, Svetlana. I'd love some.'

She got up and went into the kitchen. I followed her. What was going on here?

'Anton, we have a provisional analysis . . .'

I thought I glimpsed the white silhouette of a bird through the curtained window — it flitted along the wall, following Svetlana.

'Ignat followed the usual plan. Compliments, interest, infatuation, love. She liked it, but it made the vortex grow. You're using a different approach — sympathy. Passive sympathy.'

No recommendations followed, which meant the analysts hadn't reached any conclusions yet. But at least now I knew what I had to do next. Look at her sadly, smile sympathetically, drink tea and say: 'Your eyes look tired, Sveta . . .'

We'd be talking to each other like friends, right? Of course we would. I was sure of that.

'Anton?'

I'd been staring at her too long. Svetlana was standing by the cooker, not moving, holding a kettle with its shiny surface dulled by condensation. She wasn't exactly frightened, that feeling was already beyond her, completely drained out of her by the black vortex. It was more like she was embarrassed.

'Is something wrong?' she asked.

'Yes. It feels awkward, Svetlana. I just turned up in the middle of the night, dumped my problems on you and now I'm hanging around, waiting for tea . . .'

'Anton, please stay. You know, I've had such a strange day, and being here alone . . . Let's call it my fee for the consultation, shall we? That is, you staying for a while and talking to me,' she explained hastily.

I nodded. Any word might be a mistake.

'The vortex has shrunk another fifteen centimetres. You've chosen the right tactic, Anton.'

But I hadn't chosen anything, why couldn't those lousy analysts understand that? I'd used the powers of an Other to enter someone else's home, I'd interfered with someone else's memory so I could stay there longer . . . and now I was just going with the flow.

And hoping the current would bring me out where I needed to be.

'Would you like some jam, Anton?'

'Yes . . .'

A mad tea party! Move over, Lewis Carroll. The maddest tea parties aren't the ones in the rabbit's burrow, with the Mad Hatter, the Dormouse and the March Hare round the table. A small kitchen in a small apartment, tea left over from the morning, topped up with boiling water, raspberry jam from a three-litre jar – this is the stage on which unknown actors play out genuinely mad tea parties. This is the place, the only place where they say the words that they would never say otherwise. This is where they pull nasty little secrets out of the darkness with a conjuror's flourish, where they take the family skeletons out of the closet, where they discover the cyanide sprinkled in the sugar bowl. And you can never find a reason to get up and leave, because every time they pour you more tea, offer you jam and move the sugar bowl a bit closer . . .

'Anton, I've known you for a year already . . .'

A shadow, a brief, perplexed shadow in Svetlana's eyes. Her memory obligingly fills in the blanks, her memory hands her explanations for why a man as likeable and good as me is still no more than her patient.

'Only from my work, of course, but now . . . I feel I'd like to talk to you somehow . . . as a neighbour. As a friend. Is that okay?'

'Of course, Sveta.'

A grateful smile. It's not so easy to use the familiar form of my name. From Anton to Antosha is too big a step.

'Thank you, Anton. You know . . . I just don't know where I am. For the last three days now.'

Of course, it's not so easy to know where you are when you have the sword of Nemesis hanging over you. Blind, furious Nemesis, escaped from the power of the dead gods . . .

'Today . . . never mind . . .'

She wanted to tell me about Ignat. She didn't understand what was happening to her, why a chance encounter had almost got all the way to the bed. She felt like she was going insane. Everybody who comes within the Others' sphere of activity has thoughts like that.

'Svetlana, perhaps . . . perhaps you've fallen out with someone?'

That was a crude move. But I was in a hurry. I didn't even know why myself, as so far the vortex was stable, it was even shrinking. But I was in a hurry.

'Why do you think that?'

Svetlana wasn't surprised and she didn't think the question was too personal. I shrugged and tried to explain:

'It often happens to me.'

'No, Anton. I haven't fallen out with anyone. I've no one to fall out with, and no reason. It's something inside me . . .'

That's where you're wrong, I thought. You've no idea how wrong you are. Black vortices the size of the one hanging over you only appear once in every hundred years. And that means someone hates you with the kind of power rarely granted to anyone, even to an Other.

'You probably need a holiday,' I suggested. 'To get away somewhere, far away to the back of beyond.'

As I said that I realised there was a solution to the problem after all. Maybe not a complete solution, it would still be fatal for Svetlana. She could go away. Out into the taiga or the tundra, to the North Pole. And then it would happen there – the volcano would erupt, the asteroid would hit, or the cruise missile with the nuclear warheads would strike. The Inferno would erupt, but Svetlana would be the only one to suffer.

It's a good thing that solutions like that are as impossible for us as the murder suggested by the Dark Magician.

'What are you thinking, Anton?'

'Sveta, what's happened to you?'

'Too abrupt, Anton! Steer the conversation away from that.'

'Is it really that obvious?'

'Yes.'

Svetlana lowered her eyes. Any moment I was expecting Olga to shout that the black vortex had begun its final, catastrophic spurt of growth, that I'd ruined everything and now I'd have thousands of human lives on my conscience for ever . . . but Olga didn't say a word.

'I betrayed . . .'

'What?'

'I betrayed my mother.'

She looked at me seriously, not a trace of the posturing of someone who's pulled some really low-down trick and is boasting about it.

'I don't understand. Sveta . . .'

'My mother's ill, Anton. Her kidneys. She needs regular dialysis, but that's only a half-measure. Well, anyway, they suggested a transplant to me.'

'Why suggest that to you?' I still didn't understand.

'They suggested I should give my mother one kidney. It would almost certainly be accepted, I even had all the tests done . . . and then I refused. I'm . . . I'm afraid.'

I didn't say anything. Everything was clear now. Something about me must have clicked, something about me had made Svetlana feel she could be totally open with me. So it was her mother.

Her mother!

'Well done, Anton. The guys are already on their way.' Olga's voice sounded triumphant. And so it should – we'd found the Black Magician! *'Would you believe it, at first contact nobody felt a thing, they thought there was nothing to her . . . Well done. Calm her down, Anton, talk to her, comfort her.'*

You can't stop your ears in the Twilight. You have to listen when you're spoken to.

'Svetlana, you know no one has the right to demand—'

'Yes, of course. I told my mother, and she told me to forget about it. She said she'd kill herself if I decided to go ahead with it. She said, what difference did it make to her, when she was going to die anyway? And it wasn't worth crippling myself for her. I shouldn't have told her anything. I should have just donated the kidney. She could have found out later, after the operation. You can even give birth with one kidney . . . there have been cases.'

Kidneys. What nonsense! What a petty problem! One hour's work for a genuine Light Magician. But we weren't allowed to heal people, every genuine cure gave a Dark Magician a permit to cast a curse or put the evil eye on someone. And it was her mother, her own mother, who had cursed her, in a split-second emotional outburst, without realising what she was doing, while she was telling her daughter not even to think about having the operation.

And that had set the monstrous black vortex growing.

'I don't know what I ought to do now, Anton. I keep doing stupid things . . . Today I almost jumped into bed with a stranger.' For Svetlana to tell me that must have been almost as difficult as telling me about her mother.

'Sveta, we can think of something,' I began. 'The important thing is not just to give up, not punish yourself unnecessarily.'

'I told her on purpose, Anton! I knew what she'd say! I wanted to be told not to do it! She ought to have cursed me, the damned old fool!'

Svetlana had no idea how right she was . . . No one knows what mechanisms are involved here, what goes on in the Twilight, and how being cursed by a stranger is different from being cursed by someone you love . . . by your child or by your mother. Except that a mother's curse is the most terrible of all.

'Anton, take it easy.'

The sound of Olga's voice sobered me up instantly.

'That's too simple, Anton. Have you ever dealt with a mother's curse?'

'No,' I said. I said it out loud, answering Svetlana and Olga at the same time.

'I'm to blame,' said Svetlana, with a shake of her head. 'Thanks, Anton, but I'm to blame and no one else.'

'I have,' the voice said through the Twilight. *'Anton, my friend, this looks all wrong! A mother's curse is a blinding black explosion and a large vortex. But it always dissipates in an instant. Almost always.'*

Maybe so. I didn't argue with her. Olga was a specialist in curses and she'd seen all sorts of things. Of course, nobody would wish their own child ill . . . at least, not for long. But there were exceptions.

'Exceptions are possible,' Olga agreed. *'They'll check her mother out thoroughly now. But . . . I wouldn't count on this being over soon.'*

'Svetlana,' I asked. 'Isn't there any other solution? Some other way to help your mother? Apart from a transplant?'

'No. I'm a doctor, I know. Medicine's not all-powerful.'

'What if it wasn't medicine?'

She was puzzled.

'What do you mean, Anton?'

'Alternative medicine,' I said. 'Folk medicine.'

'Anton . . .'

'I understand, Svetlana, it's hard to believe,' I added hastily.

'There are so many charlatans, conmen and psychos out there. But is all of it really lies?'

'Anton, can you show me one person who has cured a really serious illness?' said Svetlana, looking at me ironically. 'Not just tell me about him, but show him to me. And his patients too, preferably before and after treatment. Then I'll believe, I'll believe in anything. In psychics, and healers, in white magicians and black magicians . . .'

I couldn't help squirming on my chair. She had the most magnificent proof possible of the existence of 'black' magic hanging right there over her head, a textbook case.

'I could show you one,' I said. I remembered how they'd brought Danila into the office one time. It was after an ordinary fight – not absolutely ordinary, but not so heavy either. He'd just been unlucky. They were detaining a family of werewolves for some petty violation of the Treaty. The werewolves could have given themselves up and nothing more would have come of it than a brief joint investigation by the two Watches.

But the werewolves decided to resist. They probably had an entire trail of bloody crimes behind them that the Night Watch knew nothing about – and now they never would. Danila went in first, and got badly mauled. His left lung, his heart, a deep trauma to the liver, one kidney torn right out.

The boss fixed Danila up, with a helping hand from almost everyone in the Watch who had any strength right then. I was standing in the third circle, our job was not so much to provide the boss with energy as to cut out external influences. But sometimes I took a look at Danila. He kept sinking into the Twilight, either on his own or with the boss. Every time he surfaced into reality his wounds were smaller. It was impressive, but not really all that difficult, after all the wounds were still fresh and they weren't predestined. But I had no doubt that the boss could cure Svetlana's mother. Even if the line of her destiny broke off in the near future, even if she was definitely going to die. She could be cured. Death would simply be due to other causes . . .

'Anton, aren't you afraid to talk like that?'

I shrugged. Svetlana sighed.

'If you give someone hope, you become responsible, Anton. I don't believe in miracles. But right now I just might. Doesn't that scare you?'

I looked into her eyes.

'No, Svetlana. There are lots of things that scare me. But different things.'

'Anton, the vortex is down by twenty centimetres. The boss says to tell you well done.'

There was something about her voice I didn't like. A conversation through the Twilight isn't like an ordinary one, you can sense emotion.

'What's happened?' I asked through the dead grey shroud.

'Keep going, Anton.'

'What's happened?'

'I wish I could feel so self-assured,' said Svetlana. She looked at the window: 'Did you hear that? A kind of rustling sound . . .'

'The wind,' I suggested. 'Or someone walking by.'

'Olga, tell me!'

'Anton, everything's fine with the vortex. It's slowly shrinking. You're increasing her internal resistance somehow. They calculate that by morning the vortex will I have shrunk to a theoretically safe size. Then I can get to work.'

'Then what's the problem? There is one, Olga, I can sense it!'

She didn't answer.

'Olga, are we partners or not?'

That worked. I couldn't see the owl, but I knew her eyes had glinted and she'd glanced towards the windows of our field headquarters. Into the faces of the boss and the observer from the Dark Ones.

'*Anton, there's a problem with the boy.*'

'*With Egor?*'

'Anton, what are you thinking about?' Svetlana asked. It was hard work holding simultaneous conversations in the real world and the Twilight one.

'Just wishing I could be in two places at the same time.'

'*Anton, your mission is far more important.*'

'*Tell me, Olga.*'

'I don't understand, Anton.' That was Svetlana again.

'You know, I've just realised that a friend of mine is in trouble. Big trouble,' I said, looking into her eyes.

'*The girl vampire. She's taken the boy.*'

I didn't feel a thing . . . No emotions, no pity, no anger, no sadness. I just felt cold and empty inside.

I must have been expecting it. I didn't know why, but I was.

'*But Bear and Tiger Cub are there!*'

'*It just happened.*'

'*And what's happened to him?*'

As long as she hadn't initiated him. Death, simple death. Eternal death was more terrible.

'*He's alive. She's taken him as a hostage.*'

'*What?*'

That had never happened before. It had simply never happened. Taking hostages was a game humans played.

'*The girl vampire's demanding negotiations. She wants a trial . . . she's hoping to find some way out.*'

In my head I gave the vampire ten out of ten for inventiveness. She didn't have a chance of getting away and she'd never had one. But if she could shift all the blame on to her eliminated friend, the one who'd initiated her . . . I don't know anything, I don't understand a thing. I just got bitten and turned into what I am. I didn't know the rules. I hadn't read the Treaty. I'll be a normal, law-abiding vampire . . .

It might even work! I thought. Especially if the Night Watch made a few concessions. And we would . . . we had no choice. Every human life had to be protected.

I even went limp in relief. You might say, what was the boy to me, anyway? If he'd drawn the short straw, he could have been the legitimate prey of vampires and werewolves. That's just the way life is. And I'd have walked straight by. Never mind the short straw – how many times had the Night Watch got there too late, how many people had been killed by the Dark Ones? But it was a strange thing. I was already involved in the struggle for him, I'd stepped into the Twilight and spilled blood. And it wasn't all the same to me any more. Not by a long way . . .

Conversations in the Twilight move a lot faster than they do in the human world. But I still had to divide myself between Olga and Svetlana.

'Anton, don't bother your head about my problems.'

In spite of everything, I felt like laughing. Right then there were hundreds of heads trying to deal with her problems, and Svetlana had no idea, she knew nothing about it. But it was enough to mention other people's problems, so tiny in comparison with the black Inferno vortex, and she immediately started worrying about them.

'You know,' I said, 'there's a law called the law of paired events. You have problems, but I wasn't talking about them. There's someone else who has really big problems. His own personal problems. But that doesn't make them any easier.'

She understood. I liked the fact that she wasn't embarrassed either. She just added:

'My problems are personal too.'

'Not entirely,' I said. 'At least, I don't think so.'

'And that other person – can you help him?'

'Someone else will help him,' I said.

'Are you sure? Thanks for listening to me, but it's impossible to help me. It's just my dumb destiny, I guess.'

'Is she throwing me out?' I asked through the Twilight. I didn't want to touch her mind right then.

'No,' Olga replied. *'No . . . Anton, she can feel it.'*

Did she really have some Other powers? Or was it just a freak upsurge, triggered by the Inferno being there so long?

'What can she feel?'

'That you're needed at the other place.'

'Why me?'

'That crazy bloodsucking bitch is demanding you for the negotiations. The one who killed her partner.'

That really made me feel sick. We'd done an elective on anti-terrorist tactics, more so that we could avoid having to use our powers as Others if we got caught up in human disputes than for any real requirements of the job. We'd covered terrorist psychology, and in those terms, the girl vampire was acting perfectly logically. I was the first Watch agent she had ever come across. I'd killed her mentor and wounded her. For her the image of her enemy was concentrated in me.

'How long has she been asking for me?'

'About ten minutes.'

I looked into Svetlana's eyes. Dry, calm, not a single tear. The hardest thing of all is when pain is hidden behind a mask of calm.

'Sveta, would you mind if I went now?'

She shrugged.

'This is all so stupid . . .' I said. 'It seems to me that you need help right now. At least someone who can listen to you. Or is willing to sit beside you and drink cold tea.'

A faint smile and a barely perceptible nod.

'But you're right, there is someone else who needs help.'

'Anton, you're strange.'

I shook my head:

'Not just strange. Very strange.'

'I have this feeling . . . I've known you for a long time, but it's like we'd never met before. And then – it's like you're talking to me and someone else at the same time.'

'Yes,' I said. 'That's it exactly.'

'Maybe I'm going insane.'

'No.'

'Anton . . . this wasn't just a chance visit, was it?'

I didn't answer. Olga whispered something and stopped talking. The gigantic vortex rotated slowly above Svetlana's head.

'No, it wasn't,' I said. 'I came to help.'

If the Dark Magician who had cursed her was watching us . . . That is, if it wasn't just an accidental 'mother's curse', but a calculated blow struck by a professional . . .

We looked at each other without saying anything.

I had the feeling I could almost grasp what was really going on here. The answer was there, right beside me, and all our theories were stupid nonsense, we were following the old rules and maps that the boss had asked me to disregard. But to do that, I needed to think, I had to cut myself off for at least a second from what was going on, stare at a blank wall or a mindless TV screen and stop feeling torn between the desire to help one small human being or tens or hundreds of thousands of people. Stop swinging one way then the other trying to resolve this lousy mess, which would still turn out badly whichever way the cards fell, and the only difference it would make to me was that I would die quickly when the blast of the Inferno flung me into the grey expanses of the Twilight world, or slowly and painfully, kindling the dull flame of self-contempt in my own heart.

'Sveta, I've got to go,' I said.

'Anton!' It wasn't Olga, it was the boss. *'Anton . . .'*

He stopped, he couldn't give me any orders, the situation was an ethical impasse. The girl vampire was obviously sticking to her demands and refusing to negotiate with anyone except me. If he ordered me to stay, the boss would condemn the young hostage to death. He couldn't order me, he couldn't even ask me.

'We're organising your withdrawal . . .'

'Better just tell the vampire I'm coming.'

Svetlana reached out and touched my hand:

'Are you going away for ever?'

'Till the morning,' I said.

'I don't want you to go,' she said simply.

'I know.'

'Who are you?'

An express introduction to the mysteries of the universe? The same scene all over again?

'I'll tell you in the morning. Okay?'

'You're out of your mind,' said the boss's voice.

'Do you really have to go away?'

'Don't say that!' Olga shouted. She'd sensed what I was thinking. But I said it anyway.

'Sveta, when they suggested you should mutilate yourself to prolong your mother's life, and you refused . . . You did what was right, what was rational, didn't you? But now you're suffering. And the pain's so bad, it would have been better to act irrationally.'

'If you don't go now, will you suffer?'

'Yes.'

'Then go. Only come back, Anton.'

I got up from the table, leaving my cold tea. The Inferno vortex swayed above us.

'I will, for sure,' I said. 'And believe me . . . the situation isn't hopeless.'

Neither of us said another word. I went out of the apartment and began walking down the stairs. Svetlana closed the door behind me. That silence . . . That deathly silence, even the dogs had howled themselves out that night.

Irrational, I thought, I'm being irrational. If there's no ethically correct solution, act irrationally. Did someone tell me that? Have I just remembered a line from my old course notes, a phrase from a lecture? Or am I looking for excuses?

'*The vortex* . . .' Olga whispered. Her voice was almost unrecognisable, husky. I wanted to press her head against my shoulder.

I pushed the door to the building open and stepped out on to the icy pavement. The owl circled above my head like a bundle of white fluff.

The Inferno vortex had shrunk, it was shorter. Not a lot, relative to its overall height, but enough so that I could see it, maybe one and a half or two metres.

'*Did you know that would happen?*' asked the boss.

I looked up at the vortex and shook my head. Just what was going on here? Why had the Inferno reacted by growing larger and stronger when Ignat showed up? Putting people into a mellow state of mind was his speciality. Why had my aimless conversation and unexpected departure made the vortex shrink?

'*It's time I sacked that group of analysts,*' said the boss. I realised he'd said it to everyone, not just me. '*When will we have a working hypothesis for what's going on?*'

A car suddenly appeared from the direction of Zelyony Avenue, catching me in the glare of its headlights. Its tyres squealed as it bounced clumsily over the bumps of broken tarmac and stopped beside me. The hot-orange, low-slung, sporty cabriolet looked ridiculous, surrounded by the prefabricated, multi-storey blocks of a city where the best way of getting around was still a jeep.

Semyon stuck his head out on the driver's side and nodded:

'Get in. I've been told to drive you like the wind.'

I looked round at Olga and she sensed my glance.

'I've got a job to do here. Go.'

I walked round the car and got into the front. Ilya was sprawled in the back – the boss must have decided the Tiger Cub-Bear double act needed reinforcements.

'*Anton,*' said Olga's voice, pursuing me through the Twilight. '*Remember . . . you made a deal today. Don't forget that, not for a single moment . . .*'

I didn't understand at first what she was talking about. The witch from the Day Watch? What had she got to do with anything?

The car jerked, scraping across the hummocks of ice. Semyon swore with relish as he twisted the wheel and the car began crawling toward the avenue with an indignant roar.

'What halfwit did you get this car from?' I asked. 'Driving around in this in this weather . . .'

Ilya laughed.

'Shshsh! Boris Ignatievich has lent you his very own car.'

'Are you serious?' I asked, turning to face him. The boss was always delivered to work in his office BMW. I'd never realised he had a penchant for impractical luxury.

'It's the truth. Antosha, how did you manage that?' Ilya nodded in the direction of the vortex hanging above the houses. 'I never realised you had powers like that!'

'I never touched it. Just talked to the girl.'

'Talked? You mean you didn't fuck her?'

That was Ilya's usual way of talking when he was feeling tense about something. And he had plenty of reasons for feeling tense just then. But it still made me wince. I thought what he said sounded strained . . . or maybe he just hit a raw nerve.

'No. Ilya, don't talk like that.'

'Sorry,' he said flippantly. 'So what did you do?'

'I just talked.'

The car finally hurtled out onto the avenue.

'Hold tight,' said Semyon curtly. I was pressed back in my seat. Ilya lolled about behind me, taking out a cigarette and lighting up.

Twenty seconds later I realised that my previous ride had been no more than a lazy jaunt.

'Semyon, has the probability of an accident been deleted?' I shouted. The car hurtled through the night, as if it was trying to overtake the beams of its own headlights.

'I've been driving for seventy years,' Semyon said contemptuously. 'I drove trucks on the Road of Life during the siege of Leningrad!'

There was no reason to doubt what he said, but the thought crossed my mind that those journeys had been less dangerous. He hadn't been moving this fast, and predicting where a bomb's going to fall is no great challenge for an Other. There weren't many cars around now, but there were some, the road was terrible, to put it mildly, and our sports car was never meant for conditions like this.

'Ilya, what happened over there?' I asked, trying to tear my eyes away from a truck swerving out of our path. 'Have you been posted on that?'

'You mean with the vampire and the kid?'

'Yes.'

'We did something stupid, that's what happened,' said Ilya, and then he swore. 'Maybe not really all that stupid . . . We'd done everything right. Tiger Cub and Bear introduced themselves to the kid's parents as their favourite distant relatives.'

'"We're from the Urals"?' I asked, remembering our course on social contacts and how to get to know people.

'Yes. Everything was going fine. The table was set, the drink was flowing, they were pigging out on Urals delicacies . . . from the nearest supermarket . . .'

'They were really having a great time.' That note in Ilya's voice didn't sound like envy, more like enthusiastic approval of his colleagues. 'Everything was just fine. The kid sat with them some of the time, some of the time he was in his room . . . How could they know he was already able to enter the Twilight?'

I felt a cold shudder.

Well, how could they have known?

I hadn't told them. And I hadn't told the boss. Or anyone. I'd been satisfied with pulling Egor out of the Twilight and sacrificing a little of my own blood. A hero. The solitary warrior in the field.

Ilya went on, not suspecting a thing.

'The vampire hooked him with the Call. Very neatly too, the guys felt nothing. And firmly . . . the kid never made a sound. He entered the Twilight and climbed up on to the roof.'

'How?'

'Over the balconies. He only had to climb up three floors. The vampire was already waiting for him. And she knew the boy was under guard – the moment she took him, she revealed herself. Now the parents are sound asleep and the vampire's standing there with her arms round the kid, while Tiger Cub and Bear are going out of their minds.'

I didn't say anything. I didn't have anything to say.

'Our stupid mistake,' Ilya concluded. 'And a combination of unforeseen circumstances with potentially fatal consequences. Nobody had even initiated the kid . . . How could anyone know he could enter the Twilight?'

'I knew.'

Perhaps it was my memories that did it, or perhaps I was just frightened by our terrible speed as the car raced along the highway, but I looked into the Twilight.

People are so lucky that they can't see this – ever! And so unlucky that they will never be able to see it.

A high, grey sky, where there have never been any stars, a sky as glutinous as milk jelly, glowing with a ghastly, wan light. The outlines of everything have softened and dissolved – the buildings, covered with a carpet of blue moss, and the trees, with branches that sway regardless of which way the wind's blowing, and the streetlamps, with the birds circling above them, barely moving their short wings. The cars coming towards you move really slow, the people walking along the street are hardly even moving their feet. Everything appears through a grey light filter, everything sounds as if your ears are plugged with cotton wool. A silent, black and white movie, an eerie, elegant director's cut. The world from which we draw our strength. The world that drinks our life. The Twilight. Whoever you really are when you enter it, that's who you are when you come out. The grey gloom dissolves the shell that has been growing over you all your life, extracts the core that people call the soul and tests its quality. And that's when you'll feel yourself crunching in the jaws of the Twilight, you'll feel the chilly, piercing wind, as corrosive as snake venom . . . and you'll become an Other.

And choose which side to take.

'Is the boy still in the Twilight?' I asked.

'They're all in the Twilight,' said Ilya, diving in there after me. 'Anton, why didn't you tell them?'

'It never occurred to me. I didn't think it was that important. I'm not a field operative, Ilya.'

He shook his head.

We find it impossible, or almost impossible, to reproach each other. Especially when someone's really messed up. There's no need, our punishment is always there, all around us. The Twilight gives us more strength than humans can ever have, it gives us a life that is almost immortal in human terms. And it also takes it all away when the time comes.

In one sense we all live on borrowed time. Not just the vampires and werewolves who have to kill in order to prolong their strange existence. The Dark Ones can't afford to do good. And we can't afford the opposite.

'If I don't pull this off . . .' I didn't finish the sentence. Everything was already clear anyway.

CHAPTER 8

SEEN THROUGH the Twilight it actually looked beautiful. Up on the roof, the flat roof of that absurd 'box on stilts', I could see different-coloured patches of light. The only things that have any colour in there are our emotions. And there were plenty of those around.

The brightest of all was the column of crimson flame that pierced the sky – the vampire's fear and fury.

'She's powerful,' Semyon said simply, glancing up at the roof and kicking the car door shut. He sighed and started taking off his coat.

'What are you doing?' I asked.

'I'll go up the wall . . . over the balconies. I advise you to do the same, Ilya. Only you go in the Twilight, it's easier.'

'And how are you going?'

'The ordinary way. There's less chance she'll notice. And don't you two worry . . . I was climbing mountains for sixty years. I took the fascist flag down from Mount Elbrus.'

Semyon stripped to his shirt and threw his clothes on to the bonnet. Then he cast a swift protective spell to cover the clothes and the car.

'Are you sure?' I asked.

Semyon laughed, did a few squats and swung his arms around like an athlete warming up. Then he jogged across to the building, with the fine snow settling on his shoulders.

'Will he make it?' I asked Ilya. I knew how to climb the wall of a building in the Twilight. In theory. But an ascent in the ordinary world, and with no equipment . . .

'He ought to,' said Ilya, but he didn't really sound convinced. 'When he swam through the underground channel of the River Yauza . . . I didn't think he'd make it then, either.'

'Thirty years practising underwater swimming,' I said glumly.

'Forty . . . I'll get going then, Anton. How are you going up, in the lift?'

'Yup.'

'Okay . . . don't keep us waiting.'

He shifted into the Twilight and ran after Semyon. They were probably going to climb different walls, but I didn't really want to know who was going which way. My route was waiting for me, and it wasn't likely to prove any easier.

'Why did you ever have to find me, boss?' I whispered as I ran up to the building. The snow crunched under my feet, the blood pounded in my ears. I took my pistol out of its holster on the run and took off the safety catch. Eight explosive silver bullets. That ought to be enough. As long as I hit the target. I just had to seize the moment when I had a chance to take the vampire by surprise and not wing the boy.

'Sooner or later someone would have met you, Anton. If not us, then the Day Watch. And they had just as good a chance of taking you.'

I wasn't surprised he was keeping tabs on me. Firstly, this was a serious business. And secondly, after all, he was my first mentor.

'Boris Ignatievich, if anything happens . . .' I buttoned up my jacket

and stuck the barrel of the pistol into my belt behind my back.
'About Svetlana . . .'

'They ran an exhaustive check on her mother, Anton. No. She's not
capable of casting a curse. No powers at all.'

'No, that wasn't what I meant, Boris Ignatievich . . . I just had this
thought. I didn't pity her.'

'And what does that mean?'

'I don't know. But I didn't pity her. I didn't pay her any compliments.
I didn't make any excuses for her.'

'I understand.'

'And now . . . disappear, please. This is my job.'

'Okay. I'm sorry for turning you out into the field. Good luck,
Anton.'

I couldn't remember the boss ever apologising to anyone before.
But I had no time to be surprised, as the lift had finally arrived.

I pressed the button for the top floor and automatically reached
for my earphones dangling on their lead. Oddly, there was music
coming through them. When had I turned on the walkman?

> And what trick will chance play me?
> All will be decided later, for some he is no one,
> For me he is my lord,
> I stand in the darkness, for some I am a shadow,
> For others I am invisible

I love Picnic's music. I wonder if Shklyarsky's ever been tested
to see if he's an Other. He ought to be . . . But then, maybe not.
Let him keep singing.

> I dance out of time, I've done everything wrong,
> Not regretting the fact
> That today I'm like a shower that never fell,

A flower that never blossomed.

I, I, I – I am invisible.

I, I, I – I am invisible.

Our faces are like smoke, our faces are smoke.

And no one will learn how we conquer . . .

Maybe I could take that last line as a good omen.

The lift stopped.

I got out on to the top-floor landing and looked up at the trapdoor in the ceiling. The lock had been torn off, quite literally – the shackle was flattened and stretched. The vampire wouldn't have needed to do that, she'd probably flown to the roof. The boy had climbed up over the balconies.

So it must have been Tiger Cub or Bear. Most likely Bear – Tiger Cub would have ripped the trapdoor out completely.

I pulled off my jacket and dropped it on the floor with the murmuring walkman. I felt for the pistol behind my back – it was firmly wedged. So technology's all nonsense, is it? I thought. We'll see about that, Olga.

I cast my shadow upwards, projecting it into the air. I reached up and slid swiftly into it. Once I was in the Twilight, I started climbing the ladder. The thick, clumpy blue moss covering the rungs felt spongy under my fingers, and tried to creep away.

'Anton!'

When I stepped out on to the roof I even hunched over a bit, the wind up there was so strong. Wild, icy gusts – either an echo of the wind in the human world or some fantastic whim of the Twilight. At first I was sheltered from it by the concrete box of the lift shaft, projecting above the level of the roof, but the moment I took a step I was chilled to the bone.

'Anton, we're here!'

Tiger Cub was standing about ten metres away. For a moment

the sight of her made me envious; there was no way she was feeling the cold.

I don't know where shape-shifters and magicians get the mass for transforming their bodies. It doesn't seem to come from the Twilight, nor from the human world either. In her human form the girl weighed maybe fifty kilos, maybe a bit more. The young tigress poised ready to fight on the icy roof must have weighed a hundred and fifty kilos. Her aura was a flaming orange and there were sparks wandering lazily across the surface of her fur. Her tail was twitching left and right in a regular rhythm, the right front paw was scraping regularly at the bitumen of the roof and had scraped right through to the concrete . . . someone would get flooded come spring.

'Come closer, Anton,' the tigress growled, without turning round. 'There she is!'

Bear was standing closer to the vampire than Tiger Cub. He looked even more terrifying. For this transformation he'd chosen the form of a polar bear, but unlike the real inhabitants of the Arctic he was snowy white, just like in children's picture books. No, he had to be a magician, not a reformed shape-shifter. Shape-shifters were limited to only one form, two at most, and I'd seen Bear as a pigeon-toed brown Russian bear (when we arranged a carnival for the Watch's American guests), and as a grizzly at our demonstration classes on transformation.

The girl vampire looked terrible, a lot worse than the first time I met her. Her features were even sharper now and her cheeks were hollow. During the first stage of their body's transformation vampires require fresh blood almost constantly. But I wasn't about to be fooled by the way she looked: her exhaustion was just her appearance, it was agonising for her, but it didn't reduce her strength. The burn mark on her face was almost gone, I could just make out a faint trace.

'You!' the vampire's voice rang out triumphantly – as if she'd summoned me to be slaughtered, not to negotiate.

'Yes, me.'

Egor was standing in front of the vampire, she was using him to shield herself from our operatives. The boy was in the Twilight she'd summoned, so he hadn't lost consciousness. He stood still, not saying anything, looking from me to Tiger Cub and back. We were obviously the ones he was counting on most. The vampire had one arm round the boy's chest, holding him tight against her, and she had her other hand at his throat, with its claws extended. The situation wasn't hard to assess. Stalemate.

If Tiger Cub or Bear tried to attack the vampire, she'd tear the kid's head off with a single sweep of her hand. There's no cure for that . . . not even with our powers. On the other hand, once she killed the boy, there'd be nothing to stop us.

It's a mistake to drive your enemy into a corner. Especially if you're going to kill him.

'You wanted me to come. So I've come.' I raised my hands to show they were empty and started walking forward. When I was midway between Tiger Cub and Bear the vampire bared her fangs:

'Stop!'

'I haven't got any poplar stakes or combat amulets. I'm not a magician. And there's nothing I can do to you.'

'The amulet! The amulet on your neck!'

So that was it . . .

'That's nothing to do with you. It protects me against someone vastly superior to you.'

'Take it off!'

Oh, this was bad . . . really bad. I grabbed the chain, pulled the amulet off and dropped it at my feet. Now, if he wanted to, Zabulon could try to influence me.

'I've taken it off. Now talk. What do you want?'

The vampire twisted her head right round – her neck easily turned the full three hundred and sixty degrees. I'd never even heard of that one . . . I don't think our fighters had either: Tiger Cub growled.

'There's someone sneaking up here!' The vampire's voice was still human – the shrill, hysterical voice of a foolish girl who has acquired great strength and power by accident. 'Who is it? Who?'

She pressed her left hand, the one with the extended claws, into the boy's neck. I shuddered, picturing what would happen if one drop of blood was spilled. The vampire would lose control. She pointed to the edge of the roof with her other hand in a ludicrous gesture of accusation – like Lenin on his armoured car.

'Tell him to come out!'

I sighed and shouted:

'Ilya, come out . . .'

Fingers appeared on the edge of the roof and a moment later Ilya swung over the low barrier and stood beside Tiger Cub. Where had he been hiding? On the canopy of a balcony? Or had he been hanging there, clutching the strands of blue moss?

'I knew it!' the girl said triumphantly. 'A trick!'

It seemed like she hadn't sensed Semyon. Maybe our phlegmatic friend had spent a hundred years training in ninja techniques.

'What right have you to talk about tricks?'

'Every right!' Something human flickered briefly in the vampire's eyes. 'I know how to deceive! You don't!'

Fine, fine. You know how, we don't, I thought. Just you keep on believing that. If you believe the only place for 'white lies' is in sermons, that's just fine. If you think that the words 'good must have hard fists' belong in old poems by a ridiculed poet, you just keep on thinking that way.

'What do you want?' I asked.

She paused for a moment, as if she hadn't given it any thought:
'To live!'

'Too late. You're already dead.'

'Really? And can the dead rip people's heads off?'

'Yes. That's all they can do.'

We looked at each other, and it was strange, so pompous and theatrical – the whole conversation was absurd, after all, as we'd never be able to understand each other. She was dead. Her life was in someone else's death. I was alive. But from where she stood, it was all the other way round.

'I'm not to blame for this.' Her voice had suddenly become calmer and softer. The hand on Egor's neck relaxed slightly. 'You, the ones who call yourselves the Night Watch . . . who never sleep at night, who claim the right to protect the world against the Dark . . . where were you when my blood was drunk?'

Bear shifted forward slightly. A tiny movement, as if he hadn't shifted his powerful paws at all, just slipped when the wind pushed him. I knew he'd carry on sliding forward like that for another ten minutes, the same way he'd been doing for an entire hour since the stand-off began. Until he thought he had a good enough chance. Then he'd pounce . . . and if he was lucky, he'd be able to tear the kid out of the vampire's arms with no more harm done than a couple of broken ribs.

'We can't keep track of everybody,' I said. 'It's just not possible.'

This was terrible . . . I was starting to feel sorry for her. Not for the boy who'd been caught up in the game played between Light and Dark, not for young Svetlana, with the curse hanging over her, not for the innocent city that would bear the full brunt of that curse . . . I was feeling sorry for the vampire. It was a good question – where were we that night? The ones who call ourselves the Night Watch . . .

'In any case you still had a choice,' I said. 'And don't tell me you didn't. Initiation can only take place by mutual consent. You could have died. Died honestly. As a human being.'

'Honestly?' The vampire shook her head, scattering her hair across her shoulders. Where was Semyon? . . . How hard could it be to climb to the roof of a twelve-storey building? 'It would have been good to die – honestly. But the person who signed the licence . . . the one who earmarked me as food. Was he acting honestly?'

Light and Dark . . .

She wasn't simply the victim of a vampire on the rampage. She'd been marked down as prey, chosen by a blind throw of the dice. She had been destined to give up her life for the continuation of someone else's death. But that young guy who had crumbled into a heap of dust at my feet when he was incinerated by the seal had fallen in love with her. Really fallen in love . . . and he hadn't completely sucked out the girl's life, he'd turned her into his equal.

The dead can do more than tear off heads, they can fall in love too. The trouble is that even their love requires blood.

He'd had no choice but to conceal her, since he'd turned the girl into a vampire illegally. He'd needed to feed her, and only live blood would do for that, not the bottled blood of naïve donors.

So he'd started poaching on the streets of Moscow, and then we'd started to pay attention, the keepers of the Light, the valiant Night Watch, who hand victims over to the Dark Ones.

In a war the most dangerous thing is to understand the enemy. To understand is to forgive. And we have no right to do that – we never have had, not since the creation of the world.

'Even so, you still had a choice,' I said. 'You did. Someone else's betrayal is no excuse for your own.'

She laughed quietly.

'Yes, yes . . . good servant of the Light . . . Of course. You're right. And you can tell me a thousand times that I'm dead. That my soul has burned away and evaporated into the Twilight. But if I'm so malevolent, can you explain to me what the difference is between us? Explain that . . . make me believe it.'

The vampire lowered her head and looked into Egor's face. She spoke in an intimate, almost friendly tone:

'And you, boy, do you understand me? Answer me. Answer me honestly, don't take any notice of . . . my claws. I won't take offence.'

Bear made another tiny movement forward. I could feel his muscles tensing as he prepared to leap.

But then Semyon appeared behind the vampire, without a sound, with a movement that was smooth and quick at the same time – how did he manage to move that fast in the human world?

'Wake up, little one!' the vampire said encouragingly. 'Answer! Only honestly! And if you think he's right and I'm wrong . . . if you really believe that . . . I'll let you go.'

I caught Egor's eye.

And I knew what he was going to say.

'You're right too.'

A cold, empty feeling. No strength left for emotions. Let them show on the outside, let them blaze like a bonfire that people couldn't see.

'What do you want?' I asked. 'To exist? All right . . . give yourself up. There'll be a trial, a joint court of the Watches.'

The girl vampire looked at me and shook her head:

'No, I don't trust your court. Not the Night Watch or the Day Watch.'

'Then why did you call me here?' I asked. Semyon was moving towards the vampire, getting closer . . .

'For vengeance,' she said simply. 'You killed my friend. I'm going to kill yours . . . while you watch. And then . . . I'm going to try . . . to kill you. But even if I fail . . .' She smiled. '. . . you'll always know you didn't save the boy. Won't you, Watchman? You sign those licences without thinking about real people. And the moment you do look . . . out creeps your morality . . . your rotten, false, cheap morality . . .'

Semyon leapt.

And Bear leapt at the same time.

It was beautiful, and it was faster than any bullet or any spell, because in the end all that's left is the body striking the blow and the skill acquired over twenty, forty, a hundred years . . .

But I still pulled the pistol out from behind me and jerked the trigger, knowing that the bullet would fly through the air slowly and lazily, like a 'high-speed' shot from a cheap action movie, still leaving the vampire a chance to dodge, a chance to kill.

Semyon flattened out in the air, as if he'd hit a wall of glass, and slid down an invisible barrier, shifting into the Twilight as he went. Bear was flung off to one side – and he was far bigger. The bullet, crawling towards the vampire with all the grace of a dragonfly, flared up in a bright petal of flame and disappeared.

If it wasn't for the way the vampire's eyes were opening wider and wider, I might have thought she'd conjured up the protective shield herself. But that's something only the most powerful magicians can do.

'They are under my protection . . .' a voice said behind my back.

I swung round – and met Zabulon's gaze.

It was amazing that the vampire didn't panic. It was amazing she didn't kill Egor. The unsuccessful attack and the sudden appearance of the Dark Magician must have been much more of a surprise to her than to us, because I'd been half expecting something of the kind from the moment I took off the amulet.

I wasn't surprised he'd got there so fast. The Dark Ones have their own pathways. But why had Zabulon, the observer from the Dark Side, preferred this little tussle to staying in our headquarters?

Had he lost interest in Svetlana and the vortex hanging over her head? Did he know something that we had no way of figuring out?

That wretched habit of trying to work everything out in advance! The field operatives had it beaten out of them by the very nature of their work, which was all instant response to danger, battle, victory or defeat.

Ilya had taken out his wand. Its pale lilac glow was too bright for a third-grade magician and too steady for me to believe he could have charged it. The boss had probably charged it himself.

So he must have been expecting something.

He must have been expecting someone to turn up with powers that matched his own.

Neither Tiger Cub nor Bear changed their form. Their magic didn't require any external devices, and certainly not human bodies. Bear kept his eyes fixed on the vampire, totally ignoring Zabulon. Tiger Cub stood beside me. Semyon walked slowly round the vampire, rubbing his waist and deliberately making sure she saw him. He left the Dark Magician to us too.

'They?' Tiger Cub growled.

It took me a moment to realise what was bothering her.

'They are under my protection,' Zabulon repeated. The magician was wrapped in a shapeless black coat and his head was covered with a crumpled beret of dark fur. He had his hands in his pockets, but somehow I was certain there was nothing there, no amulets, no guns.

'Who are you?' screeched the girl vampire. 'Who are you?'

'Your protector and mentor,' said Zabulon, looking at me. Not even straight at me, more a casual glance past me. 'Your master.'

Had he gone insane? The girl vampire had no idea of the balance of forces here. She was wound up, ready to blow. She had been prepared to die . . . to end her existence. Now she suddenly had a chance to survive, but the way he spoke . . .

'I have no master!' The girl whose life depended on other people's death laughed. 'Whoever you are – from the Light, or from the Dark – remember that! I have no master and never will!'

She began backing away towards the edge of the roof, dragging Egor after her. Still clutching him with one arm, holding the other hand at his throat. A hostage . . . a good move against the forces of Light.

And maybe against the forces of Dark too?

'Zabulon, we accept,' I said, laying my hand on the tense muscles of Tiger Cub's back. 'She is yours. Take her – until the trial. We honour the Treaty.'

'I am taking *them*,' said Zabulon, gazing forward blindly. The wind was lashing into his face, but the magician's unblinking eyes remained wide open, as if they were made of glass. 'The woman and the boy are ours.'

'No. Only the vampire.'

He finally deigned to look at me.

'Agent of the Light, I am only taking what is mine. I honour the Great Treaty. The woman and the boy are ours.'

'You are stronger than any of us,' I said, 'but you are alone, Zabulon.'

The Dark Magician shook his head and smiled in mournful sympathy.

'No, Anton Gorodetsky.'

They came out from behind the lift shaft, a young man and a young woman. I knew them. Oh yes, I knew them.

Alisa and Pyotr. The witch and the warlock from Day Watch.

'Egor!' Zabulon said in a quiet voice. 'Have you understood the difference between us? Which side do you choose?'

The boy didn't answer. But perhaps only because the vampire's claws were pressed against his neck.

'Have we got a problem here?' Tiger Cub asked in a purring voice.

'Uhuh,' I confirmed.

'Your decision?' asked Zabulon. His Watch agents weren't saying anything yet, keeping out of it.

'I don't like this,' said Tiger Cub. She edged a little closer to Zabulon and her tail lashed me mercilessly across one knee. 'I don't like the Day Watch's view of what's going on here . . . not one bit.'

Bear obviously shared her opinion: when they worked as a pair, one of them spoke for both. I looked at Ilya: he was twirling the wand in his fingers, smiling darkly as if he was thinking. Like a child who's brought a loaded Uzi to a party instead of a plastic machine gun. Semyon was clearly up for anything. He didn't give a damn about petty details. He'd spent seventy years running over rooftops.

'Zabulon, do you speak for the Day Watch?' I asked.

I saw a brief flicker of doubt in the Dark Magician's eyes.

What was going on? Why had Zabulon left our headquarters, abandoning the chance to track down an unknown magician of incredible power and enlist him in the Day Watch? You didn't just abandon an opportunity like that, not even for a vampire and a kid with potentially great powers. Why was Zabulon determined to go head to head?

And why on earth was he so reluctant – I could sense it, there was no doubt about it – to speak in the name of the Day Watch?

'I speak as a private individual,' said Zabulon.

'Then we have a few little personal disagreements,' I answered.

'Yes.'

He didn't want to involve the two Watches. Right now we were just Others. We might be on duty, we might be on assignment, but Zabulon preferred not to raise the conflict to the level of an official confrontation. Why? Was he so very confident of his own powers, or was he afraid the boss might turn up?

I didn't get any of it.

And the most important question of all was why he'd left our headquarters and abandoned the hunt for the sorcerer who'd put the curse on Svetlana. The Dark Ones had insisted that the sorcerer must be handed over to them. Why would he abandon that claim so easily?

What did Zabulon know that we didn't?

'Your pitiful—' the Dark Magician began. But before he could finish, the hostage made his move.

I heard Bear's puzzled growl of confusion and looked round.

After playing hostage in the vampire's clutches for the last half-hour, Egor was dissolving, disappearing.

The kid was withdrawing deeper into the Twilight.

The vampire squeezed her arms together in an attempt to keep hold of him . . . or kill him. The sweeping movement of the clawed hand was swift, but it met no living flesh. The vampire struck herself under her left breast, in the heart.

What a pity she wasn't alive!

Like a snowdrift suddenly springing into life, Bear leapt, streaking through the empty air where Egor had just been standing and felling the vampire. The twitching body was completely covered by his massive form, with just one clawed hand protruding from under his shaggy side and twitching spasmodically.

In the same instant Ilya raised the wand. The lilac glow dimmed slightly, and then the wand exploded into a column of white flame. He looked as if he was holding a beam of light torn from the lamp of a lighthouse. It was blinding, I could almost feel its weight. With a visible effort, Ilya swung his arms, scraping the grey sky with a beam of light brighter than any seen in Moscow since the war, and swung the huge club down on Zabulon's head.

The Dark Magician cried out.

He fell, pinned down on to the roof, and the column of light tore itself out of Ilya's hands, moving of its own accord. It was no longer a beam of light, but a white snake, sprouting silvery scales as it coiled and writhed. The end of the gigantic body flattened out into a hood and a blunt head protruded from under it, with unblinking eyes the size of truck wheels. The slim, forked tongue flickered, blazing like a gas burner.

I jumped back as the tail almost caught me. The fiery cobra coiled itself into a ball and fell on Zabulon, rapidly winding the coils of its body round his head. And on the far side of the blazing coils three shadows thrashed away at each other, their rapid movements blurred into dim streaks. I hadn't noticed when Tiger Cub leaped at the witch and the warlock.

Ilya laughed quietly and took another wand from his belt. This one was less bright – he must have charged it himself.

Had he been carrying a weapon designed personally for Zabulon, then? Had the boss already known whom we'd be up against?

I looked round the roof. At first sight, everything was under control. Bear was lying on the vampire, with occasional muffled sounds emerging from beneath his body. Tiger Cub was dealing with the two Day Watch agents, and it didn't look as if she needed any help. The white cobra was throttling Zabulon.

We were left with nothing to do. Ilya was watching the struggle, holding the wand at the ready, evidently trying to decide which tussle to throw himself into. Semyon had never taken any interest in the Day Watch agents and Zabulon, and now he'd lost all interest in the vampire and was wandering along the edge of the roof, looking down. Was he worrying about new reinforcements for the Dark Side?

And I stood there like an idiot, holding the useless pistol in my hands . . .

My shadow sprang to my feet at the first attempt. I stepped into it, feeling the searing chill. Not the chill that humans know, not the chill that every Other knows – this was the chill of the deep Twilight. Here there was no wind, here the snow and ice under our feet had disappeared. Here there was no blue moss. The space was entirely filled with fog, thick and glutinous. If fog can be compared with milk, then this was curdled milk. My friends and enemies alike had all been transformed into vague shadows that were barely moving. Only the fiery cobra fighting with Zabulon was as fast and bright as ever – that battle was being fought at every level of the Twilight. Thinking about the amount of energy that must have been transferred to that wand made me feel dizzy.

But what for? Dark and Light, what for? Neither the vampire nor this young Other, the boy, were worth all this.

'Egor!' I shouted.

I was beginning to feel frozen. I'd only ever entered the second level of the Twilight twice: once in class, with an instructor beside me, and the day before, to get through the door of the apartment. I didn't carry any protection for this level, and every moment I was losing more and more strength.

'Egor!' I took a step through the fog. I could hear muffled blows behind me – the snake was pounding someone against the roof, clutching his body in its jaws . . . and I knew whose body . . .

Time down there moves even more slowly, and there was just a chance that the kid might not have lost consciousness yet. Struggling to make anything out in the gloom, I walked towards where he'd dived down to the second level of the Twilight, and I didn't see his body at my feet. I stumbled and fell, then got up, squatting on my haunches, and found myself face to face with Egor.

'You okay?' It was a stupid question to ask, because his eyes were open and he was looking at me.

'Yes.'

Our voices had a hollow, rumbling sound. There were two fluttering shadows right beside us: Bear was still struggling with the vampire. She was certainly holding in there for all she was worth.

And so was Egor.

'Let's go,' I said, reaching out and touching his shoulder. 'It's . . . tough being down here. We could get stuck here for ever.'

'So okay.'

'Don't you understand, Egor? To be dissolved in the Twilight means suffering, eternal suffering. You can't even imagine what it's like. We're leaving!'

'What for?'

'To stay alive.'

'What for?'

My fingers wouldn't bend. My pistol felt heavy, cast out of ice. I might last another minute, or two . . .

I looked into Egor's eyes.

'Everyone decides for himself. I'm leaving. I've got something to live for.'

'Why do you want to save me?' he asked curiously. 'Does your Night Watch need me?'

'I don't think you'll join our Watch,' I said, surprising even myself.

He smiled. A shadow slowly ran through us – Semyon. Had he spotted something? Was someone in trouble?

And there I was, wasting my final strength trying to prevent a little Other from committing esoteric suicide – when he was doomed anyway.

'I'm leaving,' I said. 'Goodbye.'

My shadow clutched hold of me, freezing to my fingers and growing on to my face. I began to tear myself away from it and the Twilight hissed at me.

'Help me!' said Egor. I only just caught the sound of his voice, I was almost out already. He'd left it right until the last moment.

I reached out and grabbed his hand. I was already being torn out, the fog around me was melting. All my help was purely psychological, the boy had to do the real work for himself.

And he did.

We tumbled out into the upper level of the Twilight. The cold wind struck me in the face, but this time it felt good. The listless movements on every side were transformed into a furious struggle. The blurred grey looked bright and colourful.

Something had changed during those few seconds we'd been talking. The vampire was still twitching under Bear . . . that wasn't it. The young warlock was lying on the roof, either dead or unconscious, Tiger Cub and the witch were struggling nearby . . . that wasn't it.

The snake.

The white cobra was expanding, inflating, filling a quarter of the roof. As if it had been pumped full of air and was rising, or flying up of its own accord into the low sky. Semyon was standing by the twined coils of its fiery body, half squatting in an ancient combat stance, with small orange spheres streaking from his palms into the clump of white flame. He wasn't aiming at the cobra, but at someone else beneath it, someone who should have been dead a long time ago, but was still struggling . . .

Then a sudden explosion!

A vortex of Light and scraps of Dark. I was tossed on to my back and as I fell I hit Egor and knocked him down, but I just managed to grab his hand. Tiger Cub and the witch, locked together, shot across to the edge of the roof and froze against the barrier. Bear was torn off the vampire, who was badly mauled but still alive. Semyon staggered, but remained on his feet, protected by a dimly glowing defensive shield. The only thing blown off the roof was the unconscious warlock: on his way he broke through the rusty bars of the barrier and plunged to earth in a helpless bundle.

But Ilya just carried on standing where he had been, rooted to the spot. I couldn't see any defences around him, but he just gazed curiously at what was going on, clutching his wand.

The remains of the fiery cobra soared upwards, spreading out into glowing clouds, melting away, scattering in showers of sparks and needle rays of light. Beneath this firework display Zabulon slowly rose to his feet, extending his arms in some complex magical pass. He'd lost his clothes in the struggle and was now completely naked. His body had changed, assuming the classic features of a demon: dull scales instead of skin, an irregular skull, covered with some kind of matted fur instead of hair, close-set eyes with vertical slits for pupils, a massive penis, and a short forked tail that hung from the base of his spine.

'Begone!' cried Zabulon. 'Begone!'

What must have been going on at that moment in the human world . . . Outbreaks of vicious depression and blind, irrational joy, heart attacks, bizarre behaviour, quarrels between best friends, betrayals by faithful lovers . . . People couldn't see what was happening, yet it touched their souls.

But why?

Why did the Day Watch want all this?

And at that moment I suddenly felt calm. A state of icy, rational composure I'd almost forgotten.

It was all one complex manoeuvre. If we started from one simple idea, made one initial assumption – that everything was happening according to the Day Watch's plan – and then connected up all the seemingly random events, starting with my hunt in the metro – no, starting with the moment when the young vampire had been allocated a girl to feed on, a girl he couldn't help falling in love with . . .

My thoughts were moving as fast as if I was acting as a brainstorm conductor, connected up to other people's minds, the way our analysts sometimes worked. But no, of course, that wasn't really happening, it was just that the pieces of the jigsaw had started moving around on the table in front of me, coming together.

The Day Watch didn't give a damn about the girl vampire . . .

The Day Watch wouldn't risk open conflict for the sake of a kid with potentially great powers. The Day Watch had only one reason for doing all this.

A Dark Magician of extraordinary power.

A Dark Magician who could reinforce their position, not only in Moscow, but right across the continent . . .

But then they'd already achieved that goal, we'd promised to hand over the Dark Magician . . .

The unidentified magician was the only unknown in the equation, the X. We could designate Egor as Y: his resistance to magic was far too high for any novice Other. But on the other hand, the boy was an already known quantity, with just one undetermined factor . . .

And that had been deliberately introduced into the problem, to make it more complicated.

'Zabulon!' I shouted. Behind my back Egor was scrabbling and sliding on the ice as he tried to stand up. Semyon was backing away from the magician, still maintaining his defences. Ilya was simply observing everything dispassionately. Bear was closing in on the twitching girl vampire as she tried to stand up. Tiger Cub and the witch Alisa were moving towards each other again. 'Zabulon!'

The demon looked at me.

'I know who you're fighting for!'

But I didn't know yet. I was just beginning to understand, because the pieces of the jigsaw had come together and shown me a familiar face . . .

The demon opened its jaws – they shifted to the left and the right, like a beetle's. He was looking more and more like some huge insect, his scales had grown together into a single carapace, his genitals and tail had retracted, new limbs had begun to sprout from his sides.

'Then you're dead.'

His voice was the same as before, in fact it sounded even more thoughtful and intelligent. Zabulon stretched his arm out towards me – it extended in jerks, growing new joints as it came.

'Come to me . . .' whispered Zabulon.

Everybody froze – apart from me. I started walking towards the Dark Magician. There was barely a trace left of the mental defences I'd nurtured for years. There was just no way I could not obey Zabulon.

'Stop!' roared Tiger Cub, turning away from the battered but still snarling witch. 'Stop!'

I really wished I could do as she said, but I couldn't.

'Anton . . .' I heard someone say behind me. 'Look back . . .'

That was something I could do. I turned my head, tearing my eyes away from the gaze of those amber eyes with their narrow, vertical slit pupils.

Egor was still squatting down, he didn't have the strength to get up. It was incredible that he was even conscious at all . . . after all, the external input into his energy reserves had been shut off. The external input that had attracted the boss's attention, that had been maintained from the very beginning. Factor Y. Introduced to complicate the situation.

A small ivory medallion on a copper chain dangled from Egor's hand.

'Catch!' the kid shouted.

'Don't take it!' Zabulon ordered me. But he was too late, I'd already bent down and grabbed the amulet as it came flying towards my feet. The carved medallion burned my hand when I touched it, as if I'd picked up a live coal.

I looked at the demon and shook my head:

'Zabulon, you no longer have power over me.'

The demon howled and came straight at me. His power over me was gone, but he still had plenty of strength.

'Tut-tut!' said Ilya.

A wall of white flame cut across the space between us. Zabulon howled as he hit the magical barrier and the sheet of pure white light flung him back. He shook his scorched paws, looking ridiculous now, not terrible at all.

'A complex move,' I said. 'But elementary really, isn't it?'

Everything on the roof went quiet. Tiger Cub and the witch Alisa stood side by side, not even trying to attack each other. Semyon looked at me, then at Ilya, and I couldn't tell which of us had surprised him most. The vampire was crying quietly, as she tried to get up. She was in the worst state of all, she'd used up all her strength to survive the fight with Bear, and now she was struggling to regenerate. With an incredible effort she left the Twilight, becoming a vague silhouette.

Even the wind seemed to have died away . . .

'How can you make a Dark Magician out of someone who is fundamentally pure?' I asked. 'How can you win over to the Dark Side a person who doesn't know how to hate? You can rain difficulties on him whichever way he turns . . . a little at a time, hoping that he'll become embittered . . . But that doesn't work. This person. . . . this girl . . . is too pure.'

Ilya gave a quiet laugh of approval.

'The only thing that she could hate,' I said, looking into Zabulon's eyes, now filled with nothing but powerless malice, 'is herself. And that's the clever move. Unexpected. Let her mother fall ill. Let the girl devour her very soul, despising her own weakness and refusal to help. Drive her into a corner so tight, there's nothing else she can feel but hate, even if that hate is for herself. Of course, there is a divergence of probabilities. Just a slight chance that a single Night Watch agent who doesn't really know all that much about field work—'

My knees started to buckle – I wasn't used to staying in the Twilight this long. I would have fallen on my knees in front of Zabulon, something I really didn't want to do, but Semyon slipped through the Twilight and supported me by the shoulders. He'd probably been doing that for a hundred and fifty years too.

'About field work . . .' I repeated. 'Might suddenly not behave according to plan, not trying to pity and comfort a girl for whom pity is fatal. He had to be distracted. A situation had to be created that would keep him busy. He had to be given a secondary assignment, and feel obliged to carry out that assignment for professional and personal reasons – anything that came to hand would do. An ordinary vampire could be sacrificed for that, couldn't he?'

Zabulon began transforming back to human form, assuming his former appearance as a mournful-looking intellectual.

That was odd. What for? When I'd already seen what he'd become in the Twilight, what he'd become once and for ever.

'A complex manoeuvre,' I repeated. 'I'll bet Svetlana's mother doesn't really have to die from any fatal illness at all. That was a minor intervention from your side, within the permitted limits . . . But then we have rights too.'

'She ours!' said Zabulon.

'No.' I shook my head. 'The Inferno's not going to erupt. Her mother's going to get well. I'm going straight to the girl now . . . and I'm going to tell her everything. Svetlana will join the Night Watch. You've lost, Zabulon. No matter what you do, you've lost.'

The tatters of clothes scattered across the roof crept towards the

Dark Magician, grew together and sprang up on to his body, reclothing the sad, charming intellectual grieving for the whole world.

'None of you will leave here,' said Zabulon. The Dark began thickening behind his back, like two immense black wings unfurling.

Ilya laughed again.

'I'm stronger than all of you,' said Zabulon. 'Your borrowed powers are not unlimited. You will stay here for ever, in the Twilight, deeper than you have ever dared to look . . .'

Semyon sighed and said:

'Anton, he still hasn't got the picture.'

I looked round and asked:

'Boris Ignatievich, don't you think you could drop the play-acting now?'

The bumptious young field operative shrugged:

'Of course, Antosha. But I don't often get a chance to observe the head of the Day Watch in action. Don't hold that against an old man. I hope Ilya found it just as interesting being me . . .'

Boris Ignatievich resumed his normal form. Instantly, without any theatrical intermediate stages or light effects. He was still dressed in his gown and skullcap, but he was wearing soft moccasins on his feet, with galoshes over them.

Zabulon's face was a sight.

The dark wings didn't disappear, but they stopped growing and flapped hesitantly, as if the magician was thinking about flying away, but couldn't quite make up his mind.

'Wind up this operation, Zabulon,' the boss said. 'If you withdraw immediately from this building and from Svetlana's house, we won't lodge an official protest.'

The Dark Magician didn't hesitate.

'We'll withdraw.'

The boss nodded, as if he'd never expected any other answer. Just for a moment I thought . . . He lowered the wand, and the barrier between me and Zabulon disappeared.

'I'll remember the part you played in this . . .' the Dark Magician murmured. 'For ever.'

'Do,' I said. 'It's good to remember.'

Zabulon brought his hands together – the mighty wings flapped, and the magician disappeared. But before he went, he glanced at the witch – and she nodded.

I didn't like that at all. A spiteful parting gesture may not be fatal, but it's never pleasant.

Alisa came over to me, walking with a light, dancing step completely out of keeping with her bloody face and dangling, dislocated left arm.

'You must leave too,' said the boss.

'Of course, I'll be only too delighted,' replied the witch. 'But before I do, I have one small, very small, debt to collect. Isn't that right, Anton?'

'Yes,' I send quietly. 'A seventh-degree intervention.'

Who would she strike her blow at? Not the boss, the idea was ludicrous. Tiger Cub, Bear, Semyon . . . that would be stupid. Egor? What suggestion could she implant in him at the very weakest level of intervention?

'Open yourself,' said the witch. 'Open yourself to me, Anton. A seventh-degree intervention. The head of the Night Watch is a witness: I won't overstep the mark.'

Semyon groaned, squeezing my shoulder so tight it hurt.

'She has the right,' I said. 'Boris Ignatievich . . .'

'Whatever you say,' the boss answered softly. 'I'm watching.'

I sighed and laid myself open to the witch. There was nothing she could do. Nothing. A seventh-degree intervention – she could never turn me to the Dark with that. The idea was simply ridiculous.

'Anton,' the witch said gently. 'Tell your boss what you wanted to say. Tell the truth. Act honestly and correctly. The way you ought to act.'

'Minimal intervention . . .' the boss confirmed. If there was any pain in his voice, it was so deeply hidden that I couldn't hear it.

'A complex manoeuvre,' I said, glancing at Boris Ignatievich. 'From both sides. The Day Watch sacrifices its pawns, and the Night Watch does the same. For the great goal. In order to win over to their side a sorceress of immense, unprecedented power. A young vampire who is longing for love may die. A young kid with undetermined powers may disappear for ever in the Twilight. Operatives may be hurt. But there's an end that justifies the means. Two great magicians who have opposed each other for hundreds of years cook up another little war. And the Light Magician is in the toughest spot . . . he has to stake everything. And for him to lose would be more than an inconvenience, it's a step into the Twilight, into the Twilight for all time. But still he stakes everyone's lives. His own side's and the other's. Right, Boris Ignatievich?'

'Right,' replied the boss.

Alisa laughed and walked towards the trapdoor. The witch was in no shape to fly. Tiger Cub had given her quite a mauling. But even after that she was feeling cheerful.

I looked at Semyon and he turned his eyes away. Tiger Cub slowly transformed back into a girl . . . also trying not to look me in the eye. Bear gave a short, sharp howl and trudged towards the trapdoor without changing his form. It was toughest of all for him. He was too uncompromising. Bear, the great warrior and opponent of all compromise . . .

'You're all bastards,' said Egor. He stood up, moving awkwardly – not just because he was tired, the boss was feeding his reserves now, I could see the fine thread of power running through the air

– but because at first it's always hard to tear yourself out of your shadow.

I was the next out. It wasn't difficult, during the last quarter of an hour so much energy had been splashed into the Twilight that it had lost its usual aggressive clamminess.

Almost immediately I heard an unpleasant soft thud: the warlock had fallen off the roof, hitting the tarmac below.

Then the others started to appear. An attractive, black-haired girl with a bruise under her left eye and a broken jaw; an imperturbable, stocky little man; a calm-looking businessman in an oriental robe . . . Bear had already gone. I knew what he'd be doing in his apartment – his 'lair'. Drinking surgical spirit and reading poetry. Probably out loud. And watching the happily babbling TV.

The vampire was there too. She was in really bad shape. She mumbled something, shaking her head and trying to reattach a hand that had been bitten off. The hand was making feeble efforts to grow back. Everything around her was spattered with blood – not hers, of course, it was the blood of her latest victim . . .

'Time to go,' I said, lifting the heavy pistol. My hand trembled treacherously.

The bullet smacked into the dead flesh, and a ragged wound appeared in the girl's side. She groaned and squeezed it shut with her one good hand. The other was dangling on a few threadlike tendons.

'Don't,' Semyon said softly. 'Don't, Anton . . .'

I continued, taking aim at her head. But at that moment a huge black shadow swooped down out of the sky, a bat grown to the size of a condor. It spread its wings, shielding the girl vampire and convulsing as it transformed.

'She's entitled to a trial!'

I couldn't fire at Kostya. I stood there, looking at the young vampire who lived in the apartment above me. The vampire's eyes were trained directly on me. How long had you been sneaking around after me, my friend and enemy? And what for – to save your fellow vampire or to prevent me from taking a step that would make me your mortal enemy?

I shrugged and stuck the pistol into my belt. You were right, Olga. All this equipment is pointless.

'She is,' the boss confirmed. 'Semyon, Tiger Cub, escort her.'

'All right,' said Tiger Cub. She gave me a glance, more of understanding than sympathy, and approached the vampires with a spring in her step.

'Even so, she's for the high jump,' Semyon whispered and followed her.

That was how they left the roof: Kostya carrying the groaning vampire, who had no idea what was going on, with Semyon and Tiger Cub silently walking behind him.

I was left alone with Egor and the boss.

'Son, you do have some powers,' the boss said gently. 'Not great ones, but then most don't even have what you have. I'd be happy for you to be my pupil . . .'

The boy was crying silently, struggling in vain to hold back the tears.

One little seventh-degree intervention, and he'd feel better. He'd understand that to fight the Dark, the Light has to use every possible weapon.

I looked up at the sombre sky and opened my mouth to catch the cold snowflakes. I wanted to freeze. To freeze solid. Not like in the Twilight. To become ice, not fog; not snow, but slush; to freeze, solidify and never melt again . . .

'Egor, come on, I'll see you home,' I offered.

'It's not far, I'll be okay . . .' the kid said.

I went on standing there for a long time, gulping down snow and wind, and I didn't see him leave. I heard the boss ask: 'Will you be able to wake your parents on your own?' but I didn't hear the answer.

'Anton, if it's any comfort to you at all, the boy's aura is the same as it was. Still undetermined.' He put his arm round my shoulders. He looked small now, pitiful, not at all like a well-groomed entrepreneur or a powerful magician. Just a sprightly old man who'd won another short battle in a war that had no end.

'Great.'

That's what I'd really like – to have no aura at all. To make my own destiny.

'Anton, you still have things to do.'

'I know, Boris Ignatievich.'

'Will you be able to explain everything to Svetlana?'

'Yes, I expect so . . . I will now.'

'I'm really sorry. But I have to use what I have . . . the people I have. You're linked with her. A standard mystical link, impossible to explain. No one can take your place.'

'I understand.'

The snow was settling on my face, thawing on my eyelashes, melting and running down my cheeks. It felt as if I'd almost managed to freeze solid, but I didn't have the right.

'Remember what I told you? Being with the Light is much tougher than being with the Dark . . .'

'I remember.'

'It will be even tougher for you, Anton. You'll fall in love with her. You'll live with her . . . for a while. Then Svetlana will move on. And you'll see her moving away from you, see her contacts extending into places far higher than you can reach. You'll suffer. But nothing can be done. You play your part at the beginning. That's the way it is with every Great Magician, with every Great Sorceress. They achieve greatness over the bodies of their friends and loved ones. There is no other way.'

'Yes, I understand . . . I understand everything . . .'

'Let's go then, Anton.'

I didn't answer.

'Shall we go?'

'Aren't we late already?'

'Not yet. The Light has paths of its own. I'll take you there by the short way, and after that, you follow your own path.'

'Then I'll just stand here for a while,' I said. I closed my eyes so that I could feel the snowflakes landing on my eyelids, so tenderly.

'If you only knew how many times I've stood like that,' said the boss. 'Just like that, looking up into the sky, asking for something . . . Maybe a blessing, maybe a curse.'

I said nothing, I already knew there wouldn't be any answer.

'Anton, I'm frozen,' said the boss. 'I feel cold. As a man. I want to drink a few glasses of vodka and settle down under a warm blanket. And lie there, waiting for you to help Svetlana . . . for Olga to deal with the vortex. And then take a holiday. Leave Ilya in charge here, since he's already been inside my skin, and head for Samarkand. Have you ever been to Samarkand?'

'No.'

'It's no great shakes, to be honest. Especially nowadays. There's not much good there, except memories . . . But they're enough for me.'

'Let's go, Boris Ignatievich.'

I wiped the snow off my face.

There was someone waiting for me.

And that's the only thing that stops us freezing solid.

Story Two

AMONG HIS
OWN KIND

PROLOGUE

His name was Maxim.

Not such a very unusual name, but not ordinary either, not a Sergei, Andrei or Dmitry. A name with a fine Russian ring to it, even if its roots did go back to the Greeks and the Varangians, maybe even the Scythians.

He was happy enough with his appearance. Not the cloying good looks of an actor from a TV serial, but not a dull, everyday face either. A handsome man, he stood out in a crowd. And he'd built his body too, but without overdoing it – no bulging veins, no obsessive daily workouts at the gym.

He was happy with his job as auditor for a major foreign firm, one that was profitable – he could afford to indulge his tastes, and he didn't need to concern himself with protection rackets.

It was all as if one day his guardian angel had simply decided: 'You shall be a bit better than the rest.' Only a bit, but still better. And that suited Maxim just fine. Why try to scramble higher up the ladder and fritter his life away on wanting a car with all the extras, an entree to the high life or an apartment with an extra room . . . what for? He enjoyed life for its own sake, not for the material things he could squeeze out of it.

Life was the exact opposite of money, which in itself meant nothing.

Of course, Maxim had never thought about this quite so clearly. One of the quirks of people who've managed to find a place in life that suits them perfectly is that they simply believe that's the way things ought to be. Everything just works out the way it ought to. And if someone feels short-changed by life, then he has only himself to blame. He must have been lazy and stupid. Or else he rated himself too highly and tried to 'get above himself'.

Maxim was fond of that phrase: 'getting above yourself'. It put everything into perspective. For instance, it explained why his intelligent and beautiful sister was throwing her life away on an alcoholic husband in Tambov. She'd gone off looking for someone with better prospects . . . and just look what she'd found. Or take his old school friend who'd been lying in a hospital ward for over a month now. He'd wanted to expand his business, and he had. He was lucky still to be alive, lucky his competitors happened to be so relatively restrained . . . the market in non-ferrous metals had been carved up a long time ago.

There was only one aspect of life in which Maxim could imagine the idea of 'getting above yourself' applying to him, and it was such a very strange and complicated aspect that he preferred not even to think about it. It was much easier not to think, simply to accept the weird thing that sometimes happened to him in spring, occasionally in the autumn and only very, very rarely at the height of summer, when the oppressive heat became totally unbearable, emptying his head of all logic and caution, including even those vague doubts about his psychological balance . . . Maxim didn't worry that he was in any way schizophrenic, though. He'd read books and consulted specialists . . . only, of course, without going into all the details.

No, he was normal enough. Obviously some things in life simply defied reason and couldn't be judged by the usual norms. The idea that he might be 'getting above himself' bothered him. But was that really what he was doing?

Maxim was sitting in his car, a neat, well-cared-for Toyota, with the engine running quietly. It wasn't the most expensive of cars and it didn't have all the fancy trimmings, but it was still way better than most on the road in Moscow. In the dim light of early morning, no one could have made out his face behind the steering wheel, even from just a few steps away. He'd spent the whole night like that, listening to the gentle purring sound of the engine, chilled through but determined not to turn the heater on. As usual at such times, he didn't feel like sleeping. Or smoking. He didn't feel like doing anything at all, it felt good just to sit there without moving, like a shadow in the car, parked at the kerb, waiting. The only thing that troubled him was that his wife would think he'd been with a lover. How could he prove to her that he didn't have a full-time lover and his strayings were no more than fleeting affairs at work and occasional professional services when he travelled on business . . . and he hadn't even paid for those with their family's money, they'd been provided by clients. He couldn't have refused, they'd have been offended. Or decided he was gay and offered him boys the next time . . .

The luminous green figures on the clock flickered and changed: five in the morning. Any moment now the road-sweepers would come creeping out to work. This was an old district, upmarket, they were very careful to keep things clean around here. It was a good thing it wasn't raining or snowing either, the lousy winter was over, dead and gone, and now spring was here, bringing with it its own problems, including the temptation to 'get above himself' . . .

One of the doors of a nearby building slammed. The girl who had come out stopped as she adjusted her handbag on her shoulder, about ten metres away from the car. They were ill-designed, the buildings round here, with no courtyards, inconvenient to work in and probably to live in as well: what was their smart reputation worth if the plumbing was dodgy and the metre-thick walls covered with mildew – and there were probably ghosts around as well . . .

Maxim smiled gently as he climbed out of his car. His body obeyed him without reluctance, his muscles hadn't cramped up during the night; if anything, they felt stronger than ever. And that was a sign.

But seriously, he wondered, do ghosts really exist?

'Galina!' he called.

The girl turned towards him. And that was another sign, otherwise she would have run; after all, who wouldn't be suspicious of a man lying in wait outside their door early in the morning . . .?

'I don't know you,' she said, in a voice that was both calm and curious.

'No,' Maxim asserted. 'But I know you.'

'Who are you?'

'A judge.'

He pronounced the word solemnly, rolling it off his tongue. A judge. Someone who has the right to pronounce judgement.

'And just who are you intending to judge?'

'You, Galina.' Maxim was focused, intent. Everything around him seemed to be turning dark, and that was a sign too.

'Oh, really?' She looked him over quickly, and Maxim caught a glint of yellow fire in her eyes. 'You think you'll be able to manage that?'

'Sure I will,' replied Maxim, flinging up his hand. The dagger was already in it – a long, narrow wooden blade that had once been pale but had darkened over the last three years, gradually stained . . .

The girl didn't make a sound as the wooden blade slid into her flesh and pierced her heart.

As always, Maxim felt a momentary panic, a brief, searing surge of horror – what if he'd made a mistake this time, after all?

He raised his left hand to touch the simple little wooden cross that he always wore hanging on his chest. And he continued to stand there, holding the wooden dagger in one hand and clutching the cross in the other, until the girl began to change . . .

It happened fast. It always happened fast: the transformation first into an animal and then back into a human. The animal, a black panther, lay there on the pavement for a few moments, its eyes staring blankly and its fangs exposed, a victim of the hunt, tricked out in matching skirt and jacket, tights and dainty shoes. Then the process was reversed, like a pendulum making another swing.

What Maxim found extraordinary was not the rapid transformation – too late for his victim, as usual – but the fact that there was now no wound on the dead girl. That brief moment of transfiguration had purged her and made her whole. There was only a slash in her blouse and her jacket.

'Glory be to Thee, O Lord,' Maxim whispered, looking down at the dead shape-shifter. 'Glory be to Thee.'

He didn't really resent his role in life.

But it was still a burden for a man who didn't like to get above himself.

CHAPTER 1

THAT WAS the morning I knew spring had really arrived.

The evening before, the sky had been different, with clouds drifting over the city, and the air had been filled with the scent of a chilly, damp wind and snow that hadn't fallen yet. I'd felt like snuggling down deep into my armchair, putting something cheerful and moronic – something American – in the VCR, taking a sip of cognac and just falling asleep.

But in the morning everything had changed.

Some cunning conjuror's hand had thrown a blue shawl over the city, running it over the streets and the squares and wiping away the final traces of winter. Even the heaps of brown snow left on the street corners and in the gutters didn't seem to have been overlooked by spring, they were an integral element of the decor. A memento.

I smiled as I walked to the metro.

Sometimes it feels really good to be human. That was the way I'd been living for a week now: when I got to work, I didn't go any higher than the second floor and all I did was fiddle about with the server, which had suddenly developed a number of bad habits, or install new office software for the women in accounts, even though none of us could understand what they needed it for. In the evening I went to the theatre, or to a soccer match, or to various small bars and restaurants. Anywhere at all, as long as it was noisy and crowded. Being human in a crowd is even more interesting than just being human.

Of course, at the Night Watch offices, an old four-storey building rented from our own subsidiary, there wasn't a normal human to be found. Even the three old cleaning women were Others. Even the loose-mouthed young security guards at the entrance, who were there to frighten off petty gangsters and sales reps, had some modest magical powers. Even the plumber, a classic Moscow alcoholic, was a magician . . . and he'd have been a really good magician too, if it weren't for his drinking.

But the first two floors of the building had to look entirely normal. The tax police were allowed in here, as well as our human business partners and the thugs who provided our 'protection' – the racket was actually directly controlled by our boss, but the small-fry didn't need to know that.

And the office conversation was entirely normal too. Politics, taxes, shopping, the weather, other people's love affairs and their own. The women gossiped about the men, and we gave as good as we got. There were office romances, plots were laid to unseat immediate superiors, the chances of bonuses were discussed.

Half an hour later I reached Sokol station and made my way up to street level. It was noisy and crowded, and the air was filled with exhaust fumes. But it was still spring.

There are plenty of districts in Moscow worse than the one where our office is situated. In fact, it's probably one of the best – that's not counting the Day Watch offices, of course. But then, the Kremlin wouldn't suit us, anyway: the traces of the past lie too heavy on Red Square and its ancient brick walls. Maybe some day they'll fall. But that would depend on certain developments, and there's no sign of them coming any time soon . . . no sign at all, unfortunately.

I walked from the metro, it wasn't far. The faces on every side looked friendly and welcoming, thawed by the spring sunshine. That's why I love the spring: it takes the edge off that feeling of weary helplessness. And there are fewer temptations . . .

One of the security guys was smoking outside the door. He gave me a friendly nod. Thorough checks weren't part of his job description. Plus there was also the fact that I was the one who decided whether or not they had internet access and new games on their duty room computer, or just the official information and personnel files.

'You're late, Anton,' he said.

I checked my watch.

'The boss wants everyone together in the conference room, they were looking for you.'

That was strange, I wasn't usually brought in on the morning briefings. Had one of my computer networks crashed? It wasn't likely, for that they'd have dragged me out of bed in the middle of the night without a second thought, and it wouldn't have been the first time either . . .

I nodded and started walking faster.

The building has a lift, but it's an antique, and I preferred to run up to the fourth floor. There was another security post – a rather more serious one – on the third-floor landing. Garik was on duty. As I approached he screwed up his eyes and peered into the Twilight, scanning my aura and the markings that Night Watch agents have on our bodies. Then he gave me a warm smile:

'Get a move on.'

The door of the conference room was half open. I glanced inside. There were about thirty people, mostly field agents and analysts. The boss was striding backwards and forwards in front of a map of Moscow and nodding his head, while his commercial deputy Vitaly Markovich − a very weak magician, but a born businessman − addressed the meeting.

'And so we have completely covered our current outgoings, and we have no need to resort to . . . er . . . any special varieties of financial activity. If the meeting approves my proposals, we can increase employees' allowances somewhat − in the first instance, naturally, for field operatives. Payments for temporary disability and pensions for the families of those killed on duty also need to be . . . er . . . somewhat increased. And we can afford to do that . . .'

It was bizarre to see magicians who could transmute lead into gold, coal into diamond and neat rectangles of paper into crisp bank notes, discussing business. But it actually made things easier, and for two reasons. Firstly, it created an occupation for those Others whose powers were too weak to provide them with a living. Secondly, it reduced the risks of unsettling the balance of power.

As I appeared, Boris Ignatievich nodded and said:

'Thank you, Vitaly. I think this is all quite clear, no complaints as far as your work is concerned. Shall we vote? Thank you. Now, while we have everyone here . . .'

The boss kept an eye on me as I tiptoed to an empty chair and sat down.

'. . . we can move on to the most important item of business.'

From his chair next to me, Semyon leaned over and whispered:

'The most important item of business is the payment of the Party dues for March . . .'

I couldn't help smiling. Sometime Boris Ignatievich really does act just like an old-time Party apparatchik. I find that less irritating than when he acts like a medieval inquisitor or a retired general, but maybe that's just me . . .

'The most important item is a protest I received from the Day Watch just two hours ago,' said the boss.

This didn't sink in straight away. The Day Watch and the Night Watch are always making problems for each other. There are protests every week: sometimes it's all settled at district office level, in others a case goes as far as the Berne tribunal.

Then I registered that any protest that required a full meeting of the Watch couldn't possibly be ordinary.

'The essential point of the protest . . .' said the boss, rubbing the bridge of his nose, '. . . the essential point of the protest is as follows . . . This morning one of the Dark Side's women was killed near Stoleshnikov Lane. There is a brief description of the incident . . .'

Two sheets of paper, still warm from the printer, landed in my lap. As they did in everyone else's. I ran my eyes over the words:

'Galina Rogova, twenty-four years old . . . initiated at the age of seven, her family are not Others . . . mentor – Anna Chernogorova, fourth-grade magician . . . At the age of seven Galina Rogova was identified as a were-panther. Average powers . . .'

I frowned as I read through the notes, although there wasn't really that much to frown at. Rogova had been a Dark One, but she hadn't worked for the Day Watch. She hadn't ever hunted humans, not even once. Even the two licences she'd had, when she came of age and after her wedding, had never been used. By use of magic she'd reached a senior position in the Warm Home construction company and married the vice-president. One child – a boy, no Other powers detected. She'd used her powers for self-protection a few times, and on one occasion killed her attacker. But even then she hadn't stooped to cannibalism . . .

'We could do with more shape-shifters like that, right?' asked Semyon. He turned the page and gave a little snort of surprise. Intrigued, I turned to the second page.

The report of the post-mortem examination. A cut in the blouse and the jacket . . . probably a blow with a thin-bladed dagger.

Enchanted, of course, a shape-shifter couldn't be killed with plain ordinary steel. But what was it that had surprised Semyon?

No visible wounds had been discovered on the body. Not even a scratch. The cause of death was a total drain of vital energy.

'Very neat,' said Semyon. 'I remember during the Civil War I was sent to capture a were-tiger. The bastard worked in the Cheka, and pretty high up too . . .'

'Have you familiarised yourselves with the data?' the boss asked.

'May I ask a question?' A slim arm shot into the air on the far side of the room.

'By all means, Yulia,' said the boss with a nod.

The Night Watch's youngest member stood up, adjusting her hair nervously. A pretty young girl, maybe a little childish. But assigning her to the analytical department had been a good move.

'Boris Ignatievich, the way I see it, the magical intervention here is second degree. Or even first?'

'It could be second degree,' the boss confirmed.

'That means it could have been you . . .' Yulia paused for a moment, embarrassed. 'Or perhaps Semyon . . . Ilya . . . or Garik. Right?'

'Garik couldn't have done it,' said the boss. 'But Ilya or Semyon could have.'

Semyon mumbled something, as if he'd rather have been spared the compliment.

'It's also just possible that the killer was one of the Light Ones who was just passing through Moscow,' Yulia mused out loud. 'But a magician that powerful can't arrive in town without being noticed, they're all monitored by the Day Watch. That means there are three people we need to investigate. And if they all have alibis, there are no charges to answer, right?'

'Yulia,' the boss said, shaking his head. 'No one's bringing any charges against us. What we have here is the work of a Light

Magician who is not registered in Moscow and is unaware of the Treaty.'

Now that was serious . . .

'Then . . . oh!' said Yulia. 'I'm sorry, Boris Ignatievich.'

'That's okay,' the boss said, nodding again. 'It's taken us right to the heart of the matter. There's someone we've managed to miss, everyone. We've let him slip through our fingers. We have a Light One of great power wandering loose in Moscow. He doesn't know the situation here – and he's killing Dark Ones.'

'More than one?' a voice asked.

'Yes. I checked the archives. There were similar incidents three years ago, in the spring and autumn, and two years ago, in the autumn again. On each occasion there was no physical trauma, but the victims' clothes were slashed. The Day Watch investigated, but came up with nothing. Apparently they put the deaths down to some random accident . . . so now one of the Dark Ones will be punished for it.'

'And one of the Light Ones too?'

'One of us too.'

Semyon cleared his throat and said softly:

'The gaps between the incidents are strange, Boris . . .'

'I don't think we know about all of them. Whoever this magician is, he has always killed Others with low-level powers, obviously there must have been some kind of weakness in their protection. It's very likely that a number of his victims were uninitiated or unknown Dark Others. Here's what I propose . . .'

The boss paused and glanced round the room before continuing:

'Analytical section – collate all available information from criminal records and try to identify similar incidents. Bear in mind that they may not have been classified as murder, more likely as deaths from unknown causes. Look into the results of autopsies, question the morgue staff . . . think for yourselves where you can get relevant information. Research group – send two or three agents to the Day Watch and request an examination of the body. Operations group – intensive street patrols. Try to find him, OK?'

'We're always on the lookout for someone,' Igor muttered. 'Boris Ignatievich, there's no way we could have overlooked a powerful magician. We just couldn't have!'

'He may not be initiated,' the boss snapped back. 'His powers manifest themselves sporadically . . .'

'In the spring and the autumn, just like any ordinary psycho . . .'

'Yes, Igor, that's exactly it. In the spring and in the autumn. And now, right after this latest killing, he must still be showing some trace of magic. That gives us a chance, if only a small one. Get on to it.'

'Boris, what exactly is our goal?' Semyon asked curiously.

Some of the agents had already started getting to their feet, but now they paused.

'Our goal is to find this Maverick before the Dark Ones do. To protect him, educate him and bring him over to our side. As usual.'

'Clear enough,' said Semyon and stood up.

'Anton and Olga, would you please remain?' the boss said brusquely and walked over to the window.

On their way out, agents glanced at us curiously, even enviously. A special assignment is always intriguing. I looked across the room, caught Olga's eye and smiled with just my mouth. She smiled back.

She looked nothing like the dirty-faced, barefoot young woman who'd drunk cognac with me in my kitchen in the middle of the winter. Now her hair was expensively cut, her complexion healthy and her eyes full of . . . no, the confidence had been there all the time, but now there was a certain flirtatious pride too.

Her sentence had been repealed. In part, at least.

'Anton, I don't like what's going on here,' the boss said without turning round.

Olga shrugged her shoulders and nodded for me to reply.

'I beg your pardon, Boris Ignatievich?'

'I don't like this protest lodged by the Day Watch.'

'Neither do I.'

'You don't understand, and I'm afraid none of the others do either . . . Olga, have you at least some inkling of what's going on?'

'It's very strange the Day Watch haven't been able to find the killer after all this time.'

'Yes. Do you remember Krakow?'

'I do, unfortunately. You think we're being set up?'

'It's possible . . .' The boss moved away from the window. 'Anton, do you think that could be it?'

'I don't entirely understand,' I mumbled.

'Anton, let's assume that we really do have a Maverick wandering round the city, a solitary killer. He's uninitiated. From time to time his powers suddenly surface . . . he locates one of the Dark Ones and eliminates them. Wouldn't the Day Watch be able to find him? Unfortunately, believe me, they would. So the question is: why haven't they caught him and exposed him, when Dark Ones are dying?'

'Only insignificant ones?' I suggested.

'True. Sacrificing pawns is in the tradition . . .' the boss caught my eye and paused, '. . . in the tradition of the Watch.'

'The Watches,' I said sharply.

'The Watches,' the boss echoed wearily. 'You haven't forgotten . . . Let's think where a manoeuvre like this could be leading. An accusation of incompetence against the whole of the Night Watch? No. We're supposed to keep tabs on the activities of the Dark Ones and the observance of the Treaty by known Light Ones, not go hunting for mysterious psychos. In this case it's the Day Watch who is in the wrong.'

'Which means it must be a provocation aimed at someone in particular?'

'Exactly, Anton. Remember what Yulia said? There's only a small handful of us who could have done this. That can be proved conclusively. Let's suppose the Day Watch has decided to accuse someone of violating the Treaty. To claim that one of us – someone who knows the terms of the Treaty – is meting out summary justice on his own account.'

'But that's easy to disprove. Just find the Maverick . . .'

'And if the Dark Ones find him first, but don't bother to announce the fact?'

'What about alibis?'

'And what if the killings took place at times when someone has no alibi?'

'A tribunal, with a full-scale interrogation,' I said sombrely – having your mind turned inside out isn't a pleasant experience . . .

'A powerful magician – and these killings were committed by a powerful magician – can close off his mind even against a tribunal. Not deceive the tribunal, just close himself off from it. In any case, Anton, with a tribunal that included Dark Ones, he would have to. Otherwise our enemies would learn far too much about us. And if a magician conceals himself against investigation, it's automatically regarded as a confession of guilt. With all the consequences that would follow from such a confession – both for him and for the Watch.'

'You paint a dark picture, Boris Ignatievich,' I said. 'Very dark. Almost as dark as the one you painted for me last winter, when you briefed me in my sleep. A young boy with extraordinary Other powers, an Inferno eruption that would flatten the whole of Moscow . . .'

'I understand. But I'm not lying to you, Anton.'

'What do you expect from me?' I asked bluntly. 'This isn't really my field. Am I going to give the analysts a hand? We'll be handling everything they bring in anyway.'

'Anton, I want you to work out which one of us is under threat. Who has an alibi for all the known incidents and who doesn't.'

The boss slipped his hand into his jacket pocket and took out a disk.

'Take this . . . it's a complete record for the entire three-year period. For four of us, including me.'

I swallowed hard as I took it.

'The security codes have been removed. But you understand that no one else must see this. You have no right to copy the information. Encrypt all your calculations and procedures . . . and make the key as complex as you can.'

'I could really do with some help,' I suggested hesitantly, with a glance at Olga. But then, what kind of help could she give me? Everything she knew about computers, she'd learned from playing games like Heretic and Hexen.

'You can check my database yourself,' the boss said, after a pause. 'Use Tolik for the others. All right?'

'Then what's my assignment?' asked Olga.

'You'll cover the same ground, only by asking direct questions. Interrogating people, not to put too fine a point on it. And you'll start with me. Then the other three.'

'All right, Boris.'

'Get on to it, Anton,' the boss said with a nod. 'Start immediately. You can pass everything else on to your staff, they'll cope.'

'Maybe I could fiddle about a bit with the data?' I asked. 'If someone doesn't happen to have an alibi, I could arrange one.'

The boss shook his head.

'No. You don't understand. I don't want to set up any false alibis. I want to be absolutely sure that none of us is involved in these killings.'

'Are you serious?'

'Yes. Because nothing's impossible in this world. Anton, the good thing about our work is that I can give you an assignment like this. And you'll carry it out. Regardless of who's involved.'

There was still something bothering me, but I nodded and walked towards the door, clutching the disk. My question only took shape as I was leaving. I turned back and asked:

'Boris Ignatievich . . .'

The boss and Olga instantly moved apart.

'Boris Ignatievich, you say there are four sets of data here?'

'Yes.'

'For you, Ilya, Semyon . . .'

'And you, Anton.'

'Why?' I asked dumbly.

'During that stand-off on the roof you stayed down in the second level of the Twilight for three minutes, Anton . . . that's a third-grade power.'

'Impossible,' I said.

'It happened.'

'Boris Ignatievich, you always told me I was just an average magician!'

'Well, let's just say I need an excellent programmer more than one more field operative.'

At any other moment I would have felt proud. Offended at the same time, of course, but still proud. I'd always thought that fourth-grade magic was my ceiling, and it would be a long time before I reached it. But just at that moment everything was clouded by a clammy, repellent feeling – fear. Even though in five years of working in a quiet staff position in the Watch I'd learned not to be afraid of anything: the authorities, thugs, diseases . . .

'This was a second-degree intervention . . .'

'The boundary here's very subtle, Anton. You might be capable of more.'

'But we have more than ten third-grade magicians. Why am I a suspect?'

'Because you offended Zabulon personally. And he's quite capable of setting a trap just for Anton Gorodetsky. Or rather, adapting an old trap that was being kept in reserve.'

I left without asking any more questions.

Our lab's on the fourth floor too, but in the other wing of the building. I set off hurriedly along the corridor, nodding to people I met, but remained focused, clutching that disk tighter than a romantic young man clutches the hand of the girl he loves.

Was the boss telling the truth?

Could this really be aimed at me?

Probably he was. I'd asked a straight question and been given a straight answer. Of course, as the years go by, even the most Light of magicians acquire a certain degree of cynicism and learn to play tricks with words. But the consequences of a direct lie would be too serious even for Boris Ignatievich.

I reached the entry lobby and its electronic security systems. Magicians tend to regard technology with disdain, and Semyon had once shown me how easy it was to fool the voice analyser and the iris scanner. But I'd gone ahead and bought these expensive toys anyway. Maybe they were no protection against an Other, but it seemed entirely possible that one day the guys from the Federal Security Service or the mafia would decide to check us out.

'One, two, three, four, five . . .' I muttered into the microphone, gazing into the camera lens at the same time. The electronic circuits pondered for a few seconds, then a green light came on above the door.

There was no one in the first room, where the server's cooling fans were humming gently. The air conditioners built into the wall were huffing and puffing, but it was still hot in there. And spring had only just begun . . .

I didn't go into the system analysts' lab, just walked straight through into my own office. It wasn't all mine. Tolik, my deputy, worked here too. Sometimes he lived here, spending the nights on an old leather sofa.

He was sitting at his desk, thoughtfully inspecting an old motherboard.

'Hi,' I said, sitting down on the sofa. The disk was burning my hands.

'It's a goner,' Tolik said gloomily.

'Bin it then.'

'Let me just take its brain out first.' Tolik was thrifty, a habit acquired from years of working in state-financed institutions. We had no financial problems, but he carefully stockpiled all the old hardware anyway, even if it was of no use to anyone. 'Would you believe it, I've been fiddling around with this for half an hour, and it's still dead.'

'It's a prehistoric antique, why waste time fiddling around with it? Even the technology in accounts is more up to date.'

'I could give it to someone . . . Maybe I should take the cache out too . . .'

'Tolik, we've got an urgent job to do,' I said.

'Uh?'

'Look . . .' I held up the disk. 'This is a dossier . . . a complete dossier on four members of the Watch. Including the boss.'

Tolik opened the drawer of his desk, put the motherboard in it and stared at the disk.

'Exactly. I'm going to go through three of them. And you're going to go through the fourth . . . mine.'

'So what are we looking for?'

'This,' I said, holding up the briefing notes. 'It's possible that one of the suspects may be carrying out sporadic killings of Dark Ones. Unauthorised killings. All the known incidents are listed here. We have to either eliminate this possibility, or . . .'

'Ah, so it really is you who's killing them, then?' Tolik asked.
'Pardon my irony.'

'No. But don't take my word for it. Let's get on with it.'

I didn't even look at the information about me, just downloaded
all eight hundred megabytes on to Tolik's computer and took out
the disk.

'Shall I tell you if I come across anything really interesting?'
Tolik asked. I glanced across at him as he started looking through
the text files, tugging on his left ear and clicking regularly with his
mouse.

'That's up to you.'

'Okay.'

I started with the materials on the boss. First there was an
introductory section – background information. Every line I read
brought me out in a sweat.

Of course, even this dossier didn't give the boss's real name and
origins. Facts like that weren't kept on file anywhere for Others of
his rank. But even so there was so much that I didn't know. Starting
with the fact that the boss was older than I'd thought. At least a
hundred and fifty years older. And that meant he'd been personally
involved in drawing up the Treaty between Light and Dark. I was
intrigued by the thought that all the other magicians still surviving
from that time held positions in the central office and weren't stuck
in the exhausting and tedious post of regional director.

Apart from that, I recognised a few of the names under which the
boss had figured in the history of the Watch, and learnt where he
was born. We'd wondered about that sometimes, and even placed
bets on it, always pointing to 'indisputable' proof. But somehow no
one had ever suspected that Boris Ignatievich was born in Tibet.

And even in my wildest dreams, I could never have imagined
whose mentor he had been.

The boss had been working in Europe since the fifteenth

century. From indirect references, I inferred that the reason for this move was a woman. I could even guess who it was.

I closed the introductory window and looked over at Tolik. He was watching some video footage. Of course, my biographical details were less fascinating than the boss's. I glanced at the small moving picture and blushed.

'For the first incident you have a solid alibi,' Tolik said without turning round.

'Listen . . .' I was lost for words.

'Okay, okay. I'll fast-forward it, to check the entire night . . .'

I imagined what the recording would look like at high speed and turned away. I'd always suspected the boss kept tabs on his colleagues, especially the young ones. But not that cynically!

'The alibi won't be that solid,' I said. 'I'll get dressed and go out any moment now.'

'I can see that,' Tolik confirmed.

'And I'll be gone for almost an hour and a half. I was looking for champagne . . . and while I was looking, I sobered up a bit in the fresh air. Started wondering if it was worth going back.'

'Don't worry about it,' said Tolik. 'You watch the boss's private life.'

Half an hour later, I realised Tolik was right. Maybe I had good reason to feel offended by the observers' invasion of my privacy. But Boris Ignatievich had as much reason as I did.

'The boss has an alibi,' I said. 'Indisputable. For two incidents he has four witnesses. And for one – almost the entire Watch.'

'Was that the hunt for that Dark One who went crazy?'

'Yes.'

'Well, in theory, you could have killed the Dark Ones. Quite easily. And I'm sorry, Anton, but every one of the killings happens when you're in an excited state. As if you weren't completely in control of yourself.'

'I didn't do it.'

'I believe you. What shall I do with the file?'

'Delete it.'

Tolik thought for a moment.

'I don't have anything valuable on here. I think I'll run a low-level format. The disk's long overdue for a clean-out.'

'Thanks.' I closed the dossier on the boss. 'That's it, I'll deal with the others myself.'

'Sure,' said Tolik as he overcame the computer's righteous indignation and it began digesting itself.

'Go check on the girls,' I suggested. 'And look disapproving for a change. I'm sure they're playing cards in there.'

'All in a day's work, I suppose,' Tolik agreed. 'When will you be through here?'

'In a couple of hours.'

'I'll call in.'

He went off to our 'girls', two young programmers who dealt with the Watch's official activity. I carried on working. Semyon was next.

Two and a half hours later I tore my eyes away from the computer, massaged the back of my neck with my palms – it always cramps up when I sit there hunched over the terminal like that – and turned on the coffee machine.

Neither the boss, nor Ilya, nor Semyon could be the unhinged killer of Dark Ones. They all had alibis – and some of them were absolutely watertight. For instance, Semyon had managed to spend the entire night of one of the murders negotiating with the senior management of the Day Watch. Ilya had been on secondment in Sakhalin – they'd screwed things up so badly over there that they'd needed back-up from Moscow . . .

I was the only one left under suspicion.

It wasn't that I didn't trust Tolik, but I went through the data again anyway. It was all very clear. Not a single alibi.

The coffee was disgusting, sour, the filter couldn't have been changed for ages. I gulped down the hot swill, staring at the screen, then took out my mobile and dialled the boss's number.

'Yes, Anton.'

He always knew who was calling him.

'Boris Ignatievich, only one of the four can be suspected.'

'Which one?'

The boss's voice was dry and official. But somehow I suddenly got this picture of him sitting half-naked on a leather sofa, with a glass of champagne in one hand and Olga's hand in the other, holding the phone in place with his shoulder, or levitating it beside his ear . . .

'Tut-tut,' the boss rebuked me. 'You lousy clairvoyant. So who's under suspicion?'

'I am.'

'I see.'

'You knew it,' I said.

'Why do you say that?'

'There was no need to get me to process that dossier. You could have done it yourself. That means you wanted me to be convinced of the danger.'

'That could be,' the boss said with a sigh. 'What are you going to do, Anton?'

'Start packing my bag for jail.'

'Come round to my office. In . . . er . . . in ten minutes.'

'Okay.' I switched off my phone.

First I went to see how the programmers were doing. Tolik was still there with them, and they were hard at work.

The Watch didn't really have any need for these two worthless workers. Their security clearance was low, so we still had to do almost everything ourselves. But where else could we find work for two sorceresses as low-level as these two? If only they'd have agreed to live ordinary lives . . . but no, they wanted the 'romance' of working for the Watch . . . So we'd invented jobs for them.

They mostly just whiled away the time, surfing the net and playing games, their favourites being various kinds of patience.

Tolik was at one of the spare PCs – we had plenty of hardware around the place. Yulia was sitting very close to him, twitching her mouse around on its mat.

'Is that what you call computer skills training?' I asked, gazing at the monsters hurtling round the screen.

'There's nothing better than computer games for improving skill with the mouse,' Tolik replied innocently.

'Well . . .' I couldn't think of any response.

It was a long time since I'd played video games. The same went for most other members of the Watch. Killing evil vermin in a cartoon became less interesting once you'd met it face to face. Unless, that is, you'd already lived a couple of hundred years and built up reserves of cynicism, like Olga . . .

'Tolik, I probably won't be back in today,' I said.

'Uhuh.' He nodded, without any sign of surprise. None of us has really strong powers of prevision, but we sense little things like that immediately.

'Galya, Lena, see you later,' I said to the girls. Galya twittered something polite, trying to look entirely absorbed in her work. Lena asked:

'Can I leave early today?'

'Of course.'

We don't lie to each other. If Lena asks, it means she really needs to leave early. We don't lie. But sometimes we might just leave something unsaid . . .

★   ★   ★

The boss's desk was in a state of total confusion. Pens, pencils, sheets of paper, printouts of reports, dull, exhausted magic crystals.

But the crowning glory of this mess was a lit spirit lamp, with some white powder roasting over it in a crucible. The boss was stirring it thoughtfully with the tip of his expensive ink pen, obviously expecting this to produce some kind of effect. But the powder seemed to be doggedly ignoring both the heat and his stirring.

'Here.' I put the disk down in front of the boss.

'What are we going to do?' Boris Ignatievich asked without even looking up. He wasn't wearing a jacket, his shirt was crumpled and his tie had slid to one side.

I stole a glance at the sofa. Olga wasn't in the office, but there was an empty champagne bottle standing on the floor, with two glasses.

'I don't know. I haven't killed any Dark Ones . . . not these Dark Ones. You know that.'

'Sure, I know.'

'But I can't prove it.'

'By my reckoning we've got two or three days,' said the boss. 'Then the Day Watch will bring a formal charge against you.'

'It wouldn't take much to arrange a false alibi.'

'And would you agree to that?' Boris Ignatievich enquired.

'Of course not. Can I ask one question?'

'Yes.'

'Where does this information come from? The photos and videos?'

The boss paused for a moment.

'I thought that would be it. You've seen my dossier, Anton. Was it any less intrusive?'

'No, I suppose not. That's why I'm asking. Why do you allow information like that to be gathered?'

'I can't forbid it. Monitoring is carried out by the Inquisition.'

I just managed to bite back the stupid question: 'But does it really exist?' My face probably said it for me anyway.

The boss carried on looking at me for a moment or two as if he was expecting further questions and then went on:

'Let's get to the point, Anton. From this moment on you must never be left alone. Maybe you can go to the lavatory on your own, but at all other times you must have two or three witnesses with you. If we're lucky, there could be another killing.'

'If I'm really being set up, the killing won't happen until I'm left without an alibi.'

'And we'll make sure you are left without one,' the boss said, laughing. 'What kind of old fool do you take me for?'

I nodded, still not sure, still not fully understanding.

'Olga . . .'

The door in the wall – the one I'd always assumed led into a closet – opened and Olga came in, smiling as she straightened her hair. Her jeans and blouse sat tight on her body, the way they only do after a hot shower. Behind her I caught a glimpse of an immense bathroom with a jacuzzi and a panoramic window right across one wall – it must have been one-way glass.

'Olya, can you handle this?' the boss asked, obviously referring to something they'd already talked about.

'On my own? No.'

'I didn't mean that.'

'Oh sure, of course I can.'

'Stand back to back,' the boss ordered.

I didn't feel like arguing, but I had a sick feeling in the pit of my stomach. I knew something really serious was about to happen.

'And both of you open yourselves to me,' Boris Ignatievich demanded.

I closed my eyes and relaxed. Olga's back was hot and damp,

even through her blouse. A strange sensation, standing there touching a woman who's just been making love . . . but not with you.

No, I wasn't the slightest bit in love with her. Maybe because I remembered her in her non-human form, maybe because we'd become friends and partners so quickly. Maybe because of the centuries that separated her birth from mine: what did a young body mean, when you could see the dust of the centuries in the other person's eyes? We'd become friends, and nothing more.

But standing next to a woman whose body still remembers someone else's touch, pressing yourself against her – that's a strange feeling . . .

'Right, let's begin . . .' said the boss, perhaps a bit sharply. And then he uttered some words I didn't understand, in some ancient language that hadn't been used for thousands of years.

Flying.

It really was like flying. As if the ground had slipped away from under my feet and I'd become weightless. An orgasm in free fall, LSD mainlined into the bloodstream, electrodes in the subcortical pleasure centres . . .

I was swept away by a wild, unadulterated joy that came out of nowhere, and the world dimmed and blurred. I would have fallen, but the power from the boss's raised hands held Olga and me up on invisible strings, making us arch over and press ourselves against each other.

And then the strings got tangled.

'I'm sorry, Anton,' said Boris Ignatievich, 'but we didn't have any time for hesitation or explanations.'

I didn't answer. I was dumbfounded, sitting there on the floor and staring at my hands, at those slim fingers with the two silver rings, at my legs – those long, shapely legs still damp after my shower, in jeans that were clinging too tight, at the blue and white trainers on my small feet.

'It's not for long,' the boss said.

'What the—' I almost swore, jerking forward and trying to get to my feet, but the sound of my voice made me cut it short. A low, vibrant, soft woman's voice.

'Calm down, Anton.' The young man standing beside me reached out his hand and helped me up.

If not for that, I'd probably have fallen over. My centre of balance had completely changed. I was shorter, and the world looked quite different.

'Olga?' I asked, looking at what used to be my face. My partner, now the inhabitant of my body, nodded. Totally confused, I gazed into her . . . into my face and saw I hadn't shaved properly that morning. And there was a little, angry red pimple on my forehead that would have done credit to any teenage slob going through puberty.

'Calm down, Anton. It's the first time I've ever changed sex too.'

Somehow I believed her. Despite her great age, Olga might never have found herself in this particular ticklish situation before.

'Have you got your bearings now?' the boss asked.

I looked myself over again, first raising my hands to my face and then looking at my reflection in the glass doors of the shelves.

'Let's go,' said Olga, tugging at my arm. 'Just one moment, Boris . . .' Her movements were as uncertain as mine. Perhaps she was even less steady. 'Light and Dark, how do you men walk?' she suddenly exclaimed.

It was then that the irony of the situation struck me and I started laughing. They'd hidden me, the target of the Dark Side's plot, in a woman's body. In the body of the boss's lover, who was as old as St Basil's Cathedral!

Olga pushed me into the bathroom – I couldn't help feeling quite pleased I was so strong – and bent me down over the jacuzzi. Then she squirted a jet of cold water straight in my face from the showerhead she'd left lying ready on the soft-pink ceramic surface.

I snorted and twisted free of her grip, suppressing the urge to smack her – or was it me, really? – across the face. The motor reflexes of this other body seemed to be waking up.

'I'm not hysterical,' I said. 'It really is funny.'

'Are you sure?' Olga screwed up her eyes, looking hard at me. Was that really my expression when I was trying to look benevolent and doubtful at the same time?

'Absolutely.'

'Then take a look at yourself.'

I went across to the mirror, which was on the same massive scale as everything else in this secret bathroom, and looked at myself.

It was weird. As I looked at my new shape, I began to feel entirely calm. The shock would probably have been worse if I'd been in another man's body. But this was okay, it just felt like the beginning of a fancy-dress party.

'Are you influencing me at all?' I asked. 'You or the boss?'

'No.'

'I must have pretty strong nerves then.'

'You've smudged your lipstick,' Olga commented. She laughed. 'Do you know how to put lipstick on?'

'Are you crazy? Of course not.'

'I'll teach you. It's not that hard.'

CHAPTER 2

AFTER I LEFT the office I hesitated for a moment, fighting the temptation to go back in.

I could reject the boss's plan at any moment. I only had to go back in and say a few words, and Olga and I would be returned to our own bodies. But in half an hour of conversation I'd learnt enough for me to accept that this was the only way to handle this provocation by the Dark Ones.

After all, it doesn't really make much sense to refuse life-saving treatment because the injections hurt.

I had the keys to Olga's apartment in her handbag, together with money and her credit card in a little wallet, make-up, a handkerchief, a box of Tic-Tacs, a comb, a layer of various small items scattered on the bottom, a mirror, a tiny mobile phone . . .

But the empty pockets of the jeans made me feel like I must have lost something. I rummaged in them for a second or two, trying to find at least a forgotten coin, but was soon convinced that Olga carried everything in her bag, the way most women do.

You might have thought I'd just lost things that were rather more important than the contents of my pockets. But it was a detail that irritated me, so I transferred a few banknotes from the handbag to my pocket and that made me feel a bit more confident.

It was a shame Olga didn't carry a walkman, though.

'Hi,' said Garik, coming towards me. 'Is the boss free?'

'He's . . . he's with Anton . . .' I replied.

'What's happened, Olya?' Garik asked, looking at me closely. I don't know what it was he'd sensed: a different intonation, hesitant movement, a changed aura. But if a field operative that neither Olga nor I had ever spent much time with could sense the difference, I wasn't doing too well.

And then Garik gave me a timid, uncertain smile. That was entirely unexpected: I'd never noticed Garik trying to flirt with the Watch's female employees. He even has trouble getting to know normal women, he's so unlucky in love.

'Nothing. We had a bit of an argument.' I turned away without saying goodbye and walked to the staircase.

That was my cover story for the Night Watch – in the highly unlikely event that we had one of the other side's agents among us. As far as I know, that's something that's only happened once or twice in the entire history of the Watch, but you can never tell . . . Might as well let everyone think Boris Ignatievich had fallen out with his old girlfriend.

There was a plausible reason, a good one. A hundred years of imprisonment in his office, without any chance to assume human form, partial rehabilitation, but with the loss of most of her magical powers. That was more than enough reason to take offence . . . And at least the story relieved me of the need to play the part of the boss's girlfriend, which would have been going just too far.

I walked down to the third floor, thinking things through as I went. I had to admit that Olga had made things as easy for me as she could. She'd put on jeans today, instead of her usual matching skirt and jacket or dress, and trainers instead of high heels. Even the light perfume she'd used wasn't overpowering.

I knew what I was supposed to do now, I knew how I was supposed to behave. But even so, it was still hard. Hard to turn into the modest, quiet side corridor instead of going toward the door.

And into the past.

They say hospitals have their own unforgettable smell. And of course they do. It would be strange if the mixture of bleach and pain, sterilising unit and wounds, standard-issue sheets and tasteless food didn't have some kind of smell.

But where do schools and colleges get their smell from?

Not all subjects are taught on the Watch's own premises. Some are easier to teach in the morgue, at night – we have our contacts there. Some are taught out in the field, some abroad. During my training, I spent time in Haiti, Angola, the USA and Spain.

But there are still some lectures that can only be given in the Watch's own building, securely sealed off from its foundations to its roof by magic and protective spells. Thirty years ago, when the Watch first moved into this building, they set up three small rooms, each for fifteen trainees. I still don't know what most influenced that decision – the optimism of my colleagues or the fact that the space was available. Even when I was in training – and that was a very good year – one room was enough for all of us, and even then it was always half-empty.

Right now the Watch was training four Others. And Svetlana was the only one we could be certain would join us and not prefer an ordinary human life.

It was deserted here, deserted and quiet. I walked slowly along the corridor, glancing into the empty teaching rooms, which would have been the envy of even the best-equipped and most prosperous university. A laptop on every desk, a huge TV projector in each room, shelves of books . . . If only a historian could have seen those books.

But historians never would see them.

Some of the books contained too much truth. Others contained too many lies. Humans couldn't be allowed to read them, for the sake of their peace of mind. Let them carry on living with the history they were used to.

The corridor terminated in a huge mirror that covered the entire end wall. When I casually glanced into it I saw a beautiful young woman swaying her hips as she strode along the corridor.

I staggered and almost fell: Olga had done everything possible to make things easy for me, but even she couldn't change her own centre of gravity. As long as I forgot the way I looked, everything was more or less normal, the motor reflexes took over. But the moment I saw myself from the outside, things slipped out of sync. Even my breathing changed, and the air felt different as it entered my lungs.

I walked up to the last door, a glass one, and peered through it cautiously.

The class was just finishing.

Today they'd been studying everyday magic, I knew that the moment I saw Polina Vasilievna standing by the demonstration stand. She's one of the oldest members of the Watch – to look at, that is, not by her actual age. She'd been discovered and initiated when she was already sixty-three. Who could have guessed that an old woman who earned her living by telling fortunes with cards during those wild years after the war actually possessed genuine powers? Quite considerable powers too, although only in a narrow field.

'And now, if you need to smarten up your clothes in a hurry, you can do it in a moment. Only don't forget to check first how much strength you have. Otherwise the result might be embarrassing.'

'And when the clock strikes twelve, your carriage will turn into a pumpkin,' the young guy sitting beside Svetlana said loudly. I didn't know him, this was only his second or third day of training, but already I didn't like him.

'Precisely,' Polina exclaimed delightedly, even though she heard the same witticism from every group of trainees. 'Fairy tales lie just as much as statistics do, but sometimes you can find truth in them.'

She took a neatly ironed tuxedo off the desk. It was dapper and elegant, a little old-fashioned. James Bond must have worn one like it.

'When will it turn back to rags again?' Svetlana asked in a practical tone.

'In two hours,' Polina told her briskly. She put the jacket on a hanger and hung it on the stand. 'I didn't put much into it.'

'And what's the longest you can keep it looking good?'

'About twenty-four hours.'

Svetlana nodded and suddenly looked in my direction – she'd sensed my presence. She smiled and waved. Now everyone had noticed me.

'Please come in,' said Polina, bowing her head. 'This is a great honour for us.'

Yes, she knew something about Olga that I didn't. All of us knew no more than one part of the truth about her; probably only the boss knew everything.

I went in, trying desperately to make my walk a little less provocative. It did no good. The young guy sitting next to Svetlana, and the fifteen-year-old youth who'd been stuck in the preliminary class for six months, and the tall, skinny Korean, who could have been thirty or forty – they all watched me.

With very definite interest. The atmosphere of mystery that surrounded Olga, all the rumours, and above all the fact that she was the boss's lover from way back – all provoked a distinctly noticeable response from the male section of the Watch.

'Hello,' I said. 'I hope I'm not interrupting?'

I was trying so hard to get my phrasing right, I forgot to control my tone, and my banal question came out sounding languidly mysterious, addressed to every single person there. The spotty-faced kid couldn't take his eyes off me, the young guy swallowed, and only the Korean maintained some semblance of composure.

'Olga, did you have an announcement for the students?' Polina asked.

'I need to have a word with Sveta.'

'Then class dismissed,' she declared. 'Olga, please do call in some time during class. My lectures are no substitute for your experience.'

'Certainly,' I promised generously. 'In three or four days.'

Olga could make good on my promises. I had to take the hits for her carefully cultivated sex appeal.

Svetlana and I walked towards the door. I could feel three pairs of greedy eyes drilling into my back – well, not exactly my back.

I knew that Olga and Svetlana had become close. I'd known since that night when Olga and I had explained to her the truth about the world and the Others, the Light Ones and the Dark Ones, about the Watches and the Twilight, since that dawn when she had held our hands and walked through the closed door into the field headquarters of the Night Watch. Sure, Svetlana and I were closely linked. Destiny held us together in its firm grip, but only for the time being. Svetlana and Olga were just friends – it wasn't destiny that had brought them together. They were free.

'Olya, I have to wait for Anton,' said Svetlana, taking hold of my hand. It wasn't the gesture of a younger sister clutching her elder sister's hand, looking for support and reassurance. It was the gesture of an equal. And if Olga allowed Svetlana to behave as her equal, then she really did have a great future ahead of her.

'Don't bother, Sveta,' I said.

Again there was something not quite right in the phrase or the tone. Svetlana gave me a puzzled look, and it was exactly like Garik's.

'I'll explain everything,' I said. 'But not right here. At your place.'

The new defences at her apartment were the best there were – the Watch had invested too much energy in its new member to lose her now. The boss hadn't even argued about whether I could confide in Svetlana, he'd only insisted on one thing – it had to happen at her place.

'All right.' The surprise was still there in Svetlana's eyes, but she nodded in agreement. 'Are you sure it's not worth waiting for Anton?'

'Absolutely,' I said, quite sincerely. 'Shall we take a car?'

'Aren't you driving today?'

Idiot!

I'd forgotten that Olga's favourite mode of transport was the sports car the boss had given her as a present.

'That's what I meant – shall we drive?' I asked, realising I must seem rather foolish.

Svetlana nodded. That puzzled look in her eyes was getting stronger.

At least I knew how to drive. I'd never been tempted by the dubious pleasure of owning a car in a megalopolis with lousy roads, but our training had included all sorts of things. Some things had been taught the ordinary way, some had been beaten into our heads by magic. I'd been taught how to drive like an ordinary human, but if I suddenly happened to find myself in the cabin of a helicopter or a plane, then reflex responses I couldn't even remember in an ordinary state would kick in. At least, in theory they ought to kick in.

I found the car keys in the handbag. The orange sports car, with its top down, was standing in the parking lot in front of the building, under the watchful eye of the security guards.

'Will you drive?' asked Svetlana.

I nodded without saying anything, then got into the driving seat and started the engine. I remembered that Olga always took off like a bullet, but I didn't know how to do that.

'Olga, there's something wrong with you,' said Svetlana, finally deciding to say what was on her mind. I nodded as I drove out on to Leningrad Prospect.

'Sveta, we'll talk when we get to your place.'

I'm no racing driver. We were driving for a long time, a lot longer than we ought to have been. But Svetlana didn't ask any more questions, she just sat there, leaning back in her seat and looking straight ahead. Maybe she was meditating, or maybe she was trying to look through the Twilight. Several times in the traffic jams, men tried to flirt with us from their cars – always the most expensive ones. At first I just found it annoying. Then it started to seem funny. By the end I wasn't reacting to it any longer, just like Svetlana.

'Olya, why did you make me come away? Why didn't you want me to wait for Anton?' Svetlana suddenly asked.

I shrugged. I was sorely tempted to answer: 'Because he's sitting right here beside you.' The chances were pretty small that we were being observed. The car was protected by spells too, I could sense some of them, and some of them went beyond the level of my powers.

But I restrained myself.

Svetlana hadn't done the course on information security yet, it comes three months into the training. I think it would make good sense to put it in earlier, but a specific programme has to be designed for each individual Other, and that takes time.

Once Svetlana had been through that ordeal, she'd know when to keep quiet and when to speak. They just start feeding you information, strictly measured, in a specific sequence. Some of what you hear is true, and some of it's false. They tell you some of it quite freely and openly, and some of it under a terrible oath of secrecy. And some of it you find out 'accidentally', by eavesdropping or spying.

And then everything you've learned starts to ferment inside you, making you feel pain and fear, pushing and straining so hard to break out you think your heart's going to burst, demanding some immediate, irrational reaction. In the lectures they tell you all sorts of nonsense you don't really need to know to live as an Other, while the most important training and testing is taking place in your soul.

It's rare for anyone to have a serious breakdown. It's only training, after all, not a test. And the height set for every individual is no higher than he can jump – provided he calls on every last ounce of his strength, leaving scraps of blood-stained skin behind on the razor wire along the top of the barrier.

But when the people on the course matter to you, or even if you simply like them, it starts getting to you, tearing you apart. You catch a strange glance cast in your direction and start wondering what your friend has just learned on the course. What truths? What lies?

And what the student is learning about himself, about the world around him, his parents and friends . . .

And you have a dreadful, unbearable yearning to help. To explain, to hint, to prompt.

But no one who's been through the course will ever give way to that desire. Because that's what they're learning through their own pain and suffering – what to say and when.

Generally speaking, we can and should say everything. We just have to choose the right time, otherwise the truth can be worse than a lie.

'Olya?'

'You'll understand soon,' I said. 'Just wait a while.'

I glanced through the Twilight and hurled the car forward, flitting neatly between a clumsy jeep and a military truck. The mirror cracked as it folded back after clipping the edge of the truck – I didn't care. Our car was first across the intersection, tearing out on to the Highway of Enthusiasts.

'Is he in love with me?' Svetlana suddenly asked. 'Is he, yes or no? You must know, don't you?'

I shuddered and the car swerved, but Svetlana took no notice. I sensed it wasn't the first time she'd asked that question. She and Olga must have left a difficult conversation unfinished.

'Or is he in love with you?'

That was it. I couldn't keep quiet any longer.

'Anton is very fond of Olga,' I said, speaking both of myself and the owner of my body in the third person. It was rather artificial, but it gave an impression of cool, distant politeness. 'Comrades-in-arms. Nothing more than that.'

If Svetlana asked Olga how she felt about me, it would be harder to avoid lying.

She didn't. And a moment later she touched my hand, as if she was asking me to forgive her.

But now I couldn't stop myself:

'Why do you ask?'

She answered simply, without hesitation:

'I don't understand. Anton is behaving very strangely. Sometimes he seems to be madly in love with me. And sometimes it's as if I'm just one of hundreds of Others that he knows.'

'A destiny node,' I said briefly.

'What?'

'You haven't studied that yet, Sveta.'

'Explain it to me, then!'

'You know,' I said, accelerating rapidly – that must have been the body's motor reflexes kicking in – 'you know, when he came to your place that first time—'

'I know that I was influenced. He told me,' Svetlana interrupted.

'That's not the point. The suggestion was removed when you were told the truth. But when you learn to see destiny – and you'll learn to see it a lot more clearly than I do – then you'll understand.'

'They told us that destiny is variable.'

'Destiny is polyvariable. But when he came to see you, Anton knew that if he succeeded in his assignment, he would fall in love with you.'

Svetlana didn't answer that. I thought I saw her cheeks colour slightly, but maybe that was just the wind in the open car.

'And what difference does that make?'

'Do you know what it's like to be condemned to love?'

'But isn't it always like that?' Svetlana asked, trembling with indignation. 'When people love each other, when they find each other out of thousands and millions of people. It's always destiny!'

Once again I sensed that infinitely naïve girl in her, the girl who couldn't hate anything except herself. The girl who was already beginning to disappear.

'No, Sveta, haven't you ever heard love compared to a flower?'

'Yes.'

'A flower can be grown, Sveta. But it can be bought too, or given as a gift.'

'Did Anton buy it?'

'No,' I said, rather too sharply. 'It was a gift. From destiny.'

'What difference does that make? If it is love?'

'Sveta, cut flowers are beautiful, but they don't live for long.

They're already dying, even when they're carefully placed in a vase and given fresh water.'

'He's afraid of loving me,' Svetlana said thoughtfully. 'Isn't he? I wasn't afraid, because I didn't know all this.'

I drove up to the building, weaving between the parked cars, mostly Zhigulis and Moskviches. This wasn't a smart district.

'Why did I tell you all that?' asked Svetlana. 'Why did I make you answer? Just because you're four hundred and forty-three years old?'

I shuddered. Yes, a real wealth of experience. An immense wealth. Next year Olga would be celebrating a very special kind of birthday.

I'd like to believe my body would still be in such condition, even at a quarter of that age.

I left the car without putting on the alarm. No human would ever think of trying to steal it in any case: the protective spells provide greater security than any alarm system. Svetlana and I walked briskly up the steps without speaking and went into her apartment.

Things had changed a bit, of course. Svetlana had left her job, but her study grant and the initial allowance paid to every Other when they were initiated came to far more than her modest earnings as a doctor. She had a new TV, but I couldn't imagine when she found the time to watch it. It was a flashy widescreen model, too big for her apartment. I found this sudden yen for the good life amusing. It's something everyone goes through at the beginning – probably a defensive reaction. When your world crumbles around you, when the old fears and anxieties disappear and new ones, still vague and unfamiliar, take their place, everyone starts acting out some of the dreams from their former life that seemed so unreal only recently. Some go out to expensive restaurants, others buy flashy cars or haute couture clothes. It doesn't last for long, and not just because working in the Watch won't make you a millionaire. The very needs that seemed so compelling only yesterday begin to fade, disappearing into the past. For ever.

'Olga?'

Svetlana looked into my eyes.

I sighed, gathering my strength.

'I couldn't tell you earlier. We can only talk here. Your apartment is protected against observation by the Dark Ones.'

I could see that Svetlana already suspected the truth.

'This is only Olga's body,' I said.

'Anton?'

I nodded.

The two of us must have looked absurd.

It was a good thing Svetlana was already used to absurdity.

She believed me straight away.

'You bastard!'

Spoken in a tone that would have suited the aristocratic Olga. And the slap to my face came from the same opera libretto.

It didn't hurt, but it upset me.

'What's that for?' I asked.

'For eavesdropping on other people's conversations!' Svetlana snapped.

It wasn't an entirely accurate way of putting it, but I got the idea. When Svetlana raised her other hand, I ignored the Christian teaching and dodged the second slap.

'Sveta, I promised to take care of this body!'

'I didn't!'

Svetlana breathed heavily, biting her lip. Her eyes were blazing. I'd never seen her in such a fury, never even suspected she had it in her. Just what was it that had made her so furious?

'So, you're afraid to love cut flowers?' said Svetlana, advancing on me. 'That's your problem, is it?'

I got the idea. But it took a moment or two.

'Get out of here! Get out!'

I backed away until I bumped into the door. But the moment I stopped, Svetlana stopped too. She jerked her head to one side and yelled:

'Stay in that body! It suits you better, you're not a man, you're a spineless wimp!'

I didn't answer. I didn't say a word, because I could already see how it would go. I could see the probabilities stretching out ahead of us, destiny derisively weaving its pathways together.

And when Svetlana burst into tears, suddenly robbed of all her fighting spirit, and lowered her face into her hands, when I put my arm round her and she sobbed in relief on my shoulder, I felt cold and empty inside. The cold was piercing, as if I was again standing on a snow-covered roof in a blustery winter wind.

Svetlana was still human. There wasn't enough of the Other in her yet, she didn't understand, she couldn't see the road leading off into the distance, the road we were destined to follow. And so she couldn't see how that road divided in two, running in different directions.

Love is happiness, but only when you believe it will last for ever. Even though every time it turns out to be a lie, it's only faith that gives love its strength and its joy.

Great knowledge brings great sorrow. How I wished I didn't know the inevitable future. I wished I didn't know it, and that I could love her without thinking twice, like an ordinary, mortal human being.

And what a pity that I wasn't in my own body.

To any outsider it might have looked like two women who were close friends had decided to spend a quiet evening in front of the TV taking tea with jam and chatting.

'You really like bread rolls, don't you?' Svetlana asked in surprise.

'Yes. With butter and jam,' I replied.

'I thought someone promised to take care of that body . . .'

'I'm not doing it any harm! Believe me, it's having a really great time.'

'Well,' Svetlana replied. 'You ask Olga afterwards how she takes care of her figure.'

I hesitated, but went ahead and cut another roll in half, then spread it generously with jam.

'And whose great idea was it to hide you in a woman's body?'

'The boss's, I think.'

'I thought it must be.'

'Olga supported him.'

'I should think so. She worships the ground Boris Ignatievich walks on.'

I had my doubts about that, but I kept quiet. Svetlana got up and went over to the wardrobe, opened it and looked thoughtfully at the hangers.

'Why don't you put on a robe?'

'What?' I said, choking on my roll.

'Are you going to sit around in the house like that? Those jeans are bursting on you. It must be uncomfortable.'

'Can't you find something like a tracksuit?' I asked pitifully.

Svetlana gave me a mocking glance and then relented.

'I suppose I might.'

She pulled out a tracksuit and handed it to me.

'Get changed, and I'll go make some more tea.'

She went out and I hurriedly pulled off the jeans. I started unbuttoning the blouse, fumbling with the funny little buttons that were too tight, and then glared balefully at myself in the mirror.

A good-looking girl, that was for sure. I put the new clothes on in a hurry and sat down on the sofa. There was a soap on TV– I was surprised Svetlana had chosen that channel. But then, the others were probably showing much the same stuff.

'You look great,' Svetlana said on her return.

'Don't, Sveta, please,' I begged her. 'I feel sick enough already.'

'Okay, I'm sorry,' she said lightly, sitting down beside me. 'So what have we got to do?'

'We?' I asked with gentle emphasis.

'Yes, Anton. You didn't come here by chance.'

'I had to tell you about the mess I'm in.'

'Okay. But if the boss' – Svetlana managed to pronounce the word 'boss' with respect and irony at the same time – 'has allowed you to confide in me, that means I have to help you. It must be the will of destiny.' She couldn't resist that.

I gave in.

'I mustn't be left alone. Not for a moment. The basis of the whole plan is that the Dark Ones are deliberately sacrificing their own pawns – either killing them or allowing them to die.'

'Like the other time?'

'Yes. Precisely. And if this provocation is directed at me, there's going to be another killing any time now. At some moment when they think I don't have an alibi.'

Svetlana looked at me with her chin propped on her hands and slowly shook her head.

'And then you'll jump out of this body like a jack out of his box. And it'll be clear that you couldn't have carried out these serial killings. The enemy is confounded.'

'Uhuh.'

'I'm sorry, I haven't been in the Watch for long, maybe there's something I don't understand.'

That put me on my guard. Svetlana hesitated for a second and then went on:

'When all those things happened to me, what was going on? The

Dark Ones were hoping to initiate me. They knew the Night Watch would notice, they even figured out that you could possibly get involved and help.'

'Yes.'

'That was why they played out that complex plan, sacrificing a few pieces and building up false positions of strength. And to begin with, the Night Watch was taken in. If the boss hadn't launched his counter-plan, if you hadn't gone charging straight in, taking no notice of anything . . .'

'You'd be my enemy now,' I said. 'You'd be studying with the Day Watch.'

'That's not what I meant, Anton. I'm grateful to you, and to everyone in the Night Watch, but above all to you. But that's not what I'm talking about right now. Surely you understand that what you've just told me sounds about as probable as that story did? Everything fitted together so neatly, didn't it? A pair of vampires poaching. A boy with exceptional powers. A girl under a powerful curse. A massive threat to the entire city.'

I didn't know what to say. I looked at her and felt my cheeks beginning to burn. A girl who wasn't a third of the way through the introductory course, a total novice in our line of work, was laying out the situation for me the way I ought to have laid it out for myself.

'What's happening right now?' Svetlana continued, not noticing the torment I was in. 'There's a serial killer destroying Dark Ones. You're on the list of suspects. The boss immediately makes a cunning move: you and Olga swap bodies. But just how cunning is this move, really? As far as I understand it, the practice of body-swapping is quite common. Boris Ignatievich himself used it only recently, didn't he? Has he ever used the same move twice in a row? Against the same enemy?'

'I don't know, Svetlana, they don't tell me all the details of the operations.'

'Then think for yourself. And another thing. Is Zabulon really so petty, so hysterically vengeful? He's hundreds of years old, isn't he? He's been in charge of the Day Watch for a very, very long time. If this maniac—'

'Maverick.'

'If they really have let this Maverick run loose on the streets of Moscow while they get ready to make their move, then would the head of the Day Watch really waste him on something that trivial? I'm sorry, Anton, but you're really not such an important target.'

'I understand. Officially I'm a fifth-grade magician, but the boss said I could aim for third-grade.'

'Even taking that into account.'

We looked into each other's eyes and I shrugged:

'I give up, Svetlana, you must be right. But I've told you all I know. And I can't see any other possible interpretation.'

'So you're just going to follow instructions? Walk around in a skirt, never let yourself be alone for a single moment?'

'When I joined the Watch, I knew I was giving up part of my freedom.'

'Part of it!' Svetlana snorted. 'Is that what you call it? Okay, you know best. So we're spending the night together, then?'

I nodded:

'Yes . . . But not here. It's best if I stay with people all the time.'

'What about sleeping?'

'It's not that hard to go without sleep for a few nights,' I said with a shrug. 'I expect Olga's body is trained at least as well as mine. This last few months her life's been one never-ending high-society whirl.'

'Anton, I haven't learned these tricks yet. When do I sleep?'

'During the day. In class.'

She frowned. I knew Svetlana would agree, she couldn't help

herself. With her character she couldn't even refuse to help some stranger in the street, and I certainly wasn't that.

'Why don't we go to the Maharajah?' I suggested.

'What's that?'

'An Indian restaurant, it's pretty good.'

'Is it open all night?'

'No, unfortunately. But we'll think of somewhere else to go on to afterwards.'

Svetlana stared at me so long she got under even my naturally thick skin. What had I done wrong this time?

'Thank you, Anton,' she said with real feeling. 'Thank you very much. You've just invited me to a restaurant. I've been waiting two months for that.'

She got up, went across to the wardrobe, opened it and gazed thoughtfully at the clothes hanging there.

'I don't have anything decent in your size,' she said. 'You'll have to get back into the jeans. Will they let you into the restaurant?'

'They should,' I said, not too sure of myself. But if it came to that, I could always influence the restaurant staff a little.

'If need be, I can practise implanting suggestions,' Svetlana said, as if she'd read my thoughts. 'I'll make them let you in. That will be a good deed, won't it?'

'Of course.'

'You know, Anton . . .' she said, taking a dress off a hanger, holding it up against herself and shaking her head. Then she took out a beige suit. '. . . I'm amazed at the way the members of the Watch use the interests of the Good and the Light to justify any interference in reality.'

'Not any interference!' I protested.

'Absolutely any. If necessary, they'll even claim robbery's a good deed, even murder.'

'No.'

'Imagine you're walking along the street and you see a grown-up beating a child, right there in front of you. What would you do?'

'If I had any margin left for intervention,' I said with a shrug, 'I'd perform a remoralisation. Naturally.'

'And you'd be absolutely certain that was the right thing to do? Without even thinking it over, without looking into things? What if the child deserved to be punished for what it had done? What if the punishment would have saved it from serious problems later in life, but now it will grow up to be a murderer and a bandit? You and your remoralisation!'

'Sveta, you don't understand.'

'What don't I understand?'

'Even if I didn't have any margin left for parapsychological influence, I still wouldn't just walk on by.'

Svetlana snorted.

'And you'd be certain you were right? Where's the boundary?'

'Everyone determines that for themselves. It comes with experience.'

She looked at me thoughtfully.

'Anton, every novice asks these questions. I'm right, aren't I?'

'Yes.' I smiled.

'And you're used to answering them, you have a series of ready-made answers, sophisms, historical examples and parallels.'

'No, Sveta. That's not the point. The point is that the Dark Ones never ask questions like these.'

'How do you know?'

'A Dark Magician can heal, a Light Magician can kill,' I said. 'That's the truth. Do you know what the difference is between Light and Dark?'

'No, I don't. For some reason, they don't teach us that. I expect it's hard to formulate clearly.'

'Not at all. If you always put yourself and your own interests first, then your path leads through the Dark. If you think about others, it leads towards the Light.'

'And how long will it take to reach it? The Light, I mean.'

'For ever.'

'This is all empty words, Anton. A word game. What does an experienced Dark Magician tell his novice? Maybe he uses words that are just as beautiful and true.'

'Yes. About freedom. About how everyone gets the place in life that they deserve. About how pity is degrading and true love is blind, and true kindness is useless – and true freedom is freedom from everyone else.'

'And is that a lie?'

'No,' I said with a nod. 'That's a part of the truth too. Sveta, we're not given the chance to choose absolute truth. Truth's always two-faced. The only thing we have is the right to reject the lie we find most repugnant. Do you know what I tell novices about to enter the Twilight for the first time? We enter it in order to acquire strength. And as the price for entering it we give up the part of the truth that we don't want to accept. Ordinary humans have it easier. A million times easier, even with all the disasters and problems and worries that don't exist for the Others. Humans have never had to face this choice: they can be good and bad, it all depends on the moment, on their surroundings, on the book they read yesterday, on the steak they had for dinner. That's why they're so easy to influence, even the most malicious person can easily be turned to the Light, and the kindest and most noble of men can be nudged towards the Dark. But we have made a choice.'

'I've made it too, Anton. I've already been in the Twilight.'

'Yes.'

'Then why don't I understand where the boundary is and what

the difference is between me and some witch who attends black masses? Why am I still asking these questions?'

'You'll never stop asking them. Out loud at first, and later on just to yourself. It will never stop, never. If you wanted to be free of painful questions, you chose the wrong side.'

'I chose the one I wanted.'

'I know. So now put up with it.'

'All my life?'

'Yes. It will be a long one, but you'll never get over this. You'll never stop asking yourself if every step you make is the right one.'

CHAPTER 3

MAXIM DIDN'T like restaurants. That was just his character. He felt far more comfortable and relaxed in bars and clubs, even the more expensive ones, as long as they weren't too stiff and formal. Of course, there were some people who always behaved like red commissars negotiating with the bourgeoisie, even in the most upmarket restaurants: no manners and no wish to learn any. But then who did all those New Russians in the jokes have to model themselves on?

Last night had to be smoothed over somehow, though. His wife had either believed his story about an 'important business meeting' or at least pretended that she did. But he was still suffering vague pangs of conscience. If only she knew. If she could only imagine who he really was and what it was he did.

Maxim couldn't say anything, so he had no choice but to make amends for his absence the previous night by using the same methods as any decent man after a little affair. Presents, pampering, an evening out. For instance, at a posh restaurant with exotic cuisine, foreign waiters, elegant decor and an extensive wine list.

Maxim wondered if Elena really thought he'd been unfaithful to her the night before. The question intrigued him, but not enough for him to ask it out loud. There are always some things that have to be left unsaid. Maybe some day she'd learn the truth. And then she'd be proud of him.

But his hopes on that score were probably in vain – he realised that. In a world full of the creatures of Malice and Darkness, he was the only knight of Light, eternally alone, unable to share with anyone the truth that was occasionally revealed to him. At the beginning, Maxim had still hoped to meet someone else like him: a sighted man in the kingdom of the blind, a shepherd who could sniff out the wolves in sheep's clothing from among the heedless herd.

But there wasn't anyone. He had no one to stand beside him.

Even so, he hadn't despaired.

'Do you think this is worth trying?'

Maxim glanced down at the menu. He didn't know what *malai kofta* was. But that had never prevented him from making decisions. And in any case, the ingredients were listed.

'Yes, try it. Meat with a cream sauce.'

'Beef?'

He didn't realise straight away that Elena was joking. Then he smiled back at her.

'Definitely.'

'And what if I do order something with beef?'

'Then they'll refuse politely,' said Maxim. Keeping his wife amused wasn't so difficult. He actually rather enjoyed it. But right now he would really like to take a look round the room. Something here wasn't right. He could sense a strange, cold draught blowing through the semi-darkness at his back; it made him screw up his eyes and keep looking, looking . . .

Could it really be?

The gap between his missions was usually at least a few months, maybe six. Nothing had ever come up the very next day . . .

But the symptoms were only too familiar.

Maxim reached into his inside jacket pocket, as if he was checking his wallet. What he was really concerned about was something else – the little wooden dagger, carved artlessly but with great care. It was a simple whittled weapon he'd played with as a child, without understanding what it was for at the time, thinking it was just a toy.

The dagger was waiting.

But who for?

'Max?' There was a note of reproach in Elena's voice. 'You're off in the clouds again.'

They clinked glasses. It was a bad sign for husband and wife to do that, it meant there'd be no money in the family. But Maxim wasn't superstitious.

Who was it?

At first he suspected two girls. Both attractive, even beautiful, but each in her own way. The shorter one with dark hair, who moved in a slightly angular fashion, like a man, was overflowing with energy. She positively oozed sex. The other one, the blonde, was taller, more calm and restrained. And her beauty was quite different, soothing.

Maxim felt his wife watching him and looked away.

'Lesbians,' his wife said disdainfully.

'What?'

'Well, just look at them! The small dark-haired one in jeans is totally butch.'

So she was. Maxim nodded and assumed an appropriate expression.

Not them. Not them, after all. But who was it then?

A mobile phone rang in the corner of the room and a dozen people automatically reached for their phones. Maxim located the source of the sound and caught his breath.

The man talking into the phone in rapid, quiet bursts was not simply Evil. He was enveloped in a black shroud that other people couldn't see, though Maxim could sense it.

The draught was coming from him, it smelled of danger, appalling danger, coming closer.

Maxim felt a sudden ache in his chest.

'You know what, Elena, I'd like to live on a desert island,' he blurted out before he realised what he was saying.

'Alone?'

'With you and the children. But no one else. Not a soul.'

He gulped down the rest of his wine and the waiter immediately refilled his glass.

'I wouldn't like that,' his wife said.

'I know.'

The dagger felt heavy and hot in his pocket now. The mounting excitement was acute, almost sexual. It demanded release.

'Do you remember Edgar Allen Poe?' Svetlana asked.

They'd let us in without any fuss. I hadn't been expecting that – the rules in restaurants must have changed, become more democratic, or maybe they were just short of customers.

'No. He died too long ago. But Semyon was telling me—'

'I didn't mean Poe himself. I meant his stories.'

'*The Man of the Crowd*?' I guessed.

Svetlana laughed quietly.

'Yes. You're in the same fix as him right now. You have to stick to crowded places.'

'Fortunately I'm not sick of those places just yet.'

We took a glass of Bailey's each and ordered something to eat. That probably gave the waiter ideas about why we were there – two inexperienced prostitutes looking for work – but I didn't really care.

'Was he an Other?'
'Poe? Probably an uninitiated one.'

Silence

There are some qualities—some incorporate things,
That have a double life, which thus is made
A type of that twin entity which springs
From matter and light, evinced in solid and shade.

Svetlana recited in a quiet voice.
I looked at her in surprise.
'Do you know it?' she asked.
'How can I put it?' I said. Then I raised my eyes and declaimed:

He is the corporate Silence: dread him not!
No power hath he of evil in himself;
But should some urgent fate (untimely lot!)
Bring thee to meet his shadow (nameless elf,
That haunteth the lone regions where hath trod
No foot of man), commend thyself to God!

We looked at each for a second and then both burst into laughter.

'A literary duel,' Svetlana said ironically. 'Score line: one–one. A pity we don't have an audience. But why wasn't Poe initiated?'

'A lot of poets are potential Others. But some potentials are best left to live as humans. Poe was too psychologically unstable – giving people like that special powers is like handing a pyromaniac a can of petrol. I wouldn't even try to guess which side he would have taken. He'd probably have withdrawn into the Twilight for ever, and very quickly.'

'But how do they live there? The ones who have withdrawn for ever?'

'I don't know, Svetlana. I expect no one really knows. You sometimes come across them in the Twilight world, but there's no contact in the usual sense of the word.'

'I'd like to find out,' said Svetlana, casting a thoughtful glance round the room. 'Have you noticed the Other in here?' she asked.

'The old man behind me, talking on his phone?'

'Why do you call him old?'

'He's very old. I'm not looking with my eyes.'

Svetlana bit her lip and screwed up her eyes. She was beginning to develop small ambitions of her own.

'I can't do it yet,' she admitted. 'I can't even tell if he's Light or Dark.'

'Dark. Not from the Day Watch, but Dark. A magician with middle-level powers. And by the way, he's spotted us too.'

'So what are we going to do?'

'Us? Nothing.'

'But he's Dark!'

'Yes, and we're Light. What of it? As Watch agents we have the right to check his ID. But it's bound to be in order.'

'And when will we have the right to intervene?'

'When he gets up, waves his hands through the air, turns into a demon and starts biting off people's heads . . .'

'Anton!'

'I'm quite serious. We have no right to interfere with an honest Dark Magician's pleasant evening out.'

The waiter brought our order and we stopped talking. Svetlana ate, but without any real appetite. Then, like a sulky, capricious child, she blurted out:

'And how long is the Watch going to carry on grovelling like this?'

'To the Dark Ones?'

'Yes.'

'Until we acquire a decisive advantage. Until people who become Others no longer hesitate for even a moment over what to choose: Light or Dark. Until the Dark Ones all die of old age. Until they can no longer nudge people towards Evil as easily as they do now.'

'But that's capitulation, Anton.'

'Neutrality. The status quo. Double deadlock – there's no point pretending otherwise.'

'You know, I like the solitary Maverick who's terrorising the Dark Ones a lot more. Even if he is violating the Treaty, even if he is setting us up without knowing it. He's fighting against the Dark, isn't he? Fighting! Alone, against all of them.'

'And have you thought about why he kills Dark Ones but doesn't get in touch with us?'

'No.'

'He can't see us, Svetlana. He looks straight through us.'

'He's self-taught.'

'Yes. Self-taught and talented. An Other with powers that manifest themselves chaotically. Capable of seeing Evil. Incapable of recognising Good. Don't you find that frightening?'

'No,' Svetlana said sullenly. 'I'm sorry, I can't see where you're going with this, Olga. Sorry, I mean Anton. You've started talking just like her.'

'That's okay.'

'The Dark Other's going somewhere,' said Svetlana, looking past my shoulder. 'To extract other people's energy, to cast evil spells. And we don't interfere.'

I turned my head slightly and saw the Dark One. To the unaided eye he looked about thirty years old at most. Well dressed, charming. A young woman and two children were sitting at the table he'd just left. The boy was about seven, the girl a bit younger.

'He's gone for a leak, Svetlana. And his family, by the way, are perfectly ordinary. No powers. Are you suggesting we eliminate them too?'

'Like father, like son . . .'

'Try telling that to Garik. His father's a Dark Magician. Still alive.'

'There are always exceptions.'

'Life consists of nothing but exceptions.'

Svetlana didn't answer.

'I know that itch, Sveta. The itch to do Good, to pursue Evil. Right now, to finish it for ever. That's the way I feel too. But if you can't understand that's a dead end, you'll end up in the Twilight. One of us will have to put an end to your earthly existence.'

'But at least I'd have done something.'

'You know what your actions would look like to an outsider? A psychopath killing normal, decent people at random. Chilling reports in the newspapers, with spine-chilling descriptions and grand nicknames for you, like "the new Lucretia Borgia". You'd sow more Evil in human hearts than a brigade of Dark Magicians could generate in a year.'

'How come you lot always have an answer for everything?' Svetlana asked bitterly.

'Because we've been through the training. And survived. At least most of us have.'

I called the waiter and asked for the menu.

'How about a cocktail? And then we can move on. You choose.'

Svetlana nodded as she studied the wine list. The waiter was a tall, dark young man, not Russian. He'd seen just about everything and he wasn't much bothered by one girl acting like a man with another.

'Alter Ego,' said Svetlana.

I shook my head doubtfully – it was one of the strongest cocktails. But I didn't argue.

'Two cocktails and the bill.'

We waited in oppressive silence while the barman was mixing the cocktails and the waiter was making out the bill. Eventually Svetlana asked:

'Okay, I get the picture with poets. They're potential Others. But what about the great monsters? Caligula, Hitler, the homicidal maniacs?'

'Just people.'

'All of them?'

'Mostly. We have our own monsters. Their names don't mean anything to ordinary people, but you'll be starting the history programme soon.'

'Alter Ego' was an accurate description. Two heavy, immiscible layers, black and white, swaying in the glass. A sweet plum liqueur and a dark, bitter beer.

I paid in cash – I don't like to leave an electronic trail behind me – and raised my glass.

'Here's to the Watch.'

'To the Watch,' Sveta agreed. 'And your escape from this mess.'

I felt like asking her to touch wood, but I didn't. I downed the cocktail in two gulps – first the gentle sweetness, then the mild bitterness.

'That's great,' said Svetlana. 'You know, I like it here. Maybe we could stay a bit longer.'

'There are lots of good places in Moscow. Let's find one without any Dark Magicians out on a spree.'

Sveta nodded.

'And by the way, he's not back yet.'

I looked at my watch. Yes, he'd been gone too long.

And what really bothered me was that the magician's family were still sitting at their table, and the woman was obviously getting worried.

'Sveta, I'll just be a moment.'

'Don't forget who you are!' she whispered as I left.

Yes, it would look a bit odd for me to follow the Dark Magician into the gents'.

I walked across the restaurant and took a look through the Twilight on the way. I ought to have been able to see the magician's aura, but there was nothing but a grey void lit by ordinary auras glowing different colours: pleased, concerned, lustful, drunk, happy.

He couldn't have just slipped out through the plumbing.

The only weak glimmer of light from an Other's aura was outside the building, over beside the Belorussian embassy. But it wasn't the Dark Magician, it was much weaker and a different colour.

Where had he gone to?

The narrow corridor ending in two doors was empty. I hesitated for a moment – who could tell, maybe we just hadn't noticed the magician leaving via the Twilight, or maybe he was powerful enough to teleport? Then I opened the door of the gents'.

Inside it was very clean and bright and a bit cramped, and the air had a strong smell of floral air freshener.

The Dark Magician was lying just inside the door and his outstretched arms prevented me from opening the door all the way. He had a puzzled, confused expression on his face. I spotted the gleam of a slim crystal tube in his hand. He'd reached for his weapon too late.

There was no blood. There were no signs at all, and when I took another look through the Twilight I didn't find any traces of magic.

It looked like the Dark Magician had died of a perfectly ordinary heart attack or stroke – if he'd actually been capable of dying that way.

There was just one small detail that ruled out that possibility.

A small cut on the collar of his shirt. As narrow as if it had been made by a cut-throat razor. As if someone had stuck a knife in his neck and just nicked the edge of his collar. Except that there were no signs of the blow on his skin.

'Bastards!' I whispered, not knowing who I was swearing at. 'Bastards!'

I could hardly have ended up in a worse situation than this. I'd swapped bodies and gone out to a crowded restaurant with a 'witness', only to wind up entirely alone, standing over the body of a Dark Magician killed by the Maverick.

'Come on, Pavlik,' someone said behind me.

As I looked round the woman who'd been sitting at the table with the Dark Magician came into the corridor, holding her son by the hand.

'I don't want to, Mum!' the kid yelled, acting up.

'You go in and tell your dad we're getting bored,' the woman said patiently. The next moment she looked up and saw me.

'Call someone!' I shouted desperately. 'Get help! There's a man hurt here! Take the child away and call someone!'

They obviously heard me in the restaurant – Olga had a strong voice.

The murmur of voices stopped immediately, leaving the slushy folk music to play on in the sudden silence.

Of course, she didn't do as I said. She ran forward, pushed me out of the way, collapsed on her husband's body and started keening – actually keening – at the top of her voice, already knowing what had happened while her hands were still busy unbuttoning the slit shirt collar and shaking the lifeless body. Then she started slapping the magician on the cheeks, hard, as if she hoped he was only pretending or had just fainted.

'Mum, why are you hitting Dad like that?' Pavlik cried shrilly. Not frightened, just surprised, he'd obviously never seen his parents fight. They must have been a happy family.

I took the boy by the shoulder and started gently leading him away. People were already squeezing into the corridor. I saw Sveta staring at me wide-eyed. She'd guessed what had happened.

'Take the child away,' I said to our waiter. 'I think a man's dead in there.'

'Who found the body?' the waiter asked calmly. Speaking without an accent, quite differently from when he was serving our table.

'I did.'

The waiter nodded as he smoothly handed on the boy to one of the female restaurant staff. The boy was crying now, he'd realised something had gone wrong in his happy little world.

'And what were you doing in there?'

'The door was open and I saw him on the ground,' I said, lying without even thinking about it.

The waiter nodded, accepting that it could have happened that way. But at the same time he took a firm grip of my elbow.

'You'll have to wait for the militia, lady.'

Svetlana had already pushed her way through to us. She narrowed her eyes when she heard those last words. That was all I needed now – for her to try erasing the memories of everyone there.

'Of course.' I stepped forward, and the waiter was forced to let go of my arm and follow me. 'Sveta, it's awful, there's a body in there!'

'Olya.' Sveta's reaction was the right one. She put her arm round my shoulders, gave the waiter an indignant look and led me back into the restaurant.

Just then the boy passed us, sobbing loudly as he squeezed his way through the greedy, curious crowd back to his mother. They were trying to get her away from the body – she'd taken advantage of the confusion to bend back down over her husband and start shaking him:

'Get up! Gena, get up! Get up!'

I felt Svetlana shudder at the sight and I whispered:

'Well? Do we exterminate the Dark Ones with fire and the sword?'

'Why did you do it? I would have understood without that!' Svetlana whispered furiously.

'What?'

We looked into each other's eyes.

'Then it wasn't you?' Sveta whispered uncertainly. 'I'm sorry, I believe you.'

I realised then just what a mess I was in.

The crime scene investigator didn't take any particular interest in me. I could see from his eyes that he'd already made up his mind – death from natural causes. A weak heart, drug abuse, whatever. He couldn't be expected to feel any sympathy for a man who frequented expensive restaurants.

'Was the body lying in this position?'

'Yes, just like that,' I confirmed in a weary voice. 'It was awful!'

He shrugged – he couldn't see anything really awful about a body, especially one that wasn't drenched in blood. But he was condescending.

'Yes, a terrible sight. Was there anybody else nearby?'

'Nobody. But then a woman appeared, his wife, their child.'

I was rewarded with a crooked smile for my deliberately disjointed statement.

'Thank you, Olga. Someone may be in touch with you again. Not planning to leave town at all, are you?'

I shook my head rapidly. The militia was the very last thing I was bothered about right then.

But I was bothered by the sight of the boss sitting unobtrusively at a table in the corner.

The investigator left me in peace and went to talk to the dead man's wife. Boris Ignatievich immediately made straight for our table. Nobody paid any attention to him, he was clearly protected by some mild distraction spell.

'Now you've done it,' he said simply.

'Us?' I asked, just to get things clear.

'Yes. Both of you. But especially you, Anton.'

'I followed all the instructions I was given,' I whispered, feeling furious. 'And I never laid a finger on that magician.'

The boss sighed.

'I don't doubt that. But, knowing the situation, how could you, a member of the Night Watch staff, be so stupid as to go off after a Dark One on your own?'

'Who could have foreseen this?' I asked indignantly. 'Tell me who!'

'You could. After the unprecedented measures we've taken to disguise your identity. What were your instructions? Never be left alone for a moment! Eat and sleep with Svetlana! Take your showers together! Go to the lavatory together! Every single moment you had to be . . .' The boss stopped and sighed.

'Boris Ignatievich,' Svetlana spoke up. 'None of that matters any more. Let's try to think what we can do now.'

The boss looked at her in surprise and nodded.

'You're right. Let's try to think. Starting from the fact that the situation is catastrophic now. Before, any suspicion of Anton was purely circumstantial, but now he's been caught red-handed. Don't shake your head like that! You were seen standing over a body that had just been killed. The body of a Dark

Magician, killed in the same way as all the previous victims. The Day Watch will appeal to the tribunal for your memory to be read.'

'That's very dangerous, isn't it?' asked Svetlana. 'But at least it will prove Anton isn't guilty.'

'Yes, it will, Svetlana. And in the process the Dark Ones will acquire all the information Anton has had access to. Do you realise just how much the Watch's senior programmer knows? Some things he may not even be aware of, he just glanced at the data, processed it and forgot it. But the Dark Ones have their own specialists, and when Anton comes out of that courtroom – assuming he survives having his mind turned inside out – the Day Watch will know about all our operations. Can't you see what will happen? Our teaching methods, the way we look for new Others, the way we analyse combat operations, our networks of human informers, our casualty lists, our employees' personal files, our financial plans . . .'

They were talking about me, while I just sat there as if I had nothing to do with what was going on. It wasn't just cynical frankness, it was simpler than that: the boss was consulting with Svetlana, a novice magician, and not with me, a potential magician of the third grade.

If I compared the situation with a game of chess, it was insultingly simple. I was a rook, an ordinary officer of the Watch, and Svetlana was a pawn – but a pawn about to become a queen.

And for the boss all the bad things that could happen to me meant nothing compared with the chance to give Svetlana a little practical lesson.

'Boris Ignatievich, you know I won't allow them to read my memory,' I said.

'Then you'll be found guilty.'

'I know. I swear I had nothing to do with the death of these Dark Ones. But I don't have any proof.'

'Boris Ignatievich, what if we suggest they only check Anton's memory for today?' Svetlana exclaimed joyfully. 'That would solve everything, they'd be convinced—'

'The memory can't be sliced up like that, Sveta. It spills out all in one piece. Starting from the first moment of life. With the taste of the amniotic fluid in the womb, with the smell of mother's milk.' The boss was speaking very emphatically now. 'That's the problem. Even if Anton didn't know any secrets. Imagine what it's like to remember absolutely everything and go through it all again. Swaying in that dark, viscous liquid, the walls closing in on you, the glimmer of light ahead, the pain, the choking sensation, the struggle to survive your own birth. And so on, moment by moment – you've heard it said that when you're dying your whole life flashes in front of your eyes? That's exactly what happens when they turn out your memory. And at the same time, somewhere deep inside, you still remember that all this has already happened. Can you understand that? It's hard to hold on to your sanity.'

'You say that,' Svetlana said uncertainly, 'as if—'

'I've been through it. But not in an interrogation. More than a century ago. The Watch was still studying the effects of exposing and reading the memory, and a volunteer was required. Afterwards it took them about a year to restore me to normal.'

'How?' Svetlana asked curiously.

'With new impressions. Experiences I hadn't had before. Foreign countries, unfamiliar food, surprise meetings, unfamiliar problems. And even so . . .' The boss smiled wryly. 'I still some-times catch myself thinking: What is all this – reality or just memories? Am I living it or lying on a crystal slab in the Day Watch office while they unwind my memory like a ball of string?'

He stopped.

There were people sitting at the tables around us, waiters bustling to and fro. The crime scene team had taken away the body of the Dark Magician and a man, evidently a relative, had come for the widow and the children. Nobody else seemed to be affected by what had happened. Quite the opposite, in fact. There were more customers, with bigger appetites and a greater zest for life. And nobody there was taking any notice of us: the boss's casual spell made them all look away.

What if all of this had already happened?

What if I, Anton Gorodetsky, systems administrator at the Nix trading company, and also a Night Watch magician, was lying on a crystal slab covered with ancient runes? And my memory was being unwound, examined, dissected by someone – it didn't matter who, Dark Magicians or a joint tribunal of both sides?

No!

That couldn't be right. I didn't have that feeling the boss had been talking about. I had no sense of déjà vu. I'd never been in a woman's body before, and I'd never found any bodies in restaurant lavatories.

'I've laid out the problem,' said the boss, drawing a long, slim cigarillo out of his pocket. 'Is the situation clear? What are we going to do?'

'I'm prepared to do my duty,' I said.

'Don't be in such a rush, Anton. Drop the bravado.'

'It's not bravado. It's not just that I'm prepared to protect the secrets of the Watch. I simply wouldn't survive that kind of interrogation. Better to die.'

'But we don't die the same way people do.'

'Sure, it's tougher for us. But I'm ready for that.'

The boss sighed.

'I'm sorry, ladies. Anton, let's forget the consequences for a moment and try thinking about what led up to this incident. Sometimes it's helpful to look back.'

'Okay,' I said, not feeling particularly hopeful.

'The Maverick has been poaching in the city for several years. The latest information from the analytical section indicates that these strange killings began three and a half years ago. Some of the victims are known Dark Ones. Some are probably potentials. None of the victims was higher than grade four. None of them worked for the Day Watch. It's ironic that almost all of them were moderate Dark Ones, if you can put it like that. They killed and they influenced people, but far less than they could have done.'

'They were set up, weren't they?' said Svetlana.

'They must have been. The Day Watch didn't touch this psychopath, it even laid on victims for him from the Dark Side – those it could easily spare. But what for? That's the important question: what for?'

'So they could accuse us of incompetence,' I suggested.

'The end doesn't justify the means.'

'In order to set up one of us.'

'Anton, the only member of the Night Watch who doesn't have alibis for the times of the killings is you. Why would the Day Watch go hunting for you?'

I shrugged.

'Zabulon's revenge?' said the boss, shaking his head. 'No. You only clashed with him recently, yet this was carefully planned three and a half years ago. We're still left with the question why?'

'Maybe Anton is potentially a very powerful magician,' Svetlana suggested, speaking softly. 'And the Dark Ones have realised that. It's too late to bring him over to their side, so they decided to eliminate him.'

'Anton is more powerful than he realises,' the boss replied sharply, 'but he'll never get higher than grade two.'

'What if our enemies can see further along the possible realities than we can?' I asked, looking the boss in the eye.

'And?'

'Maybe I'm a weak magician, I may be average or powerful, but what if it's enough just for me to do something in order to change the balance of power? Do something simple that has nothing to do with magic? Boris Ignatievich, the Dark Ones tried to get me away from Svetlana – that means they could see the branch of reality in which I could help her. What if they can see something else? Something in the future? What if they've been able to see it for a long time, and they've been getting ready to take me out of the game? What if the fight over Sveta is small change by comparison?'

At first the boss listened carefully. Then he frowned and shook his head.

'Anton, you're suffering from megalomania. I'm sorry, but I check the lines of everybody working in the Watch, from key staff to our plumber, Uncle Shura. And there simply aren't any great achievements in your future. Not on any of the reality lines.'

'Boris Ignatievich, are you absolutely sure you haven't missed something?'

He'd really made me angry now.

'Of course not. I'm not absolutely sure of anything. Not even of myself. But the chances of you being right are very, very slim. Believe me.'

I believed him.

Compared with the boss, my powers approximate to zero.

'So we still don't know the most important thing – the reason?'

'Right. The hit is aimed at you, there's no doubt about that now. The Maverick is being controlled, very subtly and precisely. He believes he's waging war on Evil, but he's always been a puppet, with someone else pulling the strings. Today they brought him to the same restaurant you came to. They handed him a victim. And you went right along.'

'Then what are we going to do?'

'Try to find the Maverick. It's our only chance, Anton.'

'We're actually going to kill him, though?'

'No, we're not. All we're going to do is find him.'

'All the same. No matter how bad he might be, no matter how wrong he's got everything, he's still one of us. He's fighting against Evil the best way he knows how. We just have to explain everything to him.'

'Too late, Anton. Too late. We missed him when he appeared. Now, after all he's done . . . Remember how that girl vampire died?'

I nodded: 'Laid to eternal rest.'

'And her crimes were far less serious – from the Dark Ones' point of view. She didn't understand what was going on either. But the Day Watch accepted that she was guilty.'

'Was that pure coincidence?' asked Svetlana. 'Or were they creating a precedent?'

'Who knows? Anton, you have to find the Maverick.'

I looked up, amazed.

'Find him and hand him over to the Dark Ones,' the boss said sternly.

'Why me?'

'Because you're the only who has the moral right to do it. You're the one under threat. You're only protecting yourself. For anybody else, handing over a Light One, even if he is purely acting on instinct, self-taught and misguided, would be too much of a shock. You'll survive it.'

'I'm not so sure.'

'You will. And remember, Anton. You've only got tonight. The Day Watch have no reason to drag things out. They'll bring a formal charge against you in the morning.'

'Boris Ignatievich!'

'Now remember. Remember who was in the restaurant. Who followed the Dark Magician out to the lavatory?'

'Nobody,' Svetlana put in. 'I'm sure of it. I kept looking to see when he would come out.'

'That means the Maverick was waiting for the Dark Magician in there. But he had to come out. Do you remember? Sveta, Anton?'

Neither of us said anything. I didn't remember. I'd been trying not to look at the Dark Magician.

'One man did come out,' said Svetlana. 'He was kind of . . .'

She thought about it.

'Ordinary, absolutely ordinary. An average man, as if someone had mixed a million faces together and made an average one. I just caught a glimpse and forgot him straight away.'

'Remember now,' the boss demanded.

'I can't, Boris Ignatievich. He was just a man. Middle-aged. I didn't even realise he was an Other.'

'He's an elemental Other. He doesn't even enter the Twilight, just stays right on the edge. Remember, Sveta! His face or some distinctive feature.'

Svetlana rubbed her nose with her finger.

'When he came out and sat down at his table, there was a woman there. A beautiful woman with dark blonde hair. It was dyed. And she was upset about something. She was smiling, but her smile looked wrong. As if she wanted to stay, but they had to leave.'

She started thinking again.

'The woman's aura. You remember it. Let me have the image!' the boss exclaimed, speaking more loudly and in a different tone. Of course, no one in the restaurant heard him, but for a brief moment the expressions on people's faces distorted and a waiter carrying a tray stumbled and dropped a bottle of wine and two glasses.

Svetlana shook her head sharply. The boss had put her in a trance as easily as if she was an ordinary human. Her pupils opened wide and a pale, thin, glimmering rainbow connected their two faces.

'Thank you, Sveta,' said Boris Ignatievich.

'Did I manage it?' the girl asked, surprised.

'Yes. You can consider yourself a seventh-grade magician. I'll confirm that I tested you in person. Anton!'

This time I looked into the boss's eyes.

A brief jolt.

Streaming threads of an energy unknown to ordinary humans.

An image.

No, I didn't see the face of the Maverick's female companion. I saw her aura, and that's worth far more. Blue and green layers intermingled like ice-cream in a glass, a small brown spot, a white streak. A fairly complex aura, not easy to forget, and essentially quite attractive. It upset me – she loved him.

She loved him and she was feeling hurt about something. She thought he didn't love her any more, but she was still holding on and she was prepared to keep going on like that.

By following this woman's trail I would find the Maverick. And hand him over to a tribunal – to certain death.

'No!' I said.

The boss gave me a pitying look.

'She's not guilty of anything. And she loves him, you can see that.'

That dismal music was still whining in my ears, and nobody there took any notice of my cry. I could have rolled around on the floor and dived under people's tables – they'd have just lifted their feet up and carried on with their curries.

Svetlana looked at us. She'd remembered the aura, but she hadn't been able to interpret it. That's a grade six skill.

'Then you'll die,' said the boss.

'At least I'll know what for.'

'Have you thought about the people who love you, Anton?'

'I don't have any right to do that.'

Boris Ignatievich grinned wryly:

'A hero! Oh, what great heroes we all are! Clean hands, hearts of gold, feet that have never trodden in shit. Have you forgotten the woman who was taken out of here? And the crying children, have you forgotten them? They're not Dark Ones. They're ordinary people, the ones we promised to protect. How long do we spend on getting the balance right for every operation we plan? I may curse our analysts every moment of the day, but why are they all grey-haired by the age of fifty?'

It felt like the boss was striking me across the face. He was lecturing me just as I'd lectured Svetlana so recently, with absolute confidence.

'The Watch needs you, Anton. It needs Sveta. But it doesn't need some crazy psychopath, no matter how well intentioned he might be. It's easy enough to take a little dagger and start hunting Dark Ones in back alleys and lavatories. Without thinking about the consequences or weighing up the guilt. Where's our front line, Anton?'

'Among ordinary people.' I lowered my eyes.

'Who do we protect?'

'Ordinary people.'

'There is no abstract Evil, you have to understand that! Its roots are here, all around us, in this herd that carries on chewing and having a good time only an hour after a murder. That's what you have to fight for. For people. Evil is a hydra with many heads, and the more of them you cut off, the more it grows!

Hydras have to be starved to death, don't you see? Kill a hundred Dark Ones, and a thousand more will take their place. That's why the Maverick is guilty. And that's why you, Anton, and no one else, will find him. And make sure he stands trial. Either voluntarily or forcibly—'

The boss suddenly broke off and rose abruptly to his feet.

'Let's go, ladies.'

I'd never seen him behave like that. I leapt up and grabbed my handbag – an automatic reflex response.

The boss wouldn't get jittery without good reason.

'Quickly!'

I suddenly realised I needed to visit the place where the unfortunate Dark Magician had met his end. But I didn't say a word. We moved towards the exit so fast the security guards would have been sure to stop us, if only they could have seen us.

'Too late,' the boss said quietly, right beside the door. 'We were talking too long.'

Three people walked into the restaurant as if they were sliding through the door. Two well-built young men and a woman.

I knew the woman. It was Alisa Donnikova, the witch from the Day Watch. Her eyes widened when she spotted the boss.

She was followed by two barely perceptible silhouettes moving through the Twilight.

'Would you wait a moment, please?' Alisa said in a hoarse voice, as if her throat had suddenly gone dry.

'Begone!' The boss made a swift gesture with one hand, and the Dark Ones were forced aside, towards the walls. Alisa leaned over hard, trying to resist the elastic wall of force, but her powers weren't up to it.

'Zabulon, I summon you!' she cried.

Well, well! The witch must be a real favourite of the Day Watch boss if she had the right to summon him.

The other two Dark Ones emerged from the Twilight. I identified them at a glance as warrior magicians of the third or fourth grade. Of course, they were absolutely no match for Boris Ignatievich, and I could give the boss a hand, but they could drag things out.

The boss realised that too.

'What do you want?' he asked threateningly. 'This is the time of the Night Watch.'

'A crime has been committed,' said Alisa, her eyes blazing. 'Here, not long ago. One of our brothers has been killed, killed by one of . . .' She stared hard at the boss, then at me.

'One of . . . ?' the boss asked expectantly. The witch didn't take the bait. If she'd been foolish enough to level an accusation like that at the boss, with her status and at the wrong time, he would have splattered her across the wall.

And he wouldn't have paused for a moment to wonder if such a step was reasonable or not.

'One of the Light Ones!'

'The Night Watch has no idea who the criminal is.'

'We officially request assistance.'

So. Now we had nowhere left to retreat. A refusal to render assistance to the other Watch was as good as a declaration of war.

'Zabulon, I call on you!' the witch cried again. I was beginning to hope that maybe the Dark leader couldn't hear her or was tied up with something important.

'We are willing to collaborate,' said the boss. His voice was like ice.

I glanced back into the dining area, over the shoulders of the magicians – the Dark Ones had already surrounded us, clearly intending to keep us by the door – and what was happening in the restaurant was quite incredible.

People were stuffing themselves.

They were chewing so loudly it sounded as if there were pigs at every table. Their eyes were glazed, their fingers clutched knives and forks, but they were raking up the food with their hands, choking on it, snorting and spitting it out. A respectable-looking middle-aged man who'd been dining sedately in the company of three bodyguards and a young woman was gulping wine straight from the bottle. A smart-looking young man – a yuppie type – and his pretty girlfriend were fighting over a plate, spilling the thick, orange sauce over themselves. The waiters were rushing from table to table, flinging plates, cups, bottles, braziers and dishes at the diners . . .

The Dark Ones have their own methods of distracting outsiders.

'Were any of you present in the restaurant when the murder was committed?' the witch asked triumphantly. The boss paused before he answered.

'Yes.'

'Who?'

'My companions.'

'Olga, Svetlana,' said the witch, devouring us with her eyes. 'Was there not also present another Night Watch agent, whose human name is Anton Gorodetsky?'

'Apart from us, there were no other members of the Night Watch present,' Svetlana said quickly, perhaps too quickly. Alisa frowned.

'A quiet night, isn't it?' said a voice from the doorway.

Zabulon had answered the summons.

I looked at him in despair, realising that a supreme magician would not be taken in by my disguise. He might not have recognised Ilya as the boss, but the old fox wouldn't be caught out by the same trick twice.

'Not so very quiet, Zabulon,' the boss said simply. 'Call off your minions, or I'll have to do it for you.'

The Dark Magician still looked exactly the same, as if time had stopped, as if the icy winter hadn't finally given way to a warm spring. A dark suit, a tie, a grey shirt, old-fashioned, narrow shoes. Sunken cheeks, dull eyes, short hair.

'I knew I'd find you here,' said Zabulon.

He was looking at me. And only at me.

'How stupid,' he said, shaking his head. 'What do you need all this for, eh?'

He took a step forward and Alisa darted out of his way.

'A good job, prosperity, self-esteem, all the joys of the world – all in your grasp, all you have to do is decide what you'll have this time. But you're so stubborn. I don't understand you, Anton.'

'And I don't understand you, Zabulon,' said the boss, blocking his way.

The Dark Magician reluctantly redirected his gaze.

'Then you must be getting old. The person in your lover's body is Anton Gorodetsky, the same person we suspect of the serial killings of Dark Ones. Just how long has he been hiding in there, Boris? Didn't you notice the substitution?'

He laughed.

I looked round at the Dark Ones. They still hadn't understood. They needed another second, or half a second.

Then I saw Svetlana raise her hand, with a yellow magical flame flickering in her palm.

So now she'd passed the fifth-grade test – but this was still a battle we could only lose. There were three of us and six of them. If Svetlana struck – not to save herself, but to get me out of this fix – there'd be a bloodbath.

I leapt forward.

It was a good thing Olga's body was well trained and in such good shape. It was a good thing that all of us – Light Ones and Dark Ones – weren't really used to relying on the strength of our arms and legs, on simple, crude violence. And the best thing of all was that Olga, who had been deprived of most of her magic, hadn't neglected the skills of physical combat.

Zabulon doubled up with a hoarse gasp when my fist – or rather, Olga's – sank into his stomach. I swept his legs from under him with a single kick and ran outside.

'Stop!' howled Alisa in a voice filled with admiration, loathing and love all at once.

The hunt was on.

I ran down Pokrovka Street in the direction of Zemlyanoi Val Street, with my handbag bouncing hard against my back. It was a good thing I wasn't wearing high heels. I had to get away, to disappear. I'd really enjoyed the urban survival course, but it was so short – who could have imagined a Night Watch agent would end up running and hiding, instead of chasing and catching?

I heard a screeching wail behind me.

I leapt aside in a pure reflex response, before I could even understand what was happening. A streak of crimson flame came hurtling down the street, coiling and twisting as it passed me, then it tried to stop and turn back, but its inertia was too great: the charge crashed into the wall of a building, momentarily turning the stones white hot.

I tripped and fell, glancing back. Zabulon was recharging his battle staff, but he was moving very slowly, as if there were something hindering him, slowing him down.

He was shooting to kill.

There wouldn't have been even a handful of dust left if I'd been caught by Shahab's Lash.

So the boss was wrong after all. The Day Watch didn't want what was inside my head. They wanted to eliminate me completely.

The Dark Ones were chasing after me. Zabulon was aiming his staff. The boss was restraining Svetlana as she struggled to break free. I got to my feet and started running again, already knowing there was no way I could escape. At least there was nobody around: instinctive, subconscious fear had swept everybody off the street the moment our confrontation began. Nobody else would get hurt.

I heard a squeal of brakes and looked round just in time to see the Day Watch agents jump out of the way of a car careering wildly along the street. The driver stopped for a moment, evidently thinking he'd driven into the middle of a gangland shootout, then picked up speed again.

Should I stop him? No, it wasn't allowed.

I jumped on to the pavement and squatted down, hiding from Zabulon behind an old Volga, letting the stray driver pass. The silver Toyota hurtled past me and then screeched to a halt with a smell of burning brakes.

The door on the driver's side opened and a hand beckoned to me.

Things like this just don't happen!

Heroes only get rescued by passing cars in cheap action movies.

At least that's what I was thinking as I opened the back door and jumped in.

'Get us out of here!' cried the woman sitting next to me. But the driver didn't need any encouragement, we were already moving. There was a flash behind us and the driver swerved out of the path of a streak of fire. The woman began wailing.

How did they see what was happening? As automatic gunfire? Salvos of rockets? A blast from a flame-thrower?

'Why did you come back, why?' the woman asked, trying to lean forward to hit the driver in the back. I was all set to grab her arm, but before I could the car jerked forward and tossed the woman back against the seat.

'Don't,' I said gently.

She glared at me indignantly. She had every right. What woman would be pleased to see her husband stop and risk his life for an attractive, dishevelled female stranger and take her into his car when it's being chased by a gang of armed bandits?

At least the immediate danger was past now. We came out on to Zemlyanoi Val Street and drove on in a solid stream of traffic. My friends and my enemies were both left a long way behind.

'Thanks,' I said to the short hair on the back of the driver's head.

'Did you get hit?' he asked without even turning round.

'No, thanks to you. Why did you stop?'

'Because he's a dumb fool!' the woman beside me yelled. She moved away to the far side of the car, shunning me as if I had the plague.

'Because I'm not a jerk,' the man replied calmly. 'Why were they out to get you? Never mind, it's none of my business.'

'They wanted to rape me,' I said, blurting out the first thing that came into my head. But it was a pretty good cover.

'Where do you want to go?'

'This will do fine,' I said, looking out at the flaming red letter M above the metro entrance. 'I'll make my own way home.'

'We can drop you off.'

'No need. Thanks, you've already done more than enough.'

'All right.'

He didn't argue or try to change my mind. The car braked and I got out. I looked at the woman.

'Thank you,' I said.

She snorted and jerked away, slamming the door shut.

Well, there you go.

But things like that still went to prove our work did make some kind of sense, after all, I thought.

I automatically tidied my hair and dusted down my jeans. People walking by eyed me cautiously, but they didn't shy away, so I couldn't be looking all that bad.

How much time did I have before the hunt picked up my trail? Would the boss be able to slow them down?

That would be good. Because I thought I was beginning to understand what was going on here.

And I had a chance, only a tiny one maybe, but still a chance.

I set off towards the metro, taking the cell phone out of Olga's bag on the way. I started dialling her number, then swore and dialled my own.

It rang five times, six, seven.

I ended the call and dialled my own mobile number. This time Olga answered straight away.

'Hello?' said a slightly hoarse, unfamiliar voice. My voice.

'It's me – Anton,' I shouted. A man walking past looked at me in surprise.

'You idiot!'

I wouldn't have expected anything else from Olga.

'Where are you, Anton?'

'Getting ready to go underground.'

'You'll have plenty of time for that. What can I do to help?'

'Are you up to speed on the situation?'

'Yes, I'm in parallel contact with Boris.'

'I need to get my body back.'

'Where can we meet?'

I thought for a moment.

'The station where I got off after I tried to remove that black vortex from Svetlana.'

'Sure. Boris told me where. Make it three stations further round the circle line, up and to the left.'

She was counting off stations on the plan of the metro.

'Yes, that's okay.'

'In the centre of the hall. I'll be there in twenty minutes. Want me to bring you anything?'

'Just bring me. Anything else is up to you.'

I folded away the phone, shot another look around and walked quickly into the station.

CHAPTER 4

I WAS STANDING in the centre of Novoslobodskaya station. It's a common enough sight there when it's not really late yet: a girl waiting, maybe for a bloke, maybe for a girlfriend.

In my case, I was waiting for both.

It would be harder to find me underground than on the surface. Even the cleverest of the Dark Magicians wouldn't be able to pick up my aura through the layers of earth, through all the ancient graves that Moscow stood on, among the crowd, in that dense, agitated stream of people. Of course, combing all the stations wouldn't be too hard either: just one Other with my image for each station would do it.

But I was hoping I still had an hour or at least half an hour before the Day Watch made that move.

How simple everything was, after all. How elegantly the pieces of the puzzle fitted together. I shook my head and smiled, and immediately caught the eye of a young guy dressed in punk style looking at me inquisitively. No, my friend, you're on the wrong track. This woman is only smiling at her own thoughts.

I ought to have got the picture the moment the plotlines all started converging on me. The boss was right, of course. I wasn't valuable enough. They wouldn't have come up with a risky and costly manoeuvre lasting years just for me. It was all about something else, something completely different.

They were trying to exploit our weaknesses. Our goodness and love. And it was working, or almost working.

I suddenly felt like I needed a cigarette really badly, my mouth even filled with saliva. Strange, I'd never really smoked much, it had to be a reaction from Olga's body. I imagined her a hundred years earlier – an elegant woman with a slim cigarette in a long holder, sitting in some literary salon somewhere with Alexander Blok or Gumilev. Smiling as she discussed the Freemasons, the sovereignty of the people and mankind's urge towards spiritual perfection.

Ah, here was someone at last!

'Have you got a cigarette?' I asked a young man walking past – he was dressed well enough not to smoke cheap shit like Golden Yava.

He gave me a surprised look, then held out a pack of Parliaments.

I took one, thanked him with a smile and cast a mild spell over myself. People's eyes slid off to the side.

That was better.

I concentrated, raising the temperature of the tip of the cigarette to two hundred degrees, and inhaled. So we'd wait. And we'd break a few little unquestionable rules.

People flowed past, giving me a wide berth. They sniffed the air in surprise, wondering where the smell of tobacco smoke was coming from. And I smoked, dropping the ash at my feet, eyeing the militiaman standing just five steps away and trying to figure out my chances.

They turned out to be not that bad. Pretty good, in fact. And that bothered me.

If they'd been preparing this manoeuvre for three years, one option they must have taken into account was that I'd see through it. They must have an answer for that – but what was it?

It took me a second or two to register the startled look. And when I realised who was watching me, I gasped in surprise.

Egor.

The kid, the Other with potentially great powers who'd got caught up in the battle between the two Watches three months ago. Played for a patsy by both sides. An open card that still hadn't been dealt. But players don't fight over cards like that.

His powers were strong enough to penetrate my casual cover and the meeting itself didn't really come as a shock. There are many chance events in the world, but apart from that, there's also something called predetermination.

'Hi, Egor,' I said without even pausing to think. I expanded the range of the spell to include him in the circle of distraction.

He started and looked around. Then he stared at me. Of course, he hadn't seen Olga in human form. Only as an owl.

'Who are you and how do you know me?'

Yes, he'd grown. Not on the outside, on the inside. I couldn't understand how he could have avoided making his choice for so long and still not joined either the side of the Light or the Dark. He'd already entered the Twilight, in circumstances that meant he could have gone either way. But his aura was still as pure and neutral as ever.

His destiny was his own. It must be good to have your own destiny.

'I'm Anton Gorodetsky, the Night Watch agent,' I said simply. 'Remember me?'

Of course he remembered me.

'But . . .'

'Take no notice. It's a disguise, we can swap bodies.'

I wondered for a moment if I ought to think back to the course on illusion and temporarily restore my usual appearance. But there was no need – he believed me. Maybe because he remembered the boss's body swap.

'What do you want from me?'

'Nothing, I'm just waiting for a friend, the woman this body belongs to. You just happened to meet me here by chance.'

'I hate your Watches!'

'If you say so. But I really haven't been trailing you. You can go if you want.'

The kid found that far harder to believe than the idea of swapping bodies. He looked around suspiciously and frowned.

Of course, it was hard for him to leave. He'd touched the secret and sensed powers that went beyond the human world. And he'd renounced those powers, at least for the time being.

But I could imagine how much he wanted to learn – at least just a few little things, stuff like conjuring tricks with pyrokinesis and telekinesis, suggestion, healing, cursing – I didn't know what exactly, but he must have wanted to know how to do these things, not just know about them.

'You really haven't been trailing me?' he finally asked.

'No, I haven't. And we can't lie – not directly.'

'How do I know that isn't a lie too?' the kid muttered, looking away. A logical question.

'You don't,' I agreed. 'Believe it if you want to.'

'I'd like to,' he said, still looking down at the floor. 'But I remember what happened up there on the roof. I dream about it at night.'

'You don't need to be afraid of that vampire,' I said. 'She's been laid to rest. By order of the court.'

'I know.'

'How?' I asked, surprised.

'Your boss called me. The one who swapped bodies that time.'

'I didn't know about that.'

'He rang one day when there was no one else home. He said the vampire had been executed. And he said that since I was a potential Other, even if I hadn't made a choice yet, I'd been taken off the list of humans. So I could never be selected by chance again, and I needn't be afraid.'

'Yes, of course,' I said.

'And I asked him if my parents were still on the list.'

I couldn't think of anything to say to that. I knew what the boss's answer had been.

'I'll be going, then,' said Egor, taking a step away. 'Your cigarette's finished.'

I dropped the butt and nodded.

'Where have you been? It's late.'

'Training, I swim. Tell me, is that really you?'

'You remember the trick with the broken cup?'

Egor gave a weak smile. It's always the cheapest tricks that impress people the most.

'I remember. Look—' He stopped short, staring past me.

I turned round.

It was strange to see myself from the outside. A man with my face, walking with my walk, wearing my jeans and sweater, with a walkman at his belt and a small bag in his hand. And that smile, so faint you could barely see it – that was mine. Even the eyes, those false mirrors, they were mine too.

'Hi, Anton,' said Olga. 'Good evening, Egor.'

She wasn't surprised to see the kid there. She seemed very calm altogether.

'Hello,' said Egor, looking first at her, then at me. 'Is Anton in your body now?'

'That's right.'

'How do you know me?'

'I saw you when I was in a different kind of body. Excuse us now, Anton's got serious problems and we've got to deal with them.'

'Should I go then?' Egor seemed to have forgotten that was what he'd been just about to do.

'Yes. And don't get angry, things are going to get hot around here any moment, very hot.'

The kid looked at me.

'I've got all of the Day Watch on my trail,' I explained. 'All the Dark Ones in Moscow.'

'Why?'

'It's a long story. You'd better get off back home.'

It sounded rude. Egor frowned and nodded. He glanced in the direction of the platform, where a train was just pulling in.

'But they'll protect you, won't they?' He was still finding it hard to grasp which of us was in which body. 'Your Watch will?'

'They'll try,' Olga replied gently. 'But now go, please. We haven't got much time, and it's disappearing fast.'

'Goodbye,' said Egor, turning and running towards the train. His third step took him out of the circle of distraction and he was almost knocked off his feet.

'If the boy had stayed, I might have believed he was going to join our side,' Olga said as she watched him go. 'I'd really like to check the probability lines to see why you met him in the metro.'

'By chance.'

'Nothing happens by chance. Ah, Anton, I used to be able to read reality lines like an open book, no problem.'

'I wouldn't mind having decent prevision.'

'Genuine prevision isn't something you can just order from a catalogue. Now, back to business. You want to give my body back?'

'Yes, right here.'

'As you wish.' Olga stretched out her arms – my arms – and took hold of my shoulders. It gave me a stupid, ambiguous sort of feeling. She obviously felt the same thing, because she laughed and said: 'Why did you have to get yourself into this mess so soon, Anton? I had such extravagant plans for this evening.'

'Maybe I should be grateful to the Maverick for disrupting your plans.'

Olga stopped smiling and concentrated.

'All right. Let's get on with it.'

We stood with our backs touching and held our arms out in the form of a cross. I took hold of Olga's fingers, which were also mine.

'Give back what is mine,' said Olga.

'Give back what is mine,' I repeated.

'Gesar, we return your gift!'

I started when I realised she'd spoken the boss's real name. And what a name!

'Gesar, we return your gift!' Olga repeated sternly.

'Gesar, we return your gift!'

Olga switched into some ancient language, intoning the words gently, speaking as if it was her mother tongue. It hurt to feel how hard she had to strain to perform a piece of magic that really shouldn't have been difficult with second-grade powers.

Changing bodies in reverse is like releasing a spring. Our minds had only been maintained in each other's bodies by the energy that Boris Ignatievich Gesar had transferred to us. All we had to do was relinquish that energy and we would resume our previous forms. If either of us had been a first-grade magician, we needn't even have been in physical contact, it could all have been done at a distance.

Olga's voice soared as she pronounced the final formula of renunciation.

For an instant nothing happened. Then I was racked by cramps and shooting pains, everything blurred and went grey in front of my eyes, as if I was sinking into the Twilight. For a moment I could see the whole station – the dusty stained-glass windows, the dirty floor, the slow movements of the people, the rainbows of their auras, two bodies thrashing about as if they'd been crucified on each other.

Then I was pressed and forced and squeezed into the shell of my body.

I gasped as I fell to the floor, putting my hands out just at the last moment. My muscles were twitching, my ears were ringing. The reversal had been far more uncomfortable, maybe because it wasn't performed by the boss.

'Are you okay?' Olga asked feebly. 'Anton, we've got about a quarter of an hour. Tell me everything.'

'What exactly?'

'What you've figured out. Come on. You didn't just want to get back into your own body, you've worked out some kind of plan.'

I nodded, then straightened up, dusted off my palms and brushed at my knees to clean off my jeans. The strap holding my holster was too tight under my arm, I had to loosen it. There weren't many people in the metro now, the flood tide had receded. But that meant those who were left weren't so busy manoeuvring through the crowd, and they had time to think: their auras flared up in bright rainbow colours and I caught the echoes of their owners' feelings.

They'd really limited Olga's powers. In her body it had cost me a lot of effort to observe the inner world of human feelings. But then, that was only a simple thing. Not even anything to feel proud of.

'It's not me the Day Watch want, Olga. They don't want me at all. I'm an ordinary, average magician.'

She nodded.

'But I'm the one they're hunting. There's no doubt about that. So if I'm not the quarry, I must be the bait. The same way Egor was the bait when Sveta was the quarry.'

'Have you only just realised that?' Olga shook her head. 'Of course. You're the bait.'

'For Svetlana?'

The sorceress nodded.

'I only understood it today,' I admitted. 'Just an hour ago, when Sveta wanted to stand up to the Day Watch, she shifted up to fifth-grade powers. In an instant. If a fight had broken out, she would have been killed. We can be controlled too, Olya. Human beings can be turned in different directions, towards Good or Evil, the Dark Ones can be manipulated through their meanness, their vanity, their thirst for power and fame. And we can be manipulated through love. There we're as defenceless as children.'

'Yes.'

'Is the boss in the picture?' I asked. 'Olya?'

'Yes.'

She was finding it hard to get the words out. I couldn't believe it. Light Magicians who had lived for hundreds of years didn't feel shame. They'd saved the world so often, they had all the ethical dodges off pat. Great Sorceresses didn't feel ashamed, not even former Great Sorceresses. They'd been betrayed too often themselves.

I laughed.

'Olya, did you realise straight away? As soon as the Dark Ones lodged their protest? That they were hunting me, but only in order to push Svetlana beyond her self-control?'

'Yes.'

'Yes, yes, yes. And you still didn't warn me, or her?'

'Svetlana needs to mature quickly, to skip a few steps on the way.' A bright flame flared in Olga's eyes. 'Anton, you're my friend. I'll tell you the truth, so you can understand. We don't have enough time right now to nurture a Great Sorceress properly. But we need her, we need her more than you can even imagine. She already has enough power. She'll get tougher and learn how to draw on that power and direct it and, what's even more important, she'll learn how to hold it in check.'

'And if I die, that will only strengthen her will and her hatred of the Dark.'

'Yes. But I'm sure you're not going to die. The Watch is hunting the Maverick, everybody's been drafted in. We'll turn him over to the Dark Ones and the charges against you will be dropped.'

'But a certain Light Magician who wasn't initiated at the right time will die. Miserable and alone, like an animal brought to bay, convinced he's the only one fighting against the Dark.'

'Yes.'

'You agree with everything I say today,' I said calmly. 'Olga, don't you think what you're doing might just be despicable?'

'No.' There wasn't a trace of doubt. That meant the stakes must be really high.

'How long do I have to hold out, Light One?'

She shuddered.

There was a time, a long time ago, when that was a form of address Watch members often used – 'Light One'. Why had the words lost their old meaning, why did they sound as absurd now as the word 'gentlemen' used to address the dirty street bums at the beer kiosks?

'Until morning at least.'

'The night's not our time any longer. Today all the Dark Ones will be out on the streets of Moscow. And they'll be acting within their rights.'

'Only until we locate the Maverick. Hang on in there.'

'Olga.' I took a step towards her and touched her cheek, for a moment forgetting the difference in our ages – what were a few hundred years, compared with eternal night? – and the difference in our powers and our knowledge. 'Olga, do you really believe that I'll still be alive in the morning?'

The sorceress didn't answer.

I nodded. There was nothing more to say.

> I wonder how it would be
> To lose myself in the dawn.
> To knock at the transparent doors
> And know no one will answer.

I pressed the button and set the walkman to play in random mode. Not because the song didn't suit my mood, in fact exactly the opposite.

I love the metro at night, but I don't know why. There's nothing to look at except the same old dreary adverts and the same old tired human auras. The rumble of the engine, the gusts of air coming in through the half-open windows, the jolting over the rails. The numb wait for your own station.

But I love it anyway.

I shuddered, got up and walked to the door, even though I'd been planning to go to the end of the line.

This station was Rizhskaya. The next was Alexeevskaya.

> Again that intense silence,
> Always about the same thing,
> Today the season opens
> At the lepers' club.

That was okay.

I was already on the escalator when I caught the faint sense of power ahead of me. I ran my eyes along the down escalator and saw the Dark One almost immediately.

No, he wasn't Day Watch, he was carrying himself all wrong for that. He was a low-grade magician, grade four or five, probably five: and he was concentrating hard, scanning the people around him. Still really young, not much over twenty, in a crumpled, unbuttoned jacket, with long, fair hair and an attractive face, even though it was all tensed up like that.

So what could have pushed you over the edge into the Dark? What happened before that first time you stepped into the Twilight? An argument with your girlfriend? A quarrel with your parents? Did you flunk your exams in college or get a Fail at school? Did someone tread on your foot on a trolleybus?

And the most terrible thing of all is that your appearance hasn't even changed. Maybe you're even better-looking now. Your friends were amazed to discover what a fun guy you turned out to be, how well everything went when they planned things with you. Your girlfriend discovered all sorts of good qualities in you that she couldn't see before. Your parents were overjoyed to see how serious and intelligent their son had suddenly become. Your professors were delighted with their talented student.

And nobody knows how you make the people around you pay. And just how high the price of your kindness, your jokes and your sympathy is.

I closed my eyes and leaned against the moving handrail. I was tired, I was slightly drunk, I wasn't paying any attention to anything, just listening to the music.

The Dark One's gaze slid over me, moving lower, then quivered and came to a halt.

I hadn't had any time to prepare, to change my appearance or distort my aura. I really hadn't expected the search of the metro would have started already.

A cold, piercing touch, like a gust of icy wind. The young guy was comparing me with the image that must have been distributed to all the Dark Ones in Moscow. He was working clumsily, he'd forgotten about his defences, he didn't notice my mind slipping along the pathway cleared through the Twilight and touching his thoughts.

Joy. Delight. Found. The prey. They'll give me some of the prey's power. They'll appreciate this. They'll promote me. Fame. Getting my own back. They didn't appreciate me before. Now they'll understand. They'll pay.

I'd been imagining that at least somewhere in some corner of his mind there would be some other thoughts. About me being an enemy. About me killing others like him.

But no. There was nothing. He wasn't thinking of anything but himself.

I withdrew my feelers before the young magician withdrew his own clumsy ones. All right. He didn't possess any great powers, he wouldn't be able to communicate with the Day Watch from inside the metro. And he wouldn't even want to. He thought of me as a cornered animal, and not even a dangerous one – a rabbit, not a wolf.

Bring it on, my friend.

I walked out of the metro, slipped round beside the entrance and summoned my shadow. The hazy silhouette shimmered above the ground and I stepped into it.

The Twilight.

People walking by became a transparent haze, cars started to crawl like tortoises, the streetlamps dimmed, their light turned gloomy and oppressive. It was quiet, all sounds reduced to a barely audible rumble.

I'd made my move a little too early, it would be a while before the magician could get back up after me . . . But I could feel my own power, I was pumped full of it. That must have been Olga's work. While she was in my body she'd regained her former powers and filled it with energy, without using up any of it. She would never even have thought of taking any, no matter how great the temptation might be.

'You'll understand for yourself where the boundary lies' – that's what I'd told Svetlana. Olga had known, far better than me, where the boundary lay for a long, long time.

I walked along the wall, glancing through the concrete at the inclined shaft and the belts of the escalators. There was a dark spot climbing upwards rapidly: the magician was in a hurry, running up the steps, but he was still in the human world. Saving his powers. Bring it on, bring it on.

I stopped dead.

There was a small, swirling cloud skimming toward me just above the ground, a patch of mist that had assumed the form of a human figure.

An Other. A former Other.

Maybe it had been one of us. And maybe not. The Dark Ones had to go somewhere when they died. But now it was just a hazy little cloud, an eternal wanderer in the Twilight.

'Peace be with you, fallen one,' I said. 'Whoever you may have been.'

The quivering silhouette halted in front of me. A tongue of mist freed itself from its body and extended towards me.

What did it want? The number of times inhabitants of the Twilight had tried to communicate with the living could be counted on the fingers of one hand.

The hand – if it could be called a hand – was trembling. White threads of mist came away from it, dissolving in the Twilight, scattering on to the ground.

'I'm very short of time,' I said. 'Fallen one, no matter who you were in life, Dark or Light, peace be with you. What do you want from me?'

A gust of wind seemed to ripple through the swirls of mist. The phantom turned and the outstretched hand – I no longer had any doubt that it was a hand – pointed through the Twilight towards the north-east. I turned in its direction. It was pointing to a needle-slim silhouette glimmering in the sky.

'Yes, the tower, I understand! But what does it mean?'

The mist started to blur and dissolve and a moment later the Twilight around me was as empty as usual.

I started to shiver. The dead Other had tried to communicate with me. Was it a friend or an enemy? Had it been advising me or warning me?

There was no way to tell.

I took another look through the walls of the station building – the Dark Magician had almost reached the top of the escalator, but he was still on it. So I had a moment to try to figure out what the phantom had been trying to say. I hadn't been intending to go to the Ostankino Television Tower, I had a different route in mind, a somewhat risky but surprising plan. So it didn't make any sense to warn me not to go to the tower.

Maybe I'd been given directions. But who by? Friend or foe, that was the important question. I couldn't expect all differences to be wiped out beyond the borders of life. Our dead would not abandon us in battle.

I would have to decide for myself. Only not right now.

I ran towards the entrance of the metro, taking my pistol out of my shoulder holster as I ran.

Just in time: the Dark Magician came out of the doors and immediately dived into the Twilight. He made it look easy, but I saw how he managed it. The auras of people near him flared up, scattering dark sparks in all directions.

If I'd been in the human world, I'd have seen people's faces distorted by a sudden pain in their hearts, or emotional distress – which is far more painful.

The Dark Magician gazed around, looking for my trail. He knew how to extract power from people around him, but his general technique wasn't exactly great.

'Take it easy,' I said, pressing the barrel of the pistol against the magician's spine. 'Take it easy. You've already found me. And I bet you're really pleased.'

I held his wrist tight with my other hand so that he couldn't make any passes. All these jumped-up young magicians use a standard set of spells, the simplest and most powerful. And they require the precise co-ordination of both hands.

The magician's palm was suddenly damp.

'You, you . . .' He still couldn't believe what had happened. 'You're Anton! You're outside the law!'

'Maybe so. But what good will that do you now?'

He turned his head. In the Twilight his face was distorted, it had lost that attractive, genial look. He hadn't reached the stage of the complete Twilight makeover, like Zabulon, but even so, his face was no longer human. The jaw hung down too low, the mouth was wide, like a frog's, the eyes were close-set and dull.

'You're a real ugly specimen, my friend,' I said forcing the barrel into his back again. 'This is a pistol. It's loaded with silver bullets, although that's not strictly necessary. It'll work just as well in the Twilight world as in the human one – more slowly, but that won't save you. You'll be able to feel the bullet ripping through the skin and parting the fibres of your muscles, smashing the bone, tearing the nerves apart.'

'You won't do that!'

'Why?'

'Because then there'd be no way you could get out of this!'

'Is that so? But right now there's still some kind of chance, is there? You know, the urge to squeeze this trigger is getting stronger all the time. Let's go, scumbag.'

I helped the magician along with a few kicks as I led him into the narrow passage between two kiosks. The thick growth of blue moss covering their walls started twitching. The Twilight flora was keen to taste our emotions – my fury and his fear – but the mindless plants also had a strong instinct for self-preservation.

The Dark Magician had plenty of that, too.

'Listen, what do you want from me?' he shouted. 'They gave us a briefing and told us to look for you! I was only following orders! I honour the Treaty, watchman!'

'I'm not a watchman any longer!' I said, shoving him against the wall, into the tender embrace of the moss. Let it suck out a little bit of his fear, or we wouldn't be able to have a proper talk. 'Who's leading the hunt?'

'The Day Watch.'

'More specifically?'

'The boss, I don't know his name.'

That was almost certainly true. But *I* knew the name.

'Were you sent to this particular station?'

He hesitated.

'Answer,' I said, aiming the barrel at the magician's stomach.

'Yes.'

'Alone?'

'Yes.'

'That's a lie. But it's not important. What were you ordered to do once you found me?'

'Observe.'

'Another lie. But an important one this time. Think again and try a different answer.'

The magician didn't say anything. The blue moss must have done too good a job.

I squeezed the trigger and the bullet sang sweetly as it travelled across the metre of space between us. The magician had enough time to see it – his eyes opened wide in terror – which made them look a bit more human – and he jerked away, but too late.

'That's just a flesh wound to be going on with,' I said. 'Not fatal.'

He writhed on the ground, pressing his hand against the ragged hole in his stomach. In the Twilight his blood was almost transparent, but maybe that was an optical illusion. Or maybe it was a peculiarity of this particular magician.

'Answer the question!'

I swept my free hand through the air and set the blue moss around us on fire. Enough already, now we were going to work with fear, pain, despair. Enough mercy and compassion, enough polite conversation.

This was the Dark, after all.

'We were ordered to report in and if possible to kill you.'

'Not detain me? Just kill me?'

'Yes.'

'I'll accept that answer. Your means of communication?'

'By phone, that's all.'

'Let me have it.'

'It's in my pocket.'

'Throw it.'

He reached clumsily into his pocket, found the phone and threw it as best he could – the wound wasn't deadly, and the magician's resistance was still high, but the pain he was going through was hellish.

Just the kind he deserved to suffer.

'What's the number?' I asked, catching the phone.

'It's on the emergency call key.'

I glanced at the screen.

From the initial numbers, the phone could have been absolutely anywhere. It was another mobile.

'Is that the field headquarters? Where is it?'

'I don't . . .' He paused, glancing at the pistol.

'Remember,' I encouraged him.

'They told me they'd be here in five minutes.'

All right!

I took a look back over my shoulder, at the needle blazing brightly in the sky. It fitted perfectly.

The magician moved.

No, I hadn't deliberately provoked him by looking away. But when he took a wand out of his pocket – a short, crude device he obviously hadn't made himself, some cheap trash he'd bought – I felt relieved.

'Well?' I asked when he froze, not daring to raise his weapon. 'Go for it!'

The young magician didn't move, he didn't say a word.

He knew if he tried to attack, I'd empty the entire clip into him. And that *would* be fatal. But they were probably taught how to behave in a conflict with Light Ones. So he also knew it would be hard for me to kill someone who was unarmed and defenceless.

'Stand up to me,' I said. 'Fight! You son of a bitch, it never bothered you to destroy people's lives or attack defenceless people, did it? Well? Bring it on!'

The magician licked his lips – his tongue was long and slightly forked. I suddenly realised what Twilight form he would eventually assume, and I felt sick.

'I throw myself on your mercy, watchman. I demand compassion and justice.'

'If I leave now, you'll be able to contact your base,' I said. 'Or you'll extract enough strength from people walking by to fix yourself up and get to a phone. Isn't that right? We both know it is.'

The Dark One smiled and repeated:

'I demand compassion and justice, watchman!'

I tossed the pistol from one hand to the other, looking into that smirking face. They were always ready to demand. But never to give.

'I've always had problems understanding our side's double standard of morality,' I said. 'It's a difficult thing to come to terms with. It only comes with time, and that's something I haven't got much of. Coming up with all those excuses for when you can't protect everybody. When you know that every day someone in a special department signs licences for people to be handed over to the Dark Side. It's tough, you know.'

The smile disappeared from his face. He repeated the same words, like an incantation.

'I demand compassion and justice, watchman.'

'I'm not in the Watch any more,' I said.

The pistol jerked and the breech clattered slowly, lazily spitting out the cartridge cases. The bullets slid through the air like a small swarm of angry wasps.

He only screamed once, then two bullets shattered his skull. When the pistol clicked and fell silent, I reloaded the clip slowly, mechanically.

The body on the ground in front of me was mangled and mutilated. It had already begun to emerge from the Twilight and the Twilight mask on the young face was dissolving.

I waved my hand through the air, grasping and clutching at an imperceptible something flowing through space. The outside layer of it. A copy of the Dark Magician's human appearance.

Tomorrow they'd find him. The wonderful young man every-body loved. Brutally murdered. How much Evil had I just brought into the world? How many tears, how much bitterness and blind hate? Where did the chain of future events lead?

And how much Evil had I killed? How many people would live longer and better lives? How many tears would never be spilled, how much malice would never be hoarded? How much hate would never even be born?

Maybe I'd stepped across the barrier that should never be crossed.

And maybe I'd understood where the next boundary was, the one that had to be crossed.

I put the pistol back in its holster and left the Twilight.

The sharp needle of the Ostankino Television Tower was still boring into the sky.

'Now let's try playing without any rules,' I said. 'Without any at all.'

I managed to stop a car immediately, without even needing to give the driver an attack of altruism. Maybe that was because now I was wearing such a charming face, the face of the dead Dark Magician.

'Get me to the TV Tower,' I said as I climbed into the battered model-six Lada. 'As fast as you can, before they close the doors.'

'Going out for a bit of fun?' the driver asked with a smile. He was a rather dour-looking man in glasses.

'You bet,' I answered. 'You bet.'

CHAPTER 5

THEY WERE still letting people in. I bought a ticket, paying the extra charge for the right to visit the restaurant, and set off across the green lawn round the tower. The last fifty metres of the path were covered by a feeble sort of canopy. I wondered why they'd put it there. Maybe the old building sometimes shed chunks of concrete.

The canopy ended at a booth where they checked ID. I showed mine and walked through the horseshoe frame of the metal detector – which wasn't working anyway. There were no more checks, that was all the protection this strategic target had.

I was beginning to have serious doubts. I had to admit it was a strange idea to come here. I couldn't sense any concentration of Dark Ones nearby. If they really were here, then they were very well shielded, which meant I'd have to deal with second- and third-grade magicians. And that would be suicide, pure and simple.

The headquarters. The field headquarters of the Day Watch, set up to co-ordinate the hunt for me. Where could the inexperienced Dark Magician have been expected to report his sighting of the quarry?

But I was walking straight into a set-up where there must be at least ten Dark Ones, including experienced guards. I was sticking my own head in the noose, and that was plain stupidity, not heroism – if I still had even the slightest chance of surviving. And I was very much hoping I did.

Seen from down below, under the concrete petals of its supports, the TV Tower was far more impressive than it was from a distance. But it was a certainty that most Muscovites had never been up to the observation platform and just thought of the tower as a natural part of the skyline, a utilitarian and symbolic object, rather than a place of recreation. The wind felt as strong as if I was standing in the aerodynamic pipe of some complex structure, and right at the very limit of my hearing I could just catch the low hum that was the voice of the tower.

I stood there for a moment, looking upwards at the mesh-covered openings, the shell-shaped hollows corroded into the concrete, the incredibly graceful, flexible silhouette. The tower really is flexible: rings of concrete strung on taut cables. Its strength is its flexibility.

I went in through the glass doors.

Strange. I'd have expected to find plenty of people wanting to view Moscow by night from a height of three hundred and thirty-seven metres. I was wrong. I even rode up in the lift all on my own, or rather, with a woman from the tower's staff.

'I thought there would be lots of people here,' I said, giving her a friendly smile. 'Is it always like this in the evening?'

'No, usually it's busy,' the woman said. She didn't sound very surprised, but I still caught a faint puzzled note in her voice. She touched a button and the double doors slid together. My ears instantly popped and my feet were pressed down hard against the floor as the lift went hurtling upwards – fast, but incredibly smoothly. 'Everyone just disappeared about two hours ago.'

Two hours.

Soon after my escape from the restaurant.

If that was when they set up their field headquarters, it wasn't surprising that hundreds of people who'd been planning to take a ride up to the restaurant in the sky on this warm, clear spring evening had suddenly changed their plans. Humans might not be able to see what was going on, but they could sense it.

And even the ones who had nothing to do with this whole business were smart enough not to go anywhere near the Dark Ones.

Of course, I had the young Dark Magician's appearance to protect me. But I couldn't be sure that kind of disguise would be enough. The security guard would check my appearance against the list implanted in his memory, everything would match up, and he would sense the presence of power.

But would he dig any deeper than that? Would he check the different kinds of power, check if I was Dark or Light, what grade I was?

It was fifty-fifty. He was supposed to do all that. But security guards everywhere always skip that kind of thing. Unless they just happen to be dying of boredom or they're new to the job and still keen.

But a fifty-fifty chance was pretty good, compared to my chances of hiding from the Day Watch on the streets.

The lift stopped. I hadn't even had time to think everything through properly, it had only taken about twenty seconds to get up there.

'Here we are,' the woman said, almost cheerfully. It looked pretty much like I was the Ostankino Tower's last visitor of the day.

I stepped out on to the observation platform.

This place was usually full of people. You could always tell straight away who'd just arrived and who'd already been there a while. From the uncertain way the new arrivals moved about, and how ludicrously careful they were when they approached the panoramic window, and the way they walked round the reinforced glass windows set in the floor and tested them timidly with their feet.

But this time it looked to me as if there were no more than twenty visitors. There were no children at all – I could just picture to myself the hysterics as they approached the tower, the parents' anger and confusion. Children are more sensitive to the Dark Ones.

Even the people who were on the platform seemed confused and depressed. They weren't admiring the view of the city spread out below them, with it lights glowing brightly – Moscow in its usual festive mood. Maybe it was a feast in a time of plague, but it was a beautiful feast. Right now, though, no one was enjoying it. Everything was dominated by the atmosphere of the Dark. Even I couldn't see it, but I could feel it choking me like carbon monoxide, no taste, no colour and no smell.

I looked down at my feet, pulled up my shadow and stepped into it. The guard was standing near me, just two steps away, on one of the glass windows set in the floor. He looked at me in a friendly sort of way, but slightly surprised. He obviously wasn't too comfortable hanging around in the Twilight, and I realised the other side hadn't assigned its best men to guard the field headquarters. He was young and well built, wearing a plain grey suit and a white shirt with a subdued tie – more like a bank clerk than a servant of the Dark.

'Ciao, Anton,' the magician said.

That took my breath away for a moment.

Had I really been that stupid? So ridiculously naïve?

They were waiting for me, they'd lured me here, tossed another sacrificed pawn on to the scales, and even – God only knew how – drafted in someone who'd departed into the Twilight long, long ago.

'What are you doing here?'

My heart thumped and started beating regularly again. It was all very simple after all.

The dead Dark Magician had been my namesake.

'Just something I spotted. I need some advice.'

The guard frowned darkly. Not the right turn of phrase, probably. But he still didn't catch on.

'Spit it out, Anton. Or I won't let you through, you know that.'

'You've got to let me through,' I blurted out at random. In our Watch anyone who knew the location of a field headquarters could enter it.

'Oh yeah, who says?' He was still smiling, but his left hand was already moving down towards the wand hanging on his belt.

It was charged to full capacity. Made out of a shinbone with intricate carving and a small ruby crystal in the end. Even if I dodged or shielded myself, a discharge of power like that would bring every Other in the area running.

I raised my shadow again and entered the second level of the Twilight.

Cold.

Swirling mist, or rather, clouds. Damp, heavy clouds rushing along high above the ground. There was no Ostankino Tower here, this world had shed its final resemblance to the human one. I took a step forward through the damp, along an invisible path through the droplets of water. The movement of time had slowed – I was actually falling, but so slowly that it didn't matter yet. High above me the curtain of cloud was pierced by the light of three moons – white, yellow and blood-red. A bolt of lightning appeared ahead of me and grew, sprouting branches that crept slowly through the clouds, burning out a jagged channel.

I moved close to the vague shadow that was reaching for its belt with such painful slowness. I grabbed the arm. It was heavy, unyielding, as cold as ice. I couldn't stop it. I'd have to burst back out into the first level of the Twilight and take him on face to face. At least I'd have a chance.

Light and Dark, I'm no field operative! I never wanted to end up in the front line! Give me the work I enjoy, the work I'm good at!

But the Light and the Dark didn't answer. They never do when you call on them. There was only that quiet mocking voice that speaks sometimes in every heart, whispering: 'Who ever promised you an easy life?'

I looked down at my feet. They were already about ten centimetres below the Dark Magician's. I was falling, there was nothing to support me in this reality, there were no TV towers or anything of the sort here – no cliffs that shape or trees that tall.

How I wished I had clean hands, a passionate heart and a cool head. But somehow these three qualities don't seem to get along too well. The wolf, the goat and the cabbage – what crazy ferryman would think of sticking them all in the same boat?

And when he'd eaten the goat for starters, what wolf wouldn't like to try the ferryman?

'God only knows,' I said. My voice was lost in the clouds. I lowered my hand and grabbed hold of the Dark Magician's shadow – a limp rag, a blur in space. I jerked the shadow upwards, threw it over his body and tugged the Dark One into the second level of the Twilight.

He screamed when the world suddenly became unrecognisable. He'd probably never been any lower than the first level before. The energy required for his first trip came from me, but all the sensations were quite new to him.

I braced myself on the Dark One's shoulders and pushed him

downwards, while I crept upwards, pressing my feet down hard on his hunched back.

'Great Magicians climb their way up over other people's backs.'

'You bastard, Anton! You bastard!'

The Dark Magician still hadn't realised who I was. He didn't realise it until the moment he turned over on to his back, still providing support for my feet, and saw my face. Here, in the second level of the Twilight, my crude disguise didn't work, of course. His eyes opened wide, he gave a short gasp and howled, clutching at my leg.

But he still didn't understand what I was doing and why. I kicked him over and over again, trampling his fingers and his face with my heels. It wouldn't really hurt an Other, but I wasn't trying to do him any physical damage. I wanted him lower, I wanted him to fall, move downwards on all levels of reality, through the human world and the Twilight, through the shifting fabric of space. I didn't have the time or the skill to fight a full-scale duel with him according to all the laws of the Watches, according to all the rules that had been invented for young Light Ones who still retained their faith in Good and Evil, the absolute truth of dogma and the inevitability of retribution.

When I decided I'd trampled the Dark Magician down low enough, I pushed off from his spreadeagled body, leapt up into the cold, damp mist and jerked myself out of the Twilight.

Straight out into the human world. Straight on to the observation platform.

I appeared squatting on my haunches on a slab of glass, soaking wet from head to foot, choking in an effort to suppress a sudden cough. The rain of that other world smelled of ammonia and ashes.

A faint gasp ran round the room and people staggered back, trying to get away from me.

'It's all right,' I croaked. 'Do you hear? It's all right.'

Their eyes told me they didn't agree. A man in uniform by the wall, a security guard, one of the TV Tower's faithful retainers, stared at me stony-faced and reached for his pistol holster.

'It's for your own good,' I said, choking in a new fit of coughing. 'Do you understand?'

I let my power break free and touch the people's minds. Their faces started looking more relaxed and calm. They slowly turned away and pressed their faces against the windows. The security guard froze with his hand resting on his unbuttoned holster.

Only then did I look down at my feet. And I too froze in shock.

The Dark Magician was there, under the glass. He was screaming. His eyes had turned into round black patches, forced wide open by his pain and terror. The fingertips of one hand were imbedded in the glass and he was hanging by them, with his body swaying like a pendulum in the gusts of wind. The sleeve of his white shirt was soaked in blood. The wand was still there on the magician's belt, but he'd forgotten about it. I was the only thing that existed for him right now, on the other side of that triple-reinforced glass, inside the dry, warm, bright shell of the observation platform, beyond Good and Evil. A Light Magician, sitting above him and gazing into those eyes crazy with pain and terror.

'Well, did you think we always fight fair?' I asked. Somehow I thought he might be able to hear me, even through the thick glass and the roar of the wind. I stood up and stamped my heel on the glass. Once, twice, three times – it didn't matter that the blow wouldn't reach the fingers fused into the glass.

The Dark Magician jerked, trying to tug his hand out of the way of that crushing heel – a spontaneous, instinctive, irrational reaction.

The flesh gave way.

For a moment the glass was covered with a red film of blood, but then the wind swept it away. And all I could see was the vague outline of the Dark Magician's body, getting smaller and smaller, tumbling over and over in the tower's turbulent slipstream. He was being carried in the direction of The Three Little Pigs, a fashionable establishment at the foot of the tower.

The clock ticking away in my mind gave a loud click and instantly halved the time I had left.

I stepped off the glass and walked round the platform in a circle. I wasn't looking at the people, I was gazing into the Twilight. No, there weren't any more guards here. Now I had to find out where their headquarters were. Up on top in the service area, among all the equipment? I didn't think so. Probably somewhere more comfortable.

There was another security guard, a human, standing at the top of the stairs leading down into the restaurant. One glance was enough for me to see that he'd been influenced already, and quite recently. It was a good thing they'd only influenced him superficially.

And it was a very good thing they'd decided to influence him at all. That was a trick that cut both ways.

The security guard opened his mouth, getting ready to shout.

'Quiet! Come this way!' I ordered.

The security guard followed me without saying a word.

We went into the gents' – one of the tower's free attractions, the highest urinal and toilet bowls in Moscow. Please feel free to make your mark among the clouds. I waved my hand through the air. A spotty-faced youth came scurrying out of one cubicle, zipping up his trousers, another man at the urinal grunted, broke off and went wandering out with a glassy look in his eyes.

'Take your clothes off,' I ordered the security guard and starting pulling off my wet sweater.

★   ★   ★

The guard's holster was half open, and his Desert Eagle was far older than my Makarov, but that didn't bother me. The important thing was that the uniform was almost a perfect fit.

'If you hear shooting,' I told the guard, 'go down and do your duty. Do you understand?'

He nodded.

'I turn you towards the Light,' I said, intoning the words of the enlistment formula. 'Renounce the Dark, defend the Light. I give you the vision to distinguish Good from Evil. I give you the faith to follow the Light. I give you the courage to fight against the Dark.'

I used to think I'd never get a chance to use my right to enlist volunteers. How could there be free choice in genuine Dark? How could I involve anybody in our games when the Watches themselves were established to counterattack that practice?

But now I was acting without hesitation, exploiting the loophole that the Dark Ones had left me by getting the security man to guard their headquarters, the way some people keep a small dog in their apartment: it can't bite, but it can yap. What they'd done gave me the right to sway the security man in the opposite direction and get him to follow me. After all, he wasn't either good or bad, he was a perfectly ordinary man with a wife he loved in moderation, elderly parents whom he remembered to support, a young daughter and a son from his first marriage who was almost grown up, a weak faith in God, a tangled set of moral principles and a few standard dreams – an ordinary, decent man.

A piece of cannon fodder in the war between the armies of Light and Dark.

'The Light be with you,' I said. The pathetic little man nodded and his face lit up. There was adoration in his eyes. A few hours earlier he'd gazed in exactly the same way at the Dark Magician who'd given him a casual command and shown him my photo.

A moment later the security guard was standing at the top of the stairs in my stinking clothes, and I was walking down the stairs trying to figure out what I was going to do if Zabulon was at the headquarters. Or any other magician of his level, come to that.

In that case my powers wouldn't be enough to maintain my disguise for even a second.

The Bronze Hall. I stepped through the doors and looked at the absurd ring-shaped 'restaurant car'. The ring was slowly rotating, along with the tables standing in it.

I'd been sure the Dark Ones would have set up their headquarters in either the Gold Hall or the Silver Hall. And I was quite surprised by the scene in front of me.

The waiters were drifting from table to table like lazy fish, handing out bottles of spirits, which were supposedly forbidden up here. On two tables straight ahead of me computer terminals had been set up, connected to two mobile phones. They hadn't bothered to run a cable to any of the tower's countless service outlets, which meant the headquarters had only been set up to function for a short while. Three young guys with short hair were working away intently, with their fingers leaping around all over the keyboards while the lines of type scrolled up the monitor screens and their cigarettes smoked away in the ashtrays. I'd never seen Dark programmers before, and these were only simple operators, of course. But they didn't look any different from one of our magicians sitting at a laptop plugged into the network at headquarters. Maybe they even looked a bit more respectable than some of ours.

'Sokolniki's completely covered,' one of them said. His voice wasn't loud, but it rumbled right round the ring of the restaurant, making the waiters shudder and falter in their stride.

'The Tagansko–Krasnopresnenskaya line's under surveillance,' said another. The programmers glanced at each other and laughed.

They probably had a little competition going to see who could report fastest on his sectors.

Go right ahead, keep looking!

I set off round the restaurant, making for the bar. Take no notice of me. I'm a harmless security man who just happened to be given the role of a lowly guard. And now the security man's decided he'd like a beer. Has he completely lost all sense of responsibility? Or has he decided to check that his new bosses are safe?

The young woman behind the bar was wiping glasses in a melancholy sort of way. When I reached her, she started pouring me a beer without saying a word. Her eyes were dark and empty, she'd been turned into a puppet and I had to struggle to suppress an outburst of fury. I couldn't allow it. I had no right to feelings. I was a robot too. Puppets didn't have feelings.

And then I saw the girl sitting on the tall rotating stool opposite the bar, and my heart sank again.

Why hadn't I thought of that earlier?

Every field headquarters has to be declared, and an observer sent over from the other side. It's part of the Treaty, one of the rules of the game, in the interest, supposedly, of both sides. If we had a field headquarters, then one of the Dark Ones was sitting in it right now.

The Light One here was Tiger Cub.

At first her glance slid over me with no sign of curiosity, and I was almost certain everything would be okay.

Then her eyes came back to me.

She'd already seen the security man whose appearance I'd assumed. And there was something about me that didn't match the features stored in her memory, something that bothered her. In an instant she was looking at me through the Twilight.

I stood still, without trying to shield myself.

Tiger Cub looked away and turned towards the magician sitting opposite her. I estimated his age at about a hundred and his powers as at least grade three. He wasn't low-level, just complacent.

'The actions you're taking are still a provocation,' she said to him evenly. 'The Night Watch is certain that the Maverick isn't Anton.'

'Who, then?'

'An untrained Light Magician unknown to us. A Light Magician controlled by the Dark Ones.'

'But what for?' the magician asked, genuinely surprised. 'Explain it to me. Why would we let our own people be killed, even those who are less valuable?'

'Yes, "less valuable" is the key phrase,' Tiger Cub replied in a melancholy tone.

'Maybe, just maybe, if we had a chance to eliminate the leader of the Light Ones in Moscow but, as usual, he's above all suspicion. And sacrifice twenty of our own just for one ordinary, average Light One? No way. Or do you think we're idiots?'

'No, I think you're very clever. Probably much cleverer than me.' Tiger Cub smiled her dangerous smile. 'But I'm only a field operative. Conclusions will be drawn by someone else, and they will be drawn, you can be sure!'

'We're not demanding immediate execution!' the Dark One said with a smile. 'Even now we don't exclude the possibility of error. A tribunal, a professional, impartial investigation, justice – that's all we want.'

'But isn't it strange that your leader couldn't hit Anton with Shahab's Lash?' said Tiger Cub, tilting a glass of beer with one finger. 'It's extraordinary. His favourite weapon, one he's been a master of for hundreds of years. Almost as if the Day Watch wasn't really interested in seeing Anton caught.'

'My dear girl,' said the Dark Magician, leaning across the table, 'you're being inconsistent. You can't accuse us of pursuing an innocent, law-abiding Light One and at the same time claim we're not trying to catch him!'

'Why not?'

'Such petty sadism.' The magician laughed. 'I'm genuinely enjoying this conversation. Do you really think we're a gang of crazy, bloodthirsty psychopaths?'

'No, we think you're a gang of cunning creeps.'

'Let's try comparing our methods.' I could see the Dark One was mounting hobby horse. 'Let's compare the losses the actions of the two Watches have inflicted on ordinary people, our food base.'

'It's only for you that humans are food.'

'What about you? Or are Light Ones born to Light Ones now and not picked out of the crowd?'

'For us, humans are our roots. Our roots.'

'Okay, call them roots. What's the point of arguing over words? But in that case they're our roots too. And it's no secret that the amount of sap they feed us is increasing.'

'It's no secret that our numbers aren't declining either.'

'Of course. Troubled times, all that stress and tension – people are living on the edge and it's easy to fall off. At least we're able to agree on that!'

'Yes,' Tiger Cub agreed. She didn't look in my direction again and the conversation wandered off. I realised that Tiger Cub had told me everything she needed to.

Or everything she felt it was appropriate to tell me.

I picked up the mug of beer standing in front of me and drank it in several deep, measured swallows. I really had been thirsty.

So the hunt was just a front?

Yes, and I'd realised that a long time ago. But it was important for me to know that our side understood that too.

And the Maverick hadn't been caught?

Naturally. Otherwise they would already have contacted me.

Either by phone or mentally, that was no problem for the boss. The killer would have been handed over to the tribunal, Svetlana would no longer be torn between the desire to help and the need to avoid getting drawn into a fight, and I could have laughed in Zabulon's face.

But how was it possible to find a single man in an immense city like this, when his powers manifested themselves spontaneously? Just flared up and then faded away again. Lying dormant between one killing and the next, one pointless victory over Evil and the next. And if he really was known to the Dark Ones, it was a secret kept by the very top bosses.

Not by the Dark Ones who were wasting their time up here.

I looked around in disgust.

This wasn't serious!

The guard I'd killed so easily. The third-grade magician debating so keenly with our observer and not bothering to keep his eyes open. Those young guys at the terminals, shouting out:

'Tsvetnoi Boulevard has been checked!'

'Polezhaevskaya Street is under surveillance!'

Yes, this was a field headquarters. And it was about as ludicrously unprofessional as the inexperienced Dark Ones hunting for me right across the city. Yes, the net had been cast, but no one was concerned about the gaping holes in it. The longer I could keep on dodging the round-up and the more I thrashed about, the more the Dark liked it. At the strategic level, of course. Svetlana wouldn't be able to bear it, she'd lose control. She'd try to help, because she could sense the genuine power developing inside her. None of our people would be able to restrain her – not directly. And she'd be killed.

'Volgograd Avenue.'

I could slit all their throats, or shoot them all right here and now! Every last one of them. They were the Dark's rejects and the failures, the dunces who had no prospects because they had too many shortcomings. It wasn't simply that the Dark Ones didn't feel sorry for them – they were a hindrance, they got in the way. The Day Watch was nothing like the almshouse that we sometimes resembled. The Day Watch got rid of anyone who was surplus to requirements. In fact, it usually got us to do the job, handing them a trump card, the right to respond, to redress the balance.

And the Twilight figure that had directed me to the Ostankino Tower was another product of the Dark. An insurance policy, in case I couldn't guess where I ought to go to fight my battle.

But the real action was being co-ordinated by just one Other.

Zabulon.

He didn't feel the least resentment against me. Of course not. What use would such complex and petty feelings be in a serious game like this?

He'd eaten dozens like me for breakfast, removing them from the board, sacrificing his own pawns to pay for them.

When would he decide that the game was played out and it was time for the endgame?

'Do you have a light?' I asked, putting down my beer mug and picking up a pack of cigarettes lying on the counter. Someone had forgotten them, maybe one of the restaurant's customers, fleeing in a state of panic, maybe one of the Dark Ones.

Tiger Cub's eyes lit up and she tensed her muscles. I realised the sorceress could start her battle transformation at any moment. She must have assessed the enemy's strength too. She knew we had a serious chance of success.

But there was no need.

The old third-grade Dark Magician casually held out his Ronson lighter. It gave a tuneful little click and shot out a tongue of flame, and he carried on talking.

'There's only one reason why you constantly accuse the Dark of playing a double game and organising deliberate provocations – in order to disguise the fact that you're not fit to survive. Your failure to understand the world and its laws. When you get right down to it, your failure to understand ordinary people! Once it's accepted that the diagnosis made by the Dark Side is far more accurate, then what becomes of your morality? Of your whole philosophy of life? Eh?'

I lit up, nodded politely and headed for the exit. Tiger Cub watched me go with a puzzled look. Well, you just figure out for yourself why I'm leaving.

I'd found out all I could round here.

Or rather – almost all.

I leaned down towards the short haircut of the young guy in glasses who had his nose stuck in his notebook and asked briskly:

'What districts are we closing off last?'

'Botanical Gardens and the Economic Exhibition,' he answered, without even looking up. The cursor carried on sliding across the screen. The Dark One was issuing instructions, relishing his power as he moved red dots across the map of Moscow. It would have been harder to prise him away from the exercise than to drag him away from his girlfriend.

They know how to love too, after all.

'Thanks,' I said, dropping my burning cigarette into the full ashtray. 'That's very helpful.'

'No worries,' the terminal operator said casually, without looking round. He poked the tip of his tongue out of his mouth and stuck another dot on the map: one more rank-and-file Dark One moving into the round-up. What are you so delighted about, you stupid idiot? The ones with real power will never appear on your map. You'd be better off playing with toy soldiers if power's the way you get your kicks.

I slid across to the spiral staircase. All the fury I'd felt on my way here – the determination to kill or, more likely, be killed – had disappeared. I'm sure at some point during a battle a soldier enters a state of icy calm. The same way a surgeon's hands stop trembling when the patient starts dying on the operating table.

What possible variants have you provided for, Zabulon?

That I start thrashing about in the nets closing in around me, and the commotion attracts both Light Ones and Dark Ones, all of them – and especially Svetlana?

No, that one's out.

That I give myself up or get caught and then the long, slow, exhausting trial starts, concluding in a frenzied outburst by Svetlana at the tribunal?

No, that one's out.

That I start a fight with your field headquarters operatives and kill them all, but end up trapped a third of a kilometre above the ground, and Svetlana comes racing to the tower?

No, that one's out.

Or I take a stroll round the field headquarters and figure out that no one there knows anything about the Maverick, and try to play for time?

That's a possibility.

The ring was getting tighter, I knew that. It had been closed off first round the outskirts of the city, along the Moscow Ring Road, then the city had been carved up into districts and the major transport routes had been closed off. It still wasn't too late to take a quick look around nearby districts that weren't under surveillance yet, find a hiding place and try to lie low. The only advice the boss had been able to give me was to hold out for as long as possible, while the Night Watch was racing about, trying to find the Maverick.

It's no accident that you're squeezing me into the district where we had our little scuffle last winter, is it, Zabulon? I can't help remembering it, so one way or another the way I act is bound to be affected by my memories.

The observation platform was completely empty now. The final visitors had fled, and there were no staff – only the man I'd recruited, standing by the stairs, clutching his pistol in his hand and staring downwards with his eyes blazing.

'Now we'll change clothes again,' I told him. 'The Light thanks you. Afterwards you'll forget everything we've talked about. You'll go home. All you'll remember is that it was an ordinary day, like yesterday. Nothing much happened.'

'Nothing much happened!' the security man blurted out cheerfully as he took my clothes off. It's so easy to turn humans to the Light or the Dark, but they're happiest of all when they're allowed to be themselves.

CHAPTER 6

ONCE I WAS out of the tower I stopped, stuck my hands in my pockets and stood there for a while, looking at the beams of the searchlights lancing up into the sky and the brightly lit security checkpoint.

There were just two things I didn't understand in the game being played out by the two Watches, or rather, by their leaders.

That Other who had departed into the Twilight – who was he and whose side was he on? Had he been warning me or trying to frighten me off?

And the kid, Egor – had I really met him just by chance? And if not, had our meeting been a destiny node or just another of Zabulon's moves?

I knew next to nothing about inhabitants of the Twilight. Maybe even Gesar himself knew nothing.

But at least I could think a bit about Egor.

He was a card that hadn't been dealt yet. Maybe only a low card, but a trump, like all of us. And small trumps have their uses too. Egor had already been in the Twilight – the first time when he tried to see me, the second time when he escaped from the vampire. That wasn't a very good hand, to be honest. Both times he'd been led by fear, and that should have meant his future was decided. Maybe he could linger on the borderline between human and Other for a few more years, but his path led to the Dark Ones.

It's always best to look the truth squarely in the face. It didn't make the slightest bit of difference that so far Egor was just like any other good kid. If I survived, I'd still have to ask for his ID every time I met him – or show him my own.

Zabulon could probably influence him. Send him to any place I happened to be. That reminded me that he probably had no difficulty sensing where I was either. I was prepared for that.

But I still didn't know if our 'chance' meeting had any meaning.

Going on what the Dark computer operator had said – that they weren't combing the Economics Exhibition district yet – it had. I might get the wild idea of using the boy somehow – hiding in his apartment or sending him to get help. I might head for his building. Right?

Too complicated. Way too tricky. They could take me easily enough anyway. I was missing something, something crucially important.

I walked towards the road and didn't look round again at the tower that held the Dark Ones' sham headquarters of the day. I'd almost even forgotten about the shattered body of the magician who'd been guarding it, lying somewhere near the foot of the tower at that moment. What did they want me to do? What was it? That was the point I had to start from.

Act as bait. Get caught by the Day Watch. Get caught in a way that would leave no doubt that I was guilty. And that had as good as happened already.

After that, Svetlana wouldn't be able to control herself. We could protect her and her parents. The one thing we couldn't do was interfere in her own decisions. And if she started trying to save me, to pluck me out of the Day Watch's dungeons or rescue me from the tribunal, she would be killed. Swiftly and without hesitation. The whole game had been designed so she could make a wrong move. The whole game had been set up a long time ago, when the Dark Magician Zabulon had seen the appearance of a Great Sorceress in the future and the part I was destined to play. The traps had been set. The first one had failed. The second one was holding its greedy jaws wide open right now. Maybe there was a third still to come.

But where did a kid who still couldn't manifest his magical powers come into all this?

I stopped.

He was Dark, that must be it!

And who was it who killed Dark Ones? Weak, unskilled Dark Ones who didn't want to develop?

One more body laid at my door – but what was the point?

I didn't know. But I did know that the kid was doomed and the meeting in the metro hadn't been any accident. I could see that clearly now. I must have been experiencing prevision again or another piece of the jigsaw had simply fallen into place.

Egor would die.

I remembered the way he'd looked at me on the platform in the station, with his shoulders hunched over, wanting to ask me something and shout abuse at me all at the same time, to shout out loud the truth about the two Watches, the truth he'd seen too early. I remembered the way he'd turned and run for the train.

'They'll protect you, won't they? Your Watch?'

'They'll try.'

Of course they'd try. They'd keep looking for the Maverick right to the end.

That was the answer!

I stopped walking and seized hold of my head. Light and Dark, how could I be so stupid? So hopelessly naïve?

They wouldn't spring the trap as long as the Maverick was still alive. Making me look like a psychopath out on the hunt, a poacher from the Light Side, wasn't enough. They needed to kill the real Maverick as well.

The Dark Ones knew who he was — or at least Zabulon did. And more important than that — they could control him. They tossed his victims to him — members of their own kind they didn't see as particularly useful. And for the Maverick what was happening right now wasn't just one more heroic incident — he was totally absorbed in the battle against the Dark. He had Dark Ones coming at him from every side: first the female shape-shifter, then the Dark Magician in the restaurant, and now Egor. He must be thinking the whole world had gone crazy, that the Apocalypse was just round the corner, that the powers of the Dark were taking over the world. I wouldn't have liked to be in his shoes.

The female shape-shifter had been killed so they could lodge a protest with us and demonstrate who was under threat.

The Dark Magician had been killed to close off any last loopholes and allow them to bring a formal accusation and arrest me.

The kid had to be killed to get rid of the Maverick after he'd played out his part. So they could intervene at the last moment, catch him standing over the body and kill him when he resisted and tried to escape. He didn't understand that we fought according to rules, he'd never surrender, he'd ignore instructions from a 'Day Watch' he'd never even heard of.

Once the Maverick was dead I'd be left with no way out. I'd either have to agree to have my memory pulled inside out or depart into the Twilight. Either way Svetlana would blow her cool.

I shuddered.

It was cold. Really cold. I'd thought the winter was completely gone, but that had been wishful thinking.

I held up my hand and stopped the first car that came along. I looked into the driver's eyes and said:

'Let's go.'

The impulse was pretty strong, he didn't even ask where I wanted to go.

The world was coming to an end.

Something had shifted and started to move, ancient shadows had sprung to life, the long-forgotten words of ancient tongues had rung out and a trembling had shaken the earth.

Darkness was dawning over the world.

Maxim was standing on the balcony and smoking as he listened to Elena's grumbling. It had been going on for hours already, ever since the girl he'd rescued had got out of the car at the metro station. Maxim had heard more home truths about himself than he could ever have imagined.

The claim that he was a stupid idiot and a womaniser who was prepared to risk getting shot for the sake of a cute face and a long pair of legs was one that Maxim could handle. The claim that he was a pig and a bastard who flirted with a worn-out ugly prostitute in his wife's presence showed rather more imagination. Especially since he'd only spoken a couple of words to his unexpected passenger.

And now Elena had moved on to utter nonsense, dredging up those short-notice business trips, the two occasions when he'd come home drunk – really drunk – speculating on how many mistresses he had, commenting on his incredible stupidity and spinelessness, and how they'd prevented him making a career or giving his family even a half-decent life.

Maxim glanced over his shoulder.

Elena wasn't even getting worked up, and that was strange. She was just sitting on the leather sofa in front of the huge Panasonic TV and talking, almost as if she meant everything she said.

Was this what she really thought?

That he had a whole host of mistresses? That he'd saved that girl because she had a good figure, not because of those bullets that were whistling through the air? That they had a bad life, a wretched life? When three years ago they'd bought a lovely apartment, furnished it so well and gone to France for Christmas?

His wife's voice sounded confident. It was full of accusation. And it was full of pain.

Maxim flicked his cigarette off the balcony and looked out into the night.

The Dark, the Dark was advancing.

Back there in the restaurant lavatory he'd killed a Dark Magician. One of the most repulsive manifestations of universal Evil. A man who was a carrier of malice and fear. Who extracted energy from the people around him and subjugated other people's souls, transforming white into black, love into hate. Maxim knew he was alone against the world, the way he always had been.

But nothing like this had ever happened before, he'd never run into the spawn of the devil two days in a row. Either they'd all come crawling out of their foul, stinking burrows, or his vision was becoming keener.

Like right now.

As Maxim looked out from the tenth floor he didn't see the scattered lights of a city by night. That was for other people. For the blind and the feeble. He saw a small, dense cloud of darkness hanging above the ground. Not very high, maybe ten or twelve floors up.

Maxim was seeing yet another manifestation of the Dark.

The usual way. The same way as ever. But why so often now? Why one after another? This was the third! The third time in twenty-four hours!

The Dark glimmered and swayed and shifted. The Dark was alive.

And behind him Elena went on reciting his sins in a weary, miserable, hurt voice. She got up and came across to the door of the balcony, as if she wanted to make sure Maxim was listening. Okay, that was fine. At least she wouldn't wake the kids – if they were sleeping anyway. Somehow Maxim doubted it.

If only he believed in God. Genuinely believed. But there was almost nothing left now of the weak faith that had once consoled Maxim after every act of purification. God could not exist in a world where Evil flourished.

But if only He did, or if there was any real faith left in Maxim's soul, Maxim would have gone down on his knees right there, on the dusty, crumbling concrete, and held his hands up towards the dark night sky, the sky where even the stars shone quietly and sadly. And he would have cried out: 'Why me? Why me, Lord? This is too much, this is more than I can bear. Take this burden from me, I beg you, take it away! I'm not the one You need! I'm too weak.'

But what was the point in crying out? He hadn't taken this burden on himself. It wasn't for him to abandon it. Over there the black flame was glowing brighter and brighter. A new tentacle of the Dark.

'I'm sorry, Elena,' he said, moving his wife to one side and stepping into the room. 'I have to go out.'

She stopped speaking in mid-sentence, and the eyes that had been full of irritation and resentment suddenly looked scared.

'I'll be back.' He started walking towards the door quickly, hoping to avoid any questions.

'Maxim! Maxim, wait!'

The transition from abuse to entreaty was instant. Elena dashed after him, grabbed him by the arm and looked into his face – crumpled, desperate.

'I'm sorry, forgive me, I was so frightened! I'm sorry for saying all those horrid things, Maxim!'

He looked at his wife – suddenly deflated, all her aggression spent. She'd give anything now to stop her stupid, depraved, lousy husband leaving the apartment. Could Elena have seen something in his face – something that had frightened her even more than the gangland shoot-out they'd got mixed up in?

'I won't let you go! I won't let you go anywhere! Not at this time of night!'

'Nothing's going to happen to me,' Maxim said gently. 'Quiet, you'll wake the kids. I'll be back soon.'

'If you won't think about yourself, then at least think about the children! Think about me!' said Elena, changing tack. 'What if they remembered the number of the car? What if they turn up here looking for that bitch? Then what will I do?'

'Nobody's going to turn up here.' Somehow Maxim knew that was true. 'And even if they do, it's a strong door. And you know who to call. Elena, let me past.'

His wife froze in the middle of the doorway with her arms flung out wide and her head thrown back. Her eyes were screwed up as if she was expecting him to hit her.

Maxim kissed her gently on the cheek and moved her out of the way. She looked totally confused as she watched him go out into the hall. She could hear terrible, noisy music coming from her daughter's room. She wasn't sleeping, she'd turned on her stereo to drown out their angry voices, Elena's voice.

'Don't!' his wife whispered imploringly.

He slipped on his jacket, checking quickly to make sure everything was in place in the inside pocket.

'You don't think about us at all!' Elena told him in a choking voice, speaking purely out of inertia, no longer hoping for anything. The music volume increased in her daughter's room.

'That's not true,' Maxim said calmly. 'It's you that I am thinking about now. I'm taking care of you.'

He didn't want to wait for the lift. He'd already walked down one flight of steps when his wife's last shout came. It was unexpected – she didn't like to wash their dirty linen in public and she never quarrelled outside the apartment.

'I wish you'd love us, not just take care of us!'

Maxim shrugged and started walking faster.

This was where I'd stood in the winter.

It was all just the same: the lonely alley, the noise of the cars on the road behind me, the pale light from the streetlamps. Only it had been much colder. And everything had seemed so simple and clear, I was like a fresh, young American cop going out on my first patrol.

Enforce the law. Hunt down Evil. Protect the innocent.

How wonderful it would be if everything could always be as clear and simple as it used to be when you were twelve years old, or twenty. If there really were only two colours in the world: black and white. But even the most honest, conscientious cop, raised on the resounding ideals of the Stars and Stripes, has to understand sooner or later that there's more than just Dark and Light out on the streets. There are understandings, concessions, agreements. Informers, traps, provocations. Sooner or later the time comes when you have to betray your own side, plant bags of heroin and hit people in the kidneys – carefully, so as to leave no marks behind.

And all for the sake of those simple rules.

Enforce the law. Hunt down Evil. Protect the innocent.

I'd had to come to terms with all this too.

I walked to the end of the narrow brick alley and scuffed a sheet of newsprint with my foot. This was where the unfortunate vampire had been reduced to ashes. He really had been unfortunate, the only thing he'd done wrong was to fall in love. Not with a girl vampire, not with a human, but with his victim, his food.

This was where I'd splashed the vodka out of the bottle and scalded the face of the woman who'd been handed over to feed the vampires by us, the Night Watch.

How fond the Dark Ones were of repeating the word 'Freedom!'. How often we explained to ourselves that freedom has its limits.

And that's probably just the way it ought to be. For the Dark Ones and the Light Ones who simply live among ordinary people, possessing greater powers than they have, but with the same desires and ambitions, for those who choose life according to the rules instead of confrontation.

But once you got to the borderline, the invisible borderline where the watchmen stood between the Dark and the Light . . . It was war. And war is always a crime. In every war there will always be a place not only for heroism and self-sacrifice, but also for betrayal and backstabbing. It's just not possible to wage war any other way. If you try, you've lost before you even begin.

And what was this all about, when you got right down to it? What was there worth fighting for, what gave me the right to fight when I was standing on the borderline, in the middle, between the Light and the Dark? I have neighbours who are vampires! They've never killed anyone – at least Kostya hasn't. Other people, ordinary people, think they are decent folks. If you judge them by their deeds, they are a lot more honest than the boss or Olga.

Where was the boundary? Where was the justification? Where was the forgiveness? I didn't have the answers. I didn't have anything to say, not even to myself. I drifted along, went with the flow, with the old convictions and dogmas. How could they keep fighting, those comrades of mine, the Night Watch field operatives? What justifications did they give for their actions? I didn't know that either. But their solutions wouldn't be any help to me anyway. It was every man for himself here, just like the Dark Ones' slogans said.

The worst thing was I could tell that if I failed to understand, if I couldn't get a fix on that borderline, then I was doomed. And it wasn't just me. Svetlana would die too. She'd get embroiled in a hopeless attempt to save her boss. The entire structure of the Moscow Watch would collapse.

If I didn't get the one thing right.

I went on standing there for a while, with my hand against the dirty brick wall. Digging through my memory, chewing things over, trying to find an answer. There wasn't one. That meant it was destiny.

I walked across the quiet little courtyard to the 'box on stilts'. The Soviet skyscraper made me feel strangely despondent. There was no obvious reason, but the feeling was undeniable. I'd felt the same thing before, in a train passing abandoned villages and crumbling grain silos. The sense of wasted effort. A punch thrown too hard, connecting with nothing but the air.

'Zabulon,' I said, 'if you can hear me . . .'

All was calm. The usual calm of a late evening in Moscow – car engines roaring, music playing somewhere behind the windows, empty streets.

'There's no way you can have covered every single possibility,' I said, speaking to the empty air. 'Just no way. There are always forks in the road in reality. The future isn't determined. You know that. And so do I.'

I set out across the road without looking right or left, ignoring the traffic. I was on a mission, right?

The sphere of exclusion.

A trolleybus screeched to a halt on the rails. Cars braked and skidded round an empty space with me at its centre. Nothing else existed for me now, only that building where we'd done battle on the roof three months before, in the darkness, those bright flashes of an energy that human eyes couldn't see.

And that power, visible to so few, was increasing.

I was right, this was the eye of the hurricane. This was where they'd been leading me all this time. Great. Now I'd arrived. So you didn't forget that shabby little defeat after all, Zabulon? You haven't forgotten the way you were sent down in front of your underlings.

Apart from all his exalted goals – and I understood that for him they were exalted – the Dark Magician harboured another burning desire. Once it had been a simple human weakness but now it had been increased immeasurably by the Twilight.

The desire for revenge. To get even.

To play the battle out all over again.

All you Great Magicians share this, Light and Dark – this boredom with ordinary battle, this desire to win *elegantly*. To humiliate your opponent. You're weary of simple victories, you've had plenty of those already. The great confrontation has developed into an endless game of chess. Gesar, the great Light Magician, was playing it when he assumed another's appearance and took such delight in taunting Zabulon.

But for me the confrontation still hadn't turned into a game.

And maybe that was exactly where my chance lay.

I took the pistol from its holster and clicked the safety catch off. I took a deep, deep breath as if I was about to dive into water. It was time.

Maxim could sense that this time it would all be over quickly.

He wouldn't spend all night lying in wait. He wouldn't spend hours tracking down his prey. This time the flash of inspiration had been too bright. More than just a sense of an alien, hostile presence – a clear direction to his target.

He drove as far as the intersection of Galushkin Street and Yaroslavskaya Street and parked in the courtyard of a high-rise. He watched the black flame glimmering as it slowly moved about inside the building.

The Dark Magician was in there. Maxim could already feel him as a real person, he could almost see him. A man. His powers were weak. Not a werewolf or a vampire or an incubus. A straight-forward Dark Magician. The level of his powers was so low, he wouldn't cause any problems. The problem was something else.

Maxim could only hope and pray that this wouldn't keep happening so often. The strain of killing the creatures of the Dark day after day wasn't just physical. There was also that terrible moment when the dagger pierced his enemy's heart. The moment when everything started to shudder and sway, when colours and sounds faded away and everything started moving slowly. What would he do if he ever made a mistake? If he killed someone who wasn't an enemy of the human race, but just an ordinary person?

But there was nothing he could do, since he was the only one in the entire world who could tell the Dark Ones from ordinary people. Since he was the only one who'd been given a weapon – by God, by destiny, by chance.

Maxim took out his wooden dagger and looked at the toy with a heavy heart, feeling slightly confused. He wasn't the one who'd whittled this dagger, he wasn't the one who'd given it the high-flown name of a 'misericord'.

They were only twelve at the time, he and Petka, his best friend, in fact his only childhood friend and – why not admit it? – the only friend he'd ever had. They used to play at knights in battle – not for very long, mind you, they had plenty of other ways to amuse themselves when they were kids, even without all these computer games. All the kids on the block had played the game for just one short summer, whittling swords and daggers, pretending to stab at each other with all their strength, but really being careful. They had enough sense to realise that even a wooden sword could take someone's eye out or draw blood. It was strange how he and Petka had always ended up on opposite sides. Maybe that was because Petka was a bit younger and Maxim felt slightly embarrassed about having him as a friend, the adoring way he gazed at Maxim and trailed around after him as if he was in love. It was just an ordinary moment in one of their battles when Maxim knocked Petka's wooden sword out of his hands – his friend had hardly even tried to resist – and cried: 'You're my prisoner!'

But then something odd had happened. Petka had handed him this dagger and said that the valiant knight had to take his life with it rather than humiliate him by taking him prisoner. It was a game, of course, only a game, but Maxim had shuddered inside when he pretended to strike with the wooden dagger. And there had been one brief, agonising moment when Petka had looked at Maxim's hand holding the dagger just short of his grubby white t-shirt and then glanced into Maxim's eyes. And then he'd blurted out: 'Keep it, you can have it as a trophy.'

Maxim had been happy to accept the wooden dagger. But for some reason he'd never used it in the game again. He'd kept it at home and tried to forget about it, as if he felt ashamed of the unexpected gift and his own sentimentality. But he'd never forgotten it. Even when he grew up and got married and his own first child was growing up, he'd never forgotten it. The toy weapon always lay in the drawer with the photo albums of the children, the envelopes with locks of hair and all that sentimental nonsense. Until the day Maxim first felt the presence of the Dark in the world.

It was as if the wooden dagger had summoned him. And it had proved to be a genuine weapon, pitiless, merciless, invincible.

But Petka was gone now. They'd grown apart when they were still young: a year is a big age difference for children, but for teenagers it's a huge gulf. And then life had separated them. They'd still smiled at each other whenever they met and shaken hands, had even enjoyed a drink together a few times and reminisced about their childhoods. Then Maxim had got married and moved away and they'd almost completely lost contact. But this winter he'd had news of Petka, purely by chance, from his mother – he phoned her regularly, just like a good son should. 'Do you remember Petka? You were such good friends when you were children, quite inseparable.'

He'd remembered. And he'd realised immediately where this was leading.

Maxim's mother told him that he'd fallen to his death from the roof of some high-rise, though God only knew what he'd been doing up there in the middle of the night. Maybe he'd committed suicide, or maybe he'd been drunk – but the doctors had said he was sober. Or maybe he'd been murdered. He had a job in some commercial organisation that paid well, he used to help his parents and drive around in a good car.

'He was probably high on drugs,' Maxim had said sternly. So sternly his mother hadn't even tried to argue. 'I suppose so, he always was strange.'

His heart hadn't contracted in sudden pain. But for some reason that evening he'd got drunk and killed a woman he'd been trying to track down for two weeks, a woman whose Dark power forced men to leave the women they loved and go back to their wives, an old witch who forced people together and forced them apart.

Petka was gone. The boy he'd been friends with had already been gone for many years, and now Pyotr Nesterov, the man he'd seen once a year or even less often, had been gone for three months. But Maxim still had the dagger Petka had given him.

There must have been some special reason for it, that awkward childhood friendship of theirs.

Maxim toyed with the wooden dagger, rolling it from one hand to the other. Why was he so alone? Why didn't he have a friend beside him to lift at least part of the burden from his shoulders? There was so much Dark all around, and so little Light.

For some reason Maxim recalled the last thing Elena had shouted at him as he was leaving: 'I wish you'd love us, not just take care of us.'

But isn't that the same thing? thought Maxim, mentally parrying the thrust.

No, it probably wasn't. But what was a man to do when his love was a battle fought against Evil, rather than for Good?

Against the Dark, not for the Light.

Not for the Light but against the Dark.

'I'm the guardian,' Maxim said to himself in a low voice, as if he was too fearful to say it out loud. Only schizos talked to themselves. And he wasn't a schizo, he was normal. He was better than normal, he could see the ancient Evil creeping and crawling into the world.

But was it creeping in, or had it already made its home here a long, long time ago?

No, this was madness. He mustn't, he absolutely mustn't allow himself to doubt. If he lost even a part of his faith, allowed himself to relax or start searching for non-existent allies, then he was finished. The wooden dagger would no longer be a luminous blade driving out the Dark. The next magician would reduce it to ashes with magic fire, a witch would cast a spell on it, a werewolf would tear it to pieces.

The guardian and the judge!

He mustn't hesitate.

The patch of Dark moving about on the ninth floor suddenly started moving downward. His heart started beating faster: the

Dark Magician was coming, to keep his appointment with destiny. Maxim climbed out of the car and glanced rapidly around him. As usual, some secret thing inside him had driven everyone away from the scene and cleared the battlefield.

Was it a battlefield? Or a scaffold?

Guardian and judge?

Or executioner?

What difference did it make?

The familiar power flooded into his body. Holding his hand inside his jacket, Maxim walked towards the building's entrance, towards the Dark Magician who was coming down in the lift.

Quickly, it had to be done quickly. It still wasn't quite night yet. Someone might see. And no one would ever believe him, the best he could hope for would be the madhouse.

Call out. Give his name. Take out his weapon.

Misericord. Mercy. He was the guardian and the judge. The warrior against evil. And not an executioner!

This courtyard was a battlefield, not a scaffold.

Maxim stopped outside the entrance to the building. He heard footsteps. The lock clicked.

He felt so wronged, he could have howled in horror and screamed curses at the heavens for his destiny and his gift.

The Dark Magician was a child.

A skinny, dark-haired little boy who looked quite ordinary – except for the quivering halo of Dark that only Maxim could see.

But why? Nothing like this had ever happened to him before. Maxim had killed women and men, young and old, but he'd never come across any children who'd sold their souls to the Dark. He'd never even thought about it, maybe because he hadn't wanted to accept that it was possible, or maybe because he'd been avoiding making any decisions in advance. He might have stayed at home if he'd known his next victim would be only twelve years old.

The boy stood in the doorway, looking at him with a puzzled expression. Just for a moment Maxim thought the kid was going to turn round and dash back in, slamming the heavy, code-locked door behind him. Run, then, run!

The boy took a step forward, holding the door so that it wouldn't slam too hard. He looked into Maxim's eyes, frowning slightly, but without any sign of fear. Maxim couldn't understand this. The boy hadn't taken him for a chance passer-by, he'd realised the man was waiting for him. And he'd come to meet him. Because he wasn't afraid? Because he had faith in his Dark power?

'You're a Light One, I can see that,' the boy said quietly but confidently.

'Yes.' He had trouble getting the word out, he had to force it out of his throat. Cursing himself for his weakness, Maxim took hold of the boy's shoulder and said: 'I am the judge.'

The boy still wasn't frightened.

'I saw Anton today.'

Who? Maxim didn't say anything, but the bewilderment showed in his eyes.

'Have you come to see me because of him?'

'No. Because of you.'

'What for?'

The boy was behaving almost aggressively, as if he'd had a long argument with Maxim, as if Maxim had done something wrong and he ought to admit it.

'I am the judge,' Maxim repeated. He felt like turning round and running away. This was all wrong, it wasn't supposed to happen like this! A child couldn't be a Dark One, not a child the same age as his own daughter! A Dark Magician should defend himself, attack, run away, but not just stand there with an offended look on his face, as if he was expecting an apology.

As if there was something that could protect him.

'What's your name?' Maxim asked.

'Egor.'

'I'm really sorry things have worked out this way,' Maxim said quite sincerely. He wasn't getting any sadistic satisfaction from dragging things out. 'Dammit. I've got a daughter the same age as you!'

Somehow that was what hurt the most.

'But if not me, then who?'

'What are you talking about?' The boy tried to remove Maxim's hand. That strengthened his resolve.

Boy, girl, adult, child . . . What difference did it make? Dark and Light – that was the only distinction.

'I have to save you,' said Maxim. He took the dagger out of his pocket with his free hand. 'I have to save you – and I will.'

CHAPTER 7

FIRST I RECOGNISED the car.

Then I recognised the Maverick, when he got out of it.

I suddenly felt desperate. It was the man who'd saved me when I was running away from the Maharajah, when I was in Olga's body.

Maybe I ought to have guessed at the time. Probably, if I'd been more experienced, with more time to think and more presence of mind. All it would have taken was to look at the aura of the woman in the car with him. Svetlana had given a detailed description of her, after all. I could have recognised the woman – and the Maverick. I could have ended it all right there in the car.

But how could I have ended it?

I dived into the Twilight when the Maverick looked in my direction. It seemed to work, and he kept walking towards the entrance to the staircase where I'd once sat by the garbage chute and had a gloomy conversation with a snowy owl.

The Maverick was on his way to kill Egor. Just as I'd expected. Just as Zabulon had planned it. The trap was right there in front of me. The tightly stretched spring had already begun to contract. One more move from me, and the Day Watch could celebrate the success of their operation.

But where are you, Zabulon?

The Twilight gave me time. The Maverick was still walking towards the apartment block, moving his feet slowly. I looked around for signs of the Dark. The slightest trace, the slightest breath, the slightest shadow . . .

There was immense magical tension all around me. The threads of reality that led into the future all came together here. This was the intersection of a hundred roads, the point at which the world decided which way it would go. Not because of me, not because of the Maverick, not because of the kid. We were only part of the trap. We were extras on the set: one of us had been told to say 'Dinner is served', another had to act out a fall, another had to mount the scaffold, proudly holding his head high. For the second time this spot in Moscow was the arena for an invisible battle. But I couldn't see any Others, Dark or Light. Only the Maverick, and even now I didn't think of him as an Other, except that he had a scintillating focus of power at his chest. At first I thought I was seeing his heart. Then I realised that it was a weapon – the one he used to kill the Dark Ones.

What's going on here, Zabulon? I suddenly felt absurdly insulted. Here I am! I'm stepping into your trap, look, I've already raised my foot, it's all just about to happen, but where are you?

Either the great Dark Magician had hidden himself so carefully that I couldn't find him, or he wasn't there at all.

I'd lost. I'd lost even before the game was over, because I hadn't understood my enemy's intentions. There ought to have been an ambush here, the Dark Ones needed to kill the Maverick the moment he killed Egor.

I couldn't let him kill Egor!

I was here, wasn't I? I'd explain to him what was going on, tell him about the Watches and the way they monitored each other, about the Treaty that meant we had to maintain a neutral stance, about humans and the Others, about the world and the Twilight.

I'd tell him everything the same way I'd told Svetlana, and he'd understand.

Or would he?

If he really couldn't see the Light!

For him the human world was a grey, mindless flock of sheep. The Dark Ones were the wolves who circled round him, picking off the fattest ones. And he was the guard dog. But he couldn't see the shepherds, he was blinded by his fear and fury. So he hurtled about crazily, just him against all of them.

He wouldn't believe me, he wouldn't let himself believe me.

I raced forward, towards the Maverick. The door was already open, and the Maverick was talking to Egor. Why had the stupid kid come out so late at night when he knew perfectly well what kind of powers rule our world? The Maverick wasn't able to summon his victims to him, was he?

Talk would be useless. Attack him from the Twilight. Pin him down. And explain everything afterwards.

The Twilight screeched with a thousand wounded voices when I crashed into the invisible barrier at full speed. Just three steps away from the Maverick, as I was already raising my hand to strike, I suddenly found myself flattened against a transparent wall. I slid down off it slowly with my ears ringing.

This was bad. He didn't understand the nature of his power. He was a self-taught magician, a psychopath on the side of Good. But when he set out to do his work, he protected himself with a magical barrier. The fact that it was purely spontaneous wasn't any comfort to me.

The Maverick said something to Egor and took his hand out from inside his jacket.

A wooden dagger. I'd heard something about that kind of magic, naïve and powerful at the same time, but this wasn't the right time to try to remember.

I slid out of my shadow into the human world and jumped the Maverick from behind.

When he raised the dagger, Maxim was knocked off his feet. The world around him had already turned grey, the boy was already moving in slow motion, Maxim could see his eyelids moving down for the last time before they would part in terror and pain. The night had been transformed into the twilit stage where he held court and passed sentence.

Suddenly someone had stopped him. Knocked him aside and pushed him down on to the tarmac. At the very last moment Maxim managed to put out his hand, roll over and jump to his feet.

A third character had appeared on the stage. Why hadn't Maxim noticed his sly approach? While he was busy with his vital work, chance witnesses and unwanted company had always been kept away by the power of the Light, the power that led him into battle. Why not this time?

The man was young, maybe a bit younger than Maxim. In jeans and a sweater, with a bag hanging over his shoulder – he shrugged it off carelessly on to the ground. He had a pistol in his hand.

'Stop,' said the man, as if Maxim had been about to run. 'Listen to me.'

A passer-by who'd taken him for an ordinary maniac? But then what about the pistol, and the way he'd crept up without being noticed? A special forces soldier out of uniform? No, he would have shot Maxim and finished him off, he wouldn't have let him get up off the ground.

Maxim peered at the stranger in horror, trying to figure out who he was. He could be another Dark One, but Maxim had never come across two at the same time.

There wasn't any Dark there. There simply wasn't, none at all!

'Who are you?' asked Maxim, almost forgetting about the boy magician, who was slowly backing away towards his rescuer.

'Anton Gorodetsky, Night Watch agent. You have to listen to me.'

Anton caught hold of Egor with his free hand and pushed him behind his back.

'Night Watch?' Maxim was still trying to detect a trace of the Dark in the stranger. He couldn't find it, and that frightened him even more. 'Are you from the Dark?'

He didn't get it. He tried to probe me: I could feel him searching fiercely and determinedly, but clumsily. I don't even know if I could have screened myself against it. I could sense some kind of primordial power in this man, or this Other – both terms could apply here – a wild, fanatical energy. I didn't even try to shield myself.

'The Night Watch? Are you from the Dark?'

'No. What's your name?'

'Maxim,' said the Maverick, walking slowly towards me. Looking at me as if he could sense that we'd already met, but I'd looked different then. 'Who are you?'

'I work for the Night Watch. I'll explain everything, just listen to me. You are a Light Magician.'

Maxim's face trembled and turned to stone.

'You kill Dark Ones. I know that. This morning you killed a female shape-shifter. This evening, in the restaurant, you killed a Dark Magician.'

'Do you do that too?'

Maybe I just imagined it. Or maybe there really was a tremor of hope in that voice. I deliberately stuck the pistol back in its holster.

'I'm a Light Magician. Although not a very powerful one. One of hundreds in Moscow. There are many of us, Maxim.'

His eyes opened wide and I realised I'd hit the target. Now he knew he wasn't a lunatic who'd imagined he was Superman and felt proud of it. He'd probably never wanted anything so much in his life as to meet a comrade-in-arms.

'We didn't spot you in time, Maxim,' I said. Was it really going to be possible to settle everything peacefully, without bloodshed, without an insane battle between two Light Magicians? 'That was our fault. You started a war of your own, and you've created a messy situation, Maxim, but things can still be put right. You didn't know about the Treaty, did you?'

He wasn't listening to me. He couldn't give a damn for some Treaty he'd never heard of. He wasn't alone, that was the only thing that mattered to him.

'You fight the Dark Ones?'

'Yes.'

'And there are many of you?'

'Yes.'

Maxim looked at me again, and I saw the piercing glint of the Twilight in his eyes again. He was trying to see the lie, to see the Dark, to see the malice and hatred – the only things he was capable of seeing.

'You're not a Dark One,' he said. It was almost a complaint. 'I can see that. I've never been wrong, never!'

'I'm a watchman,' I repeated. I glanced around – there was no one to be seen. Something had frightened everyone away. That was probably one of the Maverick's powers.

'That boy . . .'

'He's an Other too,' I said quickly. 'It's not clear yet if he's going to be Light or—'

Maxim shook his head.

'He's Dark.'

I glanced at Egor. The boy slowly raised his eyes to meet mine.

'No,' I said.

I could see his aura quite clearly – bright, pure, shimmering colours, typical for very young children, but not for teenagers. His destiny was his own, his future was still undefined.

'He's Dark,' said Maxim, shaking his head again. 'Don't you see? I'm never wrong, never. You stopped me from exterminating an envoy of the Dark.'

He wasn't likely to be lying. He might not have been given many skills but the ones he had were powerful. Maxim could see the Dark, he could spot the tiniest hints of it in other people's souls. In fact, he saw the Dark that was just being born more clearly than any other kind.

'We don't just kill every Dark One we come across.'

'Why not?'

'We have a truce, Maxim.'

'But there can be no truce with the Dark.'

I shuddered. I hadn't heard the faintest note of doubt in his voice.

'Any war is worse than peace.'

'Except this one.' Maxim raised the hand holding the dagger. 'You see this? It was a present from a friend of mine. He was killed, maybe people like this boy were responsible. The Dark is cunning!'

'You think you need to tell me that?'

'Of course. You may be a Light One . . .' His face twisted in a bitter grin. 'But if you are, your Light faded a long time ago. There can be no forgiveness for Evil. There can be no truce with Evil.'

'No forgiveness for Evil?' Now I was really angry. 'After you stabbed the Dark Magician, you should have tried hanging around for another ten minutes. Or didn't you want to see his children screaming and his wife crying? They're not Dark Ones, Maxim. They're ordinary people who don't have our powers. You saved that girl they were shooting at . . .'

He flinched, but his face remained as implacably stony as ever.

'Well done! But did you know they were trying to kill her because of the crime you'd committed? Well?'

'This is war.'

'You've started your own war,' I whispered. 'You're like a child, with your toy dagger. You can't make an omelette without breaking eggs, is that it? No holds barred in the great struggle for the Light?'

'I don't fight for the Light,' he said in a quiet voice. 'I fight against the Dark. That's all I'm capable of. Do you understand? And you're wrong, it isn't a matter of eggs and omelettes for me. I didn't ask for this power, I didn't dream of having it. But since it has come to me, I can't act any other way.'

Just who was it who hadn't noticed him in time?

Why hadn't we found Maxim straight away, as soon as he became an Other?

He'd have made a first-class field operative. After long arguments and explanations. After months of training, after years of exercises, after tantrums, mistakes, bouts of drinking, attempts to kill himself. Eventually he would have understood the rules of the confrontation – not with his heart, he wasn't capable of that, but with his cold, uncompromising reason. The rules that govern the struggle between the Light and the Dark, that mean we have to turn a blind eye to werewolves hunting their victims and kill our own people who can't do that.

There he was, right in front of me. A Light Magician who'd killed more Dark Ones in a few years than a field operative with a hundred years of experience. Alone, cornered. Knowing only how to hate, incapable of love.

Egor just stood there quietly behind me, listening intently. I turned round, took him by the shoulders and pushed him in front of me. I said:

'Is he a Dark Magician? Probably – I'm afraid you're right. In a few more years, this kid will start to sense his own powers. As he goes through life, the Dark will creep alongside him. With every step his life will become easier and easier. And every step will be paid for by someone else's pain. Do you remember the fairy tale about the mermaid? A witch gave her legs, she could walk, but she felt like there were red-hot knives stabbing into her feet all the time. That story's about us, Maxim! We always walk over sharp knives, and that's something you can never get used to. But Hans Christian Andersen didn't tell the whole story. The witch could have done things differently: the mermaid walks, and the knives stab other people. That's the way of the Dark.'

'I carry my own pain with me,' said Maxim, and I suddenly felt an insane hope that he could understand after all. 'But that mustn't be allowed to change anything.'

'Are you prepared to kill him?' I said, nodding towards Egor. 'Tell me, Maxim. I'm a Night Watch agent, I know where the line runs between Good and Evil. You can create Evil, even by killing Dark Ones. Tell me – are you prepared to kill him?'

He didn't hesitate. He just nodded, looking straight into my eyes.

'Yes, I am, I've never let a creature of the Dark get away. I won't let this one get away.'

The invisible trap snapped shut.

It wouldn't have surprised me to see Zabulon standing there. To see him surface out of the Twilight and give Maxim a slap on the back. Or flash a mocking smile at me.

But a moment later I realised Zabulon wasn't there. He never had been.

The trap he'd set didn't need any supervision. It would work all on its own. I'd been caught, and every member of the Day Watch had a solid alibi for that moment.

I either had to let Maxim kill the boy who was going to become a Dark Magician and make myself into his accomplice – with all the obvious consequences.

Or fight the Maverick and kill him – I was far more powerful, after all. Eliminate the only witness with my own hand and kill a Light Magician into the bargain.

Maxim would never back down. This was his war, his own cross that he'd been carrying for years. He wanted victory or death.

So why should Zabulon bother to interfere in the fight?

He'd done everything right. Purged the ranks of the Dark Ones of useless ballast, built up the tension, even deliberately shot to miss. Zabulon had made me come to this spot to meet the Maverick. And now Zabulon was somewhere far away. Maybe not even in Moscow. He might even be watching what was happening: there were plenty of technical or magical devices he could use for that. Watching and laughing.

I was finished.

Whichever way I jumped, the Twilight was waiting for me.

Evil has no need to bother to eliminate Good. It's far simpler to let Good fight against itself.

I had just one chance left, a tiny one, but it was a monstrous, vile idea.

I could be too slow.

I could let Maxim kill the boy, or rather, simply fail to stop him. He'd calm down after that. He'd go to the Night Watch head-quarters with me, listen, argue and eventually give up, crushed by the boss's implacable arguments and iron logic. He'd realise what he'd done and just how fragile the balance he'd disrupted was. And he'd hand himself over to the tribunal, where he had at least a slim chance of being acquitted.

I was no field operative, after all. I'd done everything I could. I'd even seen through the Dark's game, a sequence of moves devised by someone far wiser than me. I simply hadn't been strong enough, my reactions hadn't been fast enough.

Maxim raised the hand holding the dagger.

Time suddenly slowed down, as if I'd entered the Twilight. But the colours didn't fade, they became brighter than ever. It was like moving through a stream of thick syrup. The wooden dagger glided towards Egor's chest, changing as it moved, gleaming like metal or grey flame. Maxim's face was calm and intent, only the lip held beneath his teeth betrayed how tense he was. The kid didn't understand what was happening, he didn't even try to move out of the way.

I shoved Egor to one side – my muscles almost refused to obey me, they didn't want to do something so crazy and suicidal. For the boy, the young Dark Magician, the dagger meant death. For me, it meant life. That's the way it always has been and always will be.

What means life for a Dark One means death for a Light One, and vice versa. Who was I to change . . .?

I wasn't too slow.

Egor fell, banged his head against the door and slid down into a sitting position – I'd pushed him too hard. But I was more concerned about saving him than any bruises he might get. Maxim's eyes glittered with almost childish resentment, but he could still talk.

'He's an enemy!'

'He hasn't done anything!'

'You're defending the Dark!'

Maxim wasn't arguing about whether I was Dark or Light. He could see that well enough.

It's just that he was whiter than white. And he'd never had to decide who should live and who should die.

The dagger was raised again. Not aimed at the boy this time, but at me. I dodged away, looked for my shadow, summoned it, and it came obediently towards me.

The world turned grey, sounds disappeared, movement slowed. Egor stopped squirming and became completely still, the cars crept along the street uncertainly, with their wheels turning in spurts, the branches of the trees forgot about the wind. But Maxim didn't slow down.

He'd followed me in, without knowing what he was doing. Slipped into the Twilight as easily as someone stepping off the kerb on to the road. It was all the same to him now, he was drawing strength from his own certainty, his own hatred, his lighter-than-light hatred, the fury of the colour white. He wasn't the executioner of the Dark Ones any longer. He was an Inquisitor. And he was far more terrifying than our Inquisition.

I threw my arms out, spreading my fingers in the sign of power, simple and foolproof – how the young Others laugh when they're shown that move for the first time. Maxim didn't even stop – he staggered a bit, then put his head down stubbornly and came for me again. I began to get the picture and backed away, desperately running through the magic arsenal in my mind.

Agape – the sign of love. He didn't believe in love.

The triple key – a sign that engendered trust and understanding. He didn't trust me.

Opium – a lilac symbol, the path of sleep. I felt my own eyelids starting to close.

That was how he defeated the Dark Ones. Combined with the powers of an Other, his furious faith acted like a mirror, reflecting back any blow aimed at him. It raised him up to his opponent's level. In combination with his ability to see the Dark and his ridiculous magical dagger, it made him almost invulnerable.

He couldn't reflect everything like that, though. The reflected blows didn't come back immediately. The sign of Thanatos – death – or the white sword would probably work.

But if I killed him, I'd kill myself. Set myself on the one road that we all come to in the end – into the Twilight. Into the faded dreams and colourless visions, the eternal, cold haze. He'd found it so easy to see me as an enemy, but I wouldn't be strong enough to see him that way.

We circled round each other, with Maxim sometimes making clumsy rushes at me – he'd never been in a real fight before, he was used to killing his victims quickly and easily. From somewhere far away I could hear Zabulon's mocking laughter. His soft, wheedling voice.

'So you wanted to play a game against the Dark? Play, then. You have everything you need. Enemies, friends, love, hate. Choose your weapon. Any of them. You already know what the outcome will be.'

Maybe I imagined the voice. Or maybe I really did hear it.

'You're killing yourself too!' I shouted. The holster was flapping against my body, begging to be noticed, begging me to take the pistol out and fire a swarm of little silver wasps at Maxim. As easily as I'd done it with my namesake.

He didn't hear me – he wasn't able to hear me.

Svetlana, you wanted so much to know where our barriers are, where the line runs that we mustn't cross when we fight the Dark. Why aren't you here now? You could have seen for yourself.

But there was no one anywhere near. No Dark Ones to revel in the sight of our duel. No Light Ones to help me, to jump on Maxim and pin him down, to put an end to our deadly dance in the Twilight. No one but a young kid and future Dark Magician, getting up clumsily off the ground, and an implacable executioner with a face of stone – a self-appointed paladin of the Light who'd sown as much Evil as a dozen werewolves or vampires.

I raked my fingers through the cold mist, gathering it into my hand, letting it soak into my fingers. And directed a little more power into my right hand.

A blade of white fire sprouted from it. The Twilight hissed and burned. I raised the white sword, a simple weapon, reliable. Maxim froze.

'Good or Evil,' I said, feeling a wry grin appear on my face. 'Come to me. Come, and I'll kill you. You might be lighter than Light, but that's not the point.'

With anybody else it would have worked. No doubt about it. I can imagine how it must feel to see a sword of fire appear out of nowhere for the first time. But Maxim came for me.

He took those five steps across the space between us. Calmly, not even frowning, without looking at the white sword. And I stood there, repeating to myself the words that I'd spoken so confidently out loud.

Then the wooden dagger slid in under my ribs.

In his lair somewhere far, far away, the head of the Day Watch burst out laughing.

I collapsed on to my knees, then fell on my back. I pressed my palm against my chest. It hurt, but so far that was all. The Twilight squealed indignantly at the scent of living blood and began to thin out.

This was terrible!

Or was this my only way out? To die?

Svetlana wouldn't have anyone to save now. She'd travel on along her long and glorious road, but some day even she would have to enter the Twilight for ever.

Did you know this was going to happen, Gesar? Is this what you were hoping for?

The colours came back into the world. The dark colours of night. The Twilight had rejected me, spat me out in disgust. I was half sitting, half lying on the ground, squeezing the bleeding wound with my hand.

'Why are you still alive?' Maxim asked.

That note of resentment was back in his voice, he was almost pouting. I felt like smiling, but the pain stopped me. He looked at the dagger and raised it again, uncertainly this time. The next moment Egor was there, standing between us, shielding me from Maxim. This time even the pain couldn't stop me from laughing.

A future Dark Magician saving a Light One from another Light One!

'I'm alive because your weapon is only good against the Dark,' I said. I heard an ominous gurgling sound in my chest. The dagger hadn't reached my heart, but it had punctured a lung. 'I don't know who gave it to you, but it's a weapon of the Dark. Against me it's just a sliver of wood, but even that hurts.'

'You're a Light One,' said Maxim.

'Yes.'

'He's a Dark One.' The dagger slowly turned to point at Egor.

I nodded and tried to tug the boy out of the way. He shook his head stubbornly and stayed where he was.

'Why?' asked Maxim. 'Tell me why, eh? You're Light, he's Dark . . .'

And then even he smiled for the first time, though it wasn't a very happy smile.

'Then who am I? Tell me that.'

'I'd say you're a future Inquisitor,' said a voice behind me. 'I'm almost certain of it. A talented, implacable, incorruptible Inquisitor.'

I smiled ironically and said:

'Good evening, Gesar.'

The boss gave me a nod of sympathy. Svetlana was standing behind him, and her face was as white as chalk.

'Can you hold on for five minutes?' the boss asked. 'Then I'll deal with your little scratch.'

'Sure I can,' I agreed.

Maxim was staring at the boss with crazy eyes.

'I don't think you need to worry,' the boss said to him. 'If you were an ordinary poacher, the tribunal would have you executed – you've got too much blood on your hands, and the tribunal is obliged to maintain a balance. But you're magnificent, Maxim. They can't afford to just toss someone like you away. You'll be set above us, above Light and Dark, and it won't even matter which side you came from. But don't get excited. That isn't power. It's hard labour. Drop the dagger!'

Maxim flung the weapon to the ground as if it was burning his fingers. This was a real magician, well beyond the likes of me.

'Svetlana, you passed the test,' the boss said, looking at her. 'What can I say? Grade three for self-control and restraint. No question.'

Using Egor for support, I tried to get up. I wanted to shake the boss's hand. He'd played the game his own way again. By using everybody who was there to be used. And he'd outplayed Zabulon – what a pity the Dark Magician wasn't there to see it! How I'd have liked to see his face, the face of the demon who'd turned my first day of spring into a nightmare.

'But . . .' Maxim started to say something, then stopped. He was overwhelmed by too many new impressions. I knew just how he was feeling.

'Anton, I was certain, absolutely certain that you and Svetlana could handle this,' the boss said gently. 'The most dangerous thing of all for a sorceress with the kind of power she's been given is to lose self-control. To lose sight of the fundamental criteria of the fight against the Dark, to act in haste or to hesitate for too long. And this is one stage of the training that should never be put off.'

Svetlana finally stepped towards me and took me gently by the arm. She looked at Gesar, and just for a moment her face was a mask of fury.

'Stop it,' I said. 'Sveta, don't. He's right. Today, for the very first time, I understood where the boundary runs in our fight. Don't be angry. This is only a scratch.' I took my hand away from my wound. 'We're not like ordinary people, we're a lot tougher.'

'Thank you, Anton,' said the boss. Then he looked at Egor: 'And thank you, too, kid. I really hate the idea that you'll be on the other side of the barricades, but I was sure you'd stand up for Anton.'

The boy tried to move towards Gesar, but I kept hold of his shoulder. It would be awkward if he blurted out his resentment. He didn't understand that everything Gesar had done was only a counter-move.

'There's one thing I regret, Gesar,' I said. 'Just one. That Zabulon isn't here. That I didn't see his face when the whole box of tricks fell apart.'

The boss didn't answer right away.

It must have been hard for him to say it. And I wasn't too pleased to hear it, either.

'But Zabulon had nothing to do with it, Anton. I'm sorry. He really didn't have anything to do with it at all. It was exclusively a Night Watch operation.'

Story Three

ALL FOR MY OWN KIND

PROLOGUE

THE LITTLE man had swarthy skin and narrow eyes. He was the ideal prey for any militiaman in the capital, with his confused, slightly guilty smile and a glance that was both naïve and shifty at the same time. Despite the killing heat, he was wearing a dark suit, old-fashioned but hardly even worn, and as a finishing touch an ancient tie from the Soviet period. In one hand he was carrying a shabby, bulging briefcase, the kind agronomists and chairmen of progressive collective farms used to carry around in old Soviet movies, and in the other a string bag holding a long Central Asian melon.

The little man emerged from his second-class sleeper carriage with a smile, and he kept on smiling: at the female conductor, at his fellow travellers, at the porter who jostled him, at the stallholder selling lemonade and cigarettes. He raised his eyes and gazed in delight at the roof of Kazan Station. He wandered along the platform, occasionally stopping to adjust his grip on the melon. He might have been thirty years old or he might have been fifty. It was hard for a European eye to tell.

A minute later a young man got out of a first-class sleeper carriage in the same Tashkent–Moscow train, probably one of the dirtiest and most run-down trains in the world. He looked like the little man's complete opposite. Another Central Asian type, perhaps Uzbek, but his clothes were more in the modern Moscow style: shorts and a t-shirt, with a small leather bag and a mobile phone attached to his belt. No baggage and no provincial manners. He didn't stare at everything, trying to spot the fabled letter 'M' for 'Metro'. After a quick nod to the conductor of his carriage and a gentle shake of his head in response to the offers from taxi-drivers, two more steps saw him slipping through the bustling crowd of new arrivals, with an expression of mild distaste and alienation on his face. But a moment later he was entirely part of the crowd, indistinguishable from any of the healthy cells in the organism, attracting no interest from the phagocyte militiamen or the other cells beside him.

Meanwhile, the little man with the melon and the briefcase was pushing his way through the crowd, muttering countless apologies in rather poor Russian, looking this way and that with his head hunched between his shoulders. He walked past one underpass, shook his head and set off towards a different one, then stopped in front of an advertising hoarding where the crush was less fierce. Clutching his things clumsily against his chest, he took out a crumpled piece of paper and started to study it closely. From the look on his face he knew perfectly well he was being followed.

The three people standing next to a wall nearby were quite okay with that: a strikingly beautiful redhead in a slinky, clinging silk dress, a young man in punk clothes with a bored expression in eyes that looked surprisingly old, and a rather more mature, sleek-looking man with a camp manner and long hair.

'It doesn't look like him,' the young man with the old eyes said doubtfully. 'Not like him at all. I didn't see him for very long, and it was a long time ago, but . . .'

'Perhaps you'd like to ask Djoru, just to make sure?' the girl asked derisively. 'I can see it's him.'

'You accept responsibility?' There was no surprise or wish to argue in the young man's voice. He was just checking.

'Yes,' said the girl, keeping her eyes fixed on the little man. 'Let's go. We'll take him in the underpass.'

They set out unhurriedly, walking in step. Then they separated and the girl carried on walking straight ahead, while the men went off to each side.

The little man folded up his piece of paper and set off uncertainly for the underpass.

The sudden absence of other people would have surprised a Muscovite or a frequent visitor to the capital. After all, this was the shortest and easiest route from the metro to the platform of the mainline station. But the little man took no notice. He paid no attention to the people who stopped behind him as if they'd run into an invisible barrier and walked off to the other underpasses. And there was no way he could have seen that the same thing was happening at the other end of the underpass, inside the railway station.

The sleek man came towards him, smiling. The attractive young woman and the young man with an earring and torn jeans closed in on him from behind.

The little man carried on walking.

'Hang on, Grandpa,' the sleek man said in a friendly voice that matched his appearance – high-pitched, affected. 'Don't be in such a hurry.'

The Central Asian smiled and nodded, but he didn't stop.

The sleek man made a pass with one hand, as if he was drawing a line between himself and the little man. The air shimmered and a cold breath of wind swept through the underpass. Up on the platform children started to cry and dogs to howl.

The little man stopped, looking straight ahead with a thoughtful expression. He pursed his lips, blew, and smiled cunningly at the man standing in front of him. There was a sharp, tinkling sound, like glass breaking. The sleek man's face contorted in pain and he took a step backwards.

'Bravo, *devona*,' said the young woman, coming to a halt behind the Central Asian. 'But now you definitely shouldn't be in a hurry.'

'Oh, I need to hurry, oh yes I do,' the little man jabbered rapidly. 'Would you like some melon, beautiful lady?'

The young woman smiled as she studied him. She made a suggestion:

'Why don't you come with us? We'll sit and eat your melon, drink some tea. We've been waiting for you so long, it's not polite to go running off straight away.'

The little man's face expressed intense thought. Then he nodded:

'Let's go, let's go.'

His first step knocked the sleek man off his feet. It was as if there were an invisible shield moving along in front of the little man, a wall of raging wind: the sleek man was swept along the ground with his long hair trailing behind him, his eyes screwed up in terror, a silent scream breaking from his throat.

The young punk waved his hand through the air, sending flashes of scarlet light flying at the little man. They were blindingly bright as they left his hand, but began to fade halfway to their target, and only reached the Central Asian's back as a barely visible glimmer.

'Uh!' the little man said, but he didn't stop. He twitched his shoulder blades, as if some annoying fly had landed on his back.

'Alisa!' the young man called, continuing his fruitless attack, working his fingers to compact the air, drawing the scarlet fire out of it and flinging it at the little man. 'Alisa!'

The girl leaned her head to one side as she watched the Central

Asian walking away. She whispered something and ran her hand across her dress. Out of nowhere a slim, transparent prism appeared in her hand.

The little man started to walk faster, swerving left and right and holding his head down strangely. The sleek man went tumbling along in front of him, no longer even attempting to cry out. His face was ragged and bleeding, his arms and legs were limp and useless, as if he hadn't simply slid three metres across a smooth floor, but been dragged three kilometres across the rocky steppe by a wild hurricane, or behind a galloping horse.

The girl looked at the little man through the prism.

First the Central Asian started to walk more slowly. Then he groaned and unclasped his hands – the melon smashed open with a crunch against the marble floor, the briefcase fell with a soft, heavy thud.

The man whom the girl had called *devona* gasped.

He slumped to the floor, shuddering as he fell. His cheeks collapsed inwards, his cheekbones protruded sharply, his hands were suddenly bony, the skin covered with a network of veins. His black hair didn't turn grey, but it was suddenly thinner and dusted with white. The air around him began to shimmer and currents of heat streamed towards Alisa.

'What I have not given shall henceforth be mine,' the girl hissed. 'All that is yours is mine.'

Her face flushed with colour as rapidly as the little man's body dried out. Her lips smacked as she whispered strange, breathy words. The punk frowned and lowered his hand – the final scarlet ray slammed into the floor, turning the stone dark.

'Very easy,' he said, 'very easy.'

'The boss was most displeased,' said the girl, hiding the prism away in the folds of her dress. She smiled. Her face radiated a sexual energy.

'Easy, but our Kolya was unlucky.'

The punk nodded, glancing at the long-haired man's motionless body. There was no great sympathy in his eyes, but no hostility either.

'That's for sure,' he said, walking confidently towards the little man's desiccated corpse. He ran his hand through the air above the body, which crumbled into dust. With his next pass the young man reduced the melon to a sticky mess.

'The briefcase,' said the girl. 'Check the briefcase.'

Another wave of his hand, and the worn imitation leather cracked apart and the briefcase fell open, like an oyster shell under the knife of an experienced pearl-diver. But to judge from the young man's expression, the pearl he'd been expecting wasn't there. Two clean changes of underwear, a pair of cheap cotton tracksuit bottoms, a white shirt, rubber sandals in a plastic bag, a polystyrene cup with dried Korean noodles, a spectacles case.

He made a few more passes and the polystyrene cup split open, the clothing came apart at the seams and the case opened to reveal the spectacles.

'Shit! He hasn't got anything, Alisa! Nothing at all!'

An expression of surprise slowly spread across the witch's face.

'Stasik, this is the *devona*, the courier. He couldn't have trusted what he was carrying to anyone else!'

'He must have done,' the young man said, stirring the Central Asian's ashes with his foot. 'I warned you, didn't I, Alisa? You can expect anything from the Light Ones. You took responsibility. I may be a low-level magician, but I have more experience than you – fifty years more.'

Alisa nodded. There was no confusion in her eyes now. Her hand slid over her dress again, seeking the prism.

'Yes,' she said softly. 'You're right, Stasik. But in fifty years' time our experience will be equal.'

The punk laughed, then squatted down beside the long-haired man's body and started going swiftly through his pockets.

'You think so?'

'I'm sure. You shouldn't have insisted on having your own way. I was the one who wanted to check the other passengers as well.'

The young man swung round to protest, but it was too late – the hot currents of his life energy were already streaming out of his body.

CHAPTER 1

THE OLDSMOBILE was ancient, which was why I liked it. But the open windows were no help against the insane heat rising from the road after the sun had been scorching it all day long. What was needed was an air conditioner.

Ilya was probably thinking the same thing. He was driving with one hand on the wheel, glancing round all the time and chatting to everyone. I knew a magician of his level could identify probabilities ten minutes in advance and there wasn't going to be any crash, but I was still feeling rather uneasy.

'I was thinking about putting in an air conditioner,' he told Yulia apologetically. The young girl was suffering worse than anyone from the heat, her face had come out in nasty red blotches and her eyes were glazed. I was just hoping she wasn't going to be sick. 'But it would have ruined the entire car, it wasn't meant to have one. No air conditioner, no mobile phone, no on-board computer.'

'Uhuh?' said Yulia, with a feeble smile. We'd all been working late the day before. No one had got to bed at all, we'd been working in the office until five a.m. and then stayed there for the rest of the night. I suppose it's unfair to make a thirteen-year-old

girl slave away like that with the grown-ups. But it was what she'd
wanted, no one had forced her.

From her seat in the front, Svetlana shot Yulia an anxious look.
Then she looked at Semyon disapprovingly. The imperturbable
magician almost choked on his Yava cigarette. He breathed in and
all the smoke drifting around inside the car was drawn into his
lungs. He flicked the butt out of the window. The Yava was
already a concession to popular opinion – until just recently
Semyon had preferred to smoke Flight and other equally repulsive
tobacco products.

'Close the windows,' said Semyon.

A moment later it suddenly started getting cold. There was a
subtle, salty sea smell in the air. I could even tell that it was the sea
at night, and quite close – the typical smell of the Crimean shore.
Iodine, seaweed, a subtle hint of wormwood. The Black Sea.
Koktebel.

'Koktebel?' I asked.

'Yalta,' Semyon replied. 'September tenth, 1972, about three in
the morning. After a minor storm.'

Ilya clicked his tongue enviously.

'Pretty good! How come you haven't used up a set of sensations
like that in all this time?'

Yulia gave Semyon a guilty look. Climate conservation wasn't
something every magician found easy, and the sensations Semyon
had just used would have been a hit at any party.

'Thank you, Semyon Pavlovich,' she said. For some reason Yulia
was as shy of Semyon as she was of the boss, and she always called
him by both his first name and his patronymic.

'Oh, that's nothing,' Semyon replied equably. 'My collection
includes rain in the taiga in 1913, and I've got the 1940 typhoon,
a spring morning in Jurmaala in '56, and I think there's a winter
evening in Gagry.'

Ilya laughed:

'Forget the winter evening in Gagry. But rain in the taiga . . .'

'I won't swap,' Semyon warned him. 'I know your collection, you haven't got anything nearly that good.'

'What about two, no, three for one . . .'

'I could give it to you as a present,' Semyon suggested.

'Forget it,' said Ilya, jerking on the steering wheel. 'What could I give you that would compare with that?'

'Then I'll invite you when I unseal it.'

'I suppose I should be grateful for that.'

He started sulking, naturally. I always thought of them as more or less equal in power, maybe Ilya was somewhat stronger. But Semyon had a talent for spotting the moment that was worth recording magically. And he didn't use his collection without good reason.

Of course, some people might have thought what he'd just done was a waste: brightening up the last half-hour of our journey with such a precious set of sensations.

'Nectar like that should be breathed in the evening, with kebabs on the barbecue,' said Ilya. He could be incredibly thick-skinned sometimes. Yulia tensed.

'I remember one time in the Middle East,' Semyon said unexpectedly. 'Our helicopter . . . anyway, never mind that . . . we set out on foot. Our communications equipment had been destroyed, and using magic would have been like walking through Harlem with a placard saying "Beat the niggers!" We set out on foot, across the Hadramaut. We had hardly any distance left to go to get to our regional agent, maybe a hundred kilometres. But we were all exhausted. And we had no water. And then Alyoshka – he's a nice guy who works in the Maritime Region now – said: "I can't take any more, Semyon Pavlovich, I've got a wife and two children at home, I want to get back alive." He lay down on the sand and unsealed his special stash. He had rain in it. A cloudburst, twenty minutes of it. We drank all we needed, and filled our canteens, and recovered our strength. I felt like punching him in the face for not telling us sooner, but I took pity on him.'

Nobody in the car said anything for a minute, savouring Semyon's story.

Ilya was the first to gather his wits.

'Why didn't you use your rain in the taiga?'

'What a comparison,' Semyon snorted. A collector's item from 1913 and a standard spring cloudburst collected in Moscow. It smelled of gasoline, would you believe!'

'I do.'

'Well, there you are. There's a time and place for everything. The evening I just recalled was pleasant enough, but not really outstanding. Just about right for your old jalopy.'

Svetlana laughed quietly. The faint air of tension was dispelled.

The Night Watch had been working feverishly all week long. Not that there'd been anything unusual happening in Moscow, it was just routine. The city was in the grip of a heatwave unprecedented for June, and reports of incidents had dropped to an all-time low. Neither the Light Ones nor the Dark Ones were enjoying it too much.

Our analysts spent about twenty-four hours working on the theory that the unexpectedly hot weather had been caused by some move the Dark Ones were planning. No doubt at the same time the Day Watch were investigating whether we Light Magicians had interfered with the climate. When both sides became convinced the anomalous weather was due to natural causes, we were all left with absolutely nothing to do.

The Dark Ones had turned as quiet as flies pinned down by rain. Despite all the doctors' forecasts, the number of accidents and natural deaths across the city fell. The Light Ones didn't much feel like working either, magicians squabbled over unimportant trivia, it took half a day to get the simplest documents out of the archives, and when the analysts were asked to forecast the weather they replied acidly with eighteenth-century gibberish such as: 'The water is dark in the clouds.' Boris Ignatievich wandered round the office in a stupor: even with his oriental origins and great experience of the East, he was floored by Moscow's own version of hot weather. The previous morning, Thursday, he'd called all the staff together, appointed two volunteers from the Watch to assist him and told everyone else to clear out of the city. To go anywhere, the Maldives or Greece if we wanted, down to hell's own kitchen if we liked – even that would be more comfortable. Or just to a dacha outside town. We were told not to show up in the office again until Monday lunchtime.

The boss waited for exactly a minute, until happy smiles had spread across everyone's faces, then added that it would be only fair for us to earn this unexpected break with an intensive spell of work. That way we wouldn't end up feeling guilty of having wasted the time. The title of the old classic was to the point, he said – 'Monday starts on Saturday'. So having been granted three extra days of holiday, we had to get through all the routine work in the remaining time.

And that's what we'd been doing – getting through it. Some of us almost until the morning. We'd checked up on the Dark Ones who were still in town and under special observation: vampires, werewolves, incubi and succubi, active witches, all sorts of troublesome low-level riff-raff. Everything was in order. What the vampires wanted right now wasn't hot blood, but cold beer. Instead of trying to cast spells on their neighbours, the witches were all trying to summon up a little rain over Moscow.

But now we were on our way to relax. Not as far as the Maldives, of course – the boss had been too optimistic about the finance office's generosity. But even two or three days out of town would be great. We felt sorry for the poor volunteers who'd stayed behind in the capital to keep watch with the boss.

'I've got to call home,' said Yulia. She'd really livened up after Semyon exchanged the damp heat in the car for the cool sea air. 'Sveta, can I borrow your phone?'

I was enjoying the cool too. I glanced into the cars we were overtaking: in most of them the windows were rolled down, and the people glared at us with loathing, wrongly assuming that our ancient automobile had powerful air conditioning.

'The turn's coming up soon,' I said to Ilya.

'I remember. I drove here once before.'

'Quiet!' Yulia hissed fiercely and started chatting on the phone. 'Mum, it's me! . . . Yes, I'm here already . . . Of course, it's great! There's a lake here . . . No, it's shallow. Mum, I can't talk for long, Sveta's dad lent me his phone . . . No, there's no one else . . . Sveta? Just a moment.'

Svetlana sighed and took the phone from Yulia. She gave me a dark look and I tried to put on a serious expression.

'Hello, Aunty Natasha,' Svetlana said in a squeaky child's voice. '. . . Yes, very pleased . . . Yes . . . No, with the grown-ups. Mum's a long way off, shall I call her? . . . Okay, I'll tell her. Definitely. Goodbye.'

She switched off the phone and spoke into empty space:

'So tell me, young lady, what's going to happen when your mother asks the real Sveta how the holiday went?'

'Sveta will say we had a great time.'

Svetlana sighed and glanced at Semyon as if looking for support.

'Using magical powers for personal goals leads to unexpected consequences,' Semyon declared in a dry, official voice. 'I remember one time—'

'What magic powers?' Yulia asked, genuinely surprised. 'I told my friend Sveta I was going off to a party with some guys and asked her to cover for me. She was shocked, but of course she said yes.'

In the driving seat Ilya laughed.

'Why wouldn't I want to go to a party?' Yulia asked indignantly, clearly not understanding what he found so funny. 'That's the way the human kids amuse themselves. So what are you laughing at?'

For every member of our Watch, work takes up the greater part of our lives. Not because we're workaholics – who wouldn't rather relax than work? And not because the work is so very interesting – we spend most of our time on boring patrol duty or polishing the seats of our trousers in the office. It's simply that there aren't enough of us. It's much easier for the Day Watch to keep up to strength, any Dark One is only too keen for a chance to wield power. But our situation's quite different.

Outside work, though, every one of us has his own little piece of life that he won't give up to anyone: not to the Light and not to the Dark. That's all ours . . . A little piece of life that we don't hide, and don't put on display either. What's left of our original, essential human nature.

Some go travelling whenever they can. Ilya, for instance, prefers ordinary package holidays, but Semyon likes hitchhiking. He once travelled from Moscow to Vladivostok without a single kopeck and in record time, but he didn't register his achievement with the League of Free Travellers, because he used his magical powers twice on the way.

For Ignat – and he's not the only one – holidays are always about sex. It's a stage almost all of us go through, because Others get far more opportunities than humans do. It's a well-known fact that humans feel a powerful attraction to Others, even though they may not realise it.

There are plenty of collectors among us too. From modest

collectors of penknives, key-rings, stamps and cigarette lighters to collectors of weather, smells, auras and spells. I used to collect model cars, spending big money on rare models that only had value to a few thousand idiots. I dumped the entire collection into two cardboard boxes ages ago. I ought to take them out into the court-yard and tip them into the sandpit for the kids to enjoy.

There are lots of hunters and fishermen. Igor and Garik are into extreme parachuting. Our useless programmer Galya, a sweet girl, is into growing bonsai trees. I guess we cover pretty much the entire range of entertainments that the human race has ever invented.

But what Tiger Cub did in her spare time, I had no idea, even though it was her place we were going to. I was almost as keen to find out as I had been to escape from the scorching heat in town. When you spend a bit of time at someone's place, it usually doesn't take too long to find out what their special interest is.

'Are we almost there now?' Yulia asked in a capricious tone. We'd already turned off the main highway and travelled about five kilometres along a dirt road, past a little dacha settlement and over a small river.

'Yes, we're almost there,' I answered, checking the image of the route that Tiger Cub had left with us.

'Actually, we're there already,' said Ilya, swerving the car off the road, straight at the trees. Yulia gasped and covered her face with her hands. Svetlana reacted more calmly, but even she put her hands out, expecting a crash.

The car hurtled through thick bushes, over fallen branches and crashed into a solid wall of trees. But, of course, there was no impact. We leapt straight through the magical mirage and landed on a well-surfaced road. Straight ahead there was a small lake glinting like a bright mirror in the sun, with a two-storey brick house standing by the shore, surrounded by a tall fence.

'What always amazes me about shape-shifters,' said Svetlana, 'is how obsessed they are with secrecy. Not only does she hide behind a mirage, she has a fence too.'

'Tiger Cub's not a shape-shifter!' Yulia objected. 'She's a transformer magician.'

'That's the same thing,' Sveta said gently.

Yulia looked at Semyon, clearly expecting him to back her up.

'Essentially Sveta's right. Highly specialised combat magicians are like any other shape-shifters. But with a plus sign instead of a minus. If Tiger Cub had been in a slightly different mood when she first entered the Twilight, she'd have turned into a Dark shape-shifter. There are very few people whose path is completely determined in advance. There's usually a struggle during the preparation for initiation.'

'And how was it with me?' asked Yulia.

'I've told you before,' Semyon growled. 'It was pretty easy.'

'A mild remoralisation of your teachers and parents,' Ilya said with a laugh as he stopped the car in front of the gates. 'And the little girl was immediately filled with love and kindness for the whole world.'

'Ilya!' Semyon said sharply. He was Yulia's mentor, a rather lazy mentor who almost never interfered in the young sorceress's development, but he obviously didn't appreciate Ilya's unnecessary wisecracks.

Yulia was a talented girl, and the Watch had high hopes for her. But not so high that she had to be driven through the tortuous labyrinth of moral logic at the same rate as Svetlana, a future Great Sorceress.

Sveta and I must have had the same thought at the same time – we looked at each other. And after we looked, we turned our eyes away.

We could feel a pressure on us, forcing us apart. I'd be a third-grade magician for ever. Any moment now Sveta would outgrow me and in a short time – a very short time, because the Watch's management thought it was necessary – she would become a sorceress beyond classification.

And then all we'd have left would be friendly handshakes when we met and an exchange of cards on birthdays and Christmas.

'Are they asleep in there, or what?' Ilya asked indignantly. His mind wasn't distracted by our problems. He stuck his head out the window, and the car immediately filled with up with hot air, though at least it was clean. He waved his hand, looking into the camera at the gate, and sounded his horn.

The gates started opening slowly.

'That's better,' the magician snorted as he drove through.

It was a large plot of land, thickly planted with trees. The striking thing was how they'd managed to build the house without damaging the huge pines and firs. Apart from a small flowerbed beside a little fountain that wasn't working, there were no other signs of cultivation. There were already five cars on the concrete drive in front of the house. I recognised the old Niva that Danila drove out of stubborn patriotism, and Olga's sports car – how had she managed to drive over the dirt road in that? Standing between them was the battered station wagon belonging to Tolik and two other cars I'd seen at the office, but I didn't know whose they were.

'They didn't bother to wait for us,' Ilya said crossly. 'They're already partying, while the best people in the Watch are still bouncing along the country roads.'

He switched off the engine and Yulia immediately screeched in delight:

'Tiger Cub!'

She scrambled right over me, opened the door and jumped out of the car.

Semyon swore and followed her, moving incredibly fast. Just in time.

I don't know where those dogs had been hiding. In any case, they were still camouflaged until the moment Yulia got out of the car. But as soon as her feet touched the ground, the light-brown shadows closed in on her from all sides.

Yulia shrieked. She was more than powerful enough to deal with a pack of wolves, never mind five or six dogs, but she'd never actually been in a genuine fight, and she lost her head. To be quite honest, even I hadn't been expecting an attack – not here. And especially not this kind. Dogs never attack Others. They're afraid of Dark Ones. They like Light Ones. You have to train an animal really long and hard in order to suppress its natural fear of a walking source of magic.

Svetlana, Ilya and I scrambled out of the car. But Semyon beat us all to it. He grabbed hold of Yulia with one hand and made a pass in the air with the other. I thought he would use fright magic, or withdraw into the Twilight, or reduce the dogs to dust on the spot. A reflex response usually relies on the simplest spells.

But Semyon used the temporal freeze. He caught two of the dogs in the air: their bodies were left hanging there, enveloped in a blue glow, with their narrow, snarling muzzles reaching out. Saliva dripped from their fangs like gleaming blue hail.

The three dogs who'd been frozen on the ground weren't quite so impressive.

Tiger Cub came running over to us. Her face was white, her eyes wide. She looked at Yulia for a moment, who was still whimpering, but she was getting quieter.

'Everyone okay?' Tiger Cub asked eventually.

'Fortunately,' mumbled Ilya, lowering his wand. 'What kind of animals are you keeping here?'

'They wouldn't have done anything,' Tiger Cub said ruefully.

'Oh yeah?' Semyon took Yulia out from under his arm and set

her down on the ground. He pensively ran one finger over the bared fang of a dog hanging in mid-air. The film of the time freeze was springy and elastic under his hand.

'I swear!' said Tiger Cub, pressing her hand to her heart. 'Guys, Sveta, Yulia, I'm sorry. I didn't have a chance to stop them. The dogs are trained to knock strangers down and restrain them.'

'Even Others?'

'Yes.'

'Even Light Ones?' There was a note of uncertain respect in Semyon's voice.

Tiger Cub dropped her eyes and nodded.

Yulia went over, moved up close to her, and said more or less calmly:

'I wasn't frightened. Just taken by surprise, that's all.'

'It's a good thing I was slow to react too,' Ilya commented, putting away his wand. 'Roast dog's too exotic a dish for me. But your dogs know me, Tiger Cub!'

'They wouldn't have touched you.'

The tension slowly eased. Of course, nothing too serious would have happened, we know how to heal each other, but it would have been the end of the picnic.

'I'm sorry,' Tiger Cub repeated. She looked at us all imploringly.

'But listen, why do you need all this?' asked Sveta, with a glance at the dogs. 'Can you explain that to me? Your powers are strong enough to beat off a platoon of Green Berets, what do you need Rottweilers for?'

'They're not Rottweilers, they're Staffordshire bull terriers.'

'What difference does that make?'

'They caught a burglar once. I'm only here two days a week, I can't go back and forth to town all the time.'

The explanation wasn't all that convincing. A simple frightening spell would have kept any ordinary people from coming anywhere near the place. But no one got a chance to say it – Tiger Cub got in first:

'It's just the way I am, okay?'

'How long are the dogs going to stay hanging there like that?' asked Yulia. 'I want to make friends with them. Otherwise I'll be left with a latent psychological complex that's bound to affect my personality and my sexual preferences.'

Semyon snorted. Yulia's comment had finally defused the tension – but it was anybody's guess how spontaneous or calculated it had been.

'They'll start moving again before the evening. Well, hostess, are you going to invite us in?'

We left the dogs where they were round the car and walked towards the house.

'What a great place you have, Tiger Cub!' said Yulia. She was ignoring the rest of us entirely now, clinging to the young woman. As if the sorceress was her idol and she could be forgiven for anything, even overvigilant guard dogs.

Why is it that the powers we can't develop are always the ones that become an obsession?

Yulia's a wonderful analytical sorceress. She can untangle the threads of reality and reveal the concealed magical causes of events that seem quite ordinary. She's really smart and everyone in the department loves her, not just as a sweet girl, but as a comrade-in-arms, a valued and sometimes quite irreplaceable colleague. But her idol is Tiger Cub, a shape-shifting sorceress, a combat magician. Why couldn't she look up to good-hearted old Polina Vasilievna, who worked in the analytical section part-time, or fall for the head of the department, the impressive middle-aged ladykiller Edik.

But no, she'd chosen Tiger Cub as her role model.

I started whistling as I walked along at the back of the procession. I caught Svetlana's eye and gave her a quick nod. Everything was fine. We had entire days of doing nothing ahead of us. No Dark Ones or Light Ones, no intrigues and plots, no confrontations. Just swimming in the lake, sunbathing, eating kebabs from the barbecue and washing them down with red wine. And in the evening – the bathhouse. A big house like this had to have a good bathhouse. And then Semyon and I could take a couple of bottles of vodka and a jar of pickled mushrooms, get as far away as possible from the rest of the crowd and drink ourselves stupid, gazing up at the stars and making philosophical conversation on elevated subjects.

Marvellous.

I wanted to be a human being. For twenty-four hours at least.

Semyon stopped and nodded to me.

'Let's take two bottles. Three, even. Someone else might decide to join us.'

'It's a deal,' I said. He hadn't been reading my thoughts, it was just that he had so much more experience of life than I did.

'It's easier for you,' Semyon added. 'I almost never get the chance to be a human being.'

'Do you need to?' Tiger Cub asked, halting by the door.

Semyon shrugged:

'Of course not. But I kind of like the idea.'

We went into the house.

Twenty guests was a bit too much even for this house. If we'd been ordinary people, it would have been different. But we were too noisy. Try bringing together twenty kids who've been studying hard for months, give them the free run of a well-stocked toyshop, let them do anything they like and see what you end up with.

Sveta and I were just about the only ones not really caught up in the boisterous fun and games. We each grabbed a glass of wine from the buffet table and settled down on a leather sofa in the corner of the sitting room.

Semyon and Ilya locked horns in a magical duel. Very civilised and peaceful, amusing for the others who were watching – at first, that is. Semyon must have wounded his friend's vanity in the car: now they were taking it in turns to change the climate in the room. We'd already had winter in the forest outside Moscow, and autumn mist, and summer in Spain. Tiger Cub had categorically forbidden any kind of rain, but the magicians weren't trying to summon up a violent display of the elements. They'd obviously imposed some restrictions of their own on their range and the competition was less about who could produce the most unusual natural moment ever recorded than who could deliver something that suited the mood of the moment.

Garik, Farid and Danila were playing cards. A perfectly standard game, without frills, but the air above the table was nevertheless sparkling with magic. They were using every possible magical means to cheat and protect themselves against each other's tricks.

Ignat stood by the open doors, surrounded by women from the research department, with our useless programmers in tow. Our Casanova must have suffered some kind of romantic reversal, and he was now seeking comfort in a close circle of friends.

'Anton,' Sveta asked in a low voice, 'what do you think, is all this for real?'

'What exactly?'

'All this happy mood. You remember what Semyon said, don't you?'

I shrugged:

'Can we come back to this when we get to be a hundred? I'm feeling good. It's that simple. I don't have to go running off anywhere, I don't have to do any calculations. The Watches are lying low in the shade with their tongues hanging out.'

'I feel good too,' Svetlana agreed. 'But there are only four of us here who are young, or almost young. Yulia, Tiger Cub, you and me. What are we going to be like in a hundred years? Or in three hundred?'

'We'll have to wait and see.'

'Anton, listen to me,' Sveta said, touching my cheek lightly. 'I'm very proud that I joined the Watch. I'm happy that my mother's well again. My life's better now, no doubt about it. I can even understand why the boss put you through that ordeal . . .'

'Don't, Sveta.' I took hold of her hand. 'Even I understood that, and I got the worst of it. Don't let's talk about it.'

'I wasn't going to,' Sveta said, and drained her wine glass. 'Anton, what I'm trying to say is – I can't see any real joy.'

'Where?' Sometimes I must seem incredibly thick-headed.

'Here. In the Night Watch. In our close, friendly team. After all, every day is just one more battle for us. A big one or a little one. With a crazed werewolf, with a Dark Magician, with all the powers of the Dark at once. Flex those sinews, jut out that chin, prepare to block that attack with your bare chest or squat on a hedgehog with your bare arse.'

I snorted with laughter.

'Sveta, what's so bad about all that? Yes, we're soldiers. Every last one of us, from Yulia to Gesar. Sure, it's no great fun being at war. But if we withdraw, then . . .'

'Then what?' Sveta asked. 'Will the Apocalypse come? The forces of Good and Evil have been fighting each other for a thousand years. Tearing at each other's throats, setting armies of humans against each other – and all for the highest goals. But tell me, Anton, have people really not become any better in all that time?'

'Yes, they have.'

'And what about since the Watches were set up? Anton, my dear, you've told me so many things, and not just you. That the most important battle is for people's souls, that we're preventing mass slaughter. But are we? People still kill each other. Far more than they used to two hundred years ago.'

'Are you trying to tell me that the work we do is actually harmful?'

'No,' said Sveta, with a weary shake of her head. 'No, I'm not. I'm not that conceited. I was just trying to say that maybe we're simply the Light, and that's all there is to it . . . You know, they've started selling fake New Year Tree decorations in Moscow. They look just like the real thing, but they don't bring people any joy at all.'

She told the joke with a straight face, without even changing her tone of voice. She looked into my eyes.

'Do you understand what I mean?'

'I understand.'

'Maybe you do. The Dark Ones do less Evil,' said Svetlana. 'These mutual concessions of ours, good deed for bad deed, licences for murder and healing, those can all be justified, I'm sure. The Dark Ones do less Evil than they used to, and we don't do Evil by definition. But what about humans?'

'What have they got to do with it?'

'What do you mean? It's them we're defending. Tirelessly, self-sacrificingly. So why aren't their lives getting any better? They do the work of the Dark themselves. Why? Maybe it's because we've lost something, Anton. The faith Light Magicians used to have when they sent entire armies to their deaths, and marched in the front ranks themselves? The ability not just to defend people, but to bring them joy? What good are secure walls, if they're the walls of a prison? Humans have forgotten about genuine magic, they don't believe in the Dark, but they don't believe in the Light either! Yes, Anton, we are soldiers. But people only love the army when there's a war going on.'

'There *is* a war going on.'

'Who knows about it?'

'We're not just ordinary soldiers, I suppose,' I said. It never feels good to retreat from old, familiar positions, but there was no other way. 'More like hussars. Taram, taram, taram . . .'

'The hussars knew how to smile. But we hardly ever do.'

'Then tell me what I ought to do?' I said, realising that what had promised to be a lovely day was rapidly running downhill into a dark, stinking ravine filled with old garbage. 'Tell me! You're a Great Sorceress, or you soon will be. A general in our war. I'm just a simple lieutenant. Give me my orders, and make sure they're the right ones. Tell me what I should do!'

I noticed that the entire room had fallen silent, everyone was listening to us. But at this stage I didn't care.

'Tell me to go out in the street and kill Dark Ones, and I'll go. I'm not very good at it, but I'll give it my best shot. Tell me to smile and shower Good on the people, and I'll go and do it. Good and Evil, Light and Dark, we use these words so often we lose sight of what they mean, we hang them out like flags and leave them to rot in the wind and the rain. Then give us a new word! Give us new flags! Tell me where to go and what to do!'

Her lips started to tremble. I stopped short, but it was too late.

Svetlana sat there crying, with her hands over her face.

What on earth was I doing?

Had we really forgotten how to smile at each other?

Maybe I was right, a hundred times right, but . . .

What was my truth worth, if I was prepared to defend the entire world, but not those who were close to me? If I subdued hate, but wouldn't give love a chance?

I jumped up, put my arm round Svetlana's shoulders and led her out of the room. The magicians all stood there, looking the other way. Maybe it wasn't the first time they'd seen scenes like this. Maybe they understood the whole thing.

'Anton.' Tiger Cub appeared beside me, soundlessly. She pushed me forwards and opened the door, looking at me with both reproach and unexpected understanding. Then she left us alone.

We stood there for a moment without moving. Svetlana cried quietly, sobbing into my shoulder, and I waited. It was too late for words now. I'd said far too much already.

'I'll try.'

I hadn't been expecting that. Anything at all: resentment, counter-attack, complaints, anything but that.

Svetlana took one hand away from her wet face. She shook her head and smiled.

'You're right, Antosha. Absolutely right. So far all I've done is complain and protest. I whine like a child and I don't understand anything. Everyone just sticks my nose into my porridge and let's me play with fire and waits for me to grow up a bit. So I'll just have to do it, I'll try, I'll give you new flags.'

'Sveta—'

'You're right,' she interrupted. 'Only I'm a little bit right too. But I shouldn't have let go like that in front of the others, I know that. They're only having fun the best way they know how. Today's a day off, and nothing should be allowed to spoil it. Deal?'

I felt that wall again. The invisible wall that would always stand between me and Gesar, between me and the bosses.

The wall that time would build between us. That day I'd laid a few rows of cold crystal bricks with my own hands.

'Forgive me, Sveta,' I whispered. 'Forgive me.'

'Let's forget it,' she said very firmly. 'Let's forget it. While we still can forget.'

We eventually looked around us.

'The study?' Sveta guessed.

Stained oak bookshelves with the volumes protected by dark glass. A massive desk with a computer on it.

'Yes.'

'Does Tiger Cub live alone, then?'

'I don't know,' I said, shaking my head. 'We don't usually ask about things like that.'

'It looks as if she does. Right now, at least.' Svetlana took out her handkerchief and began wiping her tears away. 'She has a nice house. Let's go, everyone must be feeling awkward.'

I shook my head:

'They must have sensed that we're not quarrelling.'

'No, they couldn't have. There are barriers between all the rooms here, you can't sense anything through them.'

I looked through the Twilight and spotted the concealed glimmering in the walls.

'I see it now. You're getting more powerful with every day.'

Svetlana smiled, tensely, but with pride. She said:

'It's strange. Why put up barriers if you live alone?'

'And why build them if you don't?' I asked in a low voice that didn't require an answer. Svetlana didn't try to give me one.

We walked out of the study back into the sitting room.

The atmosphere wasn't entirely funereal, but it was close.

Either Semyon or Ilya had made a supreme effort and filled the room with a damp, marshy smell. Ignat was standing with his arms round Lena and gazing miserably at everyone else. He liked to have fun, in any form, any quarrelling or tension was like a knife in the heart to him. The card-players were staring silently at a single card lying on the table, and as they looked at it, it twitched, changing suit and value. Yulia looked sulky. She was asking Olga something in a quiet voice.

'Will someone pour me a drink?' Sveta asked, holding me by the hand. 'Didn't you know the best medicine for hysterical women is fifty grams of cognac?'

Tiger Cub, who had been standing by the window looking unhappy, walked quickly across to the bar. Did she really blame herself for our row?

Sveta and I took a glass of cognac each, clinked glasses demonstratively and kissed each other. I caught Olga's look: not delighted, not sad, just interested. And just slightly jealous.

I suddenly had a bad feeling.

As if I'd emerged from a labyrinth I'd been wandering around in for days, for months. And all I saw when I came out was the entrance to the next set of catacombs.

CHAPTER 2

IT WAS another two hours before I got a chance to talk with Olga alone. The jollity that had seemed so forced to Svetlana had already moved outside. Semyon was in charge of the barbecue, handing out kebabs to anyone who wanted them – they seemed to cook at a speed that definitely hinted at the use of magic. There were two crates of wine standing in the shade nearby.

Olga was chatting amicably with Ilya, each of them holding a skewer of kebab and a glass of wine. It was a shame to interrupt, but . . .

'Olga, I need to have a word with you,' I said, crossing towards them. Svetlana was engrossed in an argument with Tiger Cub – an intense discussion about the Watch's traditional New Year Carnival, which they'd moved on to from the subject of the hot weather. The moment was just right.

'Excuse me, Ilya,' said Olga with a shrug. 'We'll come back to this, okay? I'm intrigued by your views on the collapse of the Soviet Union. Even though you're wrong.'

Ilya smiled exultantly and walked off.

'Ask away, Anton,' Olga said to me in exactly the same tone.

'Do you know what I'm going to ask?'

'I think I can guess.'

I glanced around. There was no one near us. It was still that brief moment at the beginning of a dacha picnic when people want to eat and they want to drink, before their stomachs and their heads start to feel heavy.

'What's going to happen to Svetlana?'

'It's not easy to read the future. Especially the future of Great Magicians and Sorceresses . . .'

'Don't avoid the issue,' I said, looking into her eyes. 'Stop it. We worked together, didn't we? We were partners? When your punishment was still in force and you didn't even have that body. And your punishment was just.'

The blood drained from Olga's face.

'What do you know about my offence?'

'Everything.'

'How?'

'I work with the data, after all.'

'You don't have high enough clearance. And what happened to me has never been entered in the electronic archive.'

'Circumstantial evidence, Olya. You've seen ripples running across water, haven't you? The stone might be lying on the bottom already, deep in the silt, but the ripples still keep on going. Eroding the banks, casting up muck and foam, even over-turning boats if the stone was really big. Let's just say I've spent a long time standing on the bank, standing and watching the waves wearing it away.'

'You're bluffing.'

'No. Olga, what happens to Sveta, after this? What stage of the training?'

The sorceress looked at me, completely forgetting her cold kebab and half-empty glass. I struck again.

'You've been through that stage, haven't you?'

'Yes.' It looked as if she was going to open up. 'I have. But I was prepared for it more slowly.'

'So what's the great hurry with Sveta?'

'Nobody was expecting another Great Sorceress to be born this century. Gesar had to improvise, make things up as he went along.'

'Is that why they let you have your old form back? Not just for doing a good job?'

'You say you understand everything!' said Olga, and her eyes glinted angrily. 'So what's the point of tormenting me?'

'Are you monitoring her training? On the basis of your own experience?'

'Yes. Satisfied?'

'Olga, we're on the same side of the barricades,' I whispered.

'Then don't try and stop your comrades getting on with the job.'

'Olga, what's the final goal? What was it you couldn't do? What is it Sveta has to do?'

'You . . .' she said, genuinely confused now. 'Anton, you *were* bluffing!'

I didn't answer.

'You don't know anything! Ripples on the water! You don't even know which way to look to see them!'

'Maybe so. But I got the most important thing right, didn't I?'

Olga looked at me and bit her lip. Then she shook her head.

'You did. A straight answer to a straight question. But I'm not going to explain anything. You shouldn't even know about it. It doesn't concern you.'

'That's where you're wrong.'

'None of us wishes Sveta any harm,' Olga said sharply. 'Is that clear?'

'We don't know how to wish anyone harm. It's just that sometimes our Good is no different from Evil.'

'Anton, let's stop right there. I have no right to answer your questions. And we shouldn't spoil this surprise holiday for the rest.'

'Just how much of a surprise is it?' I asked suggestively. 'Well, Olya?'

But she'd already pulled herself together, and her expression remained impenetrable. Much too impenetrable for a question like that.

'You've found out too much already.' Her voice was louder, it had assumed its former tone of authority.

'Olya, we've never been sent off on holiday all at the same time before. Not even for one day. Why has Gesar sent all the Light Ones out of Moscow?'

'Not all.'

'Polina Vasilievna and Andrei don't count. You know perfectly well they're just office workers. Moscow's been left without a single Watch operative!'

'The Dark Ones have gone quiet too.'

'So what?'

'Anton, that's enough.'

I nodded, realising I wouldn't be able to get another word out of her.

'Okay, Olya. Six months ago we were on equal terms, even if it was only by accident. Now we're obviously not. I'm sorry. This is a problem for someone with the proper competence to deal with.'

Olga nodded. It was so unexpected I could hardly believe it.

'You've finally got the idea.'

Was she fooling me? Or did she really believe I'd decided not to interfere?

'I'm pretty quick on the uptake,' I said. I looked at Svetlana. She was chatting happily with Tolik.

'Are you angry with me?' Olga asked.

I touched her hand, smiled and went into the house. I wanted to do something. I wanted to do something as badly as a genie who's been let out of his bottle for the first time in a thousand years. Anything at all: raise up castles, lay waste to cities, program in Basic or embroider in cross-stitch.

I opened the door without touching it, by pushing at it through the Twilight. I don't know why I did it. I don't often do things like that, just sometimes when I've drunk a lot, or when I get really angry. The former wasn't the case here.

There was no one in the sitting room. Why would anyone want to sit inside, when outside there were hot kebabs, cold wine and more than enough loungers beneath the trees.

I flopped down into an armchair, picked up my glass – or Sveta's – from the low table and filled it with cognac, then downed it in one, as if it was cheap vodka, not fifteen-year-old Prazdnichny. I poured myself another glass.

That was when Tiger Cub came in.

'Don't mind, do you?' I asked.

'Of course not.' The sorceress sat down beside me. 'Anton, has something upset you?'

'Take no notice.'

'Have you had a quarrel with Sveta?'

I shook my head.

'That's not the problem.'

'Anton, have I done something wrong? Aren't the guys having a good time?'

I stared at her in genuine amazement.

'Tiger Cub, don't be stupid! Everything's just great. Everyone's enjoying themselves.'

'And you?'

I'd never seen the shape-shifting sorceress look so uncertain of herself. Were they having a good time or weren't they? You can't please everyone.

'They're continuing with Svetlana's training,' I said.

'What for?' she asked with a slight frown.

'I don't know. For something that Olga couldn't do. For something very dangerous and very important.'

'That's good.' She reached for a glass, poured herself some cognac and took a sip.

'Good?'

'Sure. That they're training her, giving her direction.' Tiger Cub looked around, trying to find something, then frowned and looked at the music centre by the wall. 'That remote's always going missing,' she said.

The music centre lit up and Queen started to play 'It's a Kind of Magic'. I was impressed by how casually she did it. Controlling electronic circuits at a distance isn't a simple trick, it's not like drilling holes in a wall just by looking at it or keeping mosquitoes away with fireballs.

'How long did you train to work in the Watch?' I asked.

'From when I was about seven years old. At sixteen, I was already involved in field operations.'

'Nine years! And it's easier for you – your magic's natural. They're planning to turn Svetlana into a Great Sorceress in six months or a year!'

'That's tough going,' the young woman agreed. 'Do you think the boss is wrong?'

I shrugged. To say the boss was wrong would have been about as stupid as denying that the sun rises in the east in the morning. He'd been learning how not to make mistakes for hundreds – even thousands – of years. Gesar might act harshly, even cruelly. He might provoke the Dark Ones and leave the Light Ones to carry the can. He might do anything at all. Except make a mistake.

'I think he's overestimating Sveta's strength,' I ventured.

'Come off it! The boss calculates everything.'

'I know he calculates everything. He plays the old game very well.'

'And he wishes Sveta well,' the sorceress added stubbornly. 'Do you understand that? In his own way, maybe. You would have acted differently, so would I, or Semyon, or Olga. Any one of us would have done things differently. But he's in charge of the Watch. And he has every right to be.'

'So he knows best?' I asked.

'Yes.'

'And what about freedom?' I asked, pouring myself another glass. I didn't really need it, my head was already starting to hum. 'Freedom?'

'You talk like the Dark Ones do,' the young woman snorted.

'I prefer to think they talk like I do.'

'It's all very simple, Anton.' Tiger Cub leaned down over me and looked in my eyes. She smelled of cognac and something else, a light floral smell. It wasn't likely to be perfume: shape-shifters don't like anything that is scented. 'You're in love with her.'

'Sure, I'm in love with her. That's not news.'

'You know she'll soon be on a higher level of power than you.'

'If she isn't already.' I didn't mention it, but I remembered how easily Sveta had sensed the magical screens in the walls.

'She'll go way beyond you. Her powers will totally dwarf yours. Her problems will seem incomprehensible to you, they'll seem bizarre. Stay with her and you'll start to feel like a useless parasite, a gigolo, you'll be clutching at the past.'

'Yes.' I nodded and was surprised to notice my glass was already empty. My hostess watched me closely as I filled it again. 'So I shan't stay. I don't need that.'

'But there isn't anything else on offer.'

I'd never suspected that she could be so hard. I hadn't expected her to be so concerned about whether everyone liked her

hospitality and her home, and I hadn't expected to hear this bitter
truth from her either.

'I know.'

'If you know that, Anton, there's only one reason you're feeling
so outraged about the boss dragging Sveta upwards so fast.'

'My time will soon be gone,' I said. 'It's sand running through
my fingers, rain falling from the sky.'

'Your time? Yours and hers, Anton.'

'It was never ours, never.'

'Why?'

It was a good question. I shrugged.

'You know, there are some animals that don't reproduce in
captivity.'

'There you go again!' she exclaimed. 'What captivity? You
should be glad for her. Svetlana will be the pride of the Light Ones.
You were the first to discover her, it was you who saved her.'

'For what? One more battle with the Dark? An unnecessary
battle?'

'Anton, now you're talking just like a Dark One yourself. You
love her! So don't demand or expect anything in return. That's the
way of the Light!'

'Love begins where the Dark and the Light end.'

Tiger Cub was so indignant she couldn't even respond. She
shook her head sadly and said reluctantly:

'You can at least promise . . .'

'That depends on what.'

'To be sensible. To trust your superiors.'

'I promise halfway.'

Tiger Cub sighed and then said confidingly:

'Listen, Anton, you probably think I don't understand you at all.
But it's not true. I didn't want to be a shape-shifting magician. I had
healing powers, and pretty serious ones.'

'Really?' I looked at her in amazement. I'd never have thought it.

'Yes, I did. But when I had to choose which side of my powers to develop, the boss called me in. We sat and talked over tea. We talked very seriously, like adults, although I was only a little girl, younger than Yulia is now. About what the Light needed and who the Watch needed, what I could achieve. And we decided that I should develop my combat powers, even at the expense of everything else. I didn't much like the idea at first. Do you know how painful it is when you change?'

'Into a tiger?'

'No, changing into a tiger's okay, the hard part's changing back. But I stuck with it. Because I believed the boss, because I realised it was the right thing to do.'

'And now?'

'Now I'm happy,' the young woman declared passionately. 'When I see what I would have lost, what I would have been doing with my time. Herbs and spells, fiddling with distorted psychic fields, neutralising black vortices, mixing up charms . . .'

'Blood, pain, fear, death,' I said in the same tone. 'Doing battle on two or three levels of reality simultaneously. Dodging the fire, tasting the blood, going through hell and high water.'

'That's war.'

'Yes, probably. But why do you have to be the one in the front line?'

'Someone has to, don't they? And then, after all, I wouldn't have had a house like this.' Tiger Cub waved her hand round the room. 'You know yourself you don't earn much from healing. If you heal with all your power, it just means someone else keeps killing people.'

'This is a nice place,' I agreed. 'But how often are you here?'

'Whenever I can be.'

'I guess that's not very often. You take shift after shift, you're always where the action's hottest.'

'That's my path.'

I nodded. What business was it of mine? I said:

'You're right. I suppose I must be tired. That's why I'm talking such rubbish.'

Tiger Cub looked at me suspiciously, surprised I'd given in so quickly.

'I need to sit here with my glass for a while,' I added. 'Get completey drunk all on my own, fall asleep under the table and wake up with a splitting headache. Then I'll feel better.'

'Go on, then,' the sorceress said, with a slight note of nervousness in her voice. 'What did we come here for? The bar's open, you can have whatever you like. We can go and join the others. Or I could stay and keep you company.'

'No, I'll be better off on my own,' I said, slapping my hand against the pot-bellied bottle. 'In absolute misery, with no food to go with the drink and no company. Look in before you go for a swim. Just in case I'm still capable of moving.'

'Okay.'

She smiled and went out. I was left all alone – unless the bottle of Armenian cognac counted as company. Sometimes it helps to believe it does.

She was a fine girl. They were all fine and wonderful, my friends and colleagues at the Watch. I could hear their voices through the Queen song, and I liked that. I got on really well with some of them and not so well with others. But I had no enemies here and I never would have. We were a close team, and there was only one way we could ever lose each other.

So why was I so unhappy about what was going on? I was the only one – Olga and Tiger Cub approved of what the boss was up to, and if I asked the others, they'd all feel the same way.

Maybe I really wasn't being objective.

Probably.

I took a sip of cognac and then looked into the Twilight, trying to locate the pale lights of unintelligent life in the room.

There were mosquitoes, two flies and one spider, right up in a corner of the ceiling.

I shuffled my fingers and made a tiny fireball, two millimetres across. I took aim at the spider – a fixed target is best for practising on – and sent the fireball on its way.

There was nothing immoral about my behaviour. We're not Buddhists, at least most of the Others in Russia aren't. We eat meat, we kill flies and mosquitoes, we poison cockroaches: if you're too lazy to learn new frightening spells every month, the insects quickly develop immunity to your magic.

Nothing immoral. It was just funny, it was the proverbial 'using a fireball to kill a mosquito'. A favourite game with children when they're studying for the Watch. I think the Dark Ones probably do the same, except that they don't distinguish between a fly and a sparrow, a mosquito and a dog.

I fried the spider with my first shot. And the drowsy mosquitoes were no problem either.

I celebrated each victory with a glass of cognac, clinking it against the obliging bottle. Then I started trying to kill the flies, but either I'd already had too much to drink or the flies were much better at sensing the little ball of fire approaching. I wasted four shots on the first one, but even though I missed at least I managed to disperse the first three in time. I got the second fly with my sixth shot, and in the process I managed to zap two balls of lightning into the glass of the cabinet standing against the wall.

'Sorry about that,' I said repentantly, downing my cognac. I got up and the room suddenly swayed. I went over to the cabinet, which contained swords hanging on a background of black velvet.

At first glance I thought they looked German, fifteenth or sixteenth century. The cabinet light was switched off, and I didn't try to determine their age more precisely. There were little craters in the glass, but at least I hadn't hit the swords.

I thought for a while about how to put things right and couldn't come up with anything better than putting the glass that had been scattered round the room back where it had come from. It cost me more effort than if I'd dematerialised all the glass and then recreated it.

After that I went into the bar. I didn't feel like any more cognac, but a bottle of Mexican coffee liqueur looked like a good compromise between the desire to get drunk and the desire to perk myself up. Coffee and alcohol, all in the same bottle.

When I turned back round I saw Semyon sitting in my chair.

'They've all gone to the lake,' the magician told me.

'I'll be right there,' I promised, walking towards him. 'Right there.'

'Put the bottle down,' Semyon advised me.

'What for?' I asked. But I put it down.

He looked hard into my eyes. My barriers didn't go up, and when I realised it was a trick it was too late. I tried to look away, but I couldn't.

'You bastard!' I gasped, doubling over.

'Down the corridor on the right!' Semyon shouted after me. His eyes were still boring into my back, the invisible connecting thread was still trailing after me.

I reached the bathroom. Five minutes later my tormentor caught up with me.

'Feeling better?'

'Yes,' I said, breathing heavily. I got up off my knees and stuck my head into the basin. Semyon opened the tap without saying anything and slapped me on the back:

'Relax. We started with basic folk remedies, but now . . .'

A wave of heat ran through my body. I groaned, but I didn't complain any more. The dull stupefaction was already long gone and now the final toxins came flying out of me.

'What are you doing?' I asked.

'Helping your liver out. Have some water and you'll feel better.'

It helped all right.

Five minutes later I walked out of the bathroom, sweaty and wet, but utterly sober. I even tried to protest at the violation of my rights.

'What did you interfere for? I wanted to get drunk and I did.'

'You young people,' said Semyon, shaking his head reproachfully. 'He wanted to get drunk? Who gets drunk on cognac? Especially after wine. And especially that quick, half a litre in half an hour. There was this time Sasha Kuprin and I decided to get drunk—'

'Which Sasha's that?'

'You know the one, the writer. Only he wasn't a writer then. We got drunk the right way, the civilised way, totally smashed, dancing on the tables, shooting at the ceiling.'

'Was he an Other, then?'

'Sasha? No, but he was a good man. We drank a quarter of a bucket of vodka and we got the grammar-school girls drunk on champagne.'

I slumped down on to the sofa. I looked at the empty bottle and gulped, starting to feel sick again.

'A quarter of a bucket, you must have got really drunk.'

'Of course we did!' Semyon said. 'It's okay to get drunk, Anton. If you really need to. Only you have to get drunk on vodka. Cognac and wine – that's all for the heart.'

'So what's vodka for?'

'For the soul. If it's hurting real bad.'

He looked at me with gentle reproach, a funny little magician with a cunning face, with his own funny little memories about great people and great battles.

'I was wrong,' I admitted. 'Thanks for your help.'

'No problem, my man. I once sobered up another Anton three times in the same evening. When he needed to drink without getting drunk, it was work.'

'Another Anton? Chekhov?' I asked in astonishment.

'No, don't be stupid. It was another Anton, one of us. He was killed in the Far East, when the samurai . . .' Semyon flipped his hand through the air and stopped. Then he said almost affectionately 'Don't be in such a hurry. We'll do things the civilised way this evening. Right now we've got to catch up with the others. Let's go.'

I meekly followed Semyon out of the house. And I saw Sveta. She was sitting on a lounger, already wearing her swimsuit and a bright skirt, or rather, a strip of cloth round her hips.

'Are you okay?' she asked, looking at me in surprise.

'Sure. The kebabs just didn't agree with me.'

Svetlana looked hard at me. But apparently the dark flush on my face and my wet hair were the only signs I'd got drunk so quickly.

'You should have your pancreas checked out.'

'Everything's okay,' Semyon interrupted. 'Believe me, I studied healing too. It was the heat, the sour wine, the fatty kebabs – nothing more to it. What he needs now is a swim, and in the cool of the evening we'll polish off a bottle together. That's all the treatment he needs.'

Sveta got up, walked up to me and looked into my eyes sympathetically.

'Maybe we should just sit here for a while. I'll make some strong tea.'

Yes, probably. It would be good. Just to sit here. The two of us.

And drink tea. Talk or not say a word. That didn't matter. Look at her sometimes or not even look. Just hear her breathing – or stop up my ears. Simply know that we're together. Just the two of us, and not the entire Night Watch. Together because we want to be, not because of some plan hatched by Gesar.

Had I really forgotten how to smile?

I shook my head, twisting my stubborn face into a cowardly smile.

'Let's go. I'm not a doddery old veteran of the magic wars yet. Let's go, Sveta.'

Semyon had already gone on ahead, but somehow I could tell that he winked. Approvingly.

The night didn't bring any real coolness, but at least it took the edge off the heat. From about six or seven in the evening the company split up into groups. The indefatigable Ignat stayed down by the lake with Lena and, strangely enough, Olga. Tiger Cub and Yulia went off to wander in the forest. The others were scattered through the house and around.

Semyon and I occupied the large loggia on the second floor. It was cosy in there, it let the wind through better and it had wicker furniture – perfect for hot weather.

'Number one,' said Semyon, taking a bottle of Smirnovskaya vodka out of a plastic bag with an advert for Danone kids' yoghurt on the side.

'Is that good?' I asked doubtfully. I don't regard myself as a vodka expert.

'I've been drinking it for more than a hundred years. And it used to be far worse than it is now, believe me.'

The bottle was followed out of the bag by two plain glasses, a two-litre jar with pickles floating in brine under its flat tin lid and a large cellophane bag of sauerkraut.

'What about something to drink with it?' I asked.

'You don't drink anything else with vodka, my boy,' said Semyon, shaking his head. 'Only with the fake stuff.'

'There's always something new to learn.'

'You'll learn this lesson soon enough. And there's no need to worry about the vodka, Chernogolovka village is in the territory I patrol. I know this wizard who works in the distillery there, small fry, not particularly nasty. He gets me the right stuff.'

'An exchange of petty favours,' I commented.

'No exchange. I pay him money, all honest and above board. It's our private business, nothing to do with the Watches.'

Semyon deftly twisted the cap off the bottle and poured us half a glass each. His bag had been standing on the veranda all day, but the vodka was still cold.

'To good health?' I suggested.

'Too soon for that. To us.'

When he'd sobered me up that afternoon, he must have done a thorough job and not just removed the alcohol from my bloodstream, but all the metabolic side-products as well. I drank the half-glass without even shuddering, and was amazed to discover that vodka could taste good after the heat of a summer day, not only after a winter frost.

'Well now,' said Semyon with a grunt of satisfaction, settling down more comfortably. 'We should drop a hint to Tiger Cub that a pair of rocking chairs would be good up here.'

He took out his appalling Yavas and lit up. When he spotted the annoyance on my face he said:

'I'm going to carry on smoking them anyway. I'm a patriot, I love my country.'

'I'm a patriot too, I love my health,' I retorted.

Semyon chuckled.

'There was one time this foreigner I knew invited me to go round to his place,' he began.

'A long time ago?' I asked, playing along.

'Not really, last year. He invited me round so I could teach him how to drink Russian-style. He was staying in the Penta hotel. So I picked up a girlfriend of mine and her brother – he was just back from prison camp, with nowhere to go – and off we went.'

I imagined what the group must have looked like and shook my head.

'And they let you in?'

'Yes.'

'You used magic?'

'No, my foreign friend used money. He'd laid in plenty of vodka and snacks, we started drinking on the thirtieth of April and finished on the second of May. We didn't let the maids in and we never turned the television off.'

Looking at Semyon in his crumpled, Russian-made check shirt, scruffy Turkish jeans and battered Czech sandals, I could easily picture him drinking beer poured out of a three-litre metal keg. But it was hard to imagine him in the Penta.

'You reprobates,' I said, appalled.

'Why? My friend was very pleased. He said now he understood what real Russian drunkenness was all about.'

'What is it about?'

'It's about waking up in the morning with everything around you looking grey. Grey sky, grey sun, grey city, grey people, grey thoughts. And the only way out is to have another drink. Then you feel better. Then the colours come back.'

'That was an interesting foreigner you found yourself.'

'Sure was!'

Semyon poured the vodka again – this time not filling the glasses so full. Then he thought twice and filled them right up to the top.

'Let's drink, my man. Here's to not having to drink in order to see the blue sky, the yellow sun and all the colours of the city. Let's drink to that. We go in and out of the Twilight and we see that the other side of the world isn't what everyone else thinks it is. But then, there's probably more than one other side. Here's to bright colours!'

I downed half my glass, dumbfounded.

'Don't wimp out, kid,' Semyon said without changing his tone.

I drained my glass and followed the vodka with a handful of the sweet-and-sour cabbage.

I asked him:

'Semyon, why do you behave like this? Why do you need to shock people with this image of yours?'

'Those are very clever words, I don't understand them.'

'But really?'

'It's easier this way, Antosha. Everyone looks after himself the best way he can. This is my way.'

'What should I do, Semyon?' I asked, without explaining what I meant.

'Do what you ought to do.'

'And what if I don't want to do what I ought to do? If our bright, radiant truth and our watchman's oath and our wonderful good intentions stick in my throat?'

'There's one thing you've got to understand, Anton,' said the magician, crunching a pickle. 'You ought to have realised it ages ago, but you've been tucked away with those machines of yours. Our Light truth may be big and bright, but it's made up of lots and lots of little truths. And Gesar may have a forehead a yard wide and the kind of experience you could never even dream of. But he also has haemorrhoids that have been healed by magic, an Oedipus complex and a habit of rejigging old schemes that worked before to make them look new. That's just for the sake of example, I don't really know what his oddities are, he's the boss after all.'

He took out another cigarette and this time I didn't try to object.

'Anton, I'll tell you what the problem is. You're a young guy, you join the Watch and you're delighted with yourself. At last the whole world is divided up into black and white! Your dream for humanity has come true, now you can tell who's good and who's bad. So get this. That's not the way it is. Not at all. Once we all used to be together. The Dark Ones and the Light Ones. We used to sit round the campfire in our cave and look through the Twilight to see where was the nearest pasture with a grazing mammoth, sing and dance, shooting sparks from our fingers, zap the other tribes with fireballs. And as an example, just to be entirely clear, let's say there were two brothers, both Others. Maybe when the first one went into the Twilight he was feeling well fed, maybe he'd just had sex for the first time. But for the other one it was different. Some green bamboo had given given him stomach-ache, his woman had turned him down because she said she had a headache and she was tired from scraping animal skins. And that's how it started. One leads everyone to the mammoth and he's satisfied. The other demands a piece of the trunk and the chief's daughter into the bargain. That's how we became Dark Ones and Light Ones, Good and Evil. Pretty basic stuff, isn't it? It's what we teach all the Other children. But whoever told you it had all stopped?'

Semyon leaned towards me so abruptly that his chair cracked.

'That's the way it was, it still is and it always will be. For ever, Antosha. There isn't any end to it. Today if anyone runs riot and sets off through a crowd, doing Good without authorisation, we dematerialise him. Into the Twilight with him, he's a hysterical psychopath, he's disturbing the balance, into the Twilight. But what's going to happen tomorrow? In a hundred years? In a thousand? Who can see that far? You, me, Gesar?'

'So what do I do?'

'Do you have a truth of your own, Anton? Tell me, do you? Are you certain of it? Then believe in it, not in my truth, not in Gesar's.

Believe in it and fight for it. If you have enough courage. If the idea doesn't make you shudder. What's bad about Dark freedom is not just that it's freedom from others. That's another explanation for little children. Dark freedom is first and foremost freedom from yourself, from your own conscience and your own soul. The moment you can't feel any pain in your chest – call for help. Only by then it'll be too late.'

He paused to reach into the plastic bag and took out another bottle of vodka. He sighed:

'Number two. I have a feeling we're not going to get drunk after all. We won't make it. And as for Olga and what she said . . .'

How did he always manage to hear everything?

'She's not envious because Svetlana might be able to do something she didn't do. And not because Sveta still has everything ahead of her while Olga, to be frank, has it all behind her at this stage. She envies Sveta because you love her and you're there for her and you'd like to stop her. Even though you can't do a thing about it. Gesar could have done, but he didn't want to. You can't, but you want to. Maybe in the end there's no difference, but it still gets to her. It tears at her soul, no matter how old she might be.'

'Do you know what they're preparing Svetlana for?'

'Yes,' said Semyon, splashing more vodka into the glasses.

'What is it?'

'I can't answer that. I gave a written undertaking. Do you want me to take my shirt off, so you can see the sign of chastising fire on my back? If I say a word I'll go up in flames with this chair, and the ashes will fit into a cigarette pack. So I'm sorry, Anton. Don't try to squeeze it out of me.'

'Thanks,' I said. 'Let's drink. Maybe we'll get drunk after all. I certainly need it.'

'I can see that,' Semyon agreed. 'Let's get on with it.'

CHAPTER 3

I WOKE UP very early. It was quiet all around, that living silence you get in the country, with the rustle of the morning wind after it's finally turned cool. Only that didn't make me feel any better. The bed was soaking wet with sweat and my head was splitting. Semyon was snoring monotonously on the bed beside me – three of us had been put in the same room. Tolik was sleeping on the floor, wrapped up in a blanket. He'd turned down the hammock he'd been offered, saying his back was hurting – he'd injured it in some tussle in 1976 – and he'd be better off sleeping on a hard surface.

I held the back of my head in my hands to stop the sudden movement shaking it to pieces and sat up on the bed. I looked at the bedside locker and saw two aspirins and a bottle of Borzhomi mineral water. Who was this kind soul?

The evening before, we'd drunk two bottles between us. Then Tolik had turned up. Then someone else, and they'd brought some wine. But I hadn't drunk any wine, I still had enough sense left for that.

I washed down the aspirins with half a bottle of water and sat there stupidly for a while, waiting for the medicine to take effect.

The pain didn't go away. I didn't think I'd be able to stand it for long.

'Semyon,' I called in a hoarse voice. 'Semyon!'

The magician opened one eye. He looked perfectly okay. As if he hadn't drunk far more than I had the day before. So that was what another hundred years of experience could do for you.

'Sort my head, will you . . .'

'I don't have an axe handy,' he muttered.

'Ah, you . . .' I groaned. 'Will you fix the pain?'

'Anton, we drank of our free will, didn't we? Nobody forced us, did they? And you enjoyed it!'

He turned over on to his other side.

I realised I couldn't expect any help from Semyon. And anyway he was right, it was just that I couldn't take it any more. I slipped my feet into my trainers, stepped over Tolik's sleeping body and left the room.

There were two rooms just for guests, but the door of the other was locked. However, the door at the end of the corridor, leading into our hostess's bedroom, was open. Remembering what Tiger Cub had said about her healing powers, I walked straight in without hesitation.

It looked like everything was against me today. She wasn't there. And despite my suspicions, neither were Ignat and Lena. Tiger Cub had spent the night with Yulia and the young girl was sleeping like a child, with one arm and one leg dangling over the side of the bed.

I didn't care who I asked for help any more. I tiptoed across, sat down beside the huge bed and whispered her name:

'Yulia, Yulienka . . .'

The girl opened her eyes, blinked and asked sympathetically:

'Hangover?'

'Yes.' I didn't risk a nod, someone had just set a small grenade off inside my head.

'Uhuh?'

She closed her eyes, I even thought she'd dozed off again, but she kept her arm round my neck. For a few seconds nothing happened, then the pain started receding rapidly. As if someone had opened a secret tap in the back of my head and started draining the seething poisons.

'Thanks,' I whispered. 'Thanks, Yulienka.'

'Don't drink so much, you can't take it,' she mumbled and immediately started snoring softly and evenly, as if she'd simply flipped a switch from work to sleep. Only kids and computers can do that.

I stood up, delighted to see the world in colour again. Semyon had been right, of course. You have to take responsibility for your actions. But sometimes you simply don't have enough strength for that. I looked around. The entire bedroom was decorated in beige tones, even the inclined window was slightly tinted. The music centre had a golden finish, the thick, fluffy carpet on the floor was light brown.

I really shouldn't be doing this. No one had invited me.

I walked quietly towards the door and when I had already half left, I heard Yulia's voice:

'You owe me a Snickers bar, okay?'

'Two,' I agreed.

I could have gone back to finish my night's sleep, but my memories of the bed weren't very pleasant ones. It felt like all I had to do was lie down and the pain lurking in the pillow would pounce again. I just dropped back into my room to grab my jeans and shirt and put them on, standing in the doorway.

Was everybody really asleep? Tiger Cub was wandering about outside somewhere, but surely someone must have sat up until morning, talking over a bottle.

There was a little hall on the second floor. I spotted Danila and

Nastya in there, sleeping peacefully on the sofa, and beat a hasty retreat. I shook my head: Danila had a very attractive wife, and Nastya had an elderly husband who was madly in love with her.

But then, they were only people.

And we were Others, the volunteers of the Light. How could it be helped if we had a different morality? It was like a frontline, with its field army romances and the young nurses comforting the officers and the men, not only in the hospital beds. In a war the appetite for life is just too strong.

I went to the library, where I found Garik and Farid. They had spent all night talking over a bottle – and not just one. And it obviously wasn't long since they'd fallen asleep in their armchairs: Farid's pipe was still smoking faintly on the table in front of him. There were piles of books that had been pulled off the shelves lying on the floor. They must have had a long argument about something, appealing for support to writers and poets, philosophers and historians.

I went down the long wooden spiral staircase. Surely I could find someone to share this peaceful morning with me?

Everybody was still asleep in the sitting room too. I glanced into the kitchen, but there was no one there except for a dog, cowering in the corner.

'Moving again?' I asked.

The terrier bared his fangs and gave a pitiful whine.

'Well, who asked you to play soldier yesterday?' I squatted down in front of the dog and took a piece of sausage off the table. The well-trained animal hadn't dared steal it. 'Here, take it.'

The jaws clicked shut above my open palm.

'You be kind and people will be kind to you!' I explained. 'And stop cowering in corners.'

I took a piece of sausage for myself and chewed it as I walked through the sitting room into the study.

They were asleep in there too.

Even when it was opened out the sofabed in the corner was narrow, so they were lying very close. Ignat was in the middle with his muscular arms flung out wide and a sweet smile on his face. Lena was pressed up against his left side, with one hand clutching his thick shock of blond hair, and her other arm thrown across his chest with her hand on our Don Juan's other partner. Svetlana had her face buried in Ignat's armpit, with her arms reaching in under the blanket that had slipped halfway off their bodies.

I closed the door very quietly and carefully.

It was a cosy little restaurant. As its name suggested, the Sea Dog was famous for its fish dishes and its shipboard interior. And, what's more, it was right next to the metro station. And for a fragile middle class that was sometimes prepared to splash out on a restaurant, but liked to save money on taxis, that was a significant factor.

This customer had arrived by car, in an old but perfectly serviceable model-six Zhiguli. To the well-trained eyes of the waiters the man looked a lot more prosperous than his car suggested. The calm with which he drank his expensive Danish vodka without asking the price only served to reinforce this judgement.

When the waiter brought the sturgeon he'd ordered, the customer glanced at him briefly. Before that he'd been sitting there, tracing lines on the tablecloth with a toothpick, occasionally stopping and gazing at the flame of the glass-bodied oil lamp, but now he suddenly looked up.

The waiter didn't tell anyone what he thought he saw in that instant. It was as if he was gazing into two blinding well-shafts. Blinding in the way the Light blinds when it sears and becomes indistinguishable from the Dark.

'Thank you,' said the customer.

The waiter walked away, fighting the urge to walk faster. Repeating to himself: it was just the reflection of the lamplight in the gloom of the restaurant. Just the way the lamplight happened to catch his eyes.

Boris Ignatievich carried on sitting there, breaking toothpicks. The sturgeon went cold, the vodka in the crystal carafe got warm. On the other side of the partition of thick cables, fake ships' wheels and sailcloth, a large gathering was celebrating someone's birthday, there were speeches of congratulation and complaints about the heat, taxes and gangsters who weren't doing things 'the right way'.

Gesar, the chief of the Moscow office of the Night Watch, waited.

The dogs who'd stayed outside shied away at the sight of me. The freeze had been really tough on them. Their bodies had refused to obey them, they hadn't been able to draw breath or bark, the saliva had congealed in their mouths, the air had pressed down on them with a hot, heavy, delirious hand.

But their spirits were still alive.

The gates were half open; I went through them and stood for a moment, not quite sure where I was going and what I was going to do.

What difference did it make, anyway?

I didn't feel resentful. I wasn't even in pain. The two of us had never even slept together. In fact, I was the one who'd been careful to erect barriers. I didn't just live for the present moment; I wanted everything right now, but I wanted it for ever.

I found the walkman at my belt and switched it on at random. That always worked for me. Maybe because I'd been controlling the simple electronic circuits for a long time, like Tiger Cub, without knowing it.

Who's to blame if you're so tired?
And haven't found what you were longing for?
Lost everything you sought so hard,
Flown up to the sky and fallen back again?
Whose fault is it that day after day
Life walks on other people's paths
But your home has become lonely,
With darkness at its windows,
And the light dims and sounds die
And your hands seek new torment?
And if your pain should ease –
It means new disaster's on the way.

It was what I myself had wanted. I'd tried to make it happen. And now I had only myself to blame. Instead of spending all evening with Semyon, discussing the complex issues of the global conflict between Good and Evil, I ought to have stayed downstairs. Instead of getting angry with Gesar and Olga for their cunning version of truth, I ought to have insisted on my own. And never, ever have thought that it was impossible to win.

Once you start thinking like that, you've already lost.

Who's to blame, tell me, brother?
One is married, another's rich,
One is funny, another's in love.
One's a fool, another's your enemy,
And whose fault is it that there and here
They wait for each other, it's how they live,
But the day is dreary, the night is empty,
The warm places are crowded out,
And the light dims and sounds die,
And your hands seek new torment?

And if your pain should ease,
It means new disaster's on the way.

Who's to blame and what's the secret,
Why is there no grief or happiness,
No victories without defeats,
And the score of luck and disaster is even?
And whose fault is it you're alone,
And your one life so very long,
And so dreary and you're still waiting,
Hoping some day you will die?

'No,' I whispered, pulling off the earphones. 'That's not for me.'

We'd all been taught for so long to give everything and not take anything in exchange. To sacrifice ourselves for the sake of others, to face up to the machine-gun fire. Every look noble and wise, not a single empty thought, not one sinful intention. After all, we were Others. We'd risen above the crowd, unfurled our immaculately clean banners, polished up our high boots, pulled on our white gloves. Oh, yes, in our own little world we could never go too far. A justification could be found for any action, a noble and exalted justification. Here we are all in white, and everyone else is covered in shit.

I was sick of it.

A passionate heart, clean hands, a cool head . . . Surely it was no accident that during the Revolution and the Civil War, almost all the Light Ones had attached themselves to the Cheka? And most of those who didn't had died. At the hands of the Dark Ones, or even more often at the hands of those they were defending. At the hands of humans, because of human stupidity, baseness, cowardice, hypocrisy, envy. A passionate heart and clean hands. But keeping a cool head was more important. That was essential. I didn't really agree with all the rest. Why not a pure heart and hot hands? I like the sound of that better.

'I don't want to protect you,' I said into the quietness of the forest morning. 'I don't want to! Women and children, old men and morons – none of you. Live however you want, get what you deserve! Run from vampires, worship Dark Magicians, kiss the goat under its tail! If you deserved it – take it! If my love means less than your happy lives, then why should you be happy?'

They can become better, they must, they're our roots, they're our future, they're our responsibility. Little people and big people, road-sweepers and presidents, criminals and cops. They carry within them the Light that can erupt in life-giving warmth or death-dealing flame . . .

I don't believe it!

I've seen all of you. Road-sweepers and presidents, criminals and cops. Seen mothers killing their children, fathers raping their daughters. Seen sons throwing their mothers out of the house and daughters putting arsenic in their fathers' food. Seen a husband smiling as he sees his guests out, then closes the door, and punches his pregnant wife in the face. Seen a smiling wife send her drunken husband out for another bottle and turn to his best friend for a passionate embrace. It's very simple to see all this. All you have to do is look. That's why they teach us not to look before they teach us to look through the Twilight.

But we still look anyway.

They're weak, they don't live long, they're afraid of everything. We mustn't despise them and hate them, that would be wrong. They must only be loved, pitied and protected. That is our job, our duty. We are the Watch.

I don't believe it!

Nobody can be forced to commit a vicious act. You can't push anybody into the mud, people always step into it themselves. No matter what the circumstances are, there are no justifications and there never will be any. But people look for justifications and they find them. All people have been taught to do that, and they've all proved diligent pupils.

Yes, of course, there have been, there still are, and there always will be those who have not become Others, but managed somehow to remain human. But there are so few of them, so very few. Or perhaps we're simply afraid to look at them more closely. Afraid to see what we might discover.

'Am I supposed to live for your sake?' I asked. The forest didn't answer, it was already prepared to accept anything I said.

Why must we sacrifice everything? Ourselves and those we love?

For the sake of those who will neither know nor appreciate it.

And even if they did find out, all we'd get for our efforts would be an incredulous shake of the head and insults.

Perhaps it would be worth just once showing humankind who exactly the Others are. What one single Other is capable of when he's not shackled by the Treaty, when he breaks free of the Watches.

I actually smiled to myself as I imagined the scene. The overall picture, not just my place in it: I'd be stopped soon enough. So would any Great Magician or Great Sorceress who decided to violate the Treaty and reveal the Others to the world.

What chaos it would be!

Aliens landing at the Kremlin and the White House wouldn't even come close.

Impossible, of course.

Not my path.

In the first place, because I didn't want to take over the world or throw it into total anarchy.

The only thing I wanted was for them not to force the woman I loved to sacrifice herself. Because the path of the Great Ones is genuine sacrifice. The appalling powers they develop change them utterly.

None of us is quite human. But at least we remember that we used to be human. And we can still be happy and sad, can love and hate. The Great Magicians and Sorceresses move beyond the bounds of human emotions. They probably feel emotions of their own, but we can't understand them. Even Gesar, a magician beyond classification, isn't a Great One. And Olga somehow failed to become a Great One.

They'd screwed something up. Failed to pull off some grand scheme in the struggle against the Dark.

And now they were willing to hurl a new recruit into the breach.

For the sake of humans who couldn't give a damn for the Light or the Dark.

They were driving her through all the hoops an Other is supposed to jump through. They'd already raised her powers to the third grade, now they were working on her mind. Very, very fast.

There had to be a place for me somewhere in this insane pursuit of an unknown goal. Gesar made use of everything that came to hand, including me. Whatever I did – hunting vampires, chasing down the Maverick, talking to Sveta in Olga's body – all that had just been playing into the boss's hands.

Whatever I did now was bound to have been foreseen too.

My only hope was that not even Gesar was capable of foreseeing everything.

That I could find the only way that would ruin his great plan for Sveta's powers.

And avoid causing Evil in the process. Because if I did, it would be the Twilight for me.

But in any case, I'd be doing Sveta a huge favour.

I caught myself standing with my cheek pressed against the trunk of a scrawny pine tree. Standing there, hammering my fist against the wood. In fury or in grief, I couldn't tell which. I held my scratched and bloody hand. But the sound didn't stop. It was coming from somewhere in the forest, from the very edge of the magical barrier around the house. Blows in the same rhythm, a rapid, nervous drumbeat.

I lowered my head and ran between the trees, like an adult still playing at paintball. I already had a pretty good idea of what I'd see.

There was a tiger leaping around in a small clearing. Or rather, a tigress. Her black and orange coat gleamed in the rays of the rising sun. The tigress didn't notice me, right then she wasn't capable of noticing anything. She ran between the trees, the sharp daggers of her claws ripping at the bark. White scars appeared on the pine trees. Occasionally she stopped, rose up on her hind legs and started slashing at the trunks with her claws.

I set off slowly back to the house.

We all of us let off steam the best way we can. We all of us have to struggle, not just against the Dark, but against the Light too. Because sometimes it blinds us.

But don't feel sorry for us: we're proud, very proud. Soldiers in the world war between Good and Evil, eternal volunteers.

CHAPTER 4

THE YOUNG man walked into the restaurant as confidently as if he came there every day for breakfast. But that wasn't so.

He went straight over to the table where the short, swarthy-faced man was sitting, as if they'd known each other for a long time. But that wasn't true either. With his last step he sank smoothly to his knees. He didn't slump, he lowered himself calmly, without losing his dignity or bending his back.

The waiter who was walking past swallowed and turned away. He'd seen all sorts of things in his time, let alone petty incidents like a mafia underling kowtowing to his boss. Only the young man didn't look much like an underling, and the older man didn't look much like a mafia boss.

The trouble he could smell in the air threatened to be far more serious than a mobsters' shoot-out. He didn't know what exactly was going to happen, but he could feel it coming, because he was an Other himself, although he wasn't initiated.

But only a moment later he had completely forgotten the scene he'd just witnessed. He had nothing but a vague sense of unease somewhere near his heart, but he couldn't remember why.

'Get up, Alisher,' Gesar said in a low voice. 'Get up. We don't do that round here.'

The young man got up off his knees and sat down facing the Night Watch chief. He nodded.

'We don't either. Not any more. But my father asked me to go down on my knees to you, Gesar. He followed the old rules. He would have knelt. But now he never will.'

'Do you know how he died?'

'Yes. I saw with his eyes, heard with his ears, suffered his pain.'

'Give me also his pain, Alisher, son of a *devona* and a human woman.'

'Take what you ask, Gesar, Exterminator of Evil, equal of the gods, who do not exist.'

They looked into each other's eyes. Then Gesar nodded.

'I know the killers. Your father will be avenged.'

'I must be the one to do it.'

'No, you will not be able to do it, and you have no right. You have come to Moscow illicitly.'

'Take me into your Watch, Gesar.'

The head of the Night Watch shook his head.

'I was the best in Samarkand, Gesar,' the young man said, staring hard at him. 'Don't smile, I know that here I would be the lowest of the low. Take me into the Watch. As a pupil of your pupils. As a guard dog. I ask this in honour of my father's memory – take me into the Watch.'

'You are asking too much, Alisher. You are asking me to give you your death.'

'I have already died, Gesar. When they drank my father's soul, I died with him. I walked along with a smile while he distracted the Dark Ones. I walked into the metro while they were trampling his ashes underfoot. Gesar, I have a right to ask this.'

Gesar nodded.

'Let it be so. You are a member of my Watch, Alisher.'

Not a trace of emotion showed in the young man's face, but he nodded and pressed his hand to his heart for an instant.

'Where is the thing that you have brought, Alisher?'

'I have it, my lord.'

Gesar reached across the table without speaking.

Alisher opened the small bag on his belt and took out a rectangular bundle of coarse fabric, handling it with great care.

'Take it, Gesar, and relieve me of my duty.'

Gesar covered the young man's open palm with his hand and closed his fingers. When the young man withdrew his hand a moment later, it was empty.

'Your service is completed, Alisher. Now let us simply relax. Let us eat, drink and remember your father. I will tell you all that I can remember.'

Alisher nodded. It was impossible to tell if he was pleased by what Gesar said or simply willing to accept whatever he suggested.

'We will have half an hour,' Gesar stated simply. 'Then the Dark Ones will arrive. They must have picked up your trail, even if they did so too late.'

'Will there be a battle, my lord?'

'I do not know,' Gesar replied with a shrug. 'What does it matter? Zabulon is far away. I have no reason to fear the others.'

'There will be a battle,' Alisher said thoughtfully. He looked round the restaurant.

'Drive all the customers away,' Gesar advised him. 'Gently, unobtrusively. I wish to observe your technique. And we will relax while we wait for our guests.'

About eleven everyone started waking up.

I was waiting on the terrace, lazing in a lounger with my legs stretched out, taking occasional sips from a tall gin and tonic and savouring the sweet pain of a masochist. Every time someone came out through the doors, I greeted them with a friendly wave and a little rainbow that sprang from my spread fingers and went soaring up into the sky. It was a bit of childish fun, and everybody smiled. When Yulia saw my greeting, she stopped yawning, squealed and replied with a rainbow of her own. We competed with each other for a couple of minutes, and then made a rainbow together, a big one that stretched away into the forest. Yulia told me she was going to go and look for the crock of gold, and she strode off proudly under the multicoloured arch, with one of the terriers running obediently at her feet.

I was waiting for certain people.

The first to emerge was Lena. Bright and cheerful, wearing just her swimsuit. When she saw me she was embarrassed for a moment, but then she nodded and ran towards the gates. I enjoyed watching the way she moved: slim and graceful, full of life. Now she'd dive into the cool water, swim on her own for a while and come back for breakfast with a keen appetite.

Next to appear was Ignat. In his swimming trunks and flip-flops.

'Hi, Anton!' he shouted happily. He came over, pulled open the next lounger and flopped down into it. 'How're you doing?'

'I'm in fighting mood!' I told him, raising my glass.

'Good man.' Ignat looked around for a bottle and didn't see one. He reached out and took a sip from my glass. 'Too weak, too much mixer.'

'I got plastered yesterday.'

'In that case you're right, better watch yourself,' Ignat advised me. 'We were on champagne all evening. Then we moved on to cognac later. I was afraid I'd have a hangover, but I'm okay. I seem to have got away with it.'

It was impossible to be offended by him.

'Ignat, what did you want to be when you were a kid?' I asked.

'A hospital attendant.'

'What?'

'Well, they told me boys couldn't be nurses, and I wanted to help sick people. So I decided that when I grew up I was going to be a medical attendant.'

'Great,' I said. 'But why not a doctor?'

'Too much responsibility for me,' Ignat admitted. 'And you had to study for too long.'

'So did you get to be a medical attendant?'

'Yes. I was in an ambulance crew, a psychiatric team. All the doctors loved working with me.'

'Why?'

'Firstly, because I'm really charming,' Ignat explained ingenuously. 'I can talk to both men and women in a way that seems to calm them down and make them agree to go to hospital. And secondly, I could tell when someone was really ill and when he was just seeing something invisible to others. Sometimes I was able to whisper in the doctor's ear, explain that everything was okay and no injections would be required.'

'Medicine has suffered a great loss.'

'True,' Ignat said with a sigh, 'but the boss persuaded me that I'd be more useful in the Watch. And that's right, isn't it?'

'I suppose so.'

'I'm bored already,' Ignat drawled. 'Aren't you bored? I want to get back to work.'

'I think I do too. Ignat, have you got a hobby? Outside of work?'

'What are you interrogating me for?' he asked in surprise.

'I'm curious. Or is it a secret?'

'What secrets do we have?' Ignat asked with a shrug. 'I collect butterflies. I've got one of the best collections in the world. It fills two entire rooms.'

'Very worthy,' I agreed.

'Come round some time and take a look,' he suggested. 'Bring Sveta, she tells me she likes butterflies too.'

I laughed so long even Ignat got the point. He got up, smiling uncertainly, and muttered:

'I think I'll go help get breakfast ready.'

'Good luck,' was all I said. But I just couldn't help myself, and when Ignat reached the door, I called to him: 'Listen, is the boss right to be worried about Sveta?'

He propped his chin on his hand and thought for a moment.

'You know, I think he is. She's all tensed up somehow, just can't let go and relax. And she's got big things ahead of her, not like you and me.'

'You tried your best, did you?'

'What kind of question's that?' said Ignat, offended. 'Come round some time, it'd be good to see you.'

The gin had turned warm, the ice in the glass had melted. I shook my head and put the glass down.

Gesar, you can't foresee everything.

But to fight you – not in a duel of magic, that would just be ridiculous – to fight you in the only arena where I have a chance, in words and actions, I have to know what you want. I have to know how the cards lie in the deck. And what you're holding in your hand.

Who were the players?

Gesar, the originator and organiser. Olga, his lover and consultant, a sorceress punished for some crime. Svetlana, who had to complete the mission and was being prepared with great care. Me, one of the instruments of her education. Ignat, Tiger Cub, Semyon and all the other Light Ones could be left out of my calculations.

They were instruments too, but only secondary ones. And I couldn't count on them for support.

The Dark Ones?

Naturally they were involved, but not in any obvious way. Zabulon and his henchmen were concerned about Svetlana's appearance in our camp. They couldn't do anything openly right now. But they could try to sabotage things on the sly or prepare a crushing blow that would bring the Watches to the brink of war.

What else?

The Inquisition?

I drummed my fingers on the armrest of the lounger.

The Inquisition. The structure that oversees the Watches. It reviews disputes and punishes those who violate the Treaty – from either side. It is always vigilant. It collects data on every one of us. But it only intervenes in extremely rare cases and its strength lies more in secrecy than in battle. When the Inquisition considers a case involving a powerful magician, it drafts in fighters from both Watches.

But the Inquisition was involved somehow. I knew the boss. He squeezed the last drop from every opportunity. And the recent business with Maxim, the Maverick Other, the Light One who had gone to work for the Inquisition, was a good example. The boss had made use of the incident to train Svetlana and teach her the lessons of self-control and intrigue, but at the same time he'd discovered a new Inquisitor.

I wished I knew what they were preparing Svetlana for.

So far I was groping in the dark. And the worst thing of all was that the gulf between me and Sveta was getting wider and wider.

I put on the earphones and closed my eyes.

Tonight the fern will unfold its miraculous flower,
Tonight the spirits will come back home,
Clouds from the north, wind from the west,
Soon the enchantress will wave her hand to me.
I live waiting for a miracle, like a Mauser in its holster,
Like a spider in its web,
Like a tree in the desert,
Like a black fox in its hole.

I was taking a risk, a serious risk. Great Magicians become great by trampling over their own kind, but even they don't dare go against their own. Isolated individuals don't survive.

I was running through the telescopes,
    away from the frightened eyes of children,
I wanted to sleep with a mermaid,
    but I didn't know how to act with her,
I wanted to turn into a streetcar
    and drive through your window.
The wind blows from the borderlands, we don't care
    any more,
The wind blows from the borderlands, we don't care
    any more.
Be my shadow, my squeaking stair,
    my bright-coloured Sunday, my sunshine with rain,
Be my god, my birch-tree sap,
    my electric current, my bent rifle.
I can bear witness that you are the wind,
    you blow in my face and I laugh,
I do not wish to leave you
    without a battle, since you dream of me.
Be my shadow . . .

I felt a hand on my shoulder.

'Good morning, Sveta,' I said and opened my eyes.

She was wearing shorts over a swimsuit. Her hair was wet and neat. She must have taken a shower. While I, being a filthy pig, hadn't even thought of taking one.

'How are you after yesterday?' she asked.

'Okay. And you?'

'All right,' she said and turned away.

I waited. With Spleen playing in my earphones.

'What were you expecting from me?' Sveta asked sharply. 'I'm a normal, healthy young woman. I haven't had a man since last winter. I realise you've got it into your head that Gesar threw us together, like mating horses, so you're just being stubborn.'

'I wasn't expecting anything.'

'Then I'm sorry you got a surprise!'

'Did you sense me in the room? When you woke up?'

'Yes.' Svetlana awkwardly pulled a packet of cigarettes out of her pocket and lit one. 'I'm tired. Maybe I am still only learning, and not working yet, but I'm tired. And I came here to relax.'

'You were the one who started talking about everyone faking a good time . . .'

'And you were only too happy to agree.'

'True.' I nodded.

'And then you went off to knock back vodka and organise conspiracies.'

'What conspiracies?'

'Against Gesar. And against me, by the way. How absurd! Even I sensed it! Don't get the idea you're some Great Magician who can—'

She stopped short. But too late.

'I'm not a Great Magician,' I said. 'I'm third grade. Maybe second, but no higher than that. We all have limits of our own that we can't go beyond, not even if we live for a thousand years.'

'I'm sorry, I didn't mean to offend you,' Svetlana said, embarrassed. She lowered the hand holding the cigarette.

'Forget it. I've got nothing to be offended at. Do you know why the Dark Ones form families from their own kind so often, and we prefer to choose our wives and husbands from among ordinary people? The Dark Ones find it easier to cope with inequality and constant competition.'

'A human being and an Other – that's even more unequal.'

'That doesn't count. We're two different species. That means nothing counts.'

'I want you to know,' said Svetlana, taking a deep drag on her cigarette, 'that I wasn't intending to let things go so far. I was waiting for you to come down and see us and get jealous.'

'I'm sorry, I didn't know I was supposed to get jealous.'

'And then everything just went crazy and I couldn't help myself.'

'I understand everything, Sveta. It's okay.'

She looked at me in confusion.

'Okay?'

'Of course, it happens to everyone. The Watch is one big, tight-knit family. With everything that follows from that.'

'What a bastard you are!' Svetlana exclaimed. 'Anton, if only you could see yourself now from the outside! How did you ever end up on our side?'

'Sveta, you came to make up, didn't you?' I asked. 'So I'm making up. It's all okay. Nothing counts. That's life, all sorts of things happen.'

She jumped to her feet and glared icily at me for a second. I started blinking rapidly.

'You idiot!' Svetlana blurted out and went back into the house.

So what had she been expecting? Hurt feelings, accusations, sadness?

But more importantly, what had Gesar been expecting? What would change if I stopped playing the role of Sveta's ill-starred lover? Would someone else take on the role? Or was it already time for her to be left alone – all alone with her great destiny?

The goal. I had to know what Gesar's goal was.

I sprang up off the lounger and walked into the house. I immediately spotted Olga, alone in the sitting room. Standing in front of the open display case, holding out a sword with a long, narrow blade in front of her. She wasn't looking at it the way you look at an antique toy. Tiger Cub probably looked at her swords in the same kind of way. But her love of old weapons was in the abstract; Olga's wasn't.

When Gesar came to live and work in Russia – because of her, by the way – swords like that might still have been in use.

But eighty years ago, when Olga had been deprived of all her rights, wars were already fought differently.

A former Great Sorceress. A former Great Goal. Eighty years.

'It's all so well planned, isn't it?' I said.

Olga started and swung round.

'We can't defeat the Dark ourselves. The little people have to be enlightened first. Become kind and loving, industrious and intelligent. So that every Other can see nothing but the Light. What a great goal it was, how long the ripples lasted when it was drowned in blood.'

'You figured it out after all,' said Olga. 'Or did you just guess?'

'I guessed.'

'Good. Now what?'

'How did you slip up, Olga?'

'I accepted a compromise. A little compromise with the Dark. And the result was that we lost.'

'We did? We'll always survive. Adapt, fit in, find our place. And we'll carry on the old struggle. It's only humans who lose.'

'Retreats are inevitable sometimes,' said Olga, gripping the double-handed sword easily in one hand and swinging it above her head. 'Do I look like a helicopter with its rotors idling?'

'You look like a woman waving a sword around. Do we really never learn anything, Olga?'

'Sure we do. This time everything's going to be different, Anton.'

'A new revolution?'

'We didn't want the last one. It was all supposed to happen almost completely without bloodshed. You understand: we can only win through ordinary humans. When they become enlightened, when their spirit is raised up. Communism was a wonderfully well-calculated system, and it's all my fault that it wasn't realised.'

'So why aren't you in the Twilight already, if it's all your fault?'

'Because everything had been agreed. Every step approved. Even that disastrous compromise, even that seemed acceptable.'

'And now – a new attempt to change people?'

'One more in the series.'

'Why here?' I asked. 'Why in Russia again?'

'Why not?'

'How much more of this does our country have to put up with?'

'As much as it takes.'

'Come on – why here again?'

Olga sighed, deftly slipped the sword back into its scabbard and put it back on its stand.

'Because, my dear boy, in this arena it's still possible to achieve something. The potential of Europe and North America has already been exhausted. Everything that was possible has already been tried there. There are a few things being developed right now. But all those countries are already half asleep. A healthy pensioner in shorts with a video camera – that's the prosperity of the West. We need to experiment with the young ones. Russia, Asia, the Arab world – these are where present-day battles are fought. And don't look so offended, I love my country as much as you do! I've spilled more blood for it than you have flowing in your veins. What you've got to understand, Antosha, is that the battlefield is the entire world. You know that as well as I do.'

'Our war's with the Dark, not with humans!'

'Yes, with the Dark. But we can only win by creating an ideal society. A world that will be ruled by goodness, love and justice. The Watches don't exist to capture psychopathic magicians on the streets and issue licences to vampires! All those little things take up time and energy, but they're by-products, like the heat from a light bulb. Light bulbs are meant to produce light, not heat. We have to change the human world, not just neutralise the Dark's minor outbursts. That's the goal. That's the path to victory!'

'Olga, I understand that.'

'Wonderful. Then you have to understand something that's never said in so many words. We've been fighting for thousands of years. And all that time we've been trying to change the course of history. To create a new world.'

'A brave new world.'

'Don't be so ironic. We have achieved something, after all. Through all the blood and suffering the world is becoming a more humane place. But we need a real, genuine revolution.'

'Communism was our idea, then?'

'No, not ours, but we supported it. It seemed quite attractive.'

'So now what?'

'You'll see.' Olga smiled. A friendly, sincere smile. 'Anton, everything will be fine. Trust me.'

'I need to know.'

'No. That's exactly what you don't need. And you don't need to worry, we're not planning any revolutions. No prison camps, execution squads or military tribunals. We're not going to repeat our old mistakes.'

'We're going to make new ones instead.'

'Anton!' she said, raising her voice. 'Think about it, will you, what are you doing? We have a really good chance of winning. Our country has a chance to live in peace, to flourish. It could become the vanguard of humanity. Defeat the Dark. It's been twelve years in the making, Anton. And it's not just Gesar's project, the whole senior level's been working on it.'

'What?'

'Yes. Did you think it was all being done on the spur of the moment?'

'You were keeping tabs on Svetlana for twelve years?'

'Of course not! A new social model has been developed. Various elements of the plan have already been put into action. Not even I know all the details. Since then Gesar's been waiting for the key players in the plan to come together, in space and time.'

'Who exactly? Svetlana and the Inquisitor?'

The pupils of her eyes contracted, and I knew I'd guessed it. Or part of it.

'And what else? What part am I supposed to play in all this?'

'You'll find out when the time comes.'

'Olga, so far magical intervention in human life has never led to anything good.'

'Don't come up with those old schoolroom axioms,' she said, getting really worked up now. 'Don't think you're any wiser than anyone else. We've no intention of using magic. Calm down, relax.'

I nodded.

'Okay. You've explained your position. I don't agree with it.'

'Officially?'

'No. In a private capacity. And as a private individual I believe I have the right of opposition.'

'Opposition? To Gesar?' Olga's eyes opened wide and the corners of her lips curved up in a smile. 'Anton!'

I turned on my heel and went out.

Yes, it was laughable.

Yes, it was absurd.

It wasn't just a crazy project dreamed up by Gesar and Olga. It wasn't just an attempt to repeat a failed experiment. It was a meticulously prepared operation, planned over a long period, and it had been my bad luck to get caught up in it.

An operation approved at the highest level.

Approved by the Light.

Why was I getting so involved? I had no right to be. None at all. And I had absolutely no chance either. I could console myself with the wise parable about the grain of sand that stopped the clock, but right now I was a grain of sand caught between mill wheels.

And the saddest thing of all was that these were the mill wheels of my own side. Nobody would persecute me. Nobody would fight me. They'd simply stop me doing all those stupid things that wouldn't do any good in any case.

Then why did I feel this pain, this unendurable pain in my chest?

I was standing on the terrace, clenching my fists in impotent fury, when I felt a hand on my shoulder.

'Looks like you've managed to figure something out, Anton.'

I glanced at Semyon and nodded.

'Hard to take?'

'Yes,' I admitted.

'Then just remember one thing. You're not just a grain of sand. Nobody's just a grain of sand. Especially if he's an Other.'

'How long do you have to live to be able to guess what someone else is thinking like that?'

'A hundred years, Anton.'

'Then Gesar can read any of us like an open book?'

'Of course.'

'Then I'll have to learn how not to think,' I said.

'For that you have to learn how to think first. Did you know there's been a skirmish in town?'

'When?'

'A quarter of an hour ago. It's all over already.'

'What happened?'

'A courier arrived to see the boss, from somewhere out east. The Dark Ones followed him and tried to eliminate him. Right there in front of the boss.' Semyon laughed.

'That means war!'

'No, they were within their rights. The courier entered the city illegally.'

I looked around. Nobody was in any hurry to go anywhere. They weren't starting up their cars or packing their things. Ignat and Ilya were lighting up the barbecue again.

'Shouldn't we be getting back?'

'No. The boss handled things his own way. There was a small fight, without any casualties. The courier's been made a member of our Watch, and the Dark Ones had to leave empty-handed. The restaurant suffered a bit, that's all.'

'What restaurant?'

'The restaurant where the boss met the courier,' Semyon explained patiently. 'We've been told we can carry on with our holiday.'

I looked up at the blindingly blue sky, swelling with the heat.

'You know, somehow I'm not in the mood for a holiday. I think I'll go back to Moscow. I don't suppose anyone will mind too much.'

'Of course not.'

Semyon took out his cigarettes and lit up. Then he said casually:

'In your place, I'd find out exactly what the courier brought with him from the east. Maybe that's your chance.'

I laughed bitterly.

'The Dark Ones couldn't find out. Are you suggesting I should start rummaging in the boss's safe?'

'The Dark Ones couldn't take it. Whatever it was. You have no right to take what the courier brought or even touch it, of course. But just finding out . . .'

'Thanks. I really mean that.'

Semyon nodded, accepting my gratitude graciously.

'We'll settle up in the Twilight. You know, I've had enough holiday too. After lunch I'm going to borrow Tiger Cub's motorbike and go back to town. Want a lift?'

'Uhuh.'

I felt ashamed. It was the kind of shame that probably only Others can feel. We can always tell when someone's helping us out, when they're giving us something we don't deserve but can't possibly refuse.

I couldn't stay there any longer. Stay there and see Svetlana, Olga and Ignat. Listen to their truth.

I would always have my own truth.

'Can you handle a motorbike?' I asked, clumsily trying to change the subject.

'I rode one in the first Paris – Dakar rally. Let's go give the others a hand.'

I glanced sullenly at Ignat. He was chopping wood, handling the axe like a real virtuoso. After every blow he froze for a moment and looked round quickly at everyone, flexing his biceps.

He really loved himself. Sure, he loved the rest of the world too. But he came first.

'Let's do that,' I agreed. I swung back my arm and threw the sign of the triple blade through the Twilight. Several blocks of wood flew apart into neat sticks of firewood just as Ignat raised his axe for the next blow. He lost his balance and almost fell. Then he started to look around.

Naturally my blow had left a spatial trace. The Twilight was vibrating, greedily drawing in energy.

'Antosha, what did you do that for?' Ignat asked crossly. 'That's not the sporting way!'

'But it is efficient,' I said, walking down from the terrace. 'Shall I chop some more?'

'Don't bother,' said Ignat, bending down to collect up the firewood. 'Carry on like that and we'll end up grilling the kebabs with fireballs.'

I didn't feel at all guilty, but I started helping anyway. The firewood had been chopped cleanly and the cuts glittered a rich amber yellow. It seemed a shame to put something so beautiful on the fire.

Then I looked at the house and saw Olga standing at the ground-floor window.

She'd been following my little escapade very closely. Far too closely.

I waved to her.

CHAPTER 5

TIGER CUB'S motorbike was really great, if such a vague word can ever be applied to a Harley, even the most basic model. After all, there are motorbikes, and then there are Harley-Davidsons.

Why Tiger Cub needed it, I couldn't imagine. As far as I could see, it was only ridden once or twice a year. Probably for the same reason as she needed a huge house to live in at the weekend. In any case, we arrived back in town before it was even two in the afternoon.

Semyon handled the heavy two-wheeled vehicle like a master. I could never have done it, not even if I'd activated the 'extreme skills' implanted in my memory and reviewed the reality lines. I could have got there almost as fast by expending a considerable portion of my reserves of power. But Semyon simply drove – and his superiority over an ordinary human driver was down to nothing but experience.

Even riding at a hundred kilometres an hour the air still felt hot. The wind struck at my cheeks like a rough towel. It felt like we were riding through a furnace, an endless tarmac furnace full of vehicles that had already been roasted in the sun, slowly crawling along. At least three times I was sure we were going to crash into a car or an inconveniently placed pillar.

It wasn't likely that we'd be killed outright. The rest of the team would sense what had happened and come and put us back together, piece by piece, but it wouldn't exactly be fun.

We arrived without any mishaps. After the ring road Semyon used his magic about five times, but only to make highway patrolmen look the other way.

Semyon didn't ask my address, even though he'd never been to my place. He stopped outside the entrance to the building and switched off the engine. The teenagers swilling cheap beer in the kids' playground stopped talking and stared at the bike. How great it must be to have such clear and simple dreams: beer, E at the nightclub, a hot girlfriend and a Harley.

'How long have you been having premonitions?' Semyon asked.

I started. I hadn't really told anyone that I'd been having them.

'Quite a long time now.'

Semyon nodded. He looked up at my windows. He didn't tell me why he'd asked the question.

'Maybe I ought to go up with you.'

'Listen, I'm not a girl who needs to be seen all the way home to her door.'

The magician smiled.

'Hey, don't get me mixed up with Ignat. Okay, it's not such a big deal. Be careful.'

'Of what?'

'Of everything, I suppose.'

The bike's engine howled. The magician shook his head.

'There's something coming, Anton. Coming this way. Be careful.'

He zoomed off to roars of approval from the adolescents, and slipped neatly through the gap between a parked Volga and a slow-moving Zhiguli. I watched him go and shook my head. I didn't need any premonitions to know that Semyon would spend the whole day zooming round Moscow. Then he'd attach himself to some group of rockers and a quarter of an hour later he'd be a fully fledged member, already creating legends about a crazy old biker.

Be careful . . .

Of what?

And more importantly, what for?

I tapped the code into the keypad, walked into the lobby and called the lift. That morning I'd been on holiday with my friends, and everything had been fine.

Nothing had changed now, except that I wasn't there any longer.

They say that when Light Magicians go off the rails, the first sign is always flashes of insight, like the ones epileptics have before a fit. Then the pointless use of power, like killing flies with fireballs and chopping firewood with combat spells. Quarrels with the people they love. Sudden disagreements with some friends and equally unexpected warm relations with others. Everyone knows that, and everyone knows what happens after a Light Magician goes off the rails.

Be careful . . .

I walked up to the door and reached for my keys.

But the door was already unlocked.

My parents had a set of keys. But they would never have come all the way from Saratov without giving me any warning. And I would have sensed that they were coming.

No ordinary human thief would ever break into my apartment, the simple sign on the threshold would have stopped him. And there were barriers against Others too. Of course, they could be overcome with sufficient power. But the sentry systems ought to have been triggered.

I stood there, looking at the narrow crack between the door and the doorpost, the crack that shouldn't have been there. I looked through the Twilight, but I didn't see anything.

I didn't have a weapon with me. My pistol was inside the apartment. So were the ten combat amulets.

I could have followed instructions. A member of the Night Watch who discovers that a home secured by magical means has been penetrated by strangers must first inform the duty operations officer and his supervisor, and then . . .

But the moment I imagined appealing to Gesar, after he'd casually scattered the entire Day Watch only two days earlier, I lost any desire to follow instructions. I folded my fingers into the sign for a rapid freeze spell, probably because I remembered how well it had worked for Semyon.

Be careful?

I pushed open the door and walked into the apartment that had suddenly stopped being mine.

And as I walked in, I realised who had enough power, authority and sheer chutzpah to come calling without an invitation.

'Good afternoon, boss!' I said, glancing into the study.

I wasn't entirely wrong.

Zabulon was sitting in a chair by the window, reading a newspaper. He raised his eyebrows in surprise and put down the paper. Then he carefully took off his spectacles with the slim gold frames.

'Good afternoon, Anton. You know, I'd be very glad to be your boss.'

He smiled. A Dark Magician beyond classification, the chief of the Moscow Day Watch. As usual, he was wearing an immaculately tailored black suit and a light grey shirt. An Other of indeterminate age, with a lean frame and close-cropped hair.

'My mistake,' I said. 'What are you doing here?'

Zabulon shrugged:

'Take your amulet. It's in the desk somewhere, I can sense it.'

I walked over to the desk, opened the drawer and took out the ivory medallion on a copper chain. I squeezed the amulet in my fist and felt it grow warm.

'Zabulon, you no longer have any power over me.'

The Dark Magician nodded:

'Good. I don't want you to have any doubts about your own safety.'

'What are you doing in a Light One's home, Zabulon? I would be within my rights to report you to the tribunal.'

'I know,' Zabulon said with a shrug. 'I know all that. I'm in the wrong. This is stupid. I'm exposing myself to reprisals and exposing the Day Watch too. But I haven't come to you as an enemy.'

I didn't say anything.

'And you don't need to worry about any observation devices,' he added casually. 'Either your own, or the ones that the Inquisition installs. I took the liberty of, shall we say, putting them to sleep. Everything we say to each other will remain just between the two of us, for ever.'

'Believe half of what a human says, a quarter of what a Light One says, and not a word of what a Dark One says,' I muttered.

'Of course, you have every right not to trust me. It's your duty not to. But please hear me out.' Zabulon suddenly smiled in a remarkably open and reassuring way. 'You're a Light One. You are obliged to assist everyone who asks for help, even me. And now I'm asking.'

I hesitated, then went across to the sofa and sat down. Without taking my shoes off, without cancelling the suspended freeze, as if it wasn't utterly absurd to imagine myself doing combat with Zabulon.

There was an outsider in my apartment. So much for 'my home is my castle' – and I'd almost started to believe it during the years I'd been working for the Watch.

'First of all, how did you get in?' I asked.

'First of all, I took a perfectly ordinary lock pick, but—'

'Zabulon, you know what I mean. The sentry systems can be destroyed, but they can't be tricked. They should have been triggered by any unauthorised entry.'

The Dark Magician sighed.

'Kostya helped me to get in. You gave him access.'

'I hoped he was my friend. Even if he is a vampire.'

'He is your friend,' Zabulon said with a smile. 'And he wants to help you.'

'In his own way.'

'In *our* own way, Anton. I've entered your home, but I have no intention of causing any harm. I haven't looked at any of the official documents you keep here. I haven't left any monitoring signs. I came to talk.'

'Then talk.'

'You and I have a problem, Anton. The same one. And today it reached critical proportions.'

The moment I saw Zabulon, I'd known what we'd be talking about, so I just nodded.

'Good, you understand.' The Dark Magician leaned forward in his chair and sighed. 'Anton, I'm not under any illusions here. We see the world differently. And we understand our duty in different ways. But even under those conditions our interests sometimes coincide. From your point of view, we Dark Ones have our failings. Sometimes our actions seem rather ambiguous. And we are obliged by our very nature to be rather less caring with people. That's all true. But note that nobody has ever accused us of attempting to change the entire destiny of humanity. Since the

Treaty was concluded we have simply lived our own lives and we'd like you to do the same.'

'Nobody has ever accused you,' I agreed, 'because whichever way you look at it, time is on your side.'

Zabulon nodded:

'And what does that mean? Perhaps we're more like human beings? Perhaps we're right? But let's not get into those arguments, there's no end to them. I repeat what I have said before. We honour the Treaty. And we often observe it far more closely than the forces of the Light.'

A standard tactic in an argument. First admit to some kind of generalised guilt. Then gently reproach your opponent for being equally guilty of the same general kind of fault. Reproach them a bit and then drop it. Let's just forget the whole thing!

And then move on to what's really important.

'But, let's deal with what's really important here,' said Zabulon, getting serious. 'There's no point in beating about the bush. In the last hundred years the forces of the Light have launched three global experiments. The revolution in Russia. The Second World War. And now this new project. Following the same scenario.'

'I don't know what you're talking about,' I said. I suddenly had this desperate aching feeling in my chest.

'Really? Let me explain. Social models are developed that should eventually – at the cost of massive upheaval and immense bloodshed – bring humanity to the ideal society. Ideal, that is, from your point of view, but I won't argue about that. Certainly not. Everyone has a right to his own dream. But your path is so very cruel . . .' Another sad smile. 'You accuse us of cruelty, and not entirely without reason, but what's one child killed in a black mass compared with any fascist children's concentration camp? And fascism was another of your inventions. Another one that got out of control. First there was internationalism and communism – that didn't work. Then there was national socialism. Another mistake? You put your heads together and examined the result. Then you sighed, wiped the slates clean and started experimenting all over again.'

'They turned out to be mistakes thanks to your efforts.'

'Of course! We do have an instinct for self-preservation, you know. We don't construct social models on the basis of our ethics. So why should we tolerate your projects?'

I didn't say anything.

Zabulon nodded, apparently satisfied.

'So you see, Anton. Maybe we're enemies. We *are* enemies. Last winter you caused us some inconvenience, serious inconvenience. This spring you frustrated me again. You eliminated two Day Watch agents. Yes, of course, the Inquisition declared that your actions were committed in self-defence and out of absolute necessity but, believe me, I was not pleased. What kind of leader is it who can't even protect his own colleagues? So, we are enemies. But now we have a unique situation. Yet another experiment. And you're indirectly involved in it.'

'I don't know what you're talking about.'

Zabulon laughed and raised his hands in the air.

'Anton, I'm not trying to coax any secrets out of you. I'm not going to ask any questions. Or ask you to do anything. Just listen to what I have to say. And then I'll go.'

I suddenly remembered how the young witch Alisa had used her right to intervene up on the high-rise roof the previous winter. A very minor intervention – all she did was allow me to speak the truth. And that truth had turned Egor over to the side of the Dark Ones.

Why did things happen that way?

Why was it that the Light acted through lies, and the Dark acted through the truth? Why was it that our truth proved powerless, but lies were effective? And why was the Dark able to manage perfectly well with the truth in order to do Evil? Whose nature was responsible, humankind's or ours?

'Svetlana's a wonderful sorceress,' said Zabulon. 'But her future is not to lead the Night Watch. They intend to use her for just one single purpose. For the mission that Olga failed to complete. You know, don't you, that a courier from Samarkand entered the city illegally this morning?'

'Yes, I know,' I admitted, without really knowing why.

'And I can tell you what he brought with him. Would you like to know?'

I gritted my teeth.

'You would,' said Zabulon, with a nod. 'The courier brought a piece of chalk.'

Never believe what the Dark Ones say. But somehow I got the feeling he wasn't lying.

'A little piece of chalk.' The Dark Magician smiled. 'You could write on a school blackboard with it. Or draw hopscotch squares on the pavement. Or chalk your pool cue with it. You could do all that, just as easily as you could use a large royal seal to crack nuts. But things change if a Great Sorceress picks up that piece of chalk – it has to be a Great One, an ordinary sorceress wouldn't be powerful enough, and it has to be a sorceress, in male hands the chalk remains nothing but chalk. And in addition to that the sorceress has to be a Light One. This artefact is useless for Dark Ones.'

Did I imagine it, or had he just sighed? I said nothing.

'A small piece of chalk.' Zabulon leaned back in his armchair. 'It's already worn down, beautiful young women with bright fire in their eyes have picked it up in their slim fingers several times already. It has been put to use, and the earth has trembled, the boundaries of states have melted away, empires have risen, shepherds have become prophets and carpenters have become gods, foundlings have been recognised as kings, sergeants have risen to become emperors, seminarians who failed to graduate and talentless artists have become tyrants. A little stub of chalk. Nothing more than that.'

Zabulon stood and spread his hands in a conclusive gesture.

'And that's all I wanted to tell you, my dear enemy. You'll understand the rest for yourself – if you really want to, that is.'

'Zabulon.' I unclenched my fist and looked at the amulet. 'You're a creature of the Dark.'

'Of course. But only of the darkness that was in me. The darkness that I chose myself.'

'Even your truth works Evil.'

'To whom? The Night Watch? Of course. But to humans? There I must beg to differ.'

He walked towards the door.

'Zabulon,' I said, calling him by name again. 'I've seen your true appearance. I know who you are and what you are.'

The Dark Magician stopped in his tracks. He slowly turned round and passed his hand over his face – for a moment it was distorted, the skin was replaced by dull scales and the eyes became narrow slits.

Then the illusion was dispersed.

'Yes. Of course you've seen it,' said Zabulon, in his human form once again. 'And I have seen you. And let me say that you were no white angel with a gleaming sword. Everything depends on the point you look from. Goodbye, Anton. Believe me, I shall be glad to eliminate you some time in the future. But for now I wish you good luck. From the depths of the soul that I don't have.'

The door slammed behind him.

And immediately, as if it had just woken up, the sentry system howled out of the Twilight. The mask of Chkhoen on the wall twisted into a ferocious scowl, with fury glinting in the wooden gashes of its eyes.

My security guards . . .

I silenced the system with two passes and hurled the freeze that I'd prepared at the mask. The spell had come in useful after all.

'A little piece of chalk,' I said.

I'd heard something like that before. But it was a very long time ago, and I hadn't really been paying attention. It could have been a few phrases thrown out by one of my tutors at a lecture, or idle social gossip, or a student myth. But there definitely had been something about a piece of chalk . . .

I got up off the sofa, raised my hand in the air and threw the amulet on to the floor.

'Gesar!' I called through the Twilight. 'Gesar, answer me!'

My shadow shot up towards me from the floor, took hold of my body and sucked me into itself. The light dimmed, the room swayed, the outlines of the furniture blurred. It was suddenly unbearably quiet. The heat had receded. I stood there with my arms thrown out wide as the greedy Twilight drank my power.

'Gesar, by your name I summon you!'

Threads of grey mist drifted through the room. I couldn't give a damn who else might be able to hear me shouting.

'Gesar, my mentor, I call on you – will you answer?'

Far away in the distance an invisible shadow sighed.

'I hear you, Anton.'

'Answer me!'

'What question do you want the answer to?'

'Zabulon – did he lie to me?'

'No.'

'Gesar, stop!'

'It's too late, Anton. Everything's going the way it's supposed to go. Trust me.'

'Gesar, stop!'

'You have no right to make any demands.'

'No right! If we are part of the Light, if we do Good, then I have every right!'

The boss didn't answer straight away. I even thought he'd decided not to say anything else to me.

'All right. I'll be waiting for you in an hour at the Para Bar.'

'Where?'

'The Parachutists' Bar. Near Turgenevskaya metro station, behind the old central post office.'

Then there was silence.

I took a step backwards, out of the Twilight. It was an odd sort of place to meet. Was that where Gesar had had his showdown with the Day Watch? No, that was supposed to have been in some restaurant.

Okay, what did it matter – the Para Bar, Rosie O'Grady's, even the Chance Club? It wasn't important. Parachutists, yuppies, gays, who cared?

But there was one other thing I had to find out before I met Gesar.

I took out my phone and dialled Svetlana's number. She answered immediately.

'Hi,' I said simply. 'Are you at the dacha?'

'No.' She seemed startled by my brisk, businesslike tone. 'I'm on my way into town.'

'Who with?'

She paused.

'With Ignat.'

'Good,' I said, quite sincerely. 'Listen, do you know anything about chalk?'

'About what?'

This time the puzzlement was obvious.

'About the magical properties of chalk. Have they taught you anything about its uses in magic?'

'No, Anton. Are you sure you're all right?'

'I'm better than that.'

'Has something happened?'

'Nothing special.'

'Do you want me . . .' She hesitated. 'Do you want me to ask Olya?'

'Is she there with you as well?'

'Yes, the three of us are coming back into town together.'

'I don't think so. Thanks.'

'Anton . . .'

'What?'

I walked over to the desk and opened the drawer with all my magical junk. I looked at the dull crystals, at the clumsily carved wand from the time when I still wanted to be a combat magician. I pushed the drawer back.

'Forgive me.'

'There's nothing I need to forgive you for, Sveta.'

'Can I come round to your place?'

'How far away are you?'

'Halfway there.'

I shook my head and answered:

'Not now, I've got an important meeting. I'll call you back later.'

I ended the call and smiled. Very often the truth can be malicious and false. For instance, when you only tell half the truth. Like telling someone you can't talk to them without explaining why.

Permit me to do Good through Evil. I don't have any other way right now.

Just to be sure, I walked round the apartment, looking into the bedroom, the bathroom and the kitchen. As far as I was able to tell, Zabulon really hadn't left any 'presents' behind him.

I went back into the study, switched on my laptop and inserted the disk with the general magic database. Typed in the password. Typed in the word 'chalk'.

I hadn't been expecting anything special to come up. What I wanted to know could easily require such a high security clearance that it had never been included in any data bases.

There were three entries for 'chalk'.

The first was a reference to a chalk quarry where a first-grade Light Magician and a first-grade Dark Magician fought a duel in the fifteenth century. Both of them died of simple exhaustion of their powers – they didn't have enough strength left to emerge from the Twilight at the end of the duel. During the following five hundred years almost three thousand people had died at the site.

The second entry referred to the use of chalk for drawing magical symbols and protective circles. There was a lot more information here, and I read through it all quickly. There was nothing of interest. Using chalk has no particular advantages over charcoal, pencil, blood or oil paint. Except maybe that it is easier to erase.

The third reference came in the section 'Myths and Unconfirmed Data'. Of course, this section was full of rubbish like the use of silver and garlic in fighting vampires, or descriptions of non-existent ceremonies and rituals.

But I'd come across times before when genuine information had been completely forgotten and hidden away among the myths.

Chalk was mentioned in the article 'The Books of Fate'.

I read halfway through it and realised I'd hit the bull's eye. The information was just lying there in full view, accessible to any novice magician – it might even be available in sources that were open to ordinary humans.

The Books of Fate. Chalk.

It fitted.

I closed the file and switched off the laptop. Then I sat there for a while, chewing things over. Then I looked at the clock.

It was almost time for me to set out for our rendezvous.

I took a shower and changed my clothes. I took three amulets with me: Zabulon's medallion, my Night Watch badge and a combat disc Ilya had given to me – an ancient round piece of bronze a bit bigger than a five-rouble coin. I'd never used the disc before. Ilya had told me the amulet only had one charge left – maybe two at the most.

I took my pistol out of its hiding place and checked the clip. Explosive silver bullets. Good against werewolves, of doubtful use against vampires, entirely effective against Dark Magicians.

As if I were going off to war, not for a talk with my boss.

My phone rang in my pocket when I was already at the door.

'Anton?'

'Sveta?'

'Olga wants to talk to you, I'll give her the phone.'

'Okay,' I agreed, unlocking the door.

'Anton, I love you very much. Please don't do anything stupid,' Svetlana said quickly.

I couldn't think of anything to say. Olga took the phone.

'Anton. I want you to know that everything's already been decided. And it's all going to happen very soon.'

'Tonight,' I said.

'How do you know that?'

'I can just feel it. That was why the Watch was sent out of town, wasn't it? And why Svetlana was put into the right mood.'

'What do you know?'

'The Book of Destiny. Chalk. I understand everything now.'

'That's bad,' Olga said curtly. 'Anton, you have to—'

'I don't have to do anything for anyone. Except for the Light inside me.'

I ended the call and switched off the phone. I'd had enough. Gesar could easily contact me without any technical devices. Olga would only carry on trying to change my mind. And Svetlana wouldn't understand what I was doing and why in any case.

I decided to see things through just as I was, all on my own.

'Sit down, Anton,' said Gesar.

The bar turned out to be tiny. Six or seven tables separated by partitions, plus the bar itself. A television with the sound switched off, showing free-fall jumps. A photograph of the same thing on the wall – bodies in bright-coloured overalls spreadeagled in flight. The air was filled with smoke. There weren't many people in there, maybe because of the time: it was too late for lunch and there was still a long time to go before the evening rush. I glanced round the tables and saw Gesar sitting at the one in the corner.

The boss was not alone. There was a bowl of fruit on the table in front of him, and he was lazily plucking grapes off a bunch. A swarthy-skinned young man was sitting a short distance away from him, with his arms crossed. Our eyes met and I felt a slight but distinct pressure.

He was an Other too.

We looked at each other for about five seconds, gradually building up the pressure. He had powers, substantial powers, but he didn't have much experience. As soon as I got the chance, I relaxed my resistance, dodged the young man's probe and scanned him before he had time to raise his defences.

Other. Light. Grade four.

The young man grimaced as if he was in pain. He looked at Gesar with the eyes of a beaten dog.

'Let me introduce you,' said Gesar. 'Anton Gorodetsky, Other, member of the Moscow Night Watch. Alisher Ganiev, Other, new member of the Moscow Night Watch.'

The courier.

I held out my hand and lowered my defences.

'A Light One, grade two,' said Alisher, looking into my eyes. He bowed.

I shook my head and answered:

'Grade three.'

The young man glanced at Gesar again. This time he looked surprised, rather than guilty.

'Grade two,' the boss confirmed. 'You're at the top of your form, Anton. I'm delighted for you. Sit down and we'll talk. Alisher, you observe.'

I took a seat opposite the boss.

'Do you know why I decided to meet here?' asked Gesar. 'Try the grapes, they're very good.'

'How should I know? Maybe they have the best grapes in Moscow?'

Gesar laughed.

'Bravo. However, that's not the important thing. We bought the fruit at the market.'

'The pleasant surroundings, then.'

'Nothing of the kind. Just one small room, and if you go through that door, there are two more tables and a pool table.'

'You're a secret parachutist.'

'I haven't jumped for twenty years now,' Gesar countered smoothly. 'Anton, my dear boy, I came in here for a bite of potato and beef Stroganoff simply in order to show you a micro-environment. A tiny little society. Just sit there for a while and relax. Alisher, a glass of beer for Anton! Take a look around, soldier. Look at the faces. Listen. Breathe in the air.'

I turned away from the boss and moved to the end of the wooden bench, so that I could at least see the other people there. Alisher was already standing at the bar, waiting for my beer.

The regulars in the Para Bar had strange faces. All alike in some odd, indefinable way. Distinctive eyes, distinctive gestures. Nothing really special, just the same stamp on every one.

'A team,' said the boss. 'And a microenvironment. We could have had this conversation in Chance, the gay club, or in the restaurant of the Central Writers' House, or in a snack bar next to some factory. It doesn't matter. What does matter was that there had to be a small, close-knit team. More or less isolated from general society. It couldn't have been McDonald's or a luxury restaurant, it had to be an official or unofficial club. And you know why? Because this is us. It's a model of our Watch.'

I didn't answer. I watched a young guy on crutches hobble up to the next table, wave away an invitation to sit down, lean on the partition and start talking. The music drowned out his words, but I could absorb the general meaning through the Twilight. A parachute that didn't open and had to be dumped. A landing with the reserve chute. A broken leg. And now six damn months without jumping!

'The public here has a very specific profile,' the boss continued calmly. 'Risk. Intense thrills. Little understanding of other people. Their own slang. Problems normal people couldn't possibly understand. And also, incidentally, regular injuries and death. Do you like it here?'

I thought for a moment and said:

'No, you have to be one of the in-crowd. There's no other way you can be here.'

'Of course. It's interesting to drop into any microenvironment like this – once. After that you either accept its laws and join its little society, or you're rejected. Well, we're no different. In essential terms, that is. Every Other who has been found and has accepted his own nature is faced with a choice. He either joins the Watch on his side, becomes a soldier, a warrior, who inevitably risks his life. Or he carries on living an almost human life, without developing his special magical powers, making use of some of the advantages of an Other, but suffering all the disadvantages of living like that. The most painful situation is when the initial choice is wrong. When for some reason the Other doesn't wish to accept the laws of the Watch. But it's almost impossible to leave our organisation. Tell me, Anton, could you live outside the Watch?'

Of course, the boss never makes abstract conversation.

'Probably not,' I admitted. 'It would be hard, almost impossible, in fact, for me to keep within the limits of what an ordinary Light Magician is allowed to do.'

'And without joining the Watch, you wouldn't be able to justify your magical actions by the interests of the struggle against the Dark. Right?'

'Right.'

'And that's where the difficulty lies, Antosha, that's the whole problem.' The boss sighed. 'Alisher, don't just stand there.'

He was really giving the young man a hard time. But it wasn't difficult to guess why: the courier had wormed his way into the Moscow Watch, and now he had to take the inevitable consequences.

'Your beer, Light One Anton.' The new Watch member put the glass in front of me with a brief nod.

I accepted the beer without saying anything. This young, talented magician wasn't to blame for anything. I was sure we could be friends. But just then I was feeling angry with him: the delivery Alisher had brought to Moscow would separate me from Svetlana for ever.

'Anton, what are we going to do?' the boss asked.

'Just what, exactly, is the problem?' I answered, looking at him with the eyes of a devoted St Bernard.

'Svetlana. You're opposing her mission.'

'Of course.'

'Anton. There are basic principles involved here. Axioms. You have no right to object to the policy of the Watch on the basis of your own personal interests.'

'What have my own personal interests got to do with it?' I asked, genuinely surprised. 'I regard the entire operation that's being planned as immoral. It won't be of any benefit to ordinary humans. Like it or not, every attempt to bring about a fundamental change in human society has been a failure.'

'Sooner or later we shall succeed. Note that I don't even claim that this attempt will bring success. But the chances are better now than ever before.'

'I don't believe it.'

'You can lodge an appeal at the highest level.'

'Will they have time to consider it before Svetlana picks up the chalk and opens the Book of Destiny?'

The boss closed his eyes and sighed.

'No, they won't. It's all happening tonight, just as soon as our time begins. Are you happy now you know when it's all going to happen?'

'Boris Ignatievich,' I said, deliberately using the name by which I'd first known him. 'Listen to me, please. You once left your homeland and came to Russia. Not to serve the interests of the Light, not for the sake of your career. But because of Olga. I don't know very much about your past history, how much hate and love, how much betrayal and nobility there is in it. But you have to understand me. Because you can.'

I don't know what kind of answer I'd been expecting. Maybe I thought he'd look away, or promise to cancel the project.

'I understand you very well, Anton,' the boss said with a nod. 'In fact, you can't even imagine how well. That's exactly why the plan will go ahead.'

'But why?'

'Because, my boy, there's such a thing as destiny. And there's nothing stronger than destiny. Some are destined to change the world. Some don't have that in their destiny. Some are destined to bring entire states to their knees, and some to stand in the wings holding the puppets' strings. Anton, I know what I'm doing. Believe me.'

'I don't believe you.'

I got up, leaving my untouched beer with its wilting cap of foam. Alisher gave the boss an enquiring look, as if he was prepared to stop me.

'You have the right to do whatever you want,' said the boss. 'The Light is in you, but the Twilight is always waiting behind you. You know where any false step will lead. And you know that I am willing to help you, I am obliged to help you.'

'Gesar, my mentor, thank you for everything that you have taught me,' I said with a bow, and the parachutists cast curious glances in my direction. 'I believe I no longer have the right to expect your help. Please accept my gratitude.'

'You are free of all obligations to me,' Gesar replied calmly. 'Act as your destiny requires of you.'

That was all. He cast off his former pupil as simply as that. I wondered how many pupils he'd had who'd failed to acknowledge his supreme goals and noble ideals.

Hundreds, thousands.

'Goodbye, Gesar,' I said. I glanced at Alisher. 'I wish you luck, new watchman.'

The young man looked at me reproachfully:

'If I may be allowed to say something . . .'

'Say it,' I told him.

'In your place, I would not be in any hurry, Light One Anton.'

'I've already lost too much time, Light One Alisher,' I said with a smile. I was used to thinking of myself as one of the most junior magicians in the Watch, but everything passes. And to this novice I was an authority. For the time being at least. 'One day you will hear the sound of time rustling as it slips through your fingers like sand. Remember me then. I wish you luck.'

CHAPTER 6

HEAT.

I was walking along Old Arbat Street. Artists sketching cartoon portraits, musicians playing hackneyed music, street traders all selling the same souvenirs, foreigners with the typical look of interest in their eyes, Muscovites in their usual irritated mood rushing past the stalls of sham craftwork.

Should I shake you all up a bit?

Should I put on a little show for you?

Juggle a few bolts of lightning? Swallow genuine fire? Make the paving stones open up to reveal a fountain of mineral water? Heal a dozen crippled beggars? Feed the homeless urchins darting around with cakes conjured up out of thin air?

What would the point be?

They'd toss me a handful of small change for the fireballs that should be used to kill creatures of Evil. The mineral water fountain would turn out to be a broken water main. These crippled beggars are already healthier and richer than most of the people walking by. And the homeless urchins would run for it, because they learned a long time ago that there's no such thing as free cake.

Yes, I could understand Gesar, I could understand all the higher magicians who'd been fighting against the Dark for thousands of years. You can't live for ever with a feeling of powerlessness. You can't carry on sitting in the trenches for ever: that kills an army more surely than enemy bullets.

But how did I come into it?

Did the banner of victory really have to be sewn out of the fabric of my love?

And how did these humans come into it?

Turning the world upside down and then turning it back again was easy enough, but who'd stop all the people from falling off?

Were we really incapable of learning anything?

I knew what Gesar was planning to do, or rather, what Svetlana was going to do on his instructions. I knew how it might turn out and I could even imagine which loopholes in the Treaty would be used to justify interference with the Book of Destiny. I had been told when the act would be performed. The only thing I didn't know was where and whose destiny was to be changed.

And that was a fatal gap in my knowledge.

Almost fatal enough to make me pay Zabulon a visit.

But then I'd be dispatched into the Twilight.

I was halfway along the Old Arbat when I sensed a surge of power – very faint, at the very limits of my sensitivity. There was magical activity taking place somewhere very close, not very strong, but even so . . .

The Dark!

Whatever I might think about Gesar, no matter how much I disagreed with him, I was still a soldier of the Night Watch.

I reached into my pocket for my amulet, summoned my shadow and stepped into the Twilight.

Oh, how neglected everything was!

It was a long time since I'd walked round the centre of Moscow in the Twilight.

Everything was covered with a thick carpet of blue moss. The slow oscillations of its threads created an illusion of trembling water. Ripples ran from where I was standing as the moss simultaneously drank in my emotions and tried to creep away from me. But I wasn't interested in the Twilight's little pranks right now.

I was not alone in the grey space under that sunless sky.

I looked for a second at the girl standing with her back to me and I could feel a wicked smile spreading across my face. A smile unworthy of a Light Magician. Some 'moderate intervention' this was!

A third-degree magical intervention?

Well, well.

That's very serious, my girl. So serious, you must be crazy. Third degree's way beyond your powers, you must be using someone else's amulet.

But I'll use my own powers to investigate.

I walked up to her and she didn't even hear my steps on the soft blue carpet of moss. The vague, shadowy forms of humans were sliding past us, and she was too absorbed in what she was doing.

'Anton Gorodetsky, Night Watch,' I said. 'Alisa Donnikova, you're under arrest.'

The young witch screeched and swung round. She was holding an amulet in her hand, a crystal prism through which she had been viewing the people walking by. Her first instinct was to try to hide the amulet, then she tried to look at me through the prism.

I grabbed her arm and forced her to stop. We stood close to each other for a second as I slowly increased the pressure, twisting the witch's wrist. A scene like that between a man and a woman would have looked shameful. But for us Others, physical strength doesn't depend on our sex, or even on how well developed our muscles are. Strength lies all around us – in the Twilight, in humans. I couldn't tell how much Alisa might have extracted from the world around her. It could be even more than I had.

But I'd caught her at the scene of the crime. And there could be other Watch members nearby. Resisting a member of the other Watch who had officially declared you under arrest was cause for immediate elimination.

'I'm not resisting,' said Alisa, and she opened her fingers. The prism fell into the soft moss, which swirled and seethed, enveloping the crystal amulet.

'The prism of power?' I asked rhetorically. 'Alisa Donnikova, you have performed a magical intervention of the third degree.'

'Fourth,' she replied quickly.

I shrugged.

'Third or fourth, that's of no real importance. It still means the tribunal, Alisa. You're in big trouble.'

'I didn't do anything.' The witch was trying hard to look calm. 'I have personal permission to carry the prism. I didn't make use of it.'

'Alisa, any higher magician can extract all the information needed from this thing.'

I reached down towards the ground, forcing the blue moss to part and the prism to leap into my hand. It was cold, very cold.

'Even I can read the history from it,' I said. 'Alisa Donnikova, Other, Dark Witch of the Day Patrol, fourth grade of power, I hereby formally accuse you of violating the Treaty. If you offer resistance I shall be obliged to eliminate you. Put your hands behind your back.'

She obeyed. And then she started talking, quickly and urgently, trying desperately to persuade me:

'Anton, wait, please, listen to me. Yes, I did try out the prism, but you must understand, it's the first time I've ever been trusted with such a powerful amulet! Anton, I'm not so stupid as to attack people in the centre of Moscow, and why would I want to? Anton, we're both Others! Can't we settle this in a friendly way? Anton!'

'Friendly?' I said, putting the prism in my pocket. 'Come on, let's go.'

'Anton, a fourth-degree intervention, or third degree! Any third-degree intervention carried out in the interests of the Light! Not like my stupid game with the prism, a genuine intervention!'

I could understand why she was panicking. This business could easily end in dematerialisation. A Day Watch agent sucking the life out of humans for her own personal ends – that would be a tremendous scandal. They'd hand Alisa over without the slightest hesitation.

'You have no authority to make such compromises. The leader of the Dark Ones will not ratify your promise.'

'Zabulon will confirm it!'

'Will he?' I was shocked by the certainty in her voice. She was probably Zabulon's lover. But even so, it was surprising. 'Alisa, I once made a friendly agreement with you.'

'Yes, and I was the one who suggested overlooking your intervention.'

'And do you remember how it all turned out?' I asked with a smile.

'This is different, I'm the one who's broken the law,' said Alisa, lowering her eyes. 'You'll have the right to strike back. You don't need permission for third-degree Light magic, do you? Or for any Light magic? You could remoralise twenty vicious criminals and make them righteous. Incinerate ten murderers on the spot. Prevent a catastrophe, create a localised time warp! Anton, isn't that worth overlooking my stupid trick? Look around, everyone here's still alive! I hadn't done anything yet. I'd only just started—'

'Everything you say can be used against you.'

'Yes, I know, I know!'

There were tears glittering in her eyes. Probably quite genuine ones too. Beneath her nature as a witch she was still a perfectly ordinary girl. A pretty girl frightened by the mistake she'd made. And was it her fault that she'd ended up on the side of the Dark?

I felt my emotional shield starting to buckle and shook my head:

'Don't try to put pressure on me!'

'Anton, please, let's settle this. Wouldn't you like the right to a third-degree intervention?'

Wouldn't I just? It was every Light Magician's dream to be given carte blanche like that. Just for a moment to feel that he was fighting like a genuine soldier and not sitting in the trenches, being eaten by lice and gazing dejectedly at the white flag of truce.

'You have no right to make such a proposition,' I said firmly.

'I shall have!' Alisa shook her head and took a deep breath. 'Zabulon!'

I waited, clutching the little combat disc in my hand.

'Zabulon, I summon you!' Her voice had become a high-pitched screech. I noticed the human shadows around us begin moving a little faster: a vague, inexplicable feeling of alarm was making the people lengthen their strides.

Would her summons reach the Dark Ones' chief again?

Like that time at the Maharajah restaurant, when Zabulon had almost killed me with Shahab's Lash?

But he hadn't killed me. He'd missed.

Even though the whole operation had been planned by Gesar, and Zabulon really seemed to believe that I was guilty of killing Dark Ones.

Did that mean he'd already had other plans for me?

Or had Gesar intervened, secretly and unobtrusively, diverted the streaks of lightning away from me?

I didn't know. As always, I didn't have enough information. I could have come up with thirty-three different explanations, each contradicting the others.

I was almost hoping Zabulon wouldn't respond. Then I'd be able to pull Alisa out of the Twilight, call in the boss or one of the operatives, hand the fool over to them and receive a bonus at the end of the month. But what did I care about bonuses right now?

'Zabulon!' There was genuine supplication in her voice. 'Zabulon!'

She was crying now, without even realising it. The mascara had run under her eyes.

'Don't waste your time,' I said. 'Let's go.'

Just at that moment a Dark portal opened only two metres away from us.

First a blast of cold chilled me to the bone, and I started thinking fondly of the heat in the human world. Then the moss burst into flames and burned all the way down the street. Naturally Zabulon hadn't set it on fire deliberately, it was just that the opening of the portal had spilled out so much power that the moss couldn't assimilate it all.

'Zabulon,' whispered Alisa.

From out of the paving stones about five metres away a ray of violet light shot up into the sky. The flash blinded me and I automatically squeezed my eyes shut. When I looked in that direction again, there was a bluish-black bubble hanging in the grey mist, with something looking vaguely like a man clambering out of it – bristling with spiny scales. Zabulon had responded to the summons by travelling through the second or third level of the Twilight. The time we were moving in would have seemed as slow there as human time did to us.

I suddenly had the old feeling of powerlessness that I thought I'd come to terms with a long time ago. The powers that Zabulon or

Gesar used so casually were so far beyond me that I simply couldn't comprehend them.

'Zabulon!' Still holding her hands behind her back, Alisa raced towards the monstrous creature and pressed herself against it, burying her face in the bristly scales. 'Help me, help me!'

Of course, Zabulon hadn't appeared in demonic form just to make an impression on me. In human form he wouldn't have survived a minute in the deep layers of the Twilight. And he'd probably had to travel for hours, if not days.

The monster cast a baleful glance at me from the narrow slits of its eyes. A long forked tongue slithered out of its mouth and slid across Alisa's head, leaving a trail of white slime on her hair. A scaly hand with long claws took hold of Alisa by the chin and gently lifted up her head. Their eyes met. The exchange of information was brief.

'Little idiot!' the demon roared. The tongue withdrew into its mouth and the jaws clacked shut, just missing it. 'Greedy little idiot!'

Well. So much for my right to a third-degree intervention.

The demon's short tail lashed Alisa across the legs, tearing the silk dress and knocking her to the ground. Its eyes flashed, the witch was enveloped in a blue glow and she froze.

So much for the help Alisa had wanted.

'May I take my prisoner away, Zabulon?' I asked.

The monster stood there, swaying on its crooked paws, with the claws on its toes sliding in and out. Then it took a step and stood between me and the motionless witch.

'I ask you to confirm the legality of the arrest,' I said. 'Otherwise I shall be obliged to summon help.'

The demon began transforming. The proportions of its body changed and its scales disappeared, its tail was drawn back into its body, and its penis stopped looking like a club studded with nails. Finally clothes appeared on Zabulon's body.

'Wait a moment, Anton.'

'What for?'

The Dark Magician's face remained inscrutable. Presumably in his demonic form he felt far more emotions, or at least he didn't feel any need to conceal them.

'I confirm the pledge made by Alisa.'

'What?'

'If this matter is not made official, the Day Watch will accept any magical intervention you make, up to and including the third degree.'

He seemed to be utterly serious.

I swallowed. A promise like that from the head of the Day Watch . . .

'Never trust the Dark Ones.'

'Any intervention up to and including the second degree.'

'Are you that eager to avoid a scandal?' I asked. 'Or do you need her for something?'

A tremor ran across Zabulon's face.

'I need her. I love her.'

'I don't believe you.'

'As the head of the Moscow Day Watch I ask you, watchman Anton, to settle this matter amicably. It is possible, since my ward Alisa Donnikova had not yet caused any significant harm to humans. As compensation for her *attempt*' – Zabulon emphasised the last word – 'to perform a magical intervention of the third degree, the Day Watch will accept any Light intervention that you may perform up to and including the second degree. I do not ask for this agreement to remain secret. I do not impose any restrictions on your actions. I confirm that for the offence she has committed Day Watch agent Alisa will be severely punished. May the Dark bear witness to my words.'

A faint trembling. A rumbling below ground, the roar of an

approaching hurricane. A tiny black ball appeared on Zabulon's open palm, spinning rapidly.

'What do you say?' asked Zabulon.

I ran my tongue over my lips and looked at Alisa's magically frozen body. She was a real bitch, no doubt about it. And I had a personal score to settle with her.

Maybe that was why I didn't feel like settling this business with a compromise. Maybe it had nothing to do with the risks of an agreement with the Dark. Alisa had tried to use the prism of power to extract part of the life energy from humans. That was third- or fourth-degree magic. I'd be able to perform a second-degree intervention, and that was a very big deal. A genuinely massive intervention. A city without a single crime for a whole day. A brilliant and unequivocally good intervention. How many times in the history of the Night Watch had we needed to make a third- or fourth-degree intervention but didn't have the right, and we'd had to just go ahead and risk it, terrified by how the other side might respond?

And now I could have a second-degree intervention for free, or as good as.

'May the Light bear witness to my words,' I said, and held my hand out to Zabulon.

It was the first time I'd ever called on the primordial powers to witness anything. I only knew it didn't require any special incantations. And there was no real guarantee that the Light would deign to become involved in our affairs.

A petal of white flame flared up on my open palm.

Zabulon flinched, but he didn't take his hand away. We sealed the agreement with a handshake, the Dark and the Light coming together. I felt a stab of pain, like a blunt needle piercing my flesh.

'The agreement is sealed,' said the Dark Magician.

He frowned too. He had also felt the pain.

'Do you hope to gain some advantage from this?' I asked.

'Of course. I always hope to gain some advantage from everything. And I usually do.'

At least Zabulon wasn't obviously delighted with the deal we'd made. Whatever he might be hoping for as a result of our agreement, he wasn't completely certain of success.

'I've found out what the courier brought to Moscow from the east and why.'

Zabulon smiled gently.

'Excellent. I find the situation trying, and it is a great relief to know that now my concern will be shared by others.'

'Zabulon, has there ever been a single case when the Night Watch and the Day Watch collaborated? Genuine collaboration, not just catching violators and psychopaths?'

'No. In any collaboration one side or the other would be the loser.'

'I'll bear that in mind.'

'You do that.'

We even bowed politely to each other. As if we weren't two magicians on opposite sides, an adept of the Light and a servant of the Dark, but two acquaintances who got on perfectly well.

Then Zabulon returned to Alisa's motionless body, lifted it easily and threw it across his shoulder. I was expecting him to withdraw from the Twilight, but instead the Dark Ones' leader gave me a condescending smile and stepped into the portal. It remained visible for a moment, and then began to fade. I was going a different way.

It was only then that I realised how tired I felt. The Twilight likes it when we enter it, and it likes it even more when we're agitated. The Twilight's insatiable, glad to take on anyone.

I chose a spot where there weren't many people and tore myself out of my shadow.

The eyes of the people walking by swung away as usual. You meet us so often during the day, you humans . . . Light Ones and Dark Ones, magicians and werewolves, witches and healers. You look at us, but you're not allowed to see us. May it always be that way.

We can live for hundreds and thousands of years. We're very hard to kill. And for us the problems that make up human life are no more than a schoolboy's distress at his bad handwriting.

But there's a downside to everything. I'd gladly trade places with you humans. Take this ability to see the shadow and enter the Twilight. Take the protection of the Watch and the ability to influence people's minds.

Give me back the peace of mind that I have lost for ever.

Someone jostled me to get me out of the way. A tough-looking man with a shaved head, a mobile at his belt and a gold chain round his neck. He looked me up and down disdainfully, muttered something through his teeth and headed on down the street. The girlfriend clinging to his arm made a rather unsuccessful attempt to imitate his glance, the kind that petty gangsters use for jerks who are a soft touch.

I laughed out loud. Yes, I probably looked a sight! Standing stock still in the middle of the street, apparently gawping at a stand covered with ugly bronze figurines, wooden *matryoshka* dolls with politicians' faces and fake Khokhloma painted boxes.

I had the right to shake up the entire street. To perform a mass remoralisation – then the man with the shaven head would take a job as an orderly in a mental hospital and his girlfriend would head for the train station to go to see the old mother she'd managed to forget, somewhere out in the sticks.

I wanted to do Good – my hands were just itching to do it!

And that was why I mustn't.

The heart might be pure and the hands might be hot, but the head still had to be cool.

I was an ordinary, rank-and-file Other. I didn't have the power granted to Gesar or Zabulon, and I never would have. Maybe that was why I took a different view of what was happening. And I couldn't even use this unexpected gift – the right to use Light magic. That would be joining in the game that was being played out above my head.

My only chance was to drop out of the game.

And take Svetlana with me.

And in the process ruin the operation the Night Watch had been preparing for so long. To stop being a field agent of the Watch. Become an ordinary Light Magician, using mere crumbs of my powers. That was the best case, of course – in the worst case scenario it was the eternal Twilight for me.

Today, today at midnight.

Where? And who? Whose Book of Destiny would the sorceress open? Olga had said they'd been planning the operation for twelve years. Twelve years spent searching for a Great Sorceress who could use the little piece of chalk that had been kept safe all that time.

But wait!

I could have howled at my own stupidity. Higher magicians plan many moves ahead. There are no accidents in their games. There are queens and there are pawns. But there are no superfluous pieces.

Egor!

The boy who had almost become a victim of illegal hunting. Who'd entered the Twilight in a state of mind that had nudged him towards the Dark Side. The boy whose destiny was still not determined, whose aura still had all the colours of a child's. A unique case. I'd been stunned when I saw him for the first time.

I'd been stunned, and then had forgotten. The moment I discovered that the kid's powers had been artificially increased by the boss – to mislead the Dark Ones and allow Egor to offer at least some resistance to the vampires.

And for me he'd become a personal failure – after all, I had been the first to discover he was an Other – and a good person, at least so far, and a future enemy in the eternal struggle between Good and Evil. The memory of his undecided destiny had remained buried somewhere deep under all the rest.

He could still become absolutely anyone. His future potential was indeterminate. An open book. A Book of Destiny.

He was the one who would stand in front of Svetlana when she picked up the piece of chalk. And he would do it gladly, once Gesar had explained what it was all about. A serious, logical explanation. The boss of the Night Watch, the leader of the Light Ones of Moscow, a great and ancient magician – he'd be able to explain everything clearly. Gesar would talk about correcting mistakes. And it would be the truth. Gesar would talk about the great future that would open up for Egor. And even that would be true! The Dark Ones could lodge a thousand protests, but the Inquisition would certainly take into account that the boy had initially suffered from their actions.

Svetlana would certainly be told that I was depressed by my failure with Egor. And that the main reason the boy had suffered was because the Watch had been busy saving her.

She wouldn't even hesitate.

She'd accept everything she was told to do.

She'd pick up the piece of ordinary chalk that could be used to draw squares for hopscotch in the street or to write '2 + 2 = 4' on a school blackboard.

And she'd start shaping a destiny that hadn't been defined yet.

What were they planning to make him into?

Who?

A chief, a leader of new parties and revolutions?

A prophet of religions that hadn't been created yet?

A thinker who would found a new school of social thought? A musician, a poet, a writer, whose work would change the consciousness of millions?

Just how many years into the future did the plan of the powers of the Light extend?

The original essential nature of an Other could not be changed. Egor would always be a very weak magician, but thanks to the intervention of the Night Watch, he would be a Light Magician.

And in order to alter the destiny of the human world, you didn't have to be an Other. It could even get in the way. It would be much better to have the support of the Watch while you led the human crowd, so much in need of the happiness we had invented for it.

And he would lead them. I didn't know how, and I didn't know where, but he would lead them. But that was when the Dark Ones would make their move. An assassin can be found for every president. And for every prophet there are a thousand interpreters to distort the essence of the religion, to replace the bright flame with the heat of the inquisitors' pyres. The time came when every book was cast into the fire, when every symphony was reduced to a popular tune and played in all the bars.

No, we hadn't learned a thing. Probably because we didn't want to.

But at least I still had a bit of time. And the right to make my move. My only move.

If only I knew what it was.

Should I appeal to Svetlana not to accept what Gesar said, not to get involved in higher magic, not to change anyone else's destiny?

But why should she agree? Everything was being done correctly. Mistakes that had been made were being put right, a positive future was being created both for a single individual and for humanity as a whole. I was being relieved of the burden of the mistake I'd made. Svetlana was being relieved of the knowledge that her good fortune had been paid for by someone else's tragedy. She was entering the ranks of the Great Sorceresses. What did my vague doubts mean compared to all that? And what were they really? How much was genuine concern, and how much petty self-interest? Where was the Light, where was the Dark?

'Hey, friend!'

The street trader who owned the stall I was standing in front of was staring at me. Not really angry, just rather annoyed.

'You buying anything?'

'Do I look like an idiot?' I asked him.

'Sure you do. If you're not buying, move on.'

From where he stood he was right. But I was in the mood to talk back.

'You don't realise how lucky you are. I'm collecting a crowd for you, attracting customers.'

He was a colourful character. Stocky, red-faced, with huge thick arms, rippling masses of fat and muscle. He sized me up, obviously didn't see anything threatening and got ready to make some caustic remark.

Then suddenly he smiled.

'Okay, if you're collecting a crowd, put a bit more effort into it. Pretend to buy something. You can even pretend to pay me some money.'

This was a pleasant surprise.

I smiled back at him:

'Would you like me to buy something for real?'

'What would you do that for? This is rubbish for the tourists.' The trader stopped smiling, but there was no tension or aggression left in his face. 'This damn heat, it's driving me crazy. I wish it would rain.'

I looked up at the sky and shrugged. Something seemed to be changing. Something had shifted in the transparent blue dome of the heavenly oven.

'I think it's going to,' I told him.

'Great.'

We nodded at each other and I walked away, slipping into the stream of people.

I didn't know what to do, but I already knew where to go. And that was a start.

CHAPTER 7

TO A LARGE extent our powers are borrowed.

The Dark Ones draw theirs from the suffering of humans. Things are a lot simpler for them. They don't even have to cause people any pain. They can just wait. Just keep their eyes open and keep absorbing people's suffering, like drinking a cocktail through a straw.

We can do the same, only with one small difference. We draw strength from people who are feeling good, when they're happy. But there's one little difficulty that makes the process easy for the Dark Ones and almost forbidden to us. Happiness and sorrow are not just two levels on a single scale of human emotions. If they were, there'd be no such thing as radiant sorrow or malicious joy. They're two parallel processes, two equal currents of power that Others can feel and use.

When a Dark Magician drinks in someone's pain, it only increases.

When a Light Magician takes someone's joy, it decreases.

We can absorb power at any moment. But we very rarely allow ourselves to.

That day I decided that I was entitled.

I took a little bit from a couple locked in each other's arms at the entrance to the metro. They were happy, very happy just then. But I could tell that the lovers were parting, and for a long time, and sadness would inevitably come to them anyway. I decided I had the right. Their joy was bright and rich, like a bouquet of scarlet roses, proud and delicate.

I touched a child as he ran past – he was happy, he didn't feel the oppressive heat, he was running to buy an ice cream. He would soon restore his power. It was as simple and pure as wild flowers. A posy of daisies that I gathered without hesitation.

I saw an old woman in a window. The shadow of death was already hovering over her, she could probably sense it herself. But she was still smiling. Her grandson had called round to see her that day. Probably only to check if his grandmother was still alive, or if the valuable apartment in the centre of Moscow was free now. She understood that too, but she was still happy. I felt ashamed, unbearably ashamed, but I touched her and took a little power. A fading orange and yellow bunch of asters and autumn leaves . . .

I walked along just as I used to in my nightmares, when I handed out happiness to everyone on all sides, making sure no one went away without his share. But the trail I left behind me now was quite different. Slightly faded smiles, wrinkled foreheads, lips pressed together in doubt.

It was pretty easy to see where I'd been.

If I met a Day Watch patrol, they wouldn't stop me.

And even if any Light Ones saw what was happening, they wouldn't say anything.

I was doing what I thought was necessary. What I believed I had a right to do. Borrowing. Stealing. And the way I used the power I'd taken would seal my destiny.

Either I'd pay back all my debts in full.

Or the Twilight would open its arms to embrace me.

When a Light Magician starts drawing power from humans, he's gambling everything on a single throw of the dice. And the usual balancing of accounts between the actions of the two Watches didn't apply.

Not only did the amount of Good that was done have to exceed the amount of Evil I had caused, I would have to be certain beyond a shadow of a doubt that I'd paid everything back in full.

The lovers, the children, the old people. The group drinking beer by the statue. I'd been afraid their happiness might turn out to be a sham, but it was genuine, and I took their power.

Forgive me.

I could apologise to every one of them three times over. I could pay for what I'd taken. But I wouldn't really mean it.

I was simply fighting for love. In the first place. And only after that for you, the humans for whom this new happiness was being prepared.

But what if I were really doing that as well?

What if, every time you fought for love, you were fighting for the whole world?

For the whole world – not against the whole world.

Power!

Power.

Power?

I gathered it in crumbs, sometimes gently, sometimes in crude haste, to prevent my hand from trembling and my eyes from looking away in shame, as I took almost all there was.

Maybe happiness was a rare experience anyway for this young man.

I didn't know.

Power!

Maybe without this smile, this woman would lose someone's love.

Power.

Maybe tomorrow this strong man with the ironic smile would die.

Power.

The amulets in my pockets wouldn't be any use. There wasn't going be a fight. The 'top form' the boss had mentioned wouldn't help me either. That wouldn't be enough. And the right to carry out a second-degree intervention that Zabulon had granted me so generously was a trap. There wasn't any doubt about that. He'd framed his own girlfriend, drawn the lines of probability together so that we'd meet and then handed me his deadly gift with a mournful expression on his face. I couldn't see far enough into the future to be sure the Good I did would never become Evil.

But if you have no weapon, accept one even from the hands of your enemy.

Power!

Power.

Power?

If I'd still been connected to Gesar by the narrow thread that maintains contact between a young magician and his mentor, he would long ago have sensed what was happening. Sensed the energy building up inside me, the massive energy I'd gathered for some unknown purpose.

What would he have done?

It made no sense to try to stop a magician who had started down this path.

I was walking in the direction of the Economic Exhibition metro. I knew where it was all going to happen. Coincidences aren't coincidences when they're controlled by higher magicians. The absurd 'box on stilts', the matchbox standing on its end – that was where Zabulon had lost the battle for Svetlana, that was where

Gesar had unmasked the Light Magician he'd assigned to the Inquisition, teaching Svetlana a lesson in the process.

The focus of power for the whole complex manoeuvre.

For the third time.

I didn't feel like eating or drinking, but I stopped once, bought a coffee and drank it. It was tasteless, as if all the caffeine had been filtered out of it. People started making way for me, even though I was walking in the ordinary world. The magical tension was rising.

There was no way I could conceal my approach.

But I didn't want to creep up on them anyway.

A pregnant woman was walking cautiously along the pavement. I shuddered when I saw she was smiling. And I almost turned away when I realised her unborn child was smiling too in its own safe little world.

Their power was like pale pink peonies – a large blossom and a round bud that hadn't unfolded yet.

I had to gather what I found along my way.

Without hesitation or pity.

There was something happening in the world around me too.

The heat seemed to have got stronger. In a single desperate surge.

The Dark and the Light Magicians must have had good reason to spend all those days trying to disperse the heat. Something was going to happen. I stopped and looked up at the sky through the Twilight.

Subtle, twisted coils of swirling air.

Sparks on the horizon.

Fading light in the south-east.

A glowing nimbus round the needle of the Ostankino TV Tower.

It was going to be a strange night.

I touched a little girl running by and took the naïve joy she felt because her father had come home sober. Like snapping off a briar branch, prickly and fragile.

Forgive me.

It was almost eleven o'clock when I reached the 'box on stilts'.

The last person I touched was a drunken factory worker, slumped against the wall in the alley. The same alley where I'd killed a Dark One for the first time. He was barely even conscious. But happy.

I took his power too. A dusty, trampled stem of coarse plantain, a crude, dirty-brown candle.

That was power too.

As I crossed the road, I realised I wasn't alone. I summoned my shadow and withdrew into the Twilight.

The building was cordoned off.

It was the oddest cordon I'd ever seen. Dark Ones and Light Ones all together. I spotted Semyon and nodded to him. He gave me a calm, slightly reproachful look. Tiger Cub, Bear, Ilya, Ignat . . .

When had they summoned them all? While I was wandering round the city, gathering power? Sorry about that holiday, guys.

And the Dark Ones. Even Alisa was there. The witch was a terrible sight: her face looked like a paper mask that had been crumpled and straightened out again. It looked as if Zabulon hadn't been lying when he told me she'd be punished. Alisher was standing beside Alisa, and when I caught his eye, I could tell the two of them would fight. Maybe not now. But some day.

I stepped through the ring.

'This is a restricted zone,' said Alisher.

'This is a restricted zone,' echoed Alisa.

'I have a right to enter.'

I had enough power in me to enter without permission. Only

the Great Magicians could stop me now, but they weren't there.

They didn't try to stop me. Someone, either Gesar or Zabulon, or maybe both, must have ordered them just to warn me.

'Good luck,' I heard someone whisper behind me. I swung round and caught Tiger Cub's eye. I nodded.

The entrance hall was empty. And the house had gone quiet, like the time when the immense Inferno vortex was spinning over Svetlana's head: the Evil that she had summoned against herself.

I walked on through the grey gloom. The floor echoed hollowly under my feet. In the Twilight world even the ground responded to magic, even the shades of human buildings did.

The trapdoor to the roof was open. Nobody was trying to put any obstacles in my way. The trouble was I didn't know if I ought to be pleased about that.

I emerged from the Twilight. I couldn't see any point in it. Not now.

I started climbing the ladder.

The first person I saw was Maxim.

He looked quite different from the way he had before, the spontaneous Light Magician, the Maverick who had killed adepts of the Dark for years. Maybe they'd done something to him. Or maybe he'd just changed. There are some people who make ideal executioners.

Maxim had been lucky. He'd become an executioner. An Inquisitor. Standing over and above the Light and the Dark, serving everybody – and nobody. He had his arms crossed on his chest and his head slightly lowered. Something about him reminded me of Zabulon, the first time I'd seen him. And something reminded me of Gesar too. When I appeared, Maxim raised his head slightly and cast a casual glance at me. Then he lowered his gaze.

So I really was allowed in on the whole show.

Zabulon was standing to one side, wrapped in a pale raincoat. He took no notice of my arrival. He'd known I'd be there anyway.

Gesar, Svetlana and Egor were standing together. They gave me a much livelier reception.

'So you came after all?' the boss asked

I nodded and looked at Svetlana. She was wearing a long white dress and her hair was loose. She had a small, glittering box made of white morocco leather in her hand. It looked as if it was meant for a brooch or a medallion.

'Anton, so you know then?' Egor shouted.

If anybody there was happy, he was. Perfectly happy.

'Yes, I know,' I answered. I walked up to him and ruffled his hair.

His power was like a yellow dandelion.

Now I felt like I'd collected all I could.

'Full up?' asked Gesar. 'Anton, what are you planning to do?'

I didn't answer. Something was bothering me. There was something wrong here.

That was it! Why wasn't Olga there?

Had the final briefing already been given? Did Svetlana already know what she had to do?

'A piece of chalk,' I said. 'A little piece of chalk, pointed at both ends. You can use it to write on anything. In a Book of Destiny, for instance. Cross out old lines, write in new ones.'

'Anton, you're not going to tell anyone here anything they don't already know,' the boss said calmly.

'Has permission been given?' I asked.

Gesar looked at Maxim. As if he could feel the glance, the Inquisitor raised his head and said in a hollow voice:

'Permission has been given.'

'The Day Watch wishes to object,' Zabulon said in a dull voice.

'Denied,' Maxim replied indifferently and lowered his head back on to his chest.

'If a Great Sorceress picks up the chalk,' I said, 'every line in the Book of Destiny will take a particle of her soul. And return it to her, changed. You can only change a person's destiny by giving away your own soul.'

'I know,' said Sveta. She smiled. 'I'm sorry, Anton. I think this is the right thing to do. It will be good for everyone.'

There was a brief glint of concern in Egor's eyes. He'd sensed something was wrong.

'Anton, you're a warrior of the Watch,' said Gesar. 'If you have objections, you may speak.'

Objections? To what? To Egor becoming a Light Magician instead of a Dark one? To an attempt, even if it was bound to fail, to bring Good to humans? To Svetlana becoming a Great Sorceress?

Even at the cost of sacrificing everything human she still had inside her.

'There's nothing I wish to say,' I said.

Did I imagine it, or was there a flash of surprise in Gesar's eyes? It was hard to tell what the Great Magician was really thinking.

'Let's begin,' he said. 'Svetlana, you know what you have to do.'

'I do,' she said, looking at me. I moved a few steps away from her. So did Gesar. Now there were just the two of them standing together – Svetlana and Egor. Both equally anxious. Equally tense. I looked across at Zabulon – he was waiting. Svetlana opened the little box – the click of the catch sounded like a gunshot – and slowly took out the piece of chalk, almost as if she didn't want to. It was tiny. Had it really been worn down so much by the Light's attempts to alter the destiny of the world over the millennia?

Gesar sighed.

Svetlana squatted down and began drawing a circle around herself and the boy.

I had nothing to say. I didn't know what to do.

I'd collected so much power that it was bursting out of me.

I had the right to do Good.

There was just one little thing missing — I didn't understand exactly how.

The wind stirred. Timidly, cautiously. Then it faded away.

I looked up and shuddered. Something was happening. Here, in the human world, the sky was covered with clouds. I hadn't even noticed them appear.

Svetlana finished drawing the circle and stood up.

I tried glancing at her through the Twilight and immediately turned away. She seemed to be holding a red-hot coal in her hand. Was she feeling any pain?

'There's a storm approaching,' Zabulon said from one side. 'A real storm, the kind we haven't had for a long time now.'

He laughed.

Nobody paid any attention. Except perhaps the wind — it started blowing more evenly, growing stronger. I looked down at the street — everything was calm. Svetlana was tracing the chalk through the air as if she was drawing something only she could see. A square outline with some design inside it.

Egor gave a quiet groan and threw his head back. I took half a step forward and stopped. I couldn't get across the barrier. And there was no point anyway.

When you don't know what to do, don't trust anything. Not your cool head, not your pure heart, not your hot hands.

'Anton!'

I looked at the boss. Gesar seemed worried.

'That's not just a storm, Anton. It's a hurricane. People will be killed.'

'The Dark Ones?' I asked simply.

'No, the elements.'

'Maybe you overdid it slightly with the concentration of power?' I asked. The boss ignored the jibe.

'Anton, what degree of magical intervention are you allowed?'

Ah, of course, he knew about my deal with Zabulon.

'Second.'

'You can stop the hurricane,' said Gesar. A simple statement of fact. 'Reduce it to no more than a cloudburst. You've collected enough power.'

The wind sprang up again. And this time it wasn't going to stop. It tore and tugged at us, as if it had decided to blow us all off the roof. The rain began to lash down.

'It looks like your last chance,' the boss added. 'But then, it's up to you.'

The defensive shield sprang up around him with a glassy tinkling sound. It was the first time I'd seen a magician use such defensive measures against the ordinary excesses of the elements.

Svetlana carried on drawing the Book of Destiny, with her dress billowing out around her. Egor didn't move a muscle, as if he was crucified on an invisible cross. Maybe he couldn't see or understand what was going on. What happens to someone when his old destiny is taken away and he still hasn't been given a new one?

'Gesar, the typhoon you're about to unleash will make this storm look like nothing,' I shouted.

The wind almost drowned out my words.

'That's inevitable,' Gesar replied. He seemed to be speaking in a whisper, but every word was perfectly clear. 'It's already happening.'

The Book of Destiny had become visible even in the human world. Of course, Svetlana hadn't been drawing it in the literal sense of the word, she'd been extracting it from the deepest levels of the Twilight. Making a copy, so that any changes she made in it would be reflected in the original. The Book of Destiny looked like a model, a replica, made out of fiery threads of flame hanging motionless in the air. The raindrops sizzled when they touched it.

And now Svetlana would start changing Egor's destiny.

And later, decades later, Egor would change the destiny of the world.

As always, trying to shift it towards the Good.

And, as always, failing.

I staggered. In a single instant, completely without warning, the strong wind had become a hurricane. The scene around me was incredible. I saw cars stop on the avenue up close against the kerb – as far away as possible from the trees. A huge advertising hoarding collapsed on to an intersection without a single sound – the roaring of the wind completely drowned out the crash. A few little figures made a belated dash for the buildings, as if they hoped to find shelter by the walls.

Svetlana stopped. The red-hot coal was still glowing in her hand.

'Anton!'

I could hardly make out what she was saying.

'Anton, what should I do? Tell me, Anton, should I do this?'

The chalk circle was protecting her but not completely – the clothes were still being torn off her body – but at least it allowed her to stay on her feet.

Everything else seemed to have disappeared. I looked at her, and at the glowing piece of chalk, already poised to change another person's destiny. Svetlana was waiting for an answer, but I had nothing to say to her. Because I didn't know the answer either.

I lifted my arms up towards the raging heavens. I saw the spectral blossoms of power in my hands.

'Can you handle it?' Zabulon asked sympathetically. 'The storm's quite wild already.'

Even through the clamour of the hurricane, I could hear his voice as clearly as the boss's.

Gesar sighed.

I opened my hands and turned the palms towards the sky – the sky where there were no stars, the sky full of dark roiling clouds, torrents of rain, flashes of lightning.

It was one of the simplest spells. Almost the first one everybody was taught.

Remoralisation.

Without any limiting conditions.

'Don't do that!' Gesar shouted. 'Don't you dare!'

In one swift movement he dashed across to shield Svetlana and Egor from me. As if that could stop the spell. There was nothing that could stop it now.

A ray of light that humans couldn't see shot from my open hands. It was the scraps that I'd gathered so mercilessly from all those people. The scarlet flame of roses, the pale pink of peonies, the yellow glow of asters, white daisies and almost black orchids.

Zabulon laughed quietly behind my back.

Svetlana stood there, holding the chalk poised over the Book of Destiny.

Egor was frozen in front of her, with his arms flung out.

Pieces on a chess board. The power was in my hands. I'd never had so much power. It was overflowing, I could direct it at anyone.

I smiled at Svetlana. And very slowly raised my palms with their fountain of rainbow light towards my own face.

'No!'

Zabulon's howl didn't cut through the roar of the hurricane, it completely drowned it. A bolt of lightning flashed across the sky. The leader of the Dark Ones rushed towards me, but Gesar stepped out to meet him, and the Dark Magician stopped. I didn't really see all this, I felt it. My face was enveloped in the shimmering colours. My head was spinning. I couldn't feel the wind any more.

There was nothing left except a rainbow, a never-ending rainbow, and I was drowning in it.

The wind raged all around me without touching me. I looked at Sveta and heard the invisible wall that had always separated us breaking down. Breaking down and forming a protective barrier around us. Her fluttering hair settled gently around her face.

'Did you use it all on yourself?'

'Yes,' I said.

'Everything you collected?'

She still couldn't believe it. Svetlana knew what the price for borrowed power was.

'All of it,' I answered. I had an incredibly light feeling.

'Why?' The sorceress held out her hand towards me. 'Why, Anton? When you could have stopped this storm? You could have brought happiness to thousands of people. How could you use it all on yourself?'

'In order to avoid making a mistake,' I explained. I felt slightly embarrassed that a Great Sorceress like her didn't understand such a minor detail.

Svetlana said nothing for a moment. Then she glanced at the piece of chalk glowing in her hand.

'What should I do, Anton?'

'You've already opened the Book of Destiny.'

'Anton! Who's right? Gesar or you?'

I shook my head.

'You decide for yourself.'

Svetlana frowned.

'Anton, is that all? Why did you take so much Light from others? What have you wasted your second-degree magic on?'

'Listen to me,' I said, not sure how much conviction there was

in my voice. Even now I wasn't entirely convinced myself. 'Sometimes the most important thing isn't to do something. Sometimes
it's more important not to do anything. Some things you have to
decide for yourself, without any advice. From me, or Gesar, or
Zabulon, or the Light or the Dark. All on your own.'

She shook her head.

'No!'

'Yes. You must decide for yourself. And nobody can relieve you
of that responsibility. And whatever you do – you'll always regret
what you didn't do.'

'Anton, I love you!'

'I know. And I love you. That's why I won't say anything.'

'And you call that love?'

'There isn't any other kind.'

'I need your advice!' she shouted. 'Anton, I need your advice!'

'We all create our own destinies,' I said. It was rather more than
I ought to have said. 'Decide.'

The piece of chalk in her hand flared up in a slim needle of fire
as she turned back to the Book of Destiny. She swept her hand
through the air and I heard the pages rustling under the blindingly
bright eraser.

Light and Dark are only spots on the pages of destiny. A flourish
of the hand. A rapid stroke.

Words of fire streaming across the page.

Svetlana opened her fingers and the chalk of Destiny fell at her
feet. As heavily as if it were a lead bullet. The hurricane tumbled it
across the roof, but I managed to bend down and put my hand
over it.

The Book of Destiny started to dissolve.

Egor staggered, doubled over and fell on his side, with his knees
pulled up to his chest, curled up into a pitiful little bundle.

The white circle around them had been washed away by the

rain, and I could walk over to them now. I squatted down and took hold of the boy's shoulders.

'You didn't write anything!' Gesar shouted. 'Svetlana, you only erased things!'

The sorceress shrugged. She looked down at me. The rain had already broken through the fading barrier and soaked her white dress, transforming it into transparent muslin that no longer concealed the form of her body. A moment earlier Svetlana had been a priestess in white robes, and now she was a young woman soaked to the skin, standing in the eye of a storm with her arms helplessly at her sides.

'That was your test,' Gesar said to her in a quiet voice. 'You've missed your chance.'

'Light One Gesar, I do not wish to serve in the Watch,' the young woman replied. 'I'm sorry, Light One Gesar, but it is not my path. Not my destiny.'

Gesar shook his head sadly. Zabulon came across to us with a few quick steps.

'Is that it?' the Dark Magician asked. He looked at me, at Sveta, at Egor. 'Didn't you do anything?' He looked at the Inquisitor, who raised his head and nodded.

Nobody answered him.

A crooked smile spread across Zabulon's face.

'All that effort, and it's all ended in a farce. And all because a hysterical girl didn't want to leave her indecisive lover. Anton, I'm disappointed in you. Svetlana, I'm delighted with *you*. Gesar,' – the Dark Magician looked at the boss – 'my congratulations on having such remarkable people on your staff.'

A portal opened behind Zabulon's back. He laughed quietly as he stepped into the black cloud.

I heard a heavy sigh rising up from the ground. Although I couldn't see, I knew what was happening. One after another the members of the Day Watch were emerging from the Twilight and racing to their cars to move them as far away as possible from the trees. Or hunching over and running to the nearest buildings.

After them the Light Magicians abandoned the cordon. Some for the same simple, human reasons. But I knew that most of them stayed where they were, looking up at the roof of the building. Tiger Cub, wearing a guilty expression just in case. Semyon, with the gloomy smile of an Other who'd seen worse storms than this one. Ignat with his eternal expression of sincere sympathy.

'I couldn't do it,' said Svetlana. 'I'm sorry, Gesar. I couldn't.'

'You never could have,' I said. 'And you were never meant to.'

I opened my hand and looked at the little piece of chalk, which while I held it was no more than that – a wet, sticky piece of chalk. Pointed at one end. Broken off unevenly at the other.

'How long ago did you realise?' asked Gesar. He came across and sat down beside me. His shield extended to cover us and the roar of the hurricane faded away.

'Only just now.'

'What's going on?' exclaimed Svetlana. 'Anton, tell me what's going on.'

Gesar answered her.

'Everyone has his or her own destiny, my dear. For some it means changing other people's lives and destroying empires. For others it simply means getting on with life.'

'While the Day Watch was waiting for you to act,' I explained, 'Olga took the other half of the chalk and rewrote someone else's destiny. The way the Light wanted it to be.'

Gesar sighed. He reached out and touched Egor. The boy stirred and tried to get up.

'No hurry, no hurry,' the boss said gently. 'It's all over now, or almost.'

I put my arm round the boy's shoulders and rested his head on my knees. He calmed down again.

'Why all this?' I asked. 'If you knew in advance what would happen?'

'Even I can't know everything.'

'But why all this?'

'Because everything had to look natural,' Gesar said, slightly annoyed. 'That was the only way Zabulon would believe what was happening. He had to believe in our plans, and believe that we failed.'

'That's not the full answer, Gesar,' I said, looking into his eyes. 'It's not even close!'

The boss sighed.

'All right. Yes, I could have done things differently. Svetlana would have become a Great Sorceress. Against her own wishes. And Egor would have become our instrument, despite the fact that the Watch was already in his debt.'

I waited. I was very interested to see if Gesar would tell the whole truth. Just once.

'Yes, I could have done it that way,' said Gesar, and sighed again. 'But you know, my boy . . . Everything that I've done in the twentieth century, apart from the great struggle between the Light and the Dark, has been dedicated to a single purpose that, naturally, brought no harm to our cause . . .'

I suddenly felt sorry for him. Incredibly sorry. Perhaps for the first time in a thousand years the Great Magician, the Most Light Gesar, destroyer of monsters and guardian of states, had been forced to tell the entire truth. Not the beautiful and exalted truth that he was used to telling.

'Don't, don't. I know!' I shouted.

But the Great Magician shook his head.

'Everything I've done was dedicated to that purpose. To force the senior levels to repeal Olga's punishment completely. To force them to restore her powers and allow her to pick up the chalk of Destiny once again. She had to become my equal. Otherwise our love was doomed. And I love her, Anton.'

Svetlana laughed. Very, very quietly. I thought she was going to slap the boss's face, but I suppose I still didn't understand her completely. Svetlana went down on her knees in front of Gesar and kissed his right hand.

The magician trembled. He seemed for a moment to have lost his infinite powers: the protective dome began shuddering and dissolving. Once more we were deafened by the roar of the hurricane.

'Are we going to change the destiny of the world again?' I asked. 'Apart from our own little personal concerns?'

He nodded and asked in return:

'Why, don't you like the idea?'

'No.'

'Well, Anton, you can't always be a winner. I haven't, and you won't be either.'

'I know that,' I said. 'Of course I know it, Gesar. But still, it would be nice.'

January–August 1998
Moscow